Legionary

Legionary

Book 1 in the Roman Rebellion Series

By Griff Hosker

Legionary
Published by Griff Hosker 2025
Copyright ©Griff Hosker

The author has asserted their moral right under the Copyright, Designs and Patents Act, 1988, to be identified as the author of this work.
All Rights reserved. No part of this publication may be reproduced, copied, stored in a retrieval system, or transmitted, in any form or by any means, without the prior written consent of the copyright holder, nor be otherwise circulated in any form of binding or cover other than that in which it is published and without a similar condition being imposed on the subsequent purchaser.

A CIP catalogue record for this title is available from the British Library.

Contents

Prologue 5
Chapter 1 11
Chapter 2 26
Chapter 3 37
Chapter 4 47
Chapter 5 57
Chapter 6 67
Chapter 7 76
Chapter 8 87
Chapter 9 97
Chapter 10 110
Chapter 11 128
Chapter 12 141
Chapter 13 151
Chapter 14 164
Chapter 15 174
Chapter 16 186
Chapter 17 196
Chapter 18 207
Chapter 19 215
Chapter 20 224
Chapter 21 233
Chapter 22 242
Epilogue 255
Glossary 257
Historical Background 258
Other books by Griff Hosker 260

Legionary

Real people in the book

Lucius Cornelius Sulla - Dictator
Gnaeus Pompeius Magnus - Pompey the Great (Roman general)
Quintus Caecilius Metellus Pius - one of Sulla's generals
Gaius Marius (aka the Younger) - Roman Consul and son of Gaius Marius the Roman army reformer
Lucius Cornelius Cinna - Marian general
Gaius Marcius Censorinus - Marian general
Gnaeus Papirius Carbo - Marian general
Marcus Licinius Crassus - Sullan general.
Marcus Lamponius - Lucanian leader
Pontius Telesinus - Samnite leader
Lucius Cornelius Scipio Asiaticus - Marian General
Gaius Norbanus - Consul and Marian General
Gaius Carrinas - Marian General
Quintus Lucretius Afella - Sullan general
Gnaeus Domitius Ahenobarbus - Marian general
Marcus Aemilius Lepidus - Roman Consul
Marcus Lucullus - Sullan General
Quintus Lutatius Catulus - Roman Consul
Marcus Junius Brutus - an ally of Lepidus and the father of Marcus Brutus, Caesar's assassin
Quintus Sertorius - Roman rebel general who took Spain from Rome
Lucius Afranius - one of Pompey's generals
Marcus Perperna - Sullan General
Lucius Hirtuleius - Sertorian General

Fictitious characters in the book

Varius Rufus Drusus - First Spear 1st Legion
Caeso Sentia Bucco - Centurion
Decimus Rufia Corbulo - Optio
Gaius Laelius Firminus - Legionary
Mamerus Porca Rufio - Legionary
Numerius Ennia Sura - Legionary
Nanus Gallia Quietus - Tesserarius
Marius Arria Gracchus - Signifer
Aulus Tarutia Avitus - Cornicen
Gnaeus Rufia Betto - Legate
Proculus Tiberius Lamia - Optio

Lucius' contuburnium

Legionary

Mettius Eustachius
Publius Aproianus
Faustus Glavias
Nonus Regatus
Marius Firminius
Appius Fullo
Caeso Dativus
Decimus Cumanus - Optio

Legionary

Roman Legion Organisation 90 BC

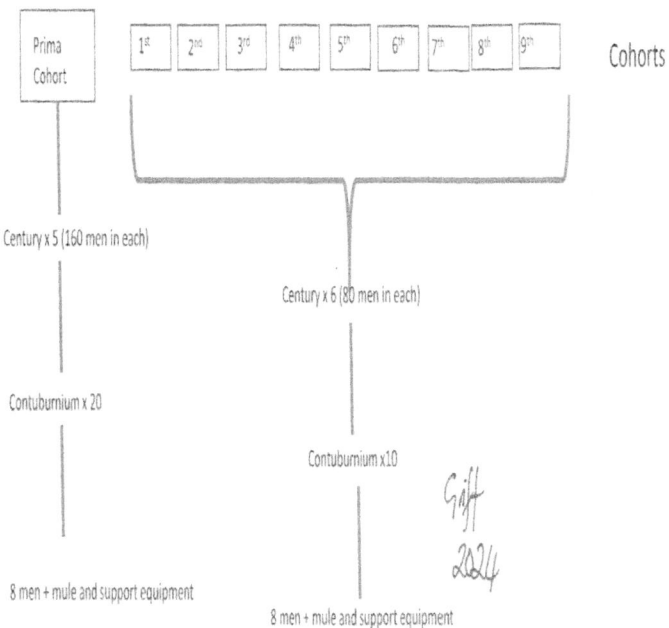

Prologue

The pigs began to die. That was, looking back, the day that my life changed from its predictable course. I can view that time a little more dispassionately now for I have lived through events that were more important. At the time, however, I thought that my world had come to an end. Indeed, it had, or the world I had known, at least. Perhaps the gods wished to change my destiny or the Fates were bored. I do not know, but all I did know was that Lucius Ulpia Porcianus did not become the farmer he had been expected to when the animals started to die. My father was also called Lucius and although he had been a soldier he was a farmer, through and through.

My family lived in the land called Picenum. We were farmers who raised pigs and beans. The pigs were not for us to eat. Such meat was a rarity for our family. We were more likely to eat animals hunted by my father and me. We were now Roman citizens but it had been in the last two generations when that had happened. My father told me that his grandfather had been of the Piceni tribe. I had grown up feeling Roman. My father had served in the legions and he had fulfilled his obligations. According to him he had only had to draw his spear in anger once. All that remained of his service now were his helmet and his sword and scabbard. When we hunted for food we used a sling or a bow. Whatever we hunted augmented the beans and greens that were our staple.

It sounds dull but life was good, especially for a young boy growing up. I got to tend the pigs and I was outdoors. My three sisters spent more time inside the house. My mother helped to fill the family coffers by making pots using the river clay we gathered from the Albula River. The girls helped. They also cooked, sewed and did all the other things that would make them good wives. My mother had married well, or relatively well. My father was good at what he did. We had a herd of six breeding pigs and each year the litters that they produced would be sold at market and bring us silver for the rest of the year. True, we had no slaves but as my father always said, slaves needed to be fed and housed. He thought we did not need them.

We lived on an isolated farm. We had enough land for the pigs and he and his father had cleared some woodland which enabled them to raise beans and other crops. The dung from the pigs and the goat we kept for milk ensured that the ground was fertile. Each year my father and I cleared a little more woodland. The wood was stored for kindling and the pigs helped to clear the ground. Every year saw a little more of our land that could be cleared.

The outdoor life and exercise gave me a broad back and strong arms. As my father said, those with slaves were weaker in the arm than we were. I had a good eye and could bring down a bird in flight. I did not miss the company of others for I liked my father and we got on. I suppose had not disaster struck us then I might have grown more and eventually sought a bride in the nearby town of Asculum Picenum. When I was not looking after pigs I was hunting. I did not bother with sandals and ran barefoot through the woods that lined the hills near our home. I used my sling to bring down birds or to catch an unwary rabbit. I covered miles each day and enjoyed the smile of my mother when I returned with food for the pot. The days when I was abroad, in the woods, were good ones. I learned to use the wind as an ally so that it took my smell from my prey and allowed me to smell them. I was able to move quietly, almost without looking so that I passed through the woodland without disturbing it. I moved slowly but purposefully when I fitted the stone to the sling and I knew how to send a ball quickly. It was rare for me to come home empty handed.

It was, I suppose, the market at Asculum Picenum that brought about the catastrophic change in not only my life but the whole family. We all visited the market. While the women sought those things that we could not make, my father and I went to the animal market. We needed a new nanny. The old one had begun to give less milk and we needed a younger one to make cheese. It was while we were there that we saw the man selling his pigs. He was from the far side of the valley and my father did not know him well but he knew he was a farmer. He was selling up and he had all of his animals with him and, being desperate to sell, his prices were low. By the time we had bought a goat he just had two pigs left. One was a young boar and we did not need him. The other was a young sow. Having just two left he was keen to sell and, although we had not planned to buy, the price was so low that my father bought her.

The first months saw her grow well. The nuts that fell from our trees fattened her. When the nanny also began to give more milk than her predecessor ever had we thanked the god, Portunus. Portunus was our household god. We celebrated the winter solstice with a meal of the old goat.

It was not long after the days began to grow a little longer when the problems came. The first sign was that the animals all became thinner. They had many cases of diarrhoea. When the sows all aborted then we knew that something was wrong. We would have no piglets to sell the next year. My father was philosophical about it all.

"We will just have to endure a year without silver. You and I shall hunt more and your mother can make more pots."

The problem was not just the abortions. The pigs began, one by one, to die. They went over a period of one month and by the time we had worked out that the cause was the pig we had bought it was too late. It was a cruel joke that she was the last to die.

As spring arrived we faced the possibility that we might starve to death. My mother and sisters could not produce enough pots to make us enough money. It took until we were almost at the summer solstice for my father to make a decision. It was one that would change my whole life.

We went to the temple to consult with the priest. We had little enough silver but my father gave some to the priest and asked for the help of the gods. Perhaps an offering would change our fortune. I did not like Aquilinus the priest. For one thing he was too fat to be honest and for another he looked down his nose at us. He took our offering and conferred with the gods. He said we had to make a sacrifice and that sacrifice was to be me. Looking back, and that is always easier, he said that I should be sold as a slave. He must have had someone who needed a fit herdsman. He said my father could use the money to restock his farm and the gods would smile on my sacrifice.

Legionary

My father listened to the priest and we left. He was quiet as we walked home and I was terrified. I did not want to be a slave yet it did not do to upset the gods. If I was made into one I would run. I dismissed the idea as soon as it came into my head for that would merely upset the gods. He took me to a high rock that was bare of trees and overlooked the valley. To the east we could see the sea and to the west, the Apennines, the line of mountains that separated us from the west and Rome.

My father pointed to the west, "First," he smiled, "I have no intention of enslaving my own son but the gods need a sacrifice. The farm does not produce enough for us all to live. Your sisters, Livia and Luculla, are old enough to be wed and I will seek husbands for them. There will be little dowry but they are attractive prospects for men who seek hard working wives. Annia can stay and help your mother until she is old enough to wed. We could do all of that and live on the vegetables we raise and the animals I hunt."

I almost knew what was coming. I had the biggest appetite in the family, even including my father. I ate more than my sisters and mother combined. If I was not in the home then they would have more to eat. The money from the pigs we sold each year had allowed us to buy extra food and grain as well as cloth to make clothes.

My father said, "There is nothing for you here, my son. I had hoped to pass on to you the same farm my father gave to me. I may be able to start again but not for some time." He picked up a piece of grass and started to chew it. "I will see my old friend Agrippa. Perhaps he will give me some credit and let me have a couple of his pigs. If not there are other things I could do." I knew what he would have to do. He would need to hunt for wild pigs and tame them. That was dangerous and time consuming.

"I can help, Father."

He shook his head, "No, that is not right. The mistake was mine and you should not have to pay." He sighed, "If the gods need you to be sacrificed then rather than enslavement I would sacrifice you to Rome. When I was young the legions were seen as a duty. Thanks to Marius, they now offer an opportunity. You are young and you are fit. You can join the legions. The son of Gnaeus Pompeius Strabo, Gnaeus Pompeius is raising a new legion. He needs strong warriors. A legionary has a future. You will be fed, clothed and housed. You will learn to be a soldier and when your enlistment is up you will be given land," he gave me a sad smile. "It is for the best. At least this way I know that you will not be starved nor abused. Legionaries are good people. They are tough but they look after their own." He shook his head, "They will be better fathers to you than me. I have failed you and the family."

Try as I could I was unable to dissuade him. My mother, when she was told, was tearful but she saw the wisdom of it. It did not do to offend the priests and the gods. Aquilinus would not make money but even he would see that I was being sacrificed. My sisters had their own problems. They would be married off to older men. They had no idea if they would be good men or not. I cursed the days the pigs died for they ended the idyll that had been my life and threw me into a future that was unknown.

The Roman World 80 BC

Legionary

Chapter 1

The recruiting for the legion took place at the port. In times past the legions had been raised when danger threatened. Gaius Marius the Elder had ended that; Rome would have a standing army and now men could join the legions and have a career. Whilst the pay of a legionary would not be a large amount there were opportunities for promotion. Such promotions would bring not only power but also more coins. I confess, as I trekked from Picenum to Ancona with my father's old spear, helmet and sword as well as my belongings hanging from the end of the spear, I did not feel particularly optimistic about any of this. I was alone and having bade farewell to my family and carrying as well as my belongings, a wine skin and some food, my spirits were as low as they could get.

I had many miles to go. I could have taken a boat from Castrum Truentinum and that would have saved my feet and three days of walking but I could not afford it. I had a couple of denarii in my purse and they were for emergencies. I knew that my family had given me all that they could afford to. I had warm clothes and my sandals were well made. In hindsight the walk was good preparation for the life of a legionary. It was not in my interest to dawdle and I hurried at what I would soon learn was called the military pace. As I did not have much food then I would also learn to go hungry. I had my sling with me and managed to hit a rabbit that first night as I camped by a small stream that tumbled and bubbled towards the sea. I could not afford lodgings and a quiet camp was just what I needed. I skinned and butchered the rabbit and cooked it on an open fire. Cooked that way it was a little tough but it augmented the bread, fruit and goat's cheese I had brought. I made water on the skin. I did not know yet what I would use it for but it seemed to me a useful object and I was joining the legion with little enough as it was. I thought perhaps I might make it into a hat for my father had said that legions had been used to fight the Gauls who lived to the north of our land. There were high mountains with snow. A hat made of a rabbit skin might keep my head warm. I boiled the bones that night and, when I rose, I added some oats to the water and made a hearty porridge. I kept the more useful bones. Some could be used to pick food from my teeth and the dagger I had would allow me to carve them. I could afford to waste nothing.

I passed few people for I avoided the roads and made my way through paths that crisscrossed the hills and woods. I had always been a solitary youth. Now I was almost a man and my character had already been formed. A man cannot change his nature. I think my father knew that when he made the decision to make me enlist. When I reached Ancona I felt as though I had entered a new world. It was far bigger than Picenum and, as a port, was filled with all manner of people. Even the language I heard sounded different. I understood all the words but the accents seemed to make the words themselves take on a new meaning.

After ascertaining where the building for recruitment was I headed for it. I contemplated finding a bath house and spending one of my denarii there but decided that if they wanted me they would take me as I was. I knew I did not smell good but I could do nothing about it. There was an old soldier seated outside at a table with a wax tablet before him. I knew he was old from the grey hairs. His helmet, which looked like the one I carried, hung from his chair. I saw that it had two black feathers in it. He watched me as I neared the table. It was quite clear what I was there to do and he studied me as I approached.

He did not make it easy for me. He simply said, "Yes, can I help you or are you lost?"

"I would like to enlist in the legion, Sir."

He shook his head, "I am not an officer, you don't need to call me sir. I don't need the flattery." I nodded, "And which legion would that be?"

The little confidence with which I had begun to speak evaporated like morning mist. I stood there with my mouth open. I did not know which legion. Did I have a choice?

He chuckled, "Let us see if you qualify first, eh? We will start with the easy questions. Name?"

"Lucius Ulpia Porcianus."

"Your father is a citizen?"

"He is. We farm northwest of Asculum Picenum and he did his military service in the legion commanded by Gnaeus Pompeius Strabo."

He wrote that down and then said, "His son is raising legions so if you meet the criteria then you would be in one of those." I nodded, "Just one more question. How old are you?"

My father had told me that this would come up. I was not yet eighteen but I needed to be eighteen to join. I was big enough to pass and so I said, without hesitation, "Eighteen."

He glanced at me as though debating if I was telling the truth and then shrugged. He stood. "Stand against the wall." As I did I saw a mark on the wall. Was I tall enough? He took out his sword and placed it on my head. He nodded. "You are tall enough, more than six pes." He pointed to a ship just entering the harbour, "The ship that is arriving, what colour is her pennant?"

"Green."

"You have good eyes then. Open our mouth." I did so and he put a vine stick in it as he examined my teeth, "Right, you have passed my bit. The next part is for you to be presented to the board of examining officers. They will need you to say sir when you speak to them. They are dining at the moment. Come back first thing this afternoon. If you are sharp enough you might be the first one in and catch them while they are still replete after food."

I smiled, "Thank you."

He frowned, "Thank me? What for? If you are successful you just become one of Marius' Mules. You will march all day, build a camp, be given a handful of food, sleep on the ground and then do it all again the next day. I am getting out, son. In one month's time I will be given a piece of land and I will be done with the army. If you take my advice you will forget this and go back home. If your father is a farmer and has land then enjoy your life."

I shook my head and stood a little straighter, "I can't do that but I wish you well in your retirement."

The smile he gave me seemed a genuine one, "Thank you for that."

I picked up my burden and felt at a slight loss. I had assumed I would present myself and then be told where to go. This board of examining officers was unexpected. My father had not mentioned it. I was loath to spend my denarii in case I was rejected. If that happened then I would need my coins. Would the gods object if I was not sacrificed? It did not bear thinking about. I wandered down to the harbour. There I would lose myself in the crowds and cacophony of noise. My father was right, I was a solitary youth but not in my head. Inside my head were conversations, questions, doubts and arguments. Others neither saw nor heard them but I did. I would let others drown out my voices for I did not need the indecision.

When I neared the waterfront I sought out a place where I could sit. I was lucky and, when a woman who had been waiting for her slave to complete the purchase of some fish stood, I pounced on the stone bollard she had used to rest. I straddled the rope which tied the small fishing ship to the stone quay. I laid my spear on the ground but hooked my foot through the rope which bound my bundle. I had few possessions but I did not want to lose them to some opportunist thief.

Most of the people I saw were busy. Some were loading and unloading ships. Some were buying and selling. All of them moved with purpose. I appeared to be the only one who was idle and that idleness was forced upon me. There was the stink of the sea and food which had fallen and rotted. There was the smell of unwashed bodies and there were more people than I had ever seen before, except on market day in Asculum Picenum. It was a strange world and filled with people who were nothing like those I saw on a daily basis. It was as my eyes scanned the crowds that I saw another who was also, to my mind, idle. He was a young patrician. His spotless white toga marked him as such. He looked to me to be in his twenties and was well groomed and dressed. He seemed incongruous in this busy place of work. He looked clean and he was in a place that reeked of dirt. He was staring out to sea. I explained his presence by assuming he was waiting for a ship to arrive. Perhaps he was a merchant who had gambled on the delivery of a cargo that would make him a fortune. I was still watching him when he turned and saw me. I saw his eyes narrow and he strode over to me. We had patricians in Picenum but I had never addressed one. We were plebians and I knew my

Legionary

place. As he neared me I stood, aware that my foot was still wrapped in the rope. I disentangled it.

I must have looked nervous for I saw the frown replaced by a smile as he stopped, "Like me, you have time to waste here, eh?"

"Yes, my lord."

"Who are you and what brings you here to this hotbed of humanity?"

"I wish to enlist, my lord, and join the legions."

He smiled, "Really? You are, if you do not mind me saying so, a little young for such a vocation."

I felt myself reddening, "I am eighteen, my lord."

"I mean no offence. What is your name?"

"Lucius, my lord."

"So, Lucius, while I have an hour to kill, tell me your tale." He waved over a man who was hawking wine. "Two beakers of wine." He spoke imperiously as though he was used to command.

The man put down his yoke and took two beakers from his belt. He poured the wine from the amphora. "Four denarii. I will give back two denarii when you have finished with the beakers."

The patrician seemed happy to pay but when he sipped the wine his face wrinkled, "Vinegar masquerading as wine. Still, it is better than the water. So, Lucius, your tale."

I sipped the wine and it was not as bad as the young man had said. The fact that he had bought the wine for me encouraged my honesty and I told him all.

When I had finished and the beakers were empty and returned he nodded, "A bad decision from your father and your lives are ruined. There is a warning for us all. The gods punish those who do not choose the wisest course of action. It was a wise decision to become a soldier rather than a slave. Well, I wish you well, Lucius Porcianus. Farewell."

Somehow the talk with the patrician, even though he had not told me one thing about himself, made me feel better and I had enjoyed the wine. I looked at the sun and realised I could make my way back to the recruiting building. The crowds had thinned a little as people were heading for places to buy food or had gone home. Mornings were always the busy times in ports and markets. The old soldier was still there but there was another young man waiting. My heart sank. I had counted on being the first one in. I felt that gave me the best chance of being accepted. The old soldier smiled, "You were a little slow," he glanced down at his wax tablet, "Lucius, Gaius Firminus here was keener."

I looked at the young man and realised that he was about the same age as me but slightly shorter. That gave me hope. He might not make the height requirement. Perhaps it would make me look even better. He was, however, broader than I was and looked to have a powerful set of shoulders.

He held out his hand, "Gaius Laelius Firminus."

"Lucius Ulpia Porcianus."

"As we are the first two here perhaps we might be accepted and train together."

The old soldier snorted, "If you are accepted," he emphasised the word *if*, "then you will be probatio. You will not become legionaries until you have passed that period."

I saw five men approach. They were a mixture of soldiers and patricians. They were clearly the examining board. The soldier took the wax tablet from the soldier, "Just two, Hostius?"

The old soldier nodded, "There were others who said they might come back this afternoon, Pilus Prior. There were four veterans. They will be in the inn."

The other soldier nodded and handed back the tablet. The other four men had entered the building. When I heard the title I looked again at the soldier who was, I could see, a centurion. I recognised the phalerae on his armour. I stood a little straighter. The centurion gave us both a disparaging look and shook his head, "Let us hope that the others are better than these two then and that they return."

My hopes were dashed by the icy water of the centurion's words. I saw the old soldier smile as the centurion entered. "Welcome to the world of centurions. Your future is in his hands and, if you are accepted, then your lives too. It is not too late to change your minds."

I looked at Gaius and saw the same determination on his face. We both shook our heads.

He sighed, "In you go. There is an antechamber on your right. Wait in there until you are called for." He nodded at our belongings. Gaius had a bundle the same size as mine, "Leave your gear here." He saw our looks, "Trust me, it will be safe with me."

Somehow I believed him and, unburdened, we entered the dark stone building. We could hear the buzz of conversation from a room ahead and we turned right. There was a table, a jug of water and four beakers. The room was small and undecorated. This was a functional building.

I was nervous and had my normal conversation with myself in my head. I was already preparing to return home and tell my father that I had failed. If they did not want me then that would be the gods rejecting my sacrifice. I thought of a hard life eking out a living by hunting and foraging until we could build up a breeding herd of pigs. The debate was so lively that when the voice shouted, "Gaius Laelius Firminus." I almost jumped.

"Good luck."

He turned, "Thank you."

I was alone and I waited in the silence with my voices. I drank a beaker of tepid water. It had been boiled I could tell that. I heard footsteps and two other young men came in. They saw me and just nodded. We stood in awkward silence. Should I be the first to speak as I was already there? Did they know each other? I was spared any more worry when I heard, "Lucius Ulpia Porcianus."

I nodded to the other two and left the room. I saw Gaius' back as he went out into the street. Had he been successful or had he failed? I walked down the corridor and entered the room. There were no openings and the room was lit by a single oil lamp. However, it was a large one and gave out a good light. Behind the men I saw a fresco painted on the wall. I had heard of such decorations but I had not time to admire it or even study it. I had to pass this test. I made out the five faces but I was aware of a figure lurking in the shadows in the corner of the room. The light was bright but the man had chosen to stay where his face would not be seen.

The centurion was in the middle and he said, "You meet the height requirement and you seem healthy enough; that is about all. Are you eighteen?"

"Yes, Pilus Prior."

"I don't think you are. You still have fluff around your chin." The other four looked bored by the whole procedure. They stank of wine and one had his eyes slightly closed as though he had enjoyed a good meal. "Did your father serve?"

"He did. He was in the legion of Gnaeus Pompeius Strabo."

I saw the centurion glance over to the figure in the corner.

The centurion leaned back and poured himself some wine from the jug, "Then go back to your father and come back next year when you have filled out and begun to shave properly."

My heart sank. I had failed in the first task given to me by my father. I opened my mouth to speak but then the figure stepped from the shadows and spoke, "I think you are being hasty Varius Drusus. This is just the sort of soldier we need. He is young and uncorrupted. He looks honest and I will have him in my legion." He held out his hand and, as he waved it, I saw it was the young patrician from the harbour. "I am Gnaeus Pompeius. If you would wait outside in the shade then you will be taken to our camp which is just four miles from here."

I left in a daze as the centurion roared, "Mamerus Porcio Rufio."

I stepped into the blinding sunlight and had to shade my eyes. Gaius said, "Well?"

"I am a legionary."

He grinned, "Me too although the centurion did not seem to want me."

"Nor me but the young patrician spoke up for me."

"And me."

The old soldier shook his head, "Aye, Gnaeus Pompeius is impetuous. They call him *'the warrior'* in the legion for he can throw a javelin a long way and he is a good rider. He is a fierce warrior and I think his legion will reflect that." He leaned forward, "You are lucky, more than three quarters of the men who are in the new legion served with his father and they are good soldiers. Mind you he was a bastard. The men hated him and when he died they dragged the body from the bier." He shook his head, "He was a greedy bastard but there was no need for that. Still, it gave young Gnaeus Pompeius the coins to equip a legion. You will join the younger ones who swell the ranks of the returning veterans."

Gaius asked, "What happens next?"

Just then the youth called Mamerus emerged from inside the building just as another four men arrived. These were older than we were. He waved an irritated hand, "You will be marched to the camp and given a proper medical. Once you pass that, you swear allegiance to Gnaeus Pompeius and start your training. Now move away. I am a busy man."

The three of us, we learned that Mamerus had been accepted too, moved around the side and, using our bundles as seats sat down.

After we had found shade we looked at each other. The other youth who had entered the building came into the light and joined us. There was awkwardness until Gaius said, "It looks like they are accepting everyone." He seemed disappointed.

"Isn't that a good thing, Gaius? It means we have a future."

"I wanted to become a legionary because I was wanted not simply because I turned up."

Just then the first of the older men emerged from inside the building. He came not long after Mamerus' companion, Sertor, had joined us. He spoke, having heard our words, "They will take almost anybody because young Gnaeus Pompeius is marching south to join Sulla. He is on his way to sort out Rome." Just then two of the other older men arrived. They had been accepted quickly. "Where is Aulus?"

One of the other older men said, "Gnaeus Pompeius recognised him as one of the men who had dragged his father's corpse from the bier at the Colline Gates. He said he might be desperate for men but not those who had dishonoured his father."

By the time darkness approached there were twenty of us. My stomach thought that my throat had been cut and Hostius and the centurion marched us to the camp. Hostius brought up the rear and the Pilus Prior led. It was a fast pace. I walked next to Gaius. We seemed to have bonded. Mamerus and Sertor were clearly friends and the older men who formed the rest had been in the legion of Gnaeus Pompeius Strabo. Hostius knew them too and we four were the only young men in the group of potential legionaries.

If I thought we would be fed when we arrived I was mistaken. We were all told to strip naked once we entered the marching camp. We four young ones were self-conscious but Hostius was unsympathetic, "You have nothing we haven't seen before. Get used to it."

I shivered. I am not sure if it was the cold or the embarrassment. The legion doctor gave us all a cursory examination. It was the same as when my father bought an animal. Our teeth were checked and our bodies patted to see if there was any fat. That done he turned to Pilus Prior, "All healthy."

"Right. Now get dressed and head over to the quartermaster and get your equipment."

Sertor asked, "Do we get fed?"

In one movement the centurion strode over and brought his vine staff up to smack between Sertor's legs, "It is Pilus Prior and you will get fed when I decide. Now get dressed."

Sertor was clearly in pain but none of us risked the wrath of the centurion by helping him. We hurried over to the quartermaster. In this we were guided by the older men. All had served in the legions before and seemed to know their way around the camp. To me it all looked strange. I would later learn that every Roman camp was identical.

The equipment was in a long tent and we moved down to collect each item. The only piece that appeared to be specifically for each of us were the caligae. A legionary looked at our feet and then handed us a pair. To be fair to him he appeared to have skill for mine were perfect. Next we were given a tunic. It was off white in colour. Mine would be loose while Gaius' and the older men would have a better fit. We were then handed a mail shirt. It was sleeveless. We were handed two leather pieces and I realised that it was a sort of harness. A helmet was handed to the others and a helmet protector as well as a pair of feathers. The feathers were not fitted. I had a helmet but not a helmet protector. "The cost of this equipment will come from your pay." The man grinned, "If you survive." I realised that the sword, helmet and spear had been wise gifts. He added, "And I would mark your helmets." I looked inside my helmet and saw my father's name scratched there. I smiled. I did not need to change it.

Legionary

The centurion had left us but Hostius remained. He said, "Right, get dressed in your gear, including the mail. You can take it off later but this way we can show you virgins how to wear it."

The older soldiers laughed at this. Once more we undressed. It was less embarrassing as there was a tent to hide us from the rest of the legion. I found that the mail was hard to put on. Gaius said, "You help me, Lucius, and I will help you." We saw that the leather protectors, which were decorated, went over the shoulders. The strap between them also made the hauberk fit a little better.

He was right and that was the start of my training as a legionary. You helped others and they helped you. I learned that a legion only survived if all the parts worked together. We watched the older soldiers fit their feather plumes and emulated them.

One of the veterans said, "These are for show. You don't wear them on the road but when someone wants to show us off or we parade then we fit them."

When it was done I felt like a soldier. We were moved to the next tent where we were given our weapons. We had been given a dagger and two belts. We watched the older men as they fitted them. I realised that the belts would help to make the mail hauberk fit tighter. We were handed a heavy pilum and a javelin. Finally, in the weapon tent we were given the curved shield in a sack. It was about four pes long. I was laden already.

If I thought we were finished then I was wrong. We went to the next tent and I groaned. We followed the veterans. We were handed a sack and a pole. Gaius and I looked at each other wondering what on earth we would use the pole for. Hostius said, "The pole is to carry your equipment." A legionary handed us a cloak. Hostius said, "Here is your sagum. It is also your blanket!" He gave us a small tool and grinned, "This is the dolabra. You might find it even more useful than your sword." He held it up. On one side was an axe and on the other a spike. "The axe cuts your wood and the spike helps you to dig. You might go many days without drawing your sword but I guarantee that you will use this every day, for every day we make a camp." He stroked the axe head, almost affectionately, "It is also a good weapon. Guard it well." We were then handed a mess tin, we learned it was called a patera and another sack, this time a smaller one and it was netted. "That is for your supplies. You won't need them yet." The last thing we were given was a leather satchel. Inside it we found tools. "Now, I will take you to your tents and then," he smiled at Sertor, "you can eat."

The tents were for eight men. We four were placed in one along with four of the older men. Hostius allocated them to us. I was relieved as the four veterans would be able to guide us. Gaius and I watched them as they laid out their cloaks and then their equipment. I saw that they stacked their pila outside and we did the same. They took off their helmets and mail and placed them next to their bedding. That done they picked up their mess tins and Gaius and I quickly copied them. We were slower but we saw them disappearing into a long tent. Once inside we saw that the rest of the legion had eaten already. It was a sort of cereal porridge with beans. There must have been a little meat in it for I recognised a meaty smell but I found no trace of it in the bowl given to me. There were also a few loaves. There was enough for us all but the fare was not what I had expected. We sat at a table with the four veterans. I saw that there was garum on the table and they liberally sprinkled the condiment on the food. We did the same and when we ate the porridge and soaked up the juices we found we were filled. There was ale too, rather than wine, and that helped too.

One of the veterans turned to the four younger ones, "Hostius, probably at the orders of the Pilus Prior, has made us into a contuburnium. That means the eight of us share a tent, a mule, a grinding stone and a cooking pot. It also means that when we fight, we fight as one." He shook his head, "I know that it is necessary but me and the lads are not happy about it. No offence but you four could get us killed."

Sertor was clearly a grumbler, "Surely that won't happen for a while. We have our training and…"

"You will have to learn to keep your mouth shut, Mouthy. Using it at the wrong time got you a vine stick in the balls and believe me, it could get worse. The training will be rudimentary at best. Sulla has landed at Brundisium. The young general will be keen to join him and show off his new legion. You will be learning how to be a legionary on the job. That means you do everything that we say." Poor Sertor had been given the nickname that would stay with him.

Gaius ventured, "You mean everything you say?"

He grinned, "Not so green as grass looking, are you, Gaius Firminus? Aye, that is right. Heed the words of Numerius Ennia Sura and you might survive your first battle."

One of the others said, "Aye, Old Man, here is a survivor." I learned then that the soldiers used nicknames. It made sense for there were many men with the same first name. The man smiled, "Don't worry, he is the Chosen Man and he will look after us all."

His words were both daunting and reassuring. His words had scared me but I knew it was in the interests of the other four to make sure we survived.

Snorting, Old Man said, "Right, we will be up early tomorrow and as Mouthy here has already attracted the attention of the Pilus Prior we will have to be perfect." We glared at the young man who looked suitably abashed. I think it was in his nature to be carping and complaining but I knew enough about the army to realise that would not do. We were shown and used the latrine. It stank and Old Man grinned when he said, "A minor punishment is filling in the old one and digging a new one." We all looked at Sertor. We were his tent mates and that meant the punishment for one would be shared by all.

As we prepared for bed Gaius asked, "What are the punishments?"

Numerius held up his fingers as he named them, "*Castigatio*, being hit by the centurion with his staff. You have had that one already, eh Mouthy? Next, reduction of rations. *Pecuniaria mulcta*, reduction in pay, fines or deductions from the pay allowance. Flogging in front of the century, cohort or legion. Whipping with the flagrum." He smiled, "That is the short whip. *Gradus deiectio*, that won't apply to you as it is a reduction in the ranks and there is none lower than us. *Missio ignominiosa*, dishonourable discharge. Loss of time in service advantages. *Militiae mutation*, relegation to inferior service or duties. *Munerum indictio*, additional duties."

He paused and I interjected, "And how much do we get paid, I mean so we know how much could be stopped?"

One of the others, Paullus, said, "Two hundred and twenty-five denarii a year." He was the only Paullus and had no nickname but as he had a lugubrious face I always thought of him as an ass.

Numerius laughed, "And of course they take out of your pay for clothing and food. You will be lucky to get paid in six months." My face fell. He laughed, "Don't worry, if you are any good you can make more than that when we win."

Sertor asked, "So is that it? They are the punishments?"

Numerius' face became serious, "They are the lesser ones." He sighed, "I might as well tell you now and then if you run, before you have sworn the oath and leave your equipment, you won't die." We all waited with bated breath. "There are two. The *fustuarium*: that is for desertion or dereliction of duty, stealing, false witness, sexual misconduct and repeating three times a same offence." He paused, "The legionary is stoned or beaten to death by cudgels, in front of the assembled troops, by his fellow soldiers. The other one is *decimation*. The sentence is carried out against an entire unit that had mutinied, deserted, or shown dereliction of duty. One out of every ten men, chosen by lots, would be beaten to death, usually by the other nine with their bare hands. I have seen men suffer the fustuarium but never a decimation." He lay down under his cloak and said, cheerfully, "Still want to be a legionary?"

Roman Roads used in the book

Chapter 2

I was exhausted but I did not sleep well. Numerius' little talk gave me nightmares. The result was I was up before the cornicen had sounded the call. We dressed in our tunics, donned our caligae and headed with our mess tins for the mess tent. It was bread and porridge although this time it was oat porridge and there was some honey. The honey soon went although because I was at the front of the queue I managed to get some.

All the new men were seated at the rear tables, reflecting our junior status. There were forty-eight of us; six conterburnia. Hostius came over, "As soon as you have eaten, dress in your mail and bring your shields and spears to the parade ground, it is time for the oath."

Sertor had not run but, after we had eaten and we dressed for the parade and the swearing in ceremony, he looked distinctly unhappy. While I had been appalled at the range and variety of punishments, I had realised that the most serious of them were well deserved. The minor ones, it seemed to me, could be avoided. The new recruits were a mixture of old and young as were our contuburnium. Most were older soldiers, veterans who had returned to the legion. Talking to Numerius I gathered that the old legions of Strabo had been disbanded when he had died. His son, so it seemed, had a better reputation already than his father had ever enjoyed. At the parade I studied the officers. The aquilifer stood with Pilus Prior and three well-dressed young officers. I did not see any centurions.

Hostius appeared. He was dressed in full armour and I saw that his helmet was that of a centurion, he had phalerae upon his armour. He had been more important than I had thought. His voice boomed as he spoke, "When you are summoned you step forward and do everything that the camp prefect asks of you. You are making a sacred oath and there will be a priest so do not take this lightly. You say, loudly, 'we do'. Understand?" I knew he was really talking to the ones they had referred to as 'virgins', the four of us and the other clean faced youths. We all nodded. "I will be watching." He left us and went to stand behind the Pilus Prior.

"Who are the men with the centurion?" I hissed.

Out of the side of his mouth Numerius said, "Narrow Band Tribunes. Young officers who will use the legion to gain power and make a name for themselves. We steer clear of them in battle. Now keep quiet. We have eyes upon us."

I saw Pilus Prior staring at us. I hoped I was not in for a beating. I resolved to do as we had advised Sertor to do and keep my mouth shut.

The legion arrived and formed neat ranks behind us. Each century had a centurion and two other officers as well as another man carrying a standard. I learned he was called a signifer. I learned that the other two men were called optio and tesserarius.

When Gnaeus Pompeius arrived, accompanied by a priest and a clerk as well as another gaggle of officers, he was dressed in magnificent armour. He had a shining cuirass and a longer sword than the other officers. The baldric and scabbard were exquisitely made. His helmet had a red horsehair plume. The legion rippled as men stood a little straighter. The Pilus Prior glared around the serried ranks but not a word was needed. There was silence punctuated only by the cluck of a fowl I saw held by a slave, behind the priest. I knew that that measured our importance. We were low down the order. A bull, or several bulls, were often sacrificed at funerals. We were only worthy of the sacrifice of a fowl.

I had spoken to the man whose banner we would follow and he had spoken quietly in a pleasant voice. Now I noticed that his tone, when he spoke to us, was different. I had once heard an orator speak and Gnaeus Pompeius used a similar style. His voice carried to everyone and he emphasised his words with gestures.

"Today we welcome the last of our recruits to this, my legion. When they have sworn their oath we have one week to prepare as a legion before we march to join General Sulla. We will wrest Rome from the Marians who think they have the right to rule. They do not." No one uttered a sound but I saw smiles on the faces of the tribunes and nods from some of the centurions. The

Pilus Prior kept a stony expression on his face. He nodded to one of the officers who stepped forward.

I learned later that the man, an older soldier, was the Camp Prefect. He had been Pilus Prior before Varius Drusus. He said, "Those who wish to serve in the legion of Gnaeus Pompeius, step forward."

We all stepped forward and the aquilifer did so too. I saw that there was an eagle upon the standard. The aquilifer was dressed as we were but on his helmet he had the pelt of an animal.

The priest stepped forward and I saw he held in his hand a knife. There would be a sacrifice. "Do you swear, before the eagle of the legion, allegiance to Gnaeus Pompeius and to fight for him and him only?"

"We do." The words seemed to echo and the silence that followed lasted longer than I had expected. The priest clearly understood drama. I saw Gnaeus Pompeius nod and the priest turned to the slave who held the fowl so that its neck was extended. The head was severed and then the fowl turned upside down. The priest sliced open the bird's belly and pulled out the heart. I was impressed for there was no hesitation. Had there been it might have been considered bad luck. He held up the heart for all to see.

Gnaeus Pompeius stepped forward and the priest said, "The gods approve."

Our commander turned to us and smiled, "Welcome to my legion."

He strode off and the tribunes and other officers, the Camp Prefect apart, hurried after him. Hostius joined him as the rest of the legion was dismissed. I saw six centurions wander over to us. When they arrived the Camp Prefect said, "You will each be assigned to a century. Hostius." The Camp Prefect obviously knew the old soldier well.

Hostius said, "When I say your name then go with the centurion I indicate."

I noticed that the first ones were in the Seventh Cohort. We were the last and we were in the Ninth Cohort and we were in the Sixth Century. It did not take a genius to work out that we were the lowest of the low. If the first century of the Prima Cohort were the best men in the legion then the Sixth Century of the Ninth Cohort had to be the worst. We were starting off at the bottom. As Caeso Sentia Bucco, our centurion, led us off, I reflected that the only way to go was up. I saw Hostius watching us as we left the parade ground. He had said he was retiring but had I seen a look in his eyes that bespoke a yearning to serve once more?

We headed for the rest of the century. They were shedding their mail shirts and their helmets. They stood watching us as we arrived. I was able to study the centurion as we walked. He was younger than I had expected. Perhaps that reflected the century's position. He was on the ladder to promotion. The centurion pointed to a legionary who had two metal disks on his baldric, "This is Decimus Corbulo. He is the optio." He smiled, "For you virgins that means he is my second in command." Corbulo did not smile. Like the centurion he was young. He would not brook any mistakes. The next man who was pointed out to us was older and had four disks on his baldric. "This is the tesserarius, Nanus Quietus. He is the third in command. He is also the keeper of the watchwords." He turned to the rest of the century, "You lot do not need me to tell you what you have to do. Instead of viewing the fresh meat get about your duties!" The centurion might be young but he commanded respect for every one of the century turned and scurried off.

The centurion turned and walked along our line. He paused at Numerius, "I know you. Did you not serve before? You were a tesserarius."

"Yes, Centurion, and you were a young recruit like these lads. Times have changed, eh, sir?"

Bucco leaned in and said, "Yes, they have, Legionary Sura." He held out his hand and Quietus handed him a wax tablet. "Which one is Porcianus?"

I shivered at the use of my name and when I spoke I croaked, "Me, sir!"

He gave a smile, "I understand you worked on your father's farm?" I nodded. He looked at the tablet and nodded, "Then you are in charge of the mule that your contuburnium will use. Tesserarius, take him to bring it and the pot and stone."

"Sir." He turned to me. "Leave your helmet, shield and spear here. Follow me." As we walked through the camp he spoke to me. "Hostius thought you had something about you, son. Was he right?"

"What, sir?"

"He said that you had the makings of a legionary. What did he mean?"

I shrugged, "I have no idea, sir."

"And you impressed Gnaeus Pompeius too."

"Is that why I am in charge of the mule, sir?"

He laughed, "In charge! You lead it and you feed it. If you want to give yourself the delusion that it is a promotion then perhaps Hostius was wrong. The centurion gave you the job as out of the four virgins you were the only one who had experience with animals. Mamerus Rufio might be given the job of cooking as his father was a baker. As for Firminius and Lamia, we have yet to see their skills."

"And the other four, sir, the veterans?"

He stopped and turned to look at me, "You virgins are about as much use as a mule turd but you have the advantage that you are raw clay. The ones you call veterans, the old hands, they know the commands and they know the calls. They can fight but they also know the ways of the legion and we have to find out if they can be trusted. Until we have fought our first fight they will be watched."

"And us, sir?"

He gave a thin smile, "Let us hope that you survive your first fight, eh?"

With those sombre words in my ears, we headed to the quartermaster's tent once more. The centurion's prompt decision to send me was rewarded by the fact that I was the first to be given a mule. Quietus, the tesserarius, identified the best. I found that I agreed with him but I was not so foolish as to tell him so.

The quartermaster said, as he handed me the panniers, "Her name is Ceres." He shrugged, "You can call her what you want."

They both looked at me as I stroked her ears. She also looked up at me. The centurion was right, I did know animals: the dog on the farm, the goat and the pigs were all treated the same by me. I spoke to them in a kindly manner unless they misbehaved and I did the same with Ceres, "No, it is a good name. The goddess of cereal was one of our house deities."

Quietus smiled, "Good." I fitted the panniers and when I had done so the clerk handed me a large cooking pot. I loaded it on one side of Ceres. The grinding stone was smaller but almost as heavy and I loaded that on the opposite side. It made sense to me but it seemed to impress Quietus for he smiled. "And now the supplies and then we are done."

Once back at the tent I unloaded Ceres and then, after ensuring she was watered I tethered her at the best piece of grass that remained. That proved to be the easiest part of the day. For the rest we were drilled by the optio and the tesserarius. The remainder of the century and the centurion were somewhere else. The first thing we learned was the march. The two officers had two pace sticks and we spent what seemed like an age learning the two paces. I watched Numerius and the veterans and picked it up quickly. It was Mamerus and not Sertor who struggled. We had a food break and then practised throwing the pilum. It was not easy. Finally, we were taught to use the sword and scutum. By the end of the day, I was exhausted but I felt a little more soldierly.

We were given just two days to work alone and then we had to learn to manoeuvre as a cohort. I did not find it hard for I had already worked out that we were the most expendable of the centuries. As such we were expected to fill a hole when necessary. It was the learning of the signals from the cornicen that was the hardest. I know that the officers in our century and the cohort were suspicious of men who had served before but Numerius was a godsend to me. He kept me straight. I realise now that it was not for altruistic reasons. He needed our contuburnium to work well. If we did not then when we fought we might all die. Gaius was also a willing pupil but the two friends, Mamerus and Sertor were always half a step behind.

After two days of manoeuvring with the cohort we were drilled as a legion and came under the baleful stare and glare of Pilus Prior as well as the scrutiny of Gnaeus Pompeius. We learned how to dig latrines, erect and dismantle a marching camp and how to load and pack our marching pole. That we were leaving soon was clear to us all. When the news came that we were to leave the next day then even the veterans became animated and as we sat outside our tent we virgins listened to their words. Even Sertor had learned to keep quiet when they spoke.

Proculus Lamia, who was in the Third Cohort, was Numerius' close friend and he shook his head, "We have barely had time to learn the names of our tent brothers and we are marching to war." He nodded to us, "And these have not had the time to learn enough."

Another of the veterans, Opiter, said, "Who knows we may not have to fight. I heard we are just going to meet Sulla and his legions. The Marians won't want to face him. Young Marius is merely a shadow of his father."

They all did as we did and looked at Numerius. Now that I knew he had been a tesserarius I respected his judgements even more. He was chewing on a piece of liquorice root. He took it from his mouth and said, "Opiter, do you think that the Marians will simply hand Rome over to Sulla? If the dictator wants it we will have to fight for it. You are right, we have not trained enough and," he looked at us and said, "no offence but I do not want to go into battle yet with you four. You might turn out to be good soldiers but I don't want to die finding that out. My hope is that as Sulla's legions have just come back from the east where they have, I am guessing, been successful that we will just be able to watch. Sulla is no fool. Gnaeus Pompeius might be a young cockerel anxious to show his martial skill but Sulla might just hold us in reserve." He shook his head, "We have the march to try to make you into soldiers."

The conversation was ended when the centurion and optio came over. They were both clearly suspicious of the veterans. While we all respected them and their views the two officers viewed them as potential troublemakers. The centurion addressed me, "On the march you lead your mule. To that end you are responsible for the loading and packing of the animal. It is in your interest that she is well balanced and not over worked. While we march it is your job to see she behaves and when we reach our marching camp, while these seven dig ditches and put in the rampart stakes, you see to her. When that is done you will erect your own tent and cook your food."

He turned to the optio who said, "Our century has the first watch. We will be relieved by the Second Century. Get what sleep you can tonight for you will just have four hours." The two officers were looking at our veterans and the faces of the four reflected the same opinion. They were unhappy that we had the first watch.

When the officers had gone we rose and headed for the tent. Gaius ventured, "Well, if we have the first watch then it stands to reason we won't have another for some time."

"Son, we are the lowest of the low. Pilus Prior will dump on us whenever he can. You can bet his precious First Cohort will not have a duty. It is us who will dig latrines and be given every shitty duty going. Until we have shown what we can do in battle then we are expendable." Numerius' voice showed his anger. Knowing he had been an officer I could understand it. Perhaps he had hoped, when he re-enlisted, that he might be given if not responsibility, then a place in a higher ranked century.

I was so nervous about my task, the next day, that even though I slept well I woke early and slipped out of the tent to make water and to prepare Ceres. My foresight in not only giving her the best grazing but also the treats of occasional handfuls of oats and old root vegetables I managed to acquire paid off. She greeted me warmly. I knew that she would be obedient on the road despite the weight she would have to bear. I went to the sack of oats that we carried and took out a small handful. I gave it to her and fussed her around her ears. I led her to the stream. Soon it would be fouled as others took their mules to be watered. I was the first there. It was not even daylight. As I was about to leave I saw another young recruit arrive with his mule.

He smiled, "I thought I would be the first."

I nodded, "I woke early. This is a big day."

"It is. My name is Marcus."

I nodded and said, "Mine is Lucius. I dare say we shall see each other on the march."

Somehow that conversation put me in good spirits. I was not the only one who felt the way I did. Breakfast was a hurried affair as we took down our tent and I began to pack the mule. Numerius and the others could have told me what to do but they did not. As they packed their own belongings they merely kept a wary eye on me as I loaded the tent, cooking pot, grinding stone and supplies on the mule. The optio's words had an effect on me

Legionary

and I was careful. I did not rush. When I was satisfied I put my marching pole and spears on the top of the rest of Ceres' burden and, after putting my scutum in its leather covering over my back, turned.

Numerius smiled, "Well I will say one thing, they have chosen a good mule man. If you can fight as well as you pack a mule then we have one virgin who might see the dawn after their first fight."

There was an order to the column and we were at the rear of it. A small unit of auxiliary cavalry led. We watched as the legionary cavalry and senior officers marched first, followed by the First Cohort. We all marched in cohort and century order. I saw our century had a ballista as did the other centuries and there was an extra mule carrying it. The rest of the auxiliary cavalry followed us. We had just two turmae. There were twenty in the one that led us and eighteen that followed us. They were Gauls and Numerius did not like them. As we marched he said to Proculus, "I remember those bastards when we fought against them. I don't like them being behind us."

Nanus Quietus had overheard him, "Get over it, Old Man. We defeated them and they signed up to serve as Roman soldiers. They don't get the same pay as you but we shall need them to scout out any enemies so accept them."

"Yes Tesserarius." I knew that Numerius did not agree but he knew how to play the game.

It soon became clear to us all that Gnaeus Pompeius was hurrying. Numerius had told us that we would normally march for five hours each day but that first day we marched for six and covered thirty miles. It might have been to test what we could do but, as I unpacked our tent and placed it where the surveyors had indicated, I spoke to one of them.

"That was a hard march, Immunis."

He was an older man and he smiled, "Aye, young 'un." He pointed ahead, "Word is that there are three armies trying to stop us joining Sulla. I would expect a hard march every day. Still, you seem to have coped well today. How are the feet?"

I looked down, "Coping well, Immunis."

"Aye, well look after them."

Legionary

I realised then that the time I had spent running in the hills and hunting, barefoot, had hardened my feet as well as making my legs stronger. Sertor and Mamerus had clearly not done the same for their feet were blistered and bleeding when they came to help the rest of our contuburnium erect the tent. Gaius' were a little better but the only one who did not ask for the vinegar flask was me. Numerius grudgingly allowed the three of them to use a little of the salve he had. It came at a price. They each had to pay him a denarius. They were learning about the life of a legionary.

We all pitched in with the cooking. When we had stopped and I had watered Ceres I had picked wild greens that I found. The veterans had discovered some nuts and they went into the cereal and bean stew that would be our meal. Mamerus was given the task of grinding the grain for the flatbreads we would eat. He showed, that first night, that he had skills. He smeared the flat rock we placed at one side of the fire with a little oil and some wild garlic I had found. The bread did not stick to the stone and tasted good when we ate it. We had plenty of salt. My mother had given me a small sack before I had left home. It was another reason that Numerius seemed to accept me more than the others.

I told the others what the immunis had said and Proculus Lamia, Numerius' friend, nodded, "Aye, that makes sense. We are a new legion with a young leader. If Gaius Marius and his men can eliminate us then they will have to face fewer men when they meet Sulla." He turned to Numerius, "We might need those Gauls, now, Old Man. Their eyes will be the only warning we have."

He snorted, "If the immunis is right then we have three armies converging on us. If they combine then no matter how good Gnaeus Pompeius is, we will be dead meat."

We had barely finished eating when the tesserarius came for us, "Right, duty time. Numerius, your tent has the duty between the porta principalis dextra and the porta decumana." I learned that because he had been an officer he was put in charge of our tent. He was the Chosen Man for our tent. He and Bucco did not like each other but the centurion recognised that Old Man had skill.

"Yes, Tesserarius." We hefted our scutum and our pilum. We went to perform our first duty.

Legionary

Numerius was professional. He assigned each of the virgins to a veteran. It made sense as that way we would be taught what to do correctly. It also meant that we got to know another member of the contuburnium better. I was with Numerius. He showed me how to hold the shield so that its weight was partly taken by my shoulder and how to rest my spear across my other shoulder. As we walked our section of the camp he nodded into the dark. "Keep your eyes fixed on the dark and mark any movement. It might be an animal but it could be someone coming to slit your throat or send an arrow in the dark." He nodded towards my chest. "Your armour and padding might stop an arrow but you would have to mend the mail. Better that you react to a movement and use your scutum."

I listened and I learned. I was afraid as we walked along the raised rampart and peered over the small palisade. I had not expected war so soon. My father had said there would be months of training. Even Hostius had implied we would have more time. I thought back to that first day at the port. Had Gnaeus Pompeius been looking for a message from a ship? Perhaps he had heard from Sulla. Whatever the reason we might have to fight and, when we did so, we would not be fully trained. Some of us would die. Would I have been better off to stay at the farm? Of course, if I had then there would have been less food for the rest of the family and we would have offended the gods. Until we had an income then the farm could not produce enough for four people. My mother, father and youngest sister might survive. As I watched our relief march up I resigned myself to the fact that, for good or ill my father had made the right decision. My fate and my future lay in the legion of Gnaeus Pompeius and in the skill of that young man.

Chapter 3

Two nights later the legion suffered its first casualty. Spies had approached the camp and unlike us the veteran who had instructed his virgins had allowed two novices to patrol together. One of the two young men was killed by an arrow. Numerius said it had been lucky or perhaps, unlucky depending upon your perspective. For the young man it was bad luck but for the legion it was good for it alerted us to the dangers of spies and scouts. The arrow had struck the young legionary in the face. He had died quickly. It was, however, a warning. The Marians were seeking us and as the assassin had not been found then the enemy knew our numbers. The noose would be tightening.

The next day we marched for seven hours and even I, despite the long walks I had taken to hunt, felt exhausted. We were racing to get to Brundisium. It was now common knowledge that there were three armies trying to get at us. Centurion Bucco gathered the century around him to tell us. He was a young officer but he was a thoughtful one. He knew that by telling us he involved everyone and by giving us as much information as he could he was preparing us.

"There are three enemy leaders who seek us: Lucius Cornelius Cinna, Gnaeus Papirius Carbo and Gaius Marius the Younger. They each have a legion and auxiliaries and they are trying to corner us so that we can be destroyed. With us destroyed they can then move on to defeat, they hope, General Sulla. We will no longer have our Gaulish horsemen behind us. We will be the rearguard. It is a place of honour. We need our horsemen to find the enemy before they find us." He smiled, "At least with our horsemen ranging far and wide we will not have to wade through horse shit." His words brought smiles, even from Numerius. "When we fight we will be on the left flank as that is our position in the line of march." He looked around the sea of faces. "When that day does come we will show that our century is every bit as good as the First Cohort." His words were well chosen and we all stood a little taller as we headed back to our tents.

Legionary

Three days later, as we neared the village of Alexina, we heard the sound of the cornicen and even I, new to the legion, recognised the call. There were enemies ahead. The centurion shouted, "Mules to the rear."

I led Ceres and sought out a tree to which to tie her. I saw a stunted, wind-blown olive tree. I doubted that it had produced olives for many years and I tied her to it. There was a little grass for grazing and she would not suffer for there was enough shade from the tree to give some respite from the sun. The breeze from the sea was also cooling. I ruffled her mane, "Hopefully I will see you after the battle, if not then I will see you in the next life." I took my scutum from its sack and my pilum and javelin. I hurried back to the century. Already the other mules, which had further to travel, were being brought back to form a long line behind the cohorts. The legion was marching into its battle lines.

I saw one of the Gaulish turma take its place to our left, along the beach. The legionary cavalry, all one hundred and twenty of them, were with the other Gaulish cavalry on our right where the men of the First Cohort were aligning themselves. Our cohort was the last on the left and we were in the third rank. We were slightly echeloned back from the Eighth Cohort. I was lucky for I was tall and I could see, between the gaps before me, the enemy as they also formed their battle lines. It was, I could see, a similar one to ours except that their cavalry were on the left flank. However, Numerius recognised their standards and he groaned, "That is just what we need. We are facing their First Cohort."

Although we were novices even we understood what that meant. Our cohort would have to face twice the number of men. First Cohort had double centuries and they would be the best of the enemy.

Sertor said, "Surely the general will shift men to give us aid."

The optio, Decimus Corbulo, roared, "Silence in the ranks or you will feel the blunt end of my pilum." He then added, a little more softly, "We have the sea to our left. If they try to outflank us they will be bogged down and they have no horsemen there."

I saw that he was right. Our auxiliaries, even though they were just a handful, would be able to get around the side of the enemy and use their javelins against the right-hand side of the enemy First Cohort. Their shields would not help them.

Someone murmured, "If we had some slingers or archers then I would be happier."

I heard a shout from the front of the cohort, "Ballistae all in position."

I said to Numerius who was next to me, "Who commands our cohort?"

He shook his head, "No one. The general will have told the centurions of every first century what their orders are. They will have passed those orders on and we obey. We listen for Centurion Bucco's orders. Today we will discover what our little Alexander can do, eh?" He took one of his spears and rammed it into the sandy soil. I did the same and then waited.

It seemed to take the enemy forever to get into line and I took heart from the fact that we had done so quicker. I saw that they had some slingers and bowmen spread out before them. That started the doubts and they assailed me from within. Was that because we had fewer men? Was their general better than ours? Did their slingers and archers give them an advantage? I was to discover that waiting was worse than any battle because in the waiting you could let a fertile mind race. My inner voices tormented me as they argued back and forth. My head was almost hurting from the conflict. When the enemy horns sounded and they advanced it was almost a relief. I heard an order from my left. The Roman officer who commanded the Gauls was telling them to stay in line. I would have been happy for them to try to rid us of the potential nuisance that was the mob of missile men heading for us. It was only then that I saw there were few of those men facing the other cohorts. The enemy was attacking the Eighth and Ninth Cohorts, first with slingers and archers and then the might of their Prima Cohort. We would be harried and then smashed by the best that the enemy had. I became resentful, even before I had used my weapon, that we were to be sacrificed by the general. I cared not if he had a wonderful plan that would defeat the enemy. If I died then my life would be meaningless. My inner voices told me to run. There was no one behind me. I could simply drop my scutum and pilum, discard my helmet and reach Ceres before I was missed. I even planned how I would shed her load and ride her north to hide in the hills. I was convinced that we would lose and no one would bother to come looking for me.

I stayed and the reason was Gaius to my left and Numerius to my right. If I ran then they might die. The contuburnium, the century and ultimately the cohort, survived in a battle because of their unity. I would stay and face my fate. The three of us would live or die together.

When the ballistae sent their bolts at the enemy the noise was terrifying. It was a long echoing crack and the bolts all flew towards the enemy. I saw one bolt strike a legionary who had raised his shield for protection but the bolt went through the shield as though it was parchment. It struck the shield and the man and the next one and the one after him. It made me look down the enemy line for their ballistae. I saw that there were none facing our part of the line and I thanked the gods for that.

We heard the command for shields to be raised. We were in the rear rank and our shields had to protect the fourth and fifth centuries before us. Suddenly all went dark. The smell of men filled my nostrils and it became hotter. When the first stones and arrows fell it was like a hailstorm. They rattled on shields. I did not feel any hit my scutum but I heard cries from the front ranks. Men had been struck. We were not ordered to take a pace forward and so I knew that none had died. There might be wounded men but they would fight.

When the command came to lower shields it was to the blinding light of the sun. It took some moments for my eyes to adjust but I saw that while we had been rained upon the enemy had moved forward. The Prima Cohort that faced us was now within charging distance. We had not yet practised this, after all we were still green recruits, but Numerius had told us that the enemy would halt, hurl their first pilum and then charge. What would the centurion of the First Century order? What had Gnaeus Pompeius instructed him to do? Would they throw their own first pilum or wait until the enemy were moving?

This time I saw the effect of the thrown spears. Men fell and legionaries stepped from the century behind to take their place. Numerius picked up his second spear and stepped into the spot vacated before him. Suddenly I had no one until Gnaeus moved next to me. I heard the command for the first and second centuries to throw their spears. I saw men in the enemy front ranks fall. I watched others whose shields, weighed down by the heavy pila, were dragged down. Even as they struck some of the enemy elite soldiers were speared. What I was not prepared for was the noise as spears and then swords hammered and clanged on swords, helmets and armour. The screams of men who had been speared and stabbed rang in the air.

I heard a horn from behind me and knew what it meant. The Eighth Cohort had been hit hard. The front two centuries echeloned to their right. It meant that the third and fourth centuries of our cohort would now have to face the enemy. The soldiers who had hurt the Eighth Cohort would be drawn even closer to us. The man before me stepped forward, and picking up my second spear and holding it in my left hand I rejoined Numerius. We were now in the second rank. If the man before me, who was from the Fourth Century fell then I would have to join the front rank. I would be fighting the best soldiers that the enemy had. I was terrified.

Numerius said, "Hold your spear to face the enemy. If you see flesh then jab."

I did so. I was grateful to be doing something rather than standing there. The man before me and his opponent were duelling with swords and the Fourth Century man was giving a good account of himself. Blood spattered me from my right but I forced myself to ignore it and concentrate on finding flesh. For a moment the elite soldier's shield dropped and drooped a little. It was like that moment when I was hunting and saw the rabbit appear before me. In that instant I had released my arrow almost without thinking and I did so now, thrusting the heavy pilum at the face of the soldier. I had a strong arm and the sharpened metal end drove into his orb and even as he screamed in pain I pushed and his scream was silenced as my spear entered his brain and ended his life.

The man who appeared before me lunged with his sword at the man who had been to the left of the fallen soldier. His sharpened weapon drove up under the arm of the enemy legionary and he was killed. They were just two deaths but I heard a cheer ripple down our line. Encouraged we all jabbed and poked our spears. The enemy responded and I saw the man before Numerius fall and Old Man had to join the front rank. As I glanced along our line I saw that Sertor was now in the second rank and when the man before him fell he stepped, somewhat nervously into the breach. He lasted less than a heartbeat. The youth who was clearly not legionary material was gutted by a savage thrust from his opponent's sword. It was Gaius who avenged him for he thrust his spear into the man's neck and he fell, the spear still attached. He picked up his second one and stepped into Sertor's place. We were now just one rank deep in places. Our only hope was that the mounting pile of bodies before us would slow down the enemy sufficiently to enable our general to come up with a plan to help us.

The legionary before me fell and before I could even think what I ought to do the legionary with the deadly looking sword came at me. I do not know why I did it. Did I panic or was the thought placed there by the milling voices in my head? Whatever the reason I jammed the spear down to impale his foot. He screamed and I punched hard with the boss of my scutum as I drew my sword. My boss struck him squarely in the face and his nose erupted as it broke. A man with a broken nose does not mean to cry but his eyes weep without any reason. He was temporarily blinded and as his shield dropped a little I drove my blade up and under his arm. It came out at his shoulder and screaming from his wounds he fell.

It was at that moment that the Gauls attacked the enemy to my left. Perhaps the officer had given the command or it may have always been the plan of the general. As it was it came at a perfect time. We were all engaged with our opponents and the Gauls hurled their spears at the men on the extreme right of the enemy Prima Cohort. Every Gaul had three javelins. The last would be used as a lance. There was just a handful of them but they killed twenty or more of the enemy and wounded others. The enemy stepped back and locked shields.

I heard Centurion Bucco shout, "Fifth and Sixth Centuries, reform." His command told me that the centurion of the Fifth Century was dead.

I took advantage of the moment to take up my spare spear from my left hand. The other was still embedded in the foot of the man I had killed. Numerius and I found ourselves flanked by Gaius and Mamerus. Somehow that made me feel better. We were still vulnerable but the attack by the Gauls had stopped them from outflanking us. I saw nothing beyond the beleaguered Eighth Cohort and our two senior centuries.

Centurion Bucco shouted, "Pass pila to the men in the front rank who do not have them."

I had one and I hefted it above my shield as the enemy began another attack. The enemy had no spears. They advanced with swords. They must have known that we had many novices and they were coming to end our time in the legion. Old Man said, "Hold firm, you two. You have both done well but the battle is not yet over. These men are not as good as they think they are."

His words gave me confidence. When they were just ten paces from us Centurion Bucco shouted, "Pila!" We had little practice throwing spears and I threw almost blindly. I threw as hard as I could and when the legionary before me raised his shield the head drove in and, as the man neared me, his shield dropped. A man could not hold a shield with a heavy pilum embedded in it. I drew my sword and punched with my scutum as he neared me. He blocked it with his sword and I back slashed and caught his unprotected upper left arm with the sword I had drawn. The weight of his shield and his wound meant he could not protect himself from his left. I saw the fear in his eyes as I pulled back my father's old sword. He tried to block the blow he knew was coming with his own weapon but I was already punching with my shield. When you have to wrestle a pig, you learn to use both hands and arms at the same time. His weapon merely grated off my boss and the tip of my sword tore through the mail links. His eyes widened as he felt the end tear into flesh and I pushed harder. I must have struck something vital for his body went limp and slid down from my sword. His body was an impediment to the man behind and the legionary behind me was able to hurl his pilum and hit the next man squarely in the face.

Once more the enemy reeled and their horn sounded for them to reform. Our line still felt very thin. There were bodies before and behind us. Old Man shouted, "Come on and feel my sword!" He seemed to have been taken over by the battle. He was like a man possessed but his words encouraged me. It was as I glanced behind that I saw an approaching column of men. I recognised the signifer of the First Century of the Second Cohort. They were marching at double speed. The ground behind was slightly lower than where we stood and I knew that the movement would be hidden from the enemy. The enemy were forming for another attack. Wounded men were being replaced by fresh ones. We did not have that luxury. I looked for a pilum to use but saw that the ones that were close were broken.

Even as the enemy formed Centurion Bucco shouted, "Fifth and Sixth centuries ten paces to your left." I heard a command from the senior centurion of the Eighth Cohort to our right. As we moved the order to charge was given and even as we headed onto the soft sand the Second Cohort, with fresh spears and unwearied arms charged the enemy First Cohort. As my feet sank into the soft sand I was able to watch the Second Cohort, eager for a victory over an enemy First Cohort, plough into them. Perhaps we had killed enough of their better legionaries. I do not know but the Second Cohort sent them packing. They fled.

Centurion Bucco shouted, "Charge!"

It was not the most elegant nor the straightest of lines. We had to cross the sand before we reached the more solid soil but we reached the flank of the fleeing legionaries and had the easier task of hacking and stabbing at the backs of men. They were Romans as we were but this was civil war and if we had lost they would have butchered us. I did not think of them as men but pigs to be slaughtered on the farm. The difference was that I had liked some of the pigs I had killed. I felt nothing for these men I did not know except that they were enemies and I had been ordered to kill them. I did.

When the order to halt came my father's sword was little better than a lump of iron. There was no edge to it. The tip still had a point but driving through mail links had blunted my weapon. I had been forced to kill the last enemy with my dagger. It had been a mercy. The man had made it from the main battle lines clutching in his guts but as he knelt before me he pleaded for a merciful death. I gave him one.

The horn that sounded the recall came not long before the sun began to set. Numerius, Gaius and Mamerus were all close and Numerius said, "Now is when we make profit. Search the dead.

Legionary

They will have coins. If they have a decent dagger or a better sword then take it."

I searched the man whose throat I had cut. He had twenty denarii but his dagger was gone as was his sword. By the time we reached our camp darkness had fallen and I was one hundred and ten denarii better off. I also had two more daggers and a good sword I had taken from a dead centurion. It meant I was adding to the weight that I would have to carry but I was one of Marius' Mules, which was now my life.

I was hungry but the smell of the burning enemy bodies took away the appetite. We had our own to bury. Mamerus took the death of his friend Sertor badly. I had been the only one who had seen the young man die and it was I who led the rest of the contuburnium to the body. We would bury our own. It was Numerius who told us that we should divide all that Sertor had amongst our section.

I thought Mamerus was going to object as did Numerius. The veteran spoke remarkably gently, as he said, "Mamerus, we could all die. Today I thought the odds were too great and that Gnaeus Pompeius had over stretched himself. I was wrong but the fact remains that when we next fight any one of us could be killed. The rest share all that we have." He took from under his belt, the leather purse that hung there. He held it up, "Here is mine." He smiled, "It will save time if you know where I keep it when searching my body. There is one gold piece in here as well as silver. Yours, I know, will not hold as much." He waved a hand at Sertor. "None of you have much but by taking a little here and there you will have. We serve the legion of Gnaeus Pompeius. He will take treasure and, hopefully, share it but he will take more and we will be lucky to get coppers. War is like that. The winners prosper and the losers," he shrugged, "they care not for they are in Elysium."

We piled wood beneath his body and using a tinderbox lit the kindling that took his body from this world to the next. He would not have an urn and there would be nowhere for his family to go to mourn. There was a comfort in knowing that if a man died in battle his family would mourn him. I determined not to die. I was now a legionary. I had survived my first battle and I would do everything in my power to survive again.

Legionary

The lesson I learned that day lived with me for the rest of my life. Numerius made out that he was a hard, uncaring man but that was a mask he wore. My opinion of him changed that day.

Chapter 4

The next day all the euphoria of the victory disappeared as we returned to the battlefield and stripped the enemy dead. Our dead had been burnt. They wore armour that could be used. They had helmets and shields. Gnaeus Pompeius was ambitious and he wanted more legions. The equipment we took could be repaired and issued to new recruits. We also collected every pilum we could. They too could be repaired. We still had a long way to go and although we had defeated one legion, there were two more looking for us. We were not out of the woods yet. That the legion we had defeated had not headed south became clear when we found no more bodies or graves after the first five miles of marching. They had headed west where they would, no doubt, join one of the other two legions searching for us. When they found us they would have vengeance in their hearts.

As we marched I noticed that while we had lost men we had not lost as many as I had expected. Of course, I saw more men sporting wounds and bandages. Those who had fallen from the line had not all perished. The loss of the centurion of the Fifth Century meant promotion for the optio of that century. Centurion Bucco had clearly benefitted from our victory as I noticed more senior officers speaking to him when we stopped for a rest. His star was rising. Numerius was still a little dismissive of him. I think it was his youth and the fact that he had known him before. Numerius might have been a centurion now had he not left the legion. He was a good soldier. I had seen that when we had fought our single battle.

The other thing I noticed, as we marched south to join Sulla, was that Ceres looked healthier than the other mules in the cohort. I took credit for that. I made sure she ate as well as she could and I was always careful not to overburden her. I brushed her coat each night and she seemed to appreciate it. Some of the other mule men appeared to regard the duty as a punishment. Perhaps, because my father had raised animals, I had a different opinion.

Legionary

We were found five more times on our way south. Each time we obeyed the horn instantly and formed ranks. Our long snake that wound down the road was vulnerable to an attack, especially an ambush. We had the handful of Gallic horsemen but we knew that if we were attacked it would be us, the rearguard, that would have to fight. The horsemen could simply ride away. Numerius was also disparaging in his comments about the auxiliaries, "They are not Roman and I do not trust them." He sniffed, "At least these are on our side. If they were on the side of the enemy then I would fear for my manhood. They are nasty fighters." Enigmatically that was all he said about our allies. However he viewed the enemy generals as incompetent. "They have three legions and we have one. No one fights three to one and survives. They are scared of our little warrior general." I noticed that his opinion of our leader was changing.

When we met Sulla and his veteran legions there was relief all around, not least because Sulla's army had proven themselves in the war against Mithridates. They were not legions who were made up largely of virgins and sprinkled with veterans. They were all veterans and they looked it. Even Numerius was impressed. That our leader had defeated a legion on the way south was greeted with great joy and Lucius Cornelius Sulla Felix, our overall leader, awarded Gnaeus Pompeius the title of Imperator, General. For one so young it was a mighty accolade.

Whilst Pompey might have been rewarded and applauded we were treated badly by the veterans of his army. They saw us as boys and there were fights. It was the older veterans from our legion who defended the honour of the rest of us. None died but there were nasty wounds inflicted. The sooner we could get back to the business of war the better, was the view of Numerius, Centurion Bucco and Optio Corbulo. They were the three men who, to me, were the most important. Gnaeus Pompeius might be the general but in battle it would be one of those three who would determine my fate and my future.

We headed up the Via Appia. The road led first to Capua and then Rome. It was a clear message. Sulla wanted Rome. When we began to march our leader left us. We learned that Sulla had tasked him with raising another legion and to find replacements for the men we had lost. We would fight alongside Sulla's five experienced legions. Even as we began to march, however, we were joined by other legions and their leaders. Marcus Licinius Crassus was the most notable amongst them although Marcus Lucullus was reputed to be a good leader too, as was Mctellus Pius. Even Numerius was impressed by Crassus, not necessarily as a general but for the fact that he had managed to become incredibly rich very quickly. His fortune was derived from the sale of slaves captured after battles. Numerius rubbed his finger and thumb together, "If he is leading our legion then we make money. He has a nose for such things."

As we turned to head north and west I was going to a new part of the land that was now called Rome. We had left Picenum when we had marched to meet Sulla but that had been on the eastern side of the mountain range that split the land in two. I would be seeing the real Rome. It was cold up in the mountains and the cloaks we wore did not seem adequate. The roads, whilst well-made could also cause problems. We had learned, when it was wet, not to march on the road. The hobnails that made our footwear last a little longer were treacherous on wet stone. The virgins copied the veterans and marched at the side of the road. We also marched hard. Sulla used the fastest speed that we could manage and his veterans took great delight in trying to break our spirit by marching hard. It was almost a competition. Another reason for not marching on the road was that our caligae lasted a little longer that way. Marcus Licinius Crassus had a legion that was also made up of veterans. These were from the Spanish campaigns and, for some reason, appeared less arrogant. When we stopped their camp was next to ours and they appeared quite friendly. As Crassus was leading our legion, too, this made sense. Numerius even found a couple of old comrades with whom he had served before and we were introduced to them. It was from these men that we learned more about our purpose.

"Our general wishes to become dictator once more. Marcus Licinius Crassus and Gnaeus Pompeius agree with him that a strong hand is needed." Agrippa pointed to the veteran legions, "I don't like them but at least they have conquered parts of Greece. We have enlarged the land ruled by Rome in Hispania but what of Lucius Cornelius Cinna, Scipio Asiaticus and Gaius Norbanus? Consul Carbo just seems intent on stopping General

Legionary

Sulla. They have done nothing with the legions that they lead. The Gauls still threaten us in the north as do the Helvetii. We need a strong Rome."

Numerius nodded, "Aye, if only to make us richer."

Gaius was a curious young man and while I sat on my tongue he was happy to ask questions, "Will we march on Rome do you think?"

Numerius deferred to Agrippa who shook his head, "Better to take the rest of the land and then have Rome beg Sulla to enter. He needs Rome to want him. He was expelled once before and this time he needs to be secure. With Crassus and Pompey at his side he has a chance."

We reached Venusia and we were welcomed. The city of Venus had been Roman for more than a hundred years. When Hannibal had taken so much of Italy, Venusia had remained loyal and our warm reception was a good omen. If we were welcomed there then other parts of Rome might do so. The town also gave us a chance to spend some of the money we had accrued. I still did not have enough to be profligate but I treated myself to some things that would be useful to me. I bought a tinderbox. Fire was a useful tool. I also bought a good whetstone. I had seen the advantage of keeping my weapons razor sharp. Numerius bought drink. I wondered if that had been his undoing the first time he had served in the legions. It would explain much.

We were heading for Capua and that was just five days away. We had been reinforced at the rear with some Boeotian auxiliaries. These were less wild looking than the Gauls and looked more like our own cavalry for they were Greeks. They were a comfort. Of course, we could not speak to them but I found that I could communicate, that was mainly because of Ceres. When we went to water our animals, usually when we camped, I often found myself close to these Greek horsemen. Unlike most of the mule men I made an effort to talk to them. They appreciated the effort and by the use of sign language, let me know they thought Ceres was well looked after. I reciprocated. The result was that they brought me oats for Ceres and shared some of their food with me. It made me feel useful. I felt guilty that I could do nothing for them but they seemed happy just to be kind to me. I managed to learn a few words and even the names of three of them.

Our enemies found us close to Capua. The land there was flatter than the mountains through which we had marched and Capua was a prosperous town. Next to Rome it was one of the most important cities in the Republic. We descended from the mountains towards the town where there would be baths, markets and, for those who wished them, lupanare and women. It was one of the horsemen who let me know. By dint of the few words I knew and sign language he let me know that there were two enemy armies approaching us and that, combined, they outnumbered us. That was all that I knew until Centurion Bucco returned from the meeting of centurions and Marcus Crassus.

Our centurion liked to tell us what he knew. I had realised early on that some of the centurions regarded legionaries as spear fodder. They did not care about them. Bucco did. He might have had his own reasons but I appreciated knowing what lay ahead. "We are to face the army of Gaius Norbanus. I have to tell you that he has sixty thousand men and we have just forty."

Before our first battle such figures would have terrified me but I now realised that while we would be armed and appear much like the men we would be facing, we had good leaders and the veterans of Sulla and Crassus would give us the edge. We had held a First Cohort when everyone thought that we would run.

"This time our legion will not be in the front rank. We will support the legion of Marcus Crassus. The attack will be initiated by the legions of General Sulla. We are on the left side of the army. There is a river and our generals hope that we can use that to our advantage." He smiled, "The sea helped us last time and I take it to be a good omen. I know we lost men in the battle by the sea but I hope that Gnaeus Pompeius will find men to replace our losses. Nonetheless we will win glory when we fight. The Fifth Century lost many men and we are to be brigaded with them. Optio Catulus is happy to be led by me."

That was good news. We would have a hundred and ten men to face the enemy as opposed to sixty if we fought as the Sixth Century.

We looked towards Capua and its walls. The city was big and even had a small amphitheatre. Numerius was disappointed that we would not see gladiatorial games. Campania was known for them. The centurion's words told us that our halt would be a brief one.

We broke camp early after a particularly frugal breakfast. Numerius did not mind, "When we win we will enjoy better rations. The ones we are fighting have come from Rome. It stands to reason that they will be well supplied. We will eat well and these Populares will have purses that are full. We are the least experienced legion in this army and yet we have enjoyed victory in battle. Norbanus has done nothing." He was a natural leader and like Bucco, knew how to inspire.

We lined up and faced the enemy. They did outnumber us. I wondered if Sulla thought they were too big a mouthful for us to take, especially when he sent some of his officers to Norbanus' camp. They returned soon after. As one of them passed Marcus Crassus who was standing nearby the officer said, "We have nothing to fear here." He pointed to Gaius and me, "Most of their men look as young as this pair!"

I found myself blushing. Numerius said, "Don't let it worry you. I know you have killed men. They don't."

Perhaps Sulla was more cunning than I gave him credit for. His emissaries had tried to make the young men from the enemy legions desert. They had failed but it might have created discord amongst the enemy and that could only help when we attacked. I knew we had to attack because of my conversation with the auxiliary cavalryman. There was an army the same size as ours coming to the aid of Norbanus. We had to fight and to win.

The initial attack would come from the five legions of Sulla. We were almost bystanders and we watched the killing machine that had defeated Mithridates hack their way through the front ranks of the enemy legions. When Norbanus sent men to stiffen his weakening line then we saw what kind of general Sulla was. He was quick thinking and skilled. Crassus was ordered to make a flank attack with his legion and that of Gnaeus Pompeius. We followed down the slope.

The slingers and archers who tried to slow us were brushed aside by the men from Hispania and then Crassus ordered us to the left of his advancing legion. It was the most difficult manoeuvre I had ever experienced. Crossing a slope downhill we had to crab behind Crassus' legion. It could not have been done without the skill of men like Bucco. When we emerged we were slightly behind the rearmost legion of General Norbanus. Even more importantly we were approaching from their right. Their shields were facing the front while the bulk of their enemies were to the left. That was the day I experienced my first charge. We halted just thirty paces from the enemy. Even as we did so they tried to turn. We were facing them slightly obliquely. The command to throw was given and the front three ranks all hurled their first pilum. The result was devastating. The spears struck flesh and men fell. Even before the spears had hit the order was given to charge. It was not a run, for that would have been a disaster, but we moved at a fast pace and the front rank, I was in the second, lunged with their spears at men who had seen those to their right die. They died too. With the pressure of Sulla's veterans and Crassus' men the front crumbled. If my first battle had been a success this second one, the one they called the Battle of Mount Tifata, was an unequivocal triumph. By the end of the day seven thousand men of the Marian army had died and six thousand had surrendered. The plunder was beyond our wildest dreams.

   We did not need to be told by Numerius what we had to do. We scoured the battlefield and took from the dead. The veteran had been right. These legions had been recently paid and still had their denarii with them. We ate their food and burned their bodies. There were simply too many to leave for the animal scavengers. We ate first and built fires that would take away the stink of death. I learned that burning bodies was necessary. Whilst the smell of burning flesh was bad it as not as bad as a camp close to rotting bodies and the sounds of animals scavenging.

   There had been losses and one of them was newly promoted Optio Catulus. His century had also lost more men than we had and, in the absence of Gnaeus Pompeius, General Crassus made the decision to amalgamate the fifth and sixth centuries into one. We had a new tent mate, Faustus Fullo. The rest of his contuburnium had all died in the battle and he took Sertor's place. He had been our only loss thus far. Although older than we were the deaths of his tent mates had affected him badly. He was morose and silent. We spent a day or so at the battlefield and all our attempts to cheer him up failed. In the end Numerius told us to leave him to face his demons himself.

"You can always help a tent mate to fight an enemy. You can defend him and protect him but the one enemy you cannot help him to fight is himself. The battle is here," he tapped the side of his head, "we will know who wins…eventually" He added mysteriously.

We wondered if we would march on Rome. The idea excited everyone, especially the younger legionaries. Even Numerius seemed animated at the thought of taking and entering the greatest city in the world. Sulla had done so before. Once more we were fed by gossip. It was not until Gnaeus Pompeius returned that the gossip became firm fact. After he had met with Sulla and Quintus Caecilius Metellus Pius along with Crassus and Marcus Lucullus, he gathered his legion around him. He knew how to inspire his men. There were new recruits for our legion with him as well as another legion that would join Sulla.

The young general looked confident and at ease as he addressed us, "It seems you do not need me to win victories." He waved a hand at the tent of Marcus Crassus, "I have heard that you did valiant work and it was my legion that helped to turn the tide of the battle. For that you shall all be rewarded. Each of you will be given one hundred denarii as a reward for your service and more will be forthcoming for we are to march north under General Pius. Norbanus has fled to Cisalpine Gaul where Gnaeus Papirius Carbo is gathering an army. If we are to enter Rome then they must be defeated. We have a long march ahead of us but I know that as Pompey's men you will not let me down." We cheered and he held his hands up for silence. "Already General Sulla's veterans speak of this legion as one of the finest they have fought alongside. We have begun to make a reputation and we shall build on it." He waved an aide over. The aide had a cushion in his hands. "We have medals to award."

This was the first such ceremony I had witnessed and, to our great delight, the first two men to be called up were Centurion Bucco and our signifer, Marius Gracchus.

"Centurion Bucco for your brave service in the battle you are awarded this phalera." He handed him the golden disk.

"Thank you, Imperator."

"And for your century, a golden battle honour to display on your standard. It will let the world know of your courage as you march into battle."

A second gold coin was handed to the signifer. They returned to our ranks. I did not hear anything else for I wanted to see the disks that, until then I had heard about and rarely seen. The ones worn by the First Spear were from the time of Pompey's father and these were the first issued by his son. They were special.

"We break camp on the morrow. I fear you will have little opportunity to spend your rewards but when the Populares and Marians are defeated we shall all enjoy the pleasures of Rome."

We celebrated well that night. The general sent us wine and we ate meat. Enemy horses had been killed and now that they were butchered we enjoyed a rare treat. Life in the army was good. We learned that General Sulla intended to deal with the Marians who were to the south of Rome. That our general had been chosen to defeat the northern rebels told us that he was viewed as a good leader.

When we marched I saw that there was a new Sixth Century. Our general had brought replacements and we were no longer the last century in the last cohort. It was promotion and along with the phalera our leader had been awarded it put a spring in our step as we marched north. The exception, of course, was our new tent mate, Faustus, who still seemed depressed. He did not join in the songs we sang as we marched. I later learned that some generals disapproved of such things but Pompey was not one of them. We had begun to call him Pompey rather than Gnaeus Pompeius as it seemed right to do so. Even Centurion Bucco referred to him that way. Our leader was young but he had charisma and as he had shown in our first battle, skill. We tried our best with Faustus Fullo but we failed.

Our route took us to the east of Rome. It was hidden from view but we all knew where it lay and our eyes were drawn to the west. One day we would march in triumph into the city and that would be our greatest accolade. We marched and made camp. As we were normally the last to leave the camp it was the duty of our cohort to take it down each morning. It was not such a hardship as it meant we normally marched a couple of hours

Legionary

after dawn and the sun had warmed the land. It also meant that we were the ones who did not have to dig the ditches and embed the stakes. That was the task of others. We ate up the miles and our diet returned to cereal and what we could forage along the road. My skills with a sling came to the fore and I was often able to bring down a rabbit. Not only did the meat enhance our food, the skins were handy too. I became a popular member of the century for I had learned to share what we had when I could.

Chapter 5

River Aesis March 83 BC

It had been a brutal winter. The euphoria of our victory had evaporated as we had endured snows and periods when we simply could not move. There were desertions and one of them was Faustus Fullo. It had been during one of the coldest nights I had ever experienced. In our tent we were all huddled tightly together, sharing the warmth of each other. We all knew when Fullo left for we were woken by the chill of the tent flap opening and closing. He was cursed. Old Man shouted, "Make water before you go to bed!" We all snuggled back to try to sleep and no one noticed that he had not returned until the morning. When he was not there then Numerius reported to the tesserarius immediately. Centurion Bucco told First Spear and our Gallic auxiliaries were sent to find him.

Numerius was, for the first time in a long time, worried, "We could be blamed."

Gaius said, "How? We did not run."

"We were his tent mates. I have heard of generals who have had tent mates executed when one of their number ran. It is a way to make sure no one else does it."

The thought terrified me. It was unfair. In the end we were not punished for two days later the frozen body of the sad man was brought back. He had fallen and broken his leg. The cold had killed him. He was not replaced. Thanks to other desertions our numbers were dwindling and we did not have the replacements we needed. I was happy for I knew the other six in our tent and I was more than happy with them. We had bonded in two battles and the march along the Via Appia. As the weather warmed so spirits rose and as the roads became easier so we were able to gain on the enemy which had eluded us over the winter.

Our scouts rode in and told us that there was an enemy army ahead. Once again most of our information came second hand but as we had marched with our scouts for some time and got to know them we knew that the news they brought was largely true.

Legionary

Gaius Carrinas was trying to prevent our crossing of the River Aesis.

During the winter and our march we had seen a change. Pompey had been given command of the cavalry. While still our leader, he had appointed a legate to command us. Gnaeus Rufia Betto was a former First Spear from one of Pompey's father's old legions. He had returned with Pompey following the recruitment drive. He was a grizzled veteran and when he was appointed, Numerius' face lit up. "We have a good leader here. Redbeard knows his business and he is a plain-speaking man."

He knew the man and was delighted that he was our leader. I also had a better picture of what to expect after his first inspection. This was before Fullo had left us. The new legate had toured our camp. He had inspected every tent and checked our equipment. When he saw Ceres a rare smile appeared on his mountain-like face, "Yours is the healthiest mule in the legion. Why is that, Legionary?"

I was nervous, "I do not know, Legate. I look after her as though she was one of my father's animals. That is all."

"Your father raises horses?"

"No Legate Betto, pigs but an animal needs care no matter what kind it is."

He grinned, "Good man. You will do well in this army." Old Man was right, Redbeard was plain speaking.

We saw the light reflecting from metal and knew we had found our enemy. When I had joined up I had not known such things. Now I did. I was far from being a veteran but I was no longer a novice. This time when we lined up we were on the two sides of the river. The water would be icy as there was still snow on the mountain tops. Our cohort was to the rear of our line. We were behind the Sixth Cohort who were behind the third. Crassus' legion was to our right. We no longer had Sulla's veterans, they were with the general around Praeneste and I was glad that we were so close to the men who had fought in Hispania. To our left were the legions of Pius and Lucullus. They were unknown but Crassus' men were like us and that comforted me.

Over the winter I had grown. I was now a man. When I had joined I was still something of a youth but the marching and the

Legionary

carrying of my load had made me stronger. We had eaten regularly. Carrying the yoke and digging ramparts had given me stronger muscles although I was still lean. I could have avoided digging as I was the mule man, it was now my nickname, but I wanted to be part of the tent. I now felt like a legionary. More importantly none of the new recruits looked raw. Our mail and cloaks were worn. The off-white tunics we wore beneath the mail were dirtier than they had been. We washed them but over time a grubby patina grew. When the enemy spied us from across the river they would see veterans. They could not know we only had one season of campaigning.

We waited and we wondered who would be ordered to attack first; them or us. When the cornicens sounded we knew it would be us. Our first cohorts marched towards the river and as our slingers, archers and javelin men attacked the enemy so the enemy responded. The first cohorts entered the river and then the order was given for the next ones to cross. We moved up and prepared to endure the icy water. Even as we marched we heard the clash and crash of pila and scutum as the front ranks collided. I saw the cohorts ahead of us rise from the river and dress their ranks at the same time as we were ordered into the river. As my feet entered the water I felt a sudden shock of cold that was painful. The water came up to my knees and I braced myself for the pain that would follow when it rose to my waist. I knew its depth from the men of the Second Century ahead of us. They were holding their scuta above the river which lapped up to their waists. My legs were numb already but once the water reached my manhood I wanted to cry out in pain. Of course, I did not. It was the mark of a veteran that you bore pain stoically. As the river shallowed I prepared to leave the water. Surprisingly, as soon as we climbed up to the bank my legs felt warmer. It was strange. Wounded men were fetched from our front and we passed the dead and wounded on the banks.

"Dress ranks."

Ahead I saw that the Sixth Cohort was now to the right of the Third Cohort and the fighting was fierce. We dressed our lines and then we followed the Second Century to bolster the junction of the Sixth and Third Cohort. We were what I had learned was a post prior century. Our job was to support the Second Century.

Centurion Bucco would choose when and where we moved. At the moment the second were not engaged but I saw a shift as the Third Cohort moved to their left and the sixth to their right. It meant that our cohort was about to engage.

We were ordered to present our pila. My left hand held my spare spear and I held my scutum so that it touched both Gaius' and Numerius'.

"Forward."

The Second Century had already moved and they hurled their spears. The two cohorts ahead of us had weakened the enemy and the spears hit shields and men who were armed with a sword. Their spears had been expended. The second spears were jammed at the faces of the enemy legionaries. Some found flesh and some found shields.

"Push into the backs of the Second Century."

I had learned that weight was vital especially when fighting men who were already tired. We had crossed a river and were yet to use any weapons. We put our shields into the backs of our fellows and our line began to move inexorably forward. When all the spears had been thrown the Second Century were ordered to fall back and we moved to take their place. We had practised this before but it was always tricky. If the enemy were alert enough they could use the disruption to launch a counterattack. Fortunately, they were not alert and I found myself in the front rank.

"Throw." The optio's voice gave the order.

I pulled back and hurled my pilum. I had learned that it did not matter if you aimed or not. The weighted end ensured that however you thew it the spear would land point first. The results would be: it would hit flesh and the man would be wounded, it would hit mail and stick in, or it would hit a shield and make the shield drop. Even before my spear had struck I had my second one ready. Some legions did not have two pila. Perhaps because he could throw one Pompey ensured that we all had two. We waited for the order from the new legate. Would we throw or advance?

Legate Betto had confidence in us and he gave the order to the cornicen for us to advance. That meant we jabbed with our spears. I was acutely aware that we had no one behind us. There were no reserves. The cavalry was with Pompey and they were not in sight. It made me realise that either I would celebrate another victory that night or I would be in Elysium. I liked the life of a legionary and Elysium could wait.

I think that General Carrinas had echeloned better legionaries into his line when his own legions had begun to buckle. The ones who now faced us were veterans and they had their spears. I would have to duel and I had not had to do so yet. I took heart from the fact that Numerius was next to me. He oozed confidence. He murmured, "Just do it the way we have in the past and we will triumph. We fight as one!"

The man I faced was smaller than I was but he was broader and he had a scarred nose. He also tried to intimidate me, "A virgin! Nothing better. I will take your head and piss in your dead skull."

I almost laughed for he could clearly not do any of that in a battle. It meant he was trying to gain an advantage over me and that also told me that he did not think he was better than I was. He was trying to terrify me. I learned that day about confidence. If you have it then it is like an extra layer of mail. You trust your mind and your body far more. I feinted with my scutum as though I was going to hit him with the boss and as his arm brought his shield up to block the blow, I lunged with my spear. I did as I had done in my first battle and aimed for an unprotected limb. I struck his leg above the knee.

"Bastard!" He screamed and as he did so I hit him with the metal boss of my shield. His arm had dropped slightly and I connected with his head. His helmet took some of the force but he still had to step back on to his good leg. I pulled up my spear and rammed it at his face. I had not given him time to think and he stepped back again as he raised his shield. My spear hit his shield with such force that he had to take another step back. I was creating a gap and Numerius and Gaius exploited it. Numerius speared his opponent and stepped next to me. On his other side Mamerus was able to advance.

I heard the optio shout, "On, Fifth Century. They are weakening."

The signifer held the standard aloft. I was keenly aware of the metal disk, given by Pompey, that it now bore. It inspired me and

Legionary

I pulled back my pilum and this time thrust so hard at the legionary that even though he raised his shield a little all that he did was to guide my spear's head under the rim of his helmet and I punched a hole in his skull. He fell like a sack of grain and I saw my chance. The next legionary was adjusting his position and I hurled my pilum. It struck him in the shield and the scutum drooped with the weight. I drew my sword and used the body of my dead enemy to leap into the air and bring the edge down on his neck. It sliced through flesh and the blood spouted and arced to shower the man fighting Numerius. He was distracted and Numerius took advantage. He rammed his spear at the man who grasped it from Numerius' grip as he fell. Numerius drew his own sword and the two of us stood side by side. In such combats speed and confidence are everything. A legionary stabbed without actually seeing where he was going to strike. I kept my eyes on the legionary I was fighting and watched his eyes. When he thrust with his pilum he was hampered by the fact that I was close to him and it was a simple move to lift my scutum and drive the haft into the air and away from flesh. My blind blow found his flesh and as it scratched and scraped through mail I twisted to enlarge the hole. I kept pushing. The man tried to step back but he was prevented from doing so by the legionary behind who was trying to get at me with his spear. The tip of my father's sword sank deeper into the man whose mouth opened in a seemingly silent scream. There was so much noise around me that I could not hear it but I kept pushing and the eyes rolled. He was dead.

It was at that moment that I heard the horns from behind the enemy. Were they sending more men in? Then I realised I recognised the call. The horns were ours and Pompey had brought the cavalry to attack the rear of the enemy line. Even as the notes ended I knew that the battle was over and that we had won. All that we had to do was to stay alive. I did not step into the space vacated by the man I had killed. I waited until Gaius, Numerius and Mamerus joined me. A few moments later we had a solid double line. The optio appeared to our right. His shield and armour were covered in blood but the look on his face told us that it was not his.

"Right lads, slow and steady. We have this lot beaten."

Legionary

He was right and more men surrendered to us than we killed. They had no way of retreating and surrender was the best option. Two of those who first surrendered were slain before Centurion Bucco shouted, "We want prisoners!"

As soon as we began to take prisoners then all resistance ended. I saw a triumphant Pompey rear his horse and raise his sword. It was his victory as much as ours.

The war did not end then, as some of us thought it might. We had lost very few men and many of the men who had surrendered to us switched sides. There were so many that General Pius formed five cohorts from them. Of course, we never trusted them but that was no matter.

The war did not end because the consul, Gnaeus Papirius Carbo, brought eight legions to face us and even though we had won the battle we could not risk fighting eight fresh legions. We waited. Thanks to our victory we had supplies and we had, of course, looted the dead. We were happy in our camp. The enemy had to be vigilant for Pompey continued to lead our cavalry to probe and harass them. We did not see much of him but we still saw ourselves as his men.

We waited for almost three weeks and then a rider rode into camp from the south. He was mud spattered for it had been raining and he looked to have almost killed his horse. We all saw his arrival and waited for news. The gossip spread within moments but we waited until Centurion Bucco brought us the official news and it was great news. Sulla had defeated a Marian army led by Gaius Marius the Younger. It had been a huge victory. The Marians had lost fifteen thousand men killed and another seven thousand who defected to General Sulla. The battle had been at Sacriportus well to the south of us. The Marians had been forced to flee to Praeneste where they were under siege.

Even as we celebrated, the enemy general Carbo broke camp, clearly having heard the same news. We were ordered to break camp as Pompey led the cavalry to pursue the eight legions to Arminium. By the time we reached the city Pompey had enjoyed yet another victory. He had caught the troops of Gaius Marcius Censorinus at Sena Gallica. He plundered the town and we all benefitted. We had more prisoners and, as we had been so victorious, more recruits for our army. Even Numerius was impressed by our success. Everything that Pompey touched seemed to turn to gold. Our Chosen Man was now an admirer of the young general. When he had first joined he had been sceptical.

There were clearly politics at work for when he returned it was not to the celebrations we had enjoyed when he met with Sulla. Metellus Pius did not give him a warm welcome. We were too busy to notice at the time for we were all enjoying the plunder taken from Sena Gallica. It was when we and Crassus' legions were ordered to break camp and head south that we knew something was amiss. Pius was left to mop up the enemy. I believe that many of the other legions regretted whatever had caused us to leave for Pompey was the one who had enjoyed the greatest success. Pius had defeated Censorinus once but it had not been like the crushing victories achieved by Pompey.

As we were heading south and away from the mountains we were quite happy. We were hardened to marching. Our constant victories meant that caligae and armour had all been replaced. We had coins and we had extra weapons. We were soldiers and were enjoying that rare experience of full bellies and purses as well as victories. Men flocked to join us as we headed south. Success breeds success as it was almost a triumphal process as we made our way to a meeting with Sulla. Metellus Pius could deal with the Populares in the north. The greater threat was Marius the Younger in the centre for it lay close to Rome and whoever controlled Rome had the better chance of winning this civil war. When I had lived on the farm the politics of Rome had meant nothing to me. My father had not fought in the civil wars and all that he was interested in was the rate at which we paid taxes. I was much more aware now of who was responsible for the decisions that would affect our day to day lives.

The road we were on, the Via Flamina, led to Rome and when we camped and sat outside our tent and talked, we debated what would happen if we reached Rome. Numerius was adamant that Marius the Younger was not the general his father had been but he accepted that there was more support in Rome for Marius than there was for Sulla.

After one heated debate there was silence until I ventured, "The difference might be Pompey."

The others looked at me. Our new tent mate, Paullus Drusus, had joined us on the road and he was an older warrior. He was nothing like Faustus had been. He said, "Pompey? He is young and has no power yet."

I smiled, "Yet he is the one with victories to equal Sulla's. He is young and he might be the acceptable face that Rome will live with."

Numerius nodded, "You could be right, Mule Man. He is certainly a better leader than his father ever was." He laughed, "He is more generous that is for sure and he does not revert to the lash as often. You may be right, Lucius, and I, for one, am pleased I chose this legion."

Gaius was surprised, "Could you have joined another?"

"Of course. Veterans like me and," he nodded to Paullus, "our new tent mate are more valuable than you youngsters. You have turned out well but remember Sertor." I saw Mamerus hang his head. They had been very close friends. "Young recruits need more training and, unlike you three, often fall in the first battle."

"Then you think we will do all right?"

Numerius shook his head, "I wouldn't go so far as that. Wait until we have a major battle and then we shall see."

"I thought we had fought some tough battles, Old Man."

"Nah, the hardest was the one on the Aesis and that was only because we had to ford a river. It was never in doubt. When Marius the Younger is finished then we can say that you have a chance of seeing five years in the legion."

Mamerus asked, "Five years?"

"Once you have done five years you can look for promotion or perhaps become an immunes."

"Then why are you just a legionary?"

"Pompey's father. I left the legion when I had served seven years. I was about to become an optio. I didn't and that was my own fault for leaving. His son has more promise. I learned my lesson and this time I might stay longer."

His words depressed me for I had thought he and I would stay and serve Pompey for a long time. It was now clear to me that

Numerius would only stay while we were victorious. What if we lost?

Chapter 6

Spoletium 82 BC
We had seven legions marching towards Rome. Marius the Younger was still under siege at Praeneste. Pompey and Crassus were great believers in the use of scouts and it was they reported our old adversary from the Aesis, Praetor Carinas, coming to the aid of Marius the Younger. They were coming from the east and so we left the Via Flamina to march towards the eight legions under the command of the praetor. Our new tent mate had served Carinas and knew the quality of the legions that were coming. "These aren't the ones you lads defeated on the Aesis. These are from Cisalpine Gaul. The are tougher than the ones you fought. They are used to fighting Gauls and the Helvetii."

Numerius was not impressed, "Hairy arsed barbarians fighting in mountains is not the same as fighting a Roman legion. Despite the youth of some of these lads we have shown that we can fight and the new recruits are all like you Paullus, veterans. Crassus' men are good too. Just so long as Pompey picks the right ground we shall win."

The place Pompey and Crassus picked to stop them was Spoletium. We headed south down the Via Flamina. The road we were following was a good road. It was the reason that Carinas was coming this way. He hoped to attack Sulla while we were still marching towards Rome. It had defied Hannibal and I think that our leaders hoped that we could reach it before the enemy. We did not but they failed to occupy it. Instead, they placed their legions across the valley. Pompey and Crassus would not be able to use our cavalry and they had won the battle at the river. Our cavalry would still be a threat but only if we won the battle. The sound of our hobnails on the road, mercifully dry, echoed and rippled as the long legionary snake wound its way to meet our enemies. I was now more accustomed to how the army marched. I had thought we would march in step but we did not. We also stopped to make water when commanded. No one left the line. If you had loose bowels you dealt with it. I knew that I was lucky to have been given the mule. I had my shield and its cover on my back, I wore the armour and carried the sword. I had my cloak about my shoulders but the others had all of that as well as a yoke, dolabra and spears. Some of the other centuries had discarded their second spear. They claimed they had lost them. Numerius was scornful, "You never know when you might need a second spear. It is hard carrying it but if it keeps me alive then I am happy."

The enemy was waiting for us before the city. That gave me confidence for they were so close that I knew they were giving themselves a bolt hole in case they lost. If they thought they could beat us they would have met us further north where the valley was narrower and there were trees and the river to stop an outflanking movement. Once they were seen we deployed. The ballistae were not unpacked but the mules carrying them were moved to the front. I tethered Ceres with the other mules and the generals' baggage. We had slingers and they too, moved to the front. We had few auxiliaries but the ones we did have were sent to the trees. They were there for defence rather than offence.

Pompey now had three legions while Crassus had four. Our legions were still at full strength and as we faced the Populare army we could tell that they were all slightly understrength. You could see that from the numbers at the rear of each legion. They were not as deep as we were. They also had fewer ballistae. That was a guess based upon the mules that they were unpacking. Our three legions were on the left but we were the ones next to Crassus' legion. We had fought alongside them before and we were comfortable with them as neighbours. The two generals were putting what they considered their best legions in the centre. The two legions on the flanks had the advantage that they had gently rising hillsides and trees to protect them and our auxiliaries had proved more than useful in such terrain. As Numerius told us, this would come down to a bloodbath in the middle and the ones who wanted to win would emerge victorious.

The success of our cohort meant that we were seen as a prior cohort and not a post prior cohort. We were in the front ranks. We were drawn up in the triplex acies formation. That meant we had three lines and could both attack and defend in depth. Until we had fought our first battle the names of these formations was a mystery but now I knew it meant four cohorts backed by four more offset cohorts with the last two cohorts ready to fill the gaps created by an enemy. That we were in the front rank was an honour. Of course, our century formed the second rank in our cohort but we did not mind.

While we had waited for the enemy to make up its mind when we had been in camp, Centurion Bucco had made us train hard. We could all throw our pila more accurately now and we had worked to fight together with the gladius and scutum. As we waited for the order to advance I felt more confident than in any other battle. Here there was no river before us; it lay to our right. The ground was generally flat, especially before us, and that would give both sides an equal opportunity to show their skills.

Mamerus had grown in confidence too and he joked, "When these are defeated and we march into Rome I shall find the prettiest maid I can and give her my seed."

Numerius laughed, "More likely some old hag who will take a couple of sestertii for a quick fumble."

Gaius and I laughed as Mamerus blushed. He was desperate to prove himself a man and that meant, in his case, with a woman. Gaius and I were not as worried about that. We intended to be in the army for a long time. Families came in the future. My father had not been a young man when he had fathered me. I had plenty of time.

The enemy horns told us that they were advancing and on they came. The legion that came at us had a wolf on its standard. Many such standards were used as it was a throwback to the founders of Rome, Romulus and Remus. It looked like a senior cohort and the standard was heading for our cohort. Our First Cohort would be able, if they were commanded, to echelon over and fight with them. I dismissed the thought as soon as it came into my head. The first battle, the one by the sea, had shown us that Gnaeus Pompeius did not fight in the same manner as the other generals.

Silence reigned on our side of the battlefield. We were now veterans and nervous chatter was for others. I took comfort from the fact that I could see heads in the enemy cohorts advancing towards us, turning as men spoke to one another. That was always a sign of nerves and a lack of discipline.

Legionary

The centurion who led the enemy century was next to the signifer and the trumpeter was behind. They were in the standard formation of eight ranks and nine files. The two centuries that followed were four ranks deep with twenty staggered files. As we were in the front rank we too had a tight eight rank formation. The cornicen, Aulus Avitus, was next to Gaius and Centurion Bucco and Signifer Gracchus were just ahead of him. I knew that we might be called upon to defend the standard as well as the centurion. I was ready. The metal disk on the standard we had won was the only battle honour we had and I was not willing to let that fall into the hands of the enemy. I saw that the auxiliaries of both armies were on the left flank. The hillsides and the woods were better suited to them than heavily armed legionaries. It would mean there would be no arrow or stone storm. The first contact would be from spears and ballista bolts followed by a vicious battle with swords. We knew what was coming and our left arms were ready to raise our scuta in the air. The first contact would show the difference between the quick and the dead.

Our slingers scored the first. The enemy did not halt to hurl their spears. They came at the run and hurled them in quick succession. They used a lighter javelin first and kept the pila until they were closer. I saw that their centurion and signifer would strike, not at Centurion Bucco but closer to us. The men in the rank before us would have to endure the spear storm. We raised our shields instinctively. In doing so those of us in the front ranks protected those behind us. However, the throwing of two spears meant that some of those in the front ranks fell for shields dropped with the weight or legionaries were hit by the heavy pila.

The command to throw was probably a heartbeat too late. The front two ranks, me included, all hurled their spears and then transferred our second spear to our right hand.

"Hold them!" Centurion Bucco's voice was firm but calm. He was not panicking.

Numerius, Gaius, Mamerus and I jabbed our spears over the shoulders of the front rank. Numerius was lucky or perhaps he was the most skilful for his spear rammed into the eye of the man about to stab upwards at the legionary standing before him.

Legionary

We were not ordered to but we knew that now was the time for our second spears to be thrown. We launched them. None of us had any way of knowing if we had hit any of the men facing us but as there were no more spears thrown at us we had to assume that the enemy had taken hits.

The legionary standing before Mamerus was one who had been wounded already and when the sword came up under his rib cage he slid to his death and Mamerus stepped into the breach. The faces of the enemy were close but my spear had been thrown and I drew my sword. I lifted my arm and poked over the top of my shield into the gap between the helmets of the two legionaries before me. I scraped alongside the enemy legionary's helmet. While it did not hurt him it distracted him and the legionary before me, Quintus, took advantage of the distraction and gutted him. Quintus said nothing; thanks would come after the battle… if we both survived.

Being in the second rank I had the luxury of being able to look along our line. The centurion and signifer were being well protected. To my right I saw that Mamerus was close to the enemy centurion and signifer. It was not the centurion who slew Mamerus but the warrior next to him. As another of the virgins fell Numerius gave a roar and stepped to his right to fill the gap. I did so too and Publius stepped from the rank behind to take my place. For the first time I did not have Gaius next to me and with Mamerus dead I began to lose some of the confidence with which I had started the battle.

Numerius was soon duelling with the veteran next to the enemy centurion. The man was also a veteran and it was hard to see who would win. I was almost distracted and when Servius, the legionary in the front rank, fell I was nearly taken by surprise. Luckily, some instinct I did not know I had took over and as his body slipped to the ground before me I used my right leg to step onto the dead body. Servius was in Elysium and he would not mind. He would want me to avenge his death. We had been taught to go for the rib cage, the face or legs when we had been trained. We had also been taught to avoid the chopping action adopted by barbarians. Thanks to the body of my dead comrade I was above the legionary who had slain Servius and none of the traditional options were open to me. The veteran I was fighting knew all of that and I saw his sword being pulled back ready to drive into my rib cage as I descended. It would be a quick death. I did the unexpected. As I stepped down I smashed my shield at his sword while hacking down at his neck. The Parcae smiled at me and, despite his helmet, I found the flesh close to the neck. It was a lucky strike. More importantly I found the vessel that sends blood around the body and the spurting fountain spattered into the air and showered both me and Numerius. As I stepped down his body fell before me and I lifted my shield to block the swords that came at me. Numerius used his shield to lock with mine.

   I took a breath. I had come as close to death as I had in any of the battles I had fought before. If blood rushed into my head I would be isolated and die. My best chance was the comfort of the legionaries next to me. Perhaps the man I had killed had been popular, I would never know but what I did know was that the enemy came at me as though I was an assassin. I had to use my quick hands to keep their blows from me. The advantage I had was that their attack meant that Numerius and those to my left could attack my attackers. One sword came at my face and as my shield was protecting my body I had no defence from the stabbing blades before me. I turned my head. The tip caught the guard of my helmet but the edge sliced into my cheek and I felt the blood dripping down. I was wounded but the man had made a mistake. His raised arm allowed me to stab up into the gap. I saw the smile of joy replaced by a look of horror as my father's sword drove up under his ribs. He slid to the ground.

   There was a gap and I saw the legionary who was alongside the cornicen. He was slightly behind the centurion who was now duelling with Numerius. The file man who was supposed to step into the gap created by my killing of the legionary was prevented when someone from behind me threw a pilum that drove into his shoulder. The cornicen was isolated and I drove my blade under his arm and he fell. The centurion sensed my presence and even as I stepped back he was trying to turn. It was not a blow we had been trained to use but I improvised and as I pulled my arm back the edge of my sword raked across the armour and baldric of the centurion. I cut some of his mail links but, more importantly, sliced through his baldric and his belt fell. It did not make him more vulnerable but, as it dropped by his feet it was a hindrance and when Numerius drove at him, he tripped. Numerius was too good to let the moment slip by and he stabbed down at the unprotected throat. Their centurion was dead.

The signifer, who wore a wolf skin over his helmet, thrust at the side of Numerius. Holding my shield on my left I turned and blocked the blow. Two other legionaries came at Numerius. All order had gone from the front ranks. There were bodies lying at awkward angles. Chaos reigned. I found myself facing a grizzled signifer who looked to be a veteran. His centurion and his cornicen had been killed and he was going to defend the standard. He must have seen me as a callow youth who was bleeding from a wound and saw his chance to have revenge. I could hear the enemy optio as he shouted, from the rear, to defend the century standard. I knew that if the standard fell then the heart would go from the enemy cohort and their legion. Taking the standard would avenge Mamerus.

He used the standard as a weapon and rammed it at my face. I flicked up my shield although my arm was already tired. Normally we would have been rotated already but the pace of the battle had taken us all by surprise. I thrust upwards with my father's sword but he was expecting the move and blocked it with his weapon. Sparks flew as our blades collided. My advantage was my shield and I punched at him. While my hand was protected by my shield, his hand, holding the standard, had no protection. I hurt his hand. I punched again and caught him by surprise as he had expected a thrust from my sword. He took a step back and then rammed the spike at the end of the standard into the ground. He would not underestimate me again and he would use a second weapon. He drew his dagger. His movement was so quick that he almost took me by surprise. He slashed with his dagger at my throat and I was barely able to raise the shield in time. I did so and then stabbed with my sword. He must have expected another thrust at his ribs but I fooled him and stabbed at his leg. I felt the end of my blade slide off his thigh bone and when he involuntarily screamed I knew that I had hurt him. Knowing he was weak I punched with my shield again and he reeled. The optio and tesserarius of the enemy century were coming from the rear to save the standard and I had no time to think. I brought up my own sword under the signifer's arm and when the tip emerged from his shoulder I knew that he was doomed.

I turned and picking up the enemy standard, roared, "Pompey!"

There was a cheer and the next thing I knew Centurion Bucco led a charge to ram into their optio and tesserarius. Their cohort was destroyed in that moment for, with all their officers dead, many of the century we had been fighting fled and our First Century drove into the side of the century waiting to move forward. The First Century was eight files wide and they ploughed through the open ranks of the waiting century. I found myself surrounded by not only my tent mates but Optio Corbulo and Tesserarius Quietus. The last three legionaries who attempted to wrest the standard from me were butchered. Gaius and Numerius were with me and though they were both bloodied and cut they were grinning.

Optio Corbulo shook his head as Centurion Bucco ordered the recall, "Bravely done but the two of you are lucky to be alive." He laughed, "The Old Man and the Mule Man."

I was too stunned to speak but Numerius was not, "Nothing to do with luck, Optio, we had skill and they did not."

I did not like to point out that a baldric had tripped the centurion and had it not then I might be dead and not them.

The destruction of the cohort was mirrored across the battlefield. They had been brave but we had more skill and, perhaps, Optio Corbulo was right, more luck. We held our expensively bought piece of ground as the surviving enemy legions were driven into Spoletium. Numerius and I had killed their colour party and the fifty survivors of our legion were happy for us to have the treasure. Centurion Bucco took the standard. He would present it to the general. Numerius held the crested helmet of the centurion and gave a cheeky look at Optio Corbulo, "Must be worth what, ten denarii?"

The optio was the next in line for a promotion and the crested helmet was in good condition. He nodded, "Ten denarii."

Numerius took the centurion's coins and his phalerae. I took the gold from the cornicen and signifer as well as the single golden disk the signifer was wearing. I also found, in the folds of the cornicen's clothes, a small Mars. I would take that too and add it to the other deities I carried with me. Only a fool did not seek the help of the gods. After taking the treasure there was a cheer from our century when I turned. It was as I turned that I saw the body of Mamerus. He would never know a woman. His dreams of a maid lay in tatters.

The stripped bodies were piled on firewood and were about to be burned when Gnaeus Pompeius rode up flanked by his guards. He looked down at the standard, "Well done, Centurion Bucco, this will mean another phalera for you and your century."

Centurion Bucco was a fair man and he shook his head, "It was Legionary Porcianus who slew the cornicen and the signifer. Legionary Sura slew the centurion."

Pompey looked down at me and smiled, "You are the recruit with the sharp eyes."

I nodded, remembering the meeting at the port, "Yes General."

I saw him trying to picture me in the line of march, "You are also the mule man." I nodded. "There will be more rewards coming to you. The century have earned another golden medal."

The men cheered as the general rode off.

Numerius sniffed, "Typical, no gold disk for us then."

Optio Corbulo said, "Numerius, you know better than any that phalerae draw men to kill you. Be grateful that you have some gold to sell and you and Mule Man are rich men." He lowered his voice, "Pompey is not like his father. You two will do well out of this."

I hoped he was right. We buried our dead. There were now just three of us left in our contuburnium. The rest had died in the bloody battle. Centurion Bucco amalgamated us with another two conterburnia. It was not the same but as we three had shown ourselves to be veterans the others deferred to us. The reorganisation of the cohort meant that we became the Third Century. The battles we had fought had cost us. We settled into a siege.

I found it quite easy to endure the siege for we did not have to constantly build and take down our camp. I found good grazing for Ceres and she put on weight. We were not called upon to assault the walls and so we had a week of what passed for leisure.

Chapter 7

Carrinas escaped from the town and his legions surrendered. Pompey was disappointed but we were not as we had a town that we were able to ransack. While others took things that they could never possibly use, I found items that I needed. I took a couple of good blankets as well as a horse blanket. I found a sack of oats that I would share between the contuburnium and Ceres. I even found, buried beneath the floor of a modest looking house, a small chest containing twenty denarii. As it coincided with payment from Pompey, my purse was bulging. When we were next near a moneyer I would change the denarii for some gold pieces. They would be easier to hide. We even found some nails. The constant marching was taking its toll on our hobnails. I was learning to be a legionary.

Pompey and Crassus were both eager for more success and scouts were sent out to find our enemy. When the orders came to break camp we knew that the scouts had been successful. We left Spoletium in good heart. Numerius and many of the others in the century had visited a whorehouse where they had spent some of their pay. Numerius often told us that he felt most at home in the lupanare. Gaius and I enjoyed good food in the taverns. We were still young. The taverns were busy but thanks to our success in battle we were treated well by other legionaries. Some even bought us wine. We had killed a centurion, a cornicen and a signifer. We had taken a standard and that brought us fame especially as we never spoke of our actions. We let others do that. We enjoyed good bread and olives as well as local cheese. It did not compare with the cheese I had enjoyed in my home. I still thought of home but the memory was fading. How would they be faring? Had my sacrifice been rewarded by the gods? A sacrifice did not guarantee that fortunes would change. Had my father managed to recover from the disaster of the dying pigs? I knew I had enough money to help him restock his farm but how could I get it to him? I smiled. I now thought of it as his farm and not our farm. I was now a legionary.

"Do you like this life now, Gaius?"

He smiled, "We have been lucky. Optio Corbulo was right in that but perhaps we are chosen by the gods to be so." He shuddered, "When I think of the slaughter of our enemies I know that we could be in the same position."

"Pompey is a good general. He is young but so are we and look at the success you and I have enjoyed."

"But not Sertor nor Mamerus."

"No, you are right but they are in Elysium now. Their troubles are over. You and I have the chance for a future."

Gaius was thoughtful, "The longer we are legionaries the more chance we have of dying and the other side of the fickle coin is even more worrying. What if we are promoted? Will a young Lucius or Gaius come after us? If we do not have to fight again then I will be happy. I have enough coins now and the pay is good. Pompey is a prompt payer. This war is almost over and I have heard rumours that our general will disband his legions. Perhaps he will share some of the wealth he will gain with us."

"Perhaps you are right and the day that Sulla becomes dictator then our lives will be easier." Even as I said it I knew that was not true. Pompey was ambitious. He would not rest on his laurels. He would take his legions and seek glory conquering lands as yet Rome's enemies. I had heard that in Hispania there were rebels. That land lay across the sea. It was beyond the mountains to the north of the lands of Italy. If I died in a foreign land would I find Elysium? It was a worrying thought.

I asked, "If you left the legion, would you go home to the farm?"

He nodded, "When we fought for the standard and I thought I would die, what came into my mind was Flavia."

"Flavia?"

He looked sheepish, "She was a girl at home but her father was wealthier than mine and I would not seek her hand as a pauper. We now have money. Unlike you I do not need it to help my family but to start one. When we can I will go home and marry her."

When we spoke to Numerius about our hopes and fears he laughed them off. The whores had been good ones and he was in a good mood. "You take each day you are alive as a gift from the gods. If you go to bed with all your limbs intact and you sleep with your tentmates then the world is good." He shrugged, "And if you are slain in battle then do not worry for you will wake and walk the fields of Elysium. Sertor and Mamerus will show you around and you will be at peace. For now we are warriors and, I hate to say it but you two are not bad soldiers. You, Quiet Boy, and you Mule Man, seem to have what it takes to be soldiers. You are both different and yet you work well together. The gods put you together for a purpose. It bodes well for the future." I noticed, as he spoke, that he fingered the small amulet he wore around his neck. It was Mars, the god of war. One did not upset the gods.

 We had word that Censorinus was bringing a large force to Praeneste. He intended to rescue Marius the Younger. He had a large number of legions and such numbers were hard to disguise. We also knew his route. We squatted on the Via Flamina and he would need to find another way to get to the town south of Rome. That meant the mountains. His legions, although they outnumbered ours, would be spread out along the road. They would not be able to march eight abreast but, more likely four. When Hannibal had caught the Roman armies at Trasimene he had employed an ambush and Pompey was well read. We heard, from Centurion Bucco, that he planned a similar ambush. If they marched down the Via Flamina his army would be heard. Even a legion could be heard many miles away as it tramped down the stone roads that were the life blood of Rome. Many legions would sound like a rumbling thunderstorm coming closer and closer. We would know when he was near yet he would have no idea where we waited. He might have numbers but we had Pompey and we had surprise. We were confident.

 The enemy legions were heading from the east and that meant taking the pass that lead to both Rome and Praeneste. We were able to use the Via Flamina and make better time than the legions of Censorinus. The enemy were being clever. By taking the road that led to Rome, Censorinus would hope for help from the people of Rome. Marius the Younger, unlike Sulla, was very popular in Rome, the centre of the known world, and his rescue would have more chance of success with the help of Romans. The route that they were taking followed the Ariani valley. The Ariani was not a particularly large river but it had cut the valley that headed east to west. We reached the small town of Vici Vari and found that Censorinus had yet to reach it. Scouts were sent to find them and we camped in the town. The people supported Marius and Carbo. Their misplaced allegiance was punished when we ate their animals, took the food and drank their wine. We had a day of leisure and then we marched out.

We took tiny trails that meandered along the valley sides. Pompey's legions headed up the northern side and Crassus' the south. It was difficult going but we did not have far to travel. We were halted where the valley narrowed and we could see the road below us. A turma of auxiliary cavalry galloped from the east. We had left our mules in Vici Vari with the Sixth Century. They were relegated to be mule guards. The rest of us were spread along the valley side, largely hidden by trees, shrubs and rocks. As we shuffled into position there were moans and complaints.

"I don't like this, Optio, we are only two ranks deep."

"Aye and in simplex acies."

Optio Corbulo snorted, "Are you virgins? We are Pompey's legion and the men we fight are Populares. They have never met us in battle. Think about it, Nanus, the only ones who can outflank us are goats. You aren't afraid of a goat are you?"

Nanus and Caeso had only been expressing the doubts in all our minds but we laughed at the scathing words of the optio.

Pompey had to have briefed the centurions well for Centurion Bucco knew exactly what we were going to do. He gathered the century around him and gave us our instructions. "We will use an open formation and we will be two ranks deep. When Crassus' horns sound we advance down the slope to attack the legions in the flank. Crassus' men will start their attack first. The attention of Censorinus' legions will be across the river. We do not shout and we move as silently as we can. When Avitus sounds the horn then we throw our pila and charge. We will only be in two ranks but their backs should be towards us. With luck and if you are skilled enough then our century should be able to account for forty or more of the enemy. We charge them and push them towards the river. Crassus' legions will hold their attention."

It seemed a remarkably simple plan. Our contribution was to attack hard and demoralise the enemy. Our eighty men were supposed to account for forty of theirs. We were a small part of the machine that was Pompey's army but if everyone did as we did then all would be well and we would win. As we went to our positions I said as much to Numerius, "Like all plans, Mule Man, it is perfect until something goes wrong. What if they know we are here and don't come down the road? What if they realise it is an ambush and have men facing us? What if they have auxiliaries flanking their line of march? It is a good plan but we know not what the gods or our enemy have planned."

Gaius laughed, "And what if the sun does not rise in the morning? It is a good plan, Numerius, and if something goes wrong then Pompey's men will deal with it." My friend was more confident now. I think it was the thought that he now had a plan. Make coins and return home to marry Flavia.

We heard the sound of hooves and saw a turma of our auxiliary cavalry galloping down the road. We were ordered to stand to. Immediately behind them came a larger number of enemy horsemen. They were Gauls and they had outnumbered the lure that was our Boeotian auxiliaries. Following them another body of auxiliaries ran down the road. Our horsemen were the bait and Censorinus had swallowed it. We heard and then saw the first legion appear soon after. They were marching at the fastest pace. They were hurrying to war. If they had looked up they might have caught the flash of light on spearpoints or helmets; perhaps the red of a centurion's crest but their attention was on the road. I realised that as the auxiliaries had not been attacked they felt safe. We were in the middle of the line of cohorts. The attack would be initiated by Crassus who waited on the other side of the river.

When the horns sounded we saw the sudden flash of colour and metal from across the river as Crassus' legions began to march down the slope. They were not charging. I smiled. Crassus and Pompey had worked things out well. The enemy horns sounded and the enemy turned to face the threat. The legions had been marching in ranks of four and they simply turned to present their shields and spears to the threat. They were four deep and Crassus was across the river. They would feel confident. They might think that Crassus had made a mistake.

Centurion Bucco ordered us forward with a simple wave of his spear. The signifer now carried a standard with two metal disks marked with the names of the battle in which they had been earned and one of them had been bought by me. The sobering thought came that they had been earned at the cost of Mamerus. We moved steadily down the slope. We all watched our feet as there were stones and roots before us. It seemed inconceivable that the enemy would not hear us but perhaps the noise they were making, allied to the cacophony of the horns from across the river, drowned out our approach. I saw the optio and tesserarius standing behind the century that we would be attacking. They seemed oblivious to our approach. They were watching Crassus' men. The sound of Avitus' horn coincided with the enemy optio turning. Perhaps a dislodged stone had rolled down the hill and given him a warning. We would never know.

The optio had little chance to sound a warning for one of our pila struck him in the chest. The rest of the century and the tesserarius were also struck. Some men were hit by two pila and some of our missiles must have missed but the overall effect was to halve the enemies we had to face. With spears held before us, we ran the last twenty or so paces to crash into men who were turning. The arrows and stones from Crassus' men hit many of the men and by the time I had plunged my spear into the nearest legionary, the survivors were surrendering. The whole combat had lasted, it seemed, moments. It was a triumph and ended any hopes that Marius the Younger might have had of being relieved.

There were men who survived and they fled east back along the road. When Pompey galloped past us with the cavalry and the auxiliaries we knew that he would pursue them until they were taken. We did not care. We had won and, unlike the last battle, we had lost not a man. We took from the dead and the prisoners. That done Marcus Crassus came to ask if any wished to join our legions. Faced with the prospect of execution the majority defected and our numbers were swollen. The ones who were not were shackled. They would become slaves. Some might join a ludus and become a gladiator. I might see them fighting in the arena when someone important died. We marched back to Vici Vari and I wondered what I would do faced with the choice of death, slavery or joining an enemy legion. I knew that I would defect and then, at the first opportunity, run. I was not Faustus and I knew how to run over rough terrain and how to hide. I hoped I would never have to make that decision for that meant we would have lost.

Life seemed to be easy in the army and we spent two days in the town enjoying comfort for a time. Pompey did not return immediately and Legate Betto continued to be our leader. It was he who told us that a huge Samnite Army, avowed enemies of Sulla and led by his arch enemy, Pontius Telesinus, had abandoned the attempt to relieve the siege of Praeneste and were heading, instead, for Rome. We were ordered to break camp and with our new legion headed towards the Via Flamina to join Sulla. We marched as quickly to Rome as the legions we had just defeated raced to Praeneste. Ceres was more than up to the task and even though she was more heavily burdened, thanks to our victories, she coped well. We marched through the night. Had it not been such a good road we might have suffered but we were able to keep up a fast pace. We were buoyed by our victories and we were well fed. We also trusted Marcus Crassus. He had enabled us to win our last battle and we had benefitted more than his men. We had no cavalry for Pompey had taken them but we had auxiliary infantry and it was they who were used as scouts.

We reached Sulla and his army just north of the city, close to the Colline Gate. It was close to dawn when we reached the city. We were all in relatively good spirits but Sulla's men, the veterans who had mocked us were exhausted after a longer march than we had endured. We discovered that the Samnites and their allies, the Lucanians, had not yet reached the city. General Sulla had sacrificed some of our cavalry to keep them from it. The gates were barred. The Marian sympathisers hated Sulla.

We set up camp near to the temple of Venus Erucina, outside the walls of Rome, not far from the Colline Gate. Sulla allowed food to be cooked but we were all stood to. His cavalry, for we had none, harassed the Samnites and it proved a good move for the enemy began to bring their huge army in battle formation towards our lines. They were not legionaries but they had similar weapons and tactics. They built a camp when they saw that we had our camp close to the walls of the city. They recognised the dangers of a night attack. It meant that there would be no immediate battle. They were building a camp and Sulla's weary army were eating and taking what rest they could. Our march had been the shortest and we were relatively fresh.

Numerius shook his head when he viewed the enemy building their camp, "The Samnites and the Lucanians are not the disordered rabble we have been fighting lately. They are good soldiers." He took a stick to pick out some food from between his teeth. He always did that before we ate, "Still, they have made a mistake here. They should have stayed inside the walls. They could have made us bleed." He nodded towards Sulla's army, arrayed to our left, "It might be that his men are too tired to fight and the Samnites know that. If that is true, then we could have another bloodbath on our hands."

When the food was brought Optio Corbulo came to speak to us, "We have a hard fight ahead of us, lads. General Pompeius is still away with the cavalry and Sulla's legions are all in. They have been besieging for some time and their march was a hard one."

Appius asked, "Will there be a battle? I mean won't the general negotiate?"

The optio pointed at the walls of Rome behind us, "Rome is within spitting distance. The Marians are done for. Metellus Pius has defeated them in the north. We have ended their threat here. All we need to do is beat these and Rome is his."

"But Numerius says the Samnites are good soldiers."

Numerius said, "And it is the truth, isn't it, Optio?"

"It is but we are better. Just look to your front, obey your orders and we will win." He grinned, "When we are in Rome you can spend your money on decent whores and good wine, eh?"

Numerius nodded. When the optio had gone he said, "He is right. Let us just do what we have done so far, eh?" He looked around at the contuburnium. There were just three of us left now from the original one. The rest looked to us three as veterans. This civil war had moulded us into one fighting unit but at the heart were the three of us, Old Man, Quiet Boy and Mule Man. The other five smiled and nodded. Numerius was still Chosen Man and our leader.

Sulla prowled the front line like a caged animal. Men were in their battle positions and taking what rest they could but their pila and scuta were neatly stacked and ready to be used instantly. This would be a battle of infantry. Most of our cavalry was with Pompey and the Sullan cavalry had been mauled when they had harassed the Samnites and Lucanians. Numerius was right, it would be a bloodbath.

On one of his prowlings Sulla stopped close to, not only our legion, but also to our century. He saw the standard with the two disks. He called over Centurion Bucco, "Tell me how this century earned those two honours. As I understand it this legion is the first one that Gnaeus Pompeius raised."

Bucco told him. He pointed over to Numerius and me as he came to our part in the story. The general waved us over. He studied me, "You are young to have killed a veteran." I know I still looked too young to be a soldier. He smiled at Numerius. "You I can believe would have the skills for your scars bespeak experience." He nodded to me, "What is your name?"

"Lucius Ulpia Porcianus, General."

"I shall keep my ears open and ask Gnaeus Pompeius about you when he returns." I did not know how to respond and I just nodded. He turned to Numerius, "You have fought many times. What do you think the outcome will be this day?"

I took a deep breath. Numerius would not lie just because this was the general and I had heard that Sulla did not brook any kind of either disloyalty or a lack of respect.

"They are a tough enemy, General. I have never fought them and I know that they will be fresher than we are." He smiled, "Hot food taken from Rome has to be better than hastily cooked rations here." I saw the general frown as though Numerius had criticised him. "But at the end of the day, and I am guessing that is when we will be fighting, they are not legionaries and we are. I don't know their leader but I know that you are a tough old general." I saw Bucco's eyes roll. "So I will say that we will be in Rome by the morrow and enjoying all that our city has to offer."

There was silence and we all waited with bated breath. The one who seemed the least concerned was Numerius himself.

Eventually a grin broke on Sulla's face, "I like honesty and your words give me hope that there will be others like you and you are right. Tomorrow we enter Rome and then heads will roll."

I shuddered for I knew he meant the words quite literally.

He pulled from his purse two aurei and flipped them in the air for the two of us to catch, "Here, in promise of more to come tomorrow."

It was a calculated act. The whole of our legion was watching him. They could not hear his words but they saw the golden coins twinkling in the winter sunlight and when we caught them there was a cheer. Sulla was a clever general who knew how to manipulate his men. We had been rewarded and if they did well then they would be too.

When he and his aides had left us Bucco said, "You skate on very thin ice Old Man."

The veteran tossed the coin in the air and deftly caught it. "Worth the risk though, Centurion."

I studied the coin. I had never seen one before for they were an uncommon currency. I saw that the coin bore the image of Sulla. I wondered if that would come back to haunt us. If we lost and our enemies took us then we would be seen as Sulla's men and it would be our heads that rolled. We both secured our treasure and ate. The food tasted better somehow. We were also reassured by the proximity of the city. We could smell the food, the people, the drains. It was a city and it was ours. If we could win then the war might be over.

Legionary

Republican Rome

Chapter 8

The Battle of the Colline Gate 1ˢᵗ November 82 BC

We were arrayed to the right of Sulla's larger army. He had more legions and we were there to support him. We lined up under the command of Marcus Crassus. We all wished that it was Pompey who commanded us because he brought us luck and victory. It was not long before the sun began to set that Sulla marched us forward to meet the enemy. Such was the battlefield that all we could see were the other two Pompeian legions at one side and Marcus Crassus' legions on the other. As we waited for our orders I studied the enemy. The first thing I realised was that none of the enemy regiments looked the same. Some had round shields and some oblong ones. Some had a scutum. Their helmets were also different. Some had ones that looked a little Roman but others had ones with fixed cheek pieces and some had plumes. They had men mailed as we were but more of the enemy wore just a bronze breastplate. Some of the regiments had long Greek spears and some had pila. How would they fight? So far we had only fought legionaries. This would be different. They did, however, have slingers, archers and men with javelins and we recognised those and understood how they would fight. Sulla's army also had slingers. Pompey's men had barely a handful. We would have to endure the attack of the enemy slingers before we could get to grips with them. Would I enjoy the aureus I had been given or would a Samnite plunder it from my dead body?

The horns sounded and we advanced as did our enemy. Night was falling and it was in everyone's interests to get the battle over as quickly as we could. I had never fought at night but I guessed that more luck than skill was involved. I worried that we had not made a sacrifice as we had intended.

Our pitifully small number of slingers fought bravely but they were soon sent packing and the handful of survivors passed through our ranks. We were in triplex acies formation and our cohort was in the rear rank. That was not a surprise. We had been in the front rank the last time we had fought and Legate Betto

Legionary

was a wise general. Our success meant that the cohorts before us would have confidence knowing that the cohort that had killed a centurion and taken a standard was behind them. The Third Cohort fought hard and were taking many casualties. The wounded passed through our ranks as we stood in the more open formation of post prior.

The fighting was hard and the Third Cohort had suffered. The Sixth Cohort rotated to take their place and we saw the bloody and battered survivors as they moved back.

"Some of them have nasty curved swords. Watch out for them! They can gut a man."

"Aye, and they stink!"

The comments showed that the Third Cohort were still in good spirits. They marched back and did not run. After a rest they would be ready to take their place again.

The fresh troops made an immediate gain and pushed back the Samnites. We knew that when we moved forward we had to negotiate the dead of the initial encounter. We had made progress. We saw nothing of Sulla and his men but we could hear their battle. It seemed to me that the sound was echoing off the walls of Rome itself. That was a worrying thought as it meant that Sulla was being forced back.

Optio Corbulo must have seen other legionaries turning to look to our left, "Never mind General Sulla and his men. We have our own battle to fight. Look to your front and wait for the order to advance." His calmness was reassuring. Darkness had fallen when the horn came for us to move. We were not rotating but our cohort was splitting in two to take its place next to the Sixth Cohort. We went with two other centuries to the right. There was a gap between the sixth and another of Pompey's legions.

Centurion Bucco roared, "Close formation!"

We shifted to form eight ranks and we were in the second rank just behind the signifer.

Numerius said, as we moved up, "Those are Lucanians ahead. We are going to stop them." He was speaking to reassure the rest of the contuburnium.

The tesserarius shouted, "Silence there."

Optio Corbulo shouted, "Ready spears!"

Legionary

The Samnites and the Lucanians were good soldiers and they fought well. The dead legionaries were a testament to that but Marcus Crassus and Gnaeus Pompeius had trained our legions well. Both generals knew how to bring fresh soldiers into the battle while it appeared the enemy just kept fighting with the same men. The Lucanians had long spears and a sword. We would throw our pila and they would have to endure the storm before we attacked. I saw that some of the Lucanians, mainly in the front rank, had lost their spears and held longer swords. They also had round shields. There would be more space for our blades to find flesh. I saw that while we all looked the same, they did not. There were differences. They also shouted and hurled insults at us but we marched silently and with purpose. The closer we came the less fearful they appeared. We were all the same and of the same mind. We had fought together for more than a year. I knew from what had been said that they had only begun to fight Sulla a few months ago. I was no longer a virgin and could work out such things. We advanced as did the Lucanians. They were trying to attack the flank of the Sixth Cohort. The cohort to our right was the Prima Cohort. They would not break.

"Halt!" Centurion Bucco was close enough to us so that I could hear the order, "Spears!"

The horns sounded and we threw our pila as one. The Lucanians came on at the fast march. They raised their shields but their design meant that more of our pila found flesh and the shields that were struck began to lower as the weight of the heavy spears dragged them down.

"Advance!" Then horns sounded and with pila held before us we advanced. The longer spears in their second and third ranks could reach us but holding a long spear with one hand was not easy. The Macedonians, we had heard, did not use a large shield but a buckler over their left hand. It meant they could use them effectively. As I thrust with my pilum at the spearless man before me I was able to flick up my scutum and deflect, easily, the long spear of the man behind. The spearless Lucanian used his longer sword to move my spear away. My father's sword would be a better weapon and I hurled the pilum into the air as I drew my blade. The cry told me that the pilum had not been wasted and I had hit someone in the supporting ranks. My enemy saw his chance and brought his sword over his head to strike at my helmet. That was the disadvantage of such a long sword. It was more unwieldy. I lifted my shield and blocked it. I was aware of Gaius and Numerius on either side of me but my attention was on the battle before me. I had a man with a sword trying to get at me and long spears poking at the gaps. It was the pila sent from behind which aided me. They fell alarmingly close to me but struck the second, third and fourth ranks of Lucanians. It allowed me to concentrate on my enemy.

I lifted my shield and blocked the strike of his sword. The blade stuck in my shield and I rammed my blade up and under his round shield. The soldier was trying to free his sword from my shield and my old sword found flesh that had no mail to guard it. It came below his breastplate and I felt the edge scrape along the metal edge of his shield and his ribs as it ended his life. I pushed my shield and his hand held the sword in death. It was pulled from my shield. As I stepped forward, along with Gaius and Numerius who had also slain their enemies, I reflected that I would need a new shield after the battle.

We had advanced and I sensed that the Prima Cohort next to us had also advanced. The Sixth Cohort was still holding. In a perfect world they would be rotated and the Third Cohort, now rested, would take their place but this crucial part of the battle was not the time for rotation. I now understood the rhythm of a battle. You pushed until the enemy's line broke and then you fell on the flanks of the others. You could never predict when that might be.

The better Lucanian warriors had been in their front ranks and we were now amongst men whose arms were weary from holding the long spears and who had felt the force of our pila. The swords we used were a comfortable weapon to hold and as we advanced the Lucanians would only see shields. Our blades were held low. I had learned to use my eyes and I stared at the young Lucanian ahead of me. It was hard to tell because of the cheek plates on his helmet but I guessed he was about my age. The difference was that I had killed many enemies and some had been veterans. His eyes showed his fear. Mine stared at him as I tried to predict what he would do. He nervously moved his spear at the three of us. The spears of the men behind were also pointed at the three of us as we advanced but when he poked his spear at me it was simplicity itself to not only block it but also render it ineffective as it was knocked over my shoulder and I stepped closer to him.

He knew that death was coming and pleaded, "No! Mercy!"

His accent was alien and he was an enemy. "Go to Elysium." We needed to end the battle and I rammed the sword into his unprotected throat. He fell and we were through to their last line of soldiers. Beyond them I saw the enemy camp.

Centurion Bucco roared, "We have them! On!"

His words inspired us. The ones behind pushed to fill gaps we had created and suddenly it was closer to forty men who were pushing and not the sixteen from a few moments earlier. The extra numbers broke the spirit of the last of the Lucanians we faced. They turned and fled. It is in the nature of victory that men follow those who flee. When their leader, Marcus Lamponius, mounted his horse and left with his aides then our battle was over.

Even as the horn sounded for us to halt we found ourselves in the Lucanian camp. I looked down the line and saw that Marcus Crassus, leading his legions and those of Gnaeus Pompeius, had destroyed the enemy left. I saw him raise his sword and shout, "Sack their camp and I will see how the general fares."

We needed no urging and we quickly entered the tents of our enemy. Luck played as much a part in this as in any night battle. Numerius, Gaius and I worked together to search the first tent we found. When some of the Sixth Cohort came to the entrance they saw us and left. We now had a reputation. We found gold as well as food and weapons. We took what we could use and discarded the rest. By the time we had searched the tent all that was worth taking had been taken and we went to the pots.

It was then that Marcus Crassus' aide galloped up, "To arms, General Sulla and his men were forced back to the walls of Rome. The battle hangs in the balance."

Pompey was not with us but Legate Betto knew his business. He had bloodied mail and his shield was dented. He had fought as hard as any. He shouted, "Close formation, on me!"

Legionary

    We dropped what we had already taken and ran to form a line. This time the walls of Rome lay to our left and not behind us. I saw a dead soldier from the Sixth Cohort and I dropped my scutum to pick up his. He would not need it and it was whole. We still had work to do. We formed a duplex acies and this time we were in the front rank with the Third Cohort to our right and the Sixth in posterior position to support us. We had lost men and so our eight files only had six ranks, nor did we have pila. This would be work for swords that were already nocked and not as sharp as they had been. We were not facing Lucanians, they had fled, but Samnites and more of them had mail. What we did have was the confidence of victory. We had won our battle and were now saving Sulla. As we advanced I could see how close they had come to the walls of Rome. I could even see that the Romans had dropped the portcullis. They did not want Sulla in the city and I knew that when we won then they would pay a heavy price.
    The Samnites had brought more men than the Lucanians and we now faced as many men as we had just defeated. The difference lay in the fact that we had victory in our nostrils and the Samnites, while they had enjoyed the best of their battle with Sulla, were now being attacked, in the dark, from two sides. The element of luck would play a larger part. The men we fought also had oblong shields and it would not be so easy to gain an advantage. The Samnites stood their ground and we advanced. We were in close formation. We had enough room to stab with our swords but we would each face just one opponent.
    The man before me had a beard which was flecked with a little grey. He was a veteran. That did not daunt me. I had slain a signifer but I would take nothing for granted. There was no fear in this man's eyes. If anything he looked supremely confident. Even as I prepared my own blow he smacked at me with his shield. It had a metal boss but my hand holding my sword was low down and I took the hit on my scutum. I was glad that I had found a replacement for my damaged one. He had a longer sword and held it over his shield to stab at me. He thought he had me as he had just forced me to block his shield with mine but my right hand brought up my father's sword and my shorter blade easily deflected his up and I was able to slash with it as I

withdrew it. His cheek guards protected most of his face but I sliced across his nose. He would be marked for life if he survived.

Gaius had slain his man and he moved forward. His shield now added pressure to mine and the Samnite's right hand did not have as much movement. I jabbed my blade under my shield but he was wise to the move and moved his shield down. My helmet had a rim and his did not. His maimed nose was gushing blood and I knew it was a distraction. I head-butted him and as his eyes were streaming he saw it late. He reeled and in that reeling signed his own death warrant. A man spreads his arms for balance when he begins to topple and even though he wore mail my sword tore through the links and into flesh. He sighed as he died.

As I stepped forward to join Gaius the man fighting Numerius made an error. He glanced at me and Numerius was too good a soldier to waste the opportunity. He gutted him. I learned that day about the Samnites' hatred for Sulla. They kept fighting. It was soon clear that they were losing. We were pushing them back and I could see Sulla's legions, now revitalised, pushing back the men who had seen the walls of Rome and victory in their sights. They kept fighting.

I was close enough now to see their leader Pontius Telesinus fighting amidst his bodyguards. It was Varius Drusus and Legate Betto who bearded him. Our Prima Cohort drove close to him and our First Spear was the one who slew the Samnite leader. The battle did not end there but its conclusion was close as word spread and the surrounded men looked for a way out. They died well and some of our century made the mistake of thinking that we had won and their overconfidence cost them dearly. The three of us were now a team. We were like a tempered sword and we worked well together. The others in our contuburnium drew confidence from our triumvirate. None of us moved too far forward until the other two were alongside us. In this way we were slow and steady as we hacked through the Samnites. We saw their camp at the same time they did. We had pushed them back from the very walls of Rome and that was enough. They broke. We were too weary to follow. My sword was scored and pitted. Just as I had found a new shield I would have to search our own dead and find one who died early. His sword would do until I could find a replacement.

We fell upon their camp and stripped it bare. By the time the sun broke we were weary beyond words. Had an enemy attacked us then we would have been easy prey. When we heard the horses galloping from the north we grabbed our weapons. We had little chance against horsemen but it was not in our nature to surrender. We would die well. When the cheer and cry, "Pompey!" went up, we knew that our leader had returned and we now had cavalry.

Gnaeus Pompeius had a mind as sharp as a razor and he waved his horsemen to take as many Samnites as he could. He reined in and grinned, "I see you do not need me. Well done Legate Betto. You have won once more."

The bloodied but unbowed legate nodded, "Aye, General, and now you can take your place behind General Sulla and next to General Crassus as you enter Rome. The city is ours!"

The city might have lowered the portcullis to stop the Sullan soldiers entering but they could not gainsay the general and the gates were opened. He had the head of Pontius Telesinus taken by General Quintus Lucretius Afella to Praeneste.

General Sulla wasted no time and we marched into the city, its inhabitants sullen but cowed. They had lost and the man they hated the most was now in control. We were weary but we were ordered to attend as Sulla summoned the senate to the Temple of Bellona on the Campus Martius. His men brought three thousand of the many Samnite and Lucanian prisoners who had surrendered and all of them were executed. It was a bloody gesture to show Rome what he would do to any who opposed him. I felt sick as they were executed. Sulla's veterans whooped and cheered. The noise added to my nausea.

I turned to Numerius, "Those men surrendered to us. They did not deserve this."

Numerius put his arm around me, "It is a fact of life, Lucius. The simple answer is not to surrender. You fight to the end or, if you know you have lost, then you run, just as fast as your legs will take you."

Gaius was sickened too, "But Pompey and Crassus took prisoners into their armies."

"And they are not Sulla. I do not like the man but he is good for Rome. The Samnites have always been against him. He lost five thousand men in this battle. He is exacting revenge and that is why his men are cheering him." He saw our looks and added, "These three thousand are just a few of the prisoners. The rest will be sold as slaves. There will be more men enslaved than killed and the generals will become even richer."

We thought that the spectacle was over until Pompey brought in the two men he had captured, Gaius Carrinas and Marcus Lamponius. They were also publicly executed. Their deaths and the manner of their execution was understandable. They had been the leaders of the battles against Sulla and Pompey. Over the next nights and weeks, the deaths of the Samnites gave me nightmares. After the executions our legions and those of Marcus Crassus were sent out of the city and we camped close to where the battles had taken place. I didn't mind as the blood bath continued in the city and the nobles' families who had opposed Sulla in Rome were executed. On one day there were nine hundred such executions. All the joy of our victory and the proximity of Rome was taken from me. A few days after our victory Marius the Younger committed suicide and his head was brought back to Rome. The fight against Sulla on the mainland was over.

We were rewarded by Sulla and also by Pompey. As the reward was paid out to the survivors and with fewer of us than had begun the battle the three of us became rich men. The rest of our contuburnium were dead and the century had lost half its numbers. I found myself longing to go home. I had hated the bloodshed but if I could give the money I had received to my family then it might all be worthwhile. That, of course, could not happen. The best that we could expect was another couple of weeks in Rome for the rumour was that Pompey was to be sent to Sicily with his legions. The last of Sulla's enemies, Carbo, had fled there. Sicily was the last hotbed of opposition to Sulla and although he was nothing like him, Gnaeus Pompeius was Sulla's man.

We were marched to Ostia to take ships to Sicily. The fleet belonged to Sulla and was the same one that had brought him back from Greece. I would be even further away from my family

Legionary

as we hunted Carbo, Gnaeus Domitius Ahenobarbus and Marcus Perperna. Our century and the Fourth Century boarded our ship and we sailed south to the land of Sicily.

Chapter 9

Sicily and Africa 81 BC

The news of our imminent arrival meant that at least one of those we hunted, Marcus Perperna, fled the island before we arrived. We knew this because we witnessed Pompey when he had a rare fit of pique and showed his anger. Our ship had been faster than the rest. The captain told us he had recently cleaned the weed from the hull and that had made his ship able to slip through the seas and take better advantage of the wind and the oars. While he did not overtake Pompey's ship, that would have caused offence, we kept pace with it and we were the second ship to dock. As there was a fleet to land then speed was of the essence when we unloaded. The two mules were taken ashore first and that meant I had the wobbly legs first but that also meant I recovered the quickest. As I waited with Ceres, stroking her mane, I saw one of Pompey's aides speaking to him.

"Perperna is gone? To Sardinia? Then even if we catch Carbo and the others we still have enemies to find."

"Sorry, General."

He was angry and his arms reflected that anger but he became angrier when his horse was led from the ship. The soldier responsible for leading her ashore was tugging at the reins and the horse did not like it. The horse reared and clattered the soldier a mortal blow to the head. The man plunged between the ships. He was dead already but his body would be crushed to a pulp. The white horse then made a prodigious leap to clatter into the bags and equipment already landed. The horse was lucky not to break a leg. I think that had he done so Pompey would have erupted like a volcano. The terrified animal looked for an escape. I did not think; I just reacted. I handed Ceres' reins to Gaius and said, "Watch her."

I saw the path the horse would take and I ran to cut it off. It was not a mule. It was a highly strung and expensive horse but it was an animal. I had learned that if you could control a pig then every other animal seemed easier. I was about to discover if that was true of an animal that weighed as much as a couple of mailed men. I raised my hands to arrest the horse's attention and then spoke. I did not shout but spoke gently and I smiled. Some men have mocked me for doing so but I believe an animal can see when a man smiles. I used a sing song tone when I spoke and my words rose and fell like the waves over which we had just passed, "Whoa! Come now, is this any way to behave? Your master is embarrassed." I walked towards the horse as I held its gaze and I talked, some would say nonsense but the animal, while it still stamped and danced, was not trying to get past me. I saw two other legionaries running and I held up my hand to stop them. I was winning but it would not take much to set the horse off again. "You have got yourself all sweaty. Still, I can understand why you are happy to be off that ship. So am I. I am betting your legs feel strange. So do mine." I reached the horse and took the reins, still speaking. "You are a fine animal." I had in my tunic some root vegetables that Ceres liked and I took one out and proffered it. The horse munched it. "There, that is better. I wish I knew your name. I shall tell you mine. I am Lucius but they call me Mule Man. My mule is called Ceres. You would like her. Let me walk you." Taking the halter I began to walk the horse in circles. There was a cheer from the soldiers being landed. The horse tossed its head and whinnied once but then let me lead it around.

Pompey came over with an aide. The aide held out his hand and I gave him the reins, "The horse needs to be walked some more, sir."

Pompey nodded, "Listen to the legionary." He looked at me. "You have talents, Legionary, as well as more courage than seems possible in one so young. If I did not already know you I would say that you are a cavalryman but you are the youth with the good eyes and the brave heart. This is another of your talents."

I nodded, "I like animals and I have learned that if you treat them well then they respond."

He studied me, "You know I did not know until this moment that you and I are similar in many ways. When I watched you with Hephaestus I remembered you, from the port and the battle."

I was so shocked at his words that I shook my head, "General, you are from a noble family and I am from humble farming stock."

"Yet both our fathers dominate our lives. I am trying to be a better soldier than my father and you sacrificed yourself for your father and his farm." He smiled, "I remembered your story. Perhaps the Parcae have thrown us together. Legate Betto tells me that you and your century helped to win the Battle of the Colline Gate." I did not know what to say. I thought that if I said anything then it would either appear arrogant or would be self-deprecating. He took an aureus out of his tunic. On it was Sulla's image. "This is for your bravery, for Hephaestus can be a wild beast. In war he terrifies everyone but you showed courage. From now on when I travel on a ship you shall be his groom. I will tell your centurion." He held out his arm, "Thank you, Legionary."

He held out his hand and I shook it, much as I did with Numerius and Gaius before and after a battle.

He turned and walked towards his aides, "Come, we have lost one prey. There are others to catch before this opposition is quashed." I was forgotten.

When I reached the century, every eye was on me. For the first time I saw something in Centurion Bucco's eyes that was akin to awe, "Legionary Porcianus, you are a man with many layers. You are the only one in this legion with whom Gnaeus Pompeius has shaken hands." He saw the aureus in my hand, "And you have been rewarded again. Does this bode well for the century?"

"I do not know, Centurion, but I am to travel, the next time we sail. with the general and care for his horse. It means someone else will need to care for Ceres on the ship."

He shook his head and he laughed, "You see what I mean? Any other man would be happy with the honour he has been given but you are concerned with an old mule."

"Ceres is not old, Centurion and..."

He put his arm around my shoulder, "And you are so serious, Mule Man. In war that is good but you should smile more and enjoy life while you can. Come we will have the chance to examine the port before the rest of the fleet docks and prices rise. Let us go before the rest of the legion arrives."

Legionary

We were not quite old soldiers but we knew how to take advantage of our early arrival. We had first choice in the markets and the taverns were empty. Prices would rise and I do not doubt we paid more than the locals but the lack of weed was like a gift from the gods and we took advantage.

Our time on Sicily consisted of tramping over mountainous roads to find what Pompey now termed, 'rebels'. Now that Sulla was dictator then those who opposed him became rebels. We travelled the island as a cohort winkling out the men who quickly surrendered when they found that their escape from the island was blocked. Pompey's warships surrounded the island and as we progressed their sails were always on the horizon. We rarely had to use a sword in anger. We found some rich men who hid in their homes and their houses yielded treasure. Sometimes it was in coin but often it was in food or fine clothes that could be sold. When Carbo was finally cornered and captured we were recalled to witness his ritual execution. He was the last of the leaders of the opposition to Sulla. Perperna still hid in Sardinia but as he had just been praetor of Sicily and the island was Pompey's it did not matter. Pompey said that Carbo's execution was necessary as payment for the crimes he had inflicted on Rome. Much as we liked Pompey we knew that was just rhetoric. Sulla had committed more crimes against Rome through the slaughter of so many of the nobles there. Our general was eliminating another rebel who might be like Sertorius or Ahenobarbus and continue the fight across the seas.

We thought we would be heading back to Rome but we were wrong. Gnaeus Domitius Ahenobarbus had taken the last Marian legions to Africa where he had taken the province for his own. This had been the land of the Carthaginians until Scipio Africanus had ended the war and repaid the enemy for the legions lost at Cannae and Trasimene. Another reason for his flight was that he had been proscribed by Sulla. If he stayed where Rome ruled he would be executed. A fleet was gathered. There would be one hundred and twenty warships and eight hundred transports. It took some time for the ships to be gathered and for the other legions we would be taking to be assembled. There would be six legions to quell what amounted to a rebellion by twenty-seven thousand rebels.

Legionary

I was summoned to the legate, "You, Legionary Porcianus, are to travel on the flagship with the general." I was not sure if Legate Betto was happy about this or not. I had learned to read Bucco and I even understood why First Spear acted the way that he did but the legate was still an unknown factor. "Serve him well for you represent this legion and I would not have the general think less of us because of an error on your part. When we land in Africa then you will rejoin your century. You will not need your gear. That can travel with the century."

I headed, wearing just my tunic and carrying my cloak, to the flagship where Hephaestus stamped an irritated hoof. Pompey was speaking to his leaders and it was a nervous looking legionary who held the war horse's reins.

Pompey glanced up and said, "Good. Take Hephaestus and secure him aboard." That was it.

The legionary handed the reins to me and then hurried away from the teeth and hooves of the horse. I smiled and took a wrinkled apple I had found. I gave it to the horse and then stroked his mane, speaking to him as I took a hold of his tether. I saw Pompey, while still talking, give me a surreptitious look and a smile appeared on his face.

"Come on then, let us board and no nonsense this time. Your master's friends are all watching not to mention the legion. I have no intention of ending my life because you had a fit of pique." All the time I was stroking the mane and Hephaestus was chewing. I walked towards the gangplank. Even Ceres had not been happy when we had boarded the first ship at Ostia and I knew that the plank would appear too narrow for the horse. The waters swirled below and made strange and unnatural noises. I used the same technique with Hephaestus as I had with Ceres. I sang as I walked up the gangplank. I did not mind appearing ridiculous. Whatever worked was necessary. The singing of the nonsense song my mother had sung to us as a lullaby seemed to be effective and Hephaestus plodded serenely up the gangplank. I did not stop singing and I walked the horse on the narrow deck, my voice rising and falling gently. I cocked my head at the seaman, whilst still singing, and he realised what I needed. He nodded and led me to a ring bolt at the prow of the ship and I moved the horse there.

I had a brush in my tunic and I began to groom him, still singing. I had learned that Ceres liked it and so did Hephaestus. It allowed me to watch the general's aides' horses as they were led aboard. One would have thought that they might have watched what I did and emulated me but they did not. The first horse came up but complained the whole way and had to be dragged by two men and two seamen. The second took two men to push it reluctantly aboard and the third, when it neared the top, suddenly reared and clattered the soldier on the back of the head. He plunged to his death between the ship and the quay. I was close enough to run and I quickly grabbed the trailing tether. I did not want the horse to hurt any of the crew who had backed off and I also did not want Hephaestus to be upset. I sang my silly song again and held the horse's gaze. He began to calm and I backed along the deck to the next available ring bolt. The crew patted my back as I tied the horse off. Luckily there were just two more horses to be boarded and lessons had been learned. I heard the men who nervously led the horses, sing as they came up.

One of the crew men brought me a beaker of wine. As he handed it to me he said, "We normally swing them aboard with a sling." He pointed to a crane, "But your general is keen to leave quickly. You did well there." He nodded to the stern where I saw the captain giving his orders, "You have made a friend of the captain. You will have a pleasant voyage."

And so it proved. I was thanked by the aide whose horse had killed the soldier and Pompey smiled and said, "Well done Mule Man", as he boarded. The best thanks came on the crossing to Africa. I enjoyed the best of wine and food. I had a more than pleasurable crossing, for not only did I have an easy time I also liked being with the animals. There was still much of my father in me. Horses are not cruel like their owners could be. They are loyal and brave and, if they are treated well, are a valuable friend. I confess I did not want the voyage to end for as we neared the heat of Africa my fertile imagination conjured up all sorts of unpleasant images. I was just wearing a tunic on the deck of a ship where the breeze kept me relatively cool and yet I still felt as though I was baking. How would I cope in the heat and dust of the African desert, wearing armour?

Legionary

The four-day voyage ended when we neared the small port of Thabraca. There was no quay and we had to beach the ships and then land the horses directly to the beach. It was easier as the beach was slightly higher than the ship and it was not as steep for the horses. After the town had been secured by legionaries I went ashore with Hephaestus and the others in charge of horses copied me exactly. They had learned from the one they all called Mule Man. My name was not an insult but an honorific.

The small beach necessitated the disembarkation by pairs of ships and was time consuming. The general commandeered houses in the town and he had one with a stable. I led Hephaestus there and was then dismissed, with thanks, by the general. I felt as though I ought to have thanked him for what had been a most pleasant voyage.

When the century landed I was, once more, back in the world of the legionary. I was given a little more respect from the officers, thanks to my service to the general but I still had all the duties I had before. Ceres, Gaius and even the taciturn Numerius were pleased to see me. Gaius rained question after question to me. By the time my account was finished Numerius shook his head, "You have more luck than a man deserves, Lucius. I should watch out for the Parcae."

He was right, of course. I knew that I ought to make a sacrifice at the temple of Mars the next time we found one. We headed first to Carthage, that ancient capital of the Carthaginian world. It was there that I found a temple of Mars. It had been used, originally, as a temple to one of the Carthaginian gods but had been converted. I bought a chicken and paid the priest to sacrifice it. It did not cost me much and that was a small price to pay to get Mars on my side for the Parcae could be precocious.

It was there that some of the legion became unruly. Carthage was famed as the home of the Carthaginians. They had ruled the sea we called the Middle Sea and they had been rich. Some of the legion, notably the Second and Third Cohorts, decided that there was buried treasure and they began to dig in the desert. Their dolabra were put to good use but in the end their tools were just blunted as they dug. We did not join them and I thought Pompey would intervene but he did not. Numerius nodded his approval, "We have had a sea voyage and the men need time to recover. These legionaries will find nothing and they will return to the ranks. Pompey is not a stupid man, Lucius. We can enjoy Carthage." I knew what that meant for Old Man.

He was right and when Pompey summoned the army to move everyone arrived. The Second and Third Cohorts, who had tried to find the treasure, had found nothing and were somewhat shame faced.

Pompey used local auxiliaries as scouts and they were sent to find General Ahenobarbus. When deserters began to pour into the city we wondered if we would have to fight at all. Gaius asked if my sacrifice had been a greater one than we had planned. Numerius laughed, "Don't be daft, lad. Mars would not hand over Africa to us just because we gave him one chicken. No, these men know that we have six legions and they are the men of Pompey and Sulla. They won't want to face us. By deserting to us they are saving their lives."

In the end seven thousand men deserted from our enemies. I wondered if Pompey would do as Sulla had done and have them executed but he proved to be a more sensible commander. He had them made into a new legion but wisely left them to defend Carthage rather than joining us to hunt down and defeat Ahenobarbus.

We were ordered from our comfortable camp at Carthage and sent to march to a place south of Utica where Ahenobarbus and his twenty thousand men awaited us. It was not a long march but I have never been either as hot or as thirsty as we trekked across that barren land. When Scipio Africanus had finally defeated the Carthaginians he had seeded the land with salt. It was recovering but slowly. We saw little vegetation except close to the coast and the sun burned down on us with such an intense heat that I am sure I could have boiled water in my helmet without the aid of a fire.

When we finally found the enemy we discovered that he had chosen a good position. He had, before him, a ravine and there appeared to be no way around it. His archers and his slingers would make mincemeat of us if we tried to cross. We waited with an armed camp behind us but we were in cohort order. The mules were tethered in the camp and it was there I saw Marius. He was the muleteer I had met the first day I had watered Ceres.

As far as I knew he was the only one left from the original mule men. He smiled, "Our paths have been different, Lucius the Mule Man, since first we met. You travel with the general and are rewarded with gold. I am just as poor as ever."

The camp prefect shouted, "You pair, stop gossiping like old women and get back to your centuries."

As we hurried back I said, "Pompey has yet to lose and I am sure that when we win we will find gold."

"I hope so, Lucius."

"May the gods favour you."

"And you."

We both took our places in our centuries.

The clouds that appeared behind us were the first we had seen since we had landed in Africa. Indeed I could not remember them in Sicily. As we waited we commented on them. "Well a drop of rain would not go amiss, eh, boys?" Gnaeus laughed.

The tesserarius continued the joke, "I would rather it was wine and not water," I liked Quietus. He knew how to lighten the mood.

It was at that moment that a wind sprang up behind us, too. We looked at the skies as the clouds began to darken and then, to our amazement, rain began to fall.

"Gnaeus Lamia, you ought to leave the army and become a seer!" Gnaeus was relatively new and in that moment gained his nickname. We had six men with the name Gnaeus and Seer was a better nickname than another Gnaeus who was called Farty for obvious reasons. For some reason I thought back to poor Sertor. His nickname, Mouthy, had been the first to be given and he had not owned it for long.

We all lifted our faces to the sky to drink in the rain. At first, one of us noticed that the enemy had left their defensive positions and, in the face of the storm, were heading back to the relative comfort of their camps. We were too busy enjoying the gift of the gods. Pompey had seen the movement and he had the horn sounded.

Centurion Bucco, who a few moments earlier had been doing as we had done and been enjoying the rain on his face barked, "Come on you shower, stand to! Have you never seen rain before?"

Legionary

The horn sounded again and we marched towards the ravine in simplex acies and in open formation. There was no way we could cross the ravine in close ranks. The rain was on our backs and it seemed to favour us rather than the Marians. They were oblivious, thanks to the storm, of our movement. The wind had whipped up the rain and it was hard rain. I wondered if it would make lakes. We reached the ravine and made our way down and then up the other side. It took some time and once we were on the top then the centurions and optios marshalled us into our centuries. This time we were in open order and we were a post prior century, behind the Second Century.

We were seen and we heard the enemy horns as their movement to their camp was arrested and they turned to march back to their battle positions, but this time they were hampered by the rain and the ground which was turning into a muddy morass. The desert was becoming a bog. Pompey waited. He was behind our legion. We had been the first that he had raised and we had earned more honours than any other of his legions. Sulla's men were on the flanks. The men who came to fight us were Romans too. They were the last of the Marians and all those with doubts had deserted and were now in Carthage. These men would fight hard. Their general also had auxiliaries; slingers and archers who ran before their legions.

Numerius chuckled, "And the rain will make their bow strings as limp as a senator's…"

He did not get to finish the insult to a senator's manhood as Centurion Bucco shouted, "Shields!"

We lifted the shields as stones flew through the air. Numerius was right. The arrows barely reached us and not a man was hurt by them. A few legionaries who were tardy to raise their scuta were struck but none fell. Now with shields in place it was like the rain had turned to hail.

Optio Corbulo was far enough back not to need his shield and he had a good view of the enemy. He roared, "Pila!"

The optio from the Second Century repeated the order ahead of us and we all presented a spear. The rain was still falling but not quite as hard and I could see the enemy legions marching purposefully towards us. Both armies had been trained the same way but the timing of the commands could make all the difference. We had just had a short climb over the ravine and we were rested. The Marians had marched from their camp and they would be more tired than we were. The centurion of the Second Century, along with the other centuries, ordered the throwing of the pila a few moments before the Marians. Two thousand spears flew through the air even as the Marians marched forward. The second pila were prepared. I saw men fall and shields droop.

"Pila!"

The second flight of pila was just as devastating and the enemy reeled and stopped to throw their own spears. They killed barely a couple of our men.

Legate Betto roared, "Rotate!" and as the Second Century moved back we moved forward. It was done seamlessly and we were in position with our unused pila ready. The Marians sent their second spears and we blocked them. I saw no one close to us fall but there were cries from further along our line that told me men had been hit. It meant that the enemy would be reduced to using their swords.

Centurion Bucco shouted, "Pila!" and we all hurled our spears just as the enemy moved forward. Moving forward whilst spears are falling is always tricky but when the ground is slippery and there are bodies before you then it is doubly worse. More of our spears found flesh than might have been expected and many others came with scuta made heavy by the pila hanging from them.

We presented our second pila as the Marians charged. It was brave but doomed to failure for our spears had a longer range than did their swords and, in addition, many had drooping shields and were easy to spear. We slew their first men and the survivors turned. They might have been rotating but I doubted that. They were glad to be away from the war machine that was our legion. The next century marched at us. Just before they reached us Numerius, Gaius and I hurled our second pila and drew our swords. Behind us the second rank poked their spears through the gaps and the enemy had to fight men with swords and men with spears. We began to hack and stab our way forward. Their better warriors had already perished and we were working our way through men who were not as skilled we were. They broke and ran.

Legionary

Men cheered and yelled, "Imperator!"

The accolade was for Pompey but our young general was having none of it, "The enemy still live! I do not want to have to fight them again. On to their camp and destroy them!"

We formed ranks, this time eight men to a file and six ranks deep. We marched towards their distant camp. They were running and we were marching. They would get there first and defend the camp. We had built similar camps and knew what to expect. There would be a ditch and a low palisade. Many of our men still had pila and they would be the ones to send their one thousand spears at an already demoralised enemy. It would be bloody work to finish them but when we did we would have the camp of Ahenobarbus to sack and who knew what riches it might hold?

Some of the fleeing Marians had not stopped at their camp. They had taken whatever horses they could and had fled. I saw their general and his leaders. They stood ready to die. If nothing else Sulla had taught the Marians that it was better to die in battle than be executed in the aftermath.

I had never assaulted a Roman camp before and I was impressed by how difficult it was. If the Marians had not lost so many men then we might have bled on it for they had interwoven thorns into the wooden stakes. As it was we managed to scale the wooden wall with just cuts and scratches and once inside then the slaughter began. The general had joined us in the assault and led from the front. Soldiers always like that and we fought even harder. When Ahenobarbus fell then the Marians surrendered. There were just a thousand of them and I saw another two thousand fleeing.

Pompey grinned and raised his sword, "Victory!" We all cheered. He gave a low bow and gestured with his sword, "And the camp is now yours!"

There was no rush to leave and we emptied the camp of everything. I found one dead Roman senator who had rings on his fingers. I had no idea of their real worth but they looked valuable and I took them. They would join the money in the chest that was guarded by Ceres. I went to search a tent that looked to have been an officer's one and found little treasure. I did find, however, the body of Marius, the mule man. He had been stabbed in the stomach. Looking around the tent I pictured the scene. He had raced ahead to get treasure and had found an officer's tent. The officer had been within and in that uneven battle the last of the mule men had died. I picked up his body and carried it, reverently to the bier with the other honoured dead. He had achieved neither glory nor gold. There was a lesson to be learned.

We left the next day to march back to Carthage. The traders there would benefit from our victory!

Chapter 10

If we thought we were done with fighting we were wrong. We spent just three days in Carthage during which time we saw many riders entering the city with messages for the general and then we marched west, towards Numidia. As usual there were rumours and there was gossip. This time our auxiliaries were locals and we could not discover the truth of the rumours. We marched. Seven days into our trek along the coast where the breeze from the sea made the march tolerable, Optio Corbulo finally gave us firm intelligence. "We are to fight a local king, Hiarbas. He is an ally of the Marians." He used his long staff to point west, "His capital is Cirta but I doubt we will have to march all the way there. We have a little battle to fight and when the enemy are defeated we can go home."

Gaius shook his head, "It is the desert, Optio, and we are on foot. Don't the locals use horses and camels?"

"They do but we have pila and shields." He nodded to me, "Besides, you have the one here who can talk to horses. Perhaps Mule Man can persuade the horses to change sides. It seems there is nothing he can't do." His tone was scathing and it hurt me.

When he had gone, Numerius sensed that I was upset by the words of the optio, "Ignore him, Lucius. The optio can't stand that you have been favoured by the general. It is jealousy. Take comfort that we are going back to Rome when this is over and we can spend some of this gold."

I was not sure I would spend the fortune I had accumulated. There was nothing I really wanted. Gaius said, "What will you spend yours on, Numerius?"

He tapped the side of his head, "Up here I have already spent it. I will go to the most expensive baths in Rome and have a slave use a strigil to clean my body. I will buy a good toga and then spend a week in the most expensive whorehouse in Rome. When the money is gone, they can throw me out."

I shook my head, "That would be a waste of the gold."

"Not for me."

"But you would have nothing left."

He sniffed loudly, "I can smell profits so long as we serve Pompey." He looked at me, "And you, Lucius Porcianus, you bring luck. A good soldier never dismisses luck. You stay alive and we shall all make a greater fortune than the one we have now." His words more than made up for the comments of the optio. That Numerius valued me was something I had never expected.

The tesserarius was close by and he said quietly, "Old Man is right. You are lucky and you bring luck to the century. Keep doing what you are doing and all will be well. It is a foolish man who tries to change his nature."

When we saw the dust cloud approaching we were ordered to halt and we heard the horn for an officers' call. The optios were left in charge and we stood to. When the legate and centurions returned it was with a new order. We had a brand-new formation; one we had never used before. The cohort formed a hollow square. The mules and the baggage were tethered in the middle. I drove the spike into the ground and made sure that Ceres was secured. We had a handful of slingers and archers and they too, sheltered in the centre. The cohorts were in duplex acies and we stood facing men from the Eighth Cohort. It felt strange to be facing friends. There was enough space between the cohorts for us all to throw our pila without hitting the enemy.

Gnaeus Lamia, the Seer, shouted, "Centurion, why are we facing our own men?"

Centurion Bucco snorted, "Just listen for the orders. This is the plan of the general and we don't question them." I could tell, from his voice, that he wondered how we would fare. I was lucky in that I was standing, not facing the other cohort but at the corner of the hollow square so that I could see the Numidians as they approached. The dust cloud settled and I saw that the army we faced was a colourful one.

Numerius said, "It is a clever plan. The barbarian horsemen like to get behind our lines. We have too few cavalry to stop them and this way they cannot find a weakness. We just need resolve."

Their king brought his army. It was largely a mounted one. He had many archers and slingers but his infantry did not look as though they would cause us trouble. The only soldiers he had who looked a danger were the three thousand or so men who had fled after the battle with Ahenobarbus. We had beaten them once and we knew we would beat them again. What worried us more were the mounted archers. They could ride around our flanks and shower us with arrows. We had no antidote to that particular poison. Even the few ballistae that still remained would not be of much use. We could only use the ones facing the enemy and when they passed between the squares our men would not be able to send their bolts. We would have to endure the arrow storm. We took comfort from the fact that Pompey knew what he was doing. We might not be able to see a way to beat them but he would. Perhaps these hollow squares would work.

The enemy had horns, drums and cymbals. They also screamed and shouted while we stood impassably silent. We heard a cacophony of noise and horses galloped towards us. "Stand to. Ready shields and pila but do not throw until you are ordered to."

The thundering hooves sounded terrifying. Thus far we had fought legionaries. They were like us and so predictable. They could throw pila and use their swords. These horsemen could use bows and throw javelins. We would have to, impotently, endure whatever they did to us and then work out a way to fight and defeat them. They would weaken us and when our spears had been expended they would send in their own infantry. For the first time since I had fought for Pompey I felt my confidence oozing away. I remembered Hephaestus as he careered around the port. I had stopped him by waving my arms but if I tried that with a warrior mounted on a horse then I would be a dead man. The horsemen raced towards us and I wondered if they would stop.

Centurion Bucco's voice was reassuring and he gave an order. Any order was welcome. "Raise shields and present spears!" Numerius, Gaius and I lifted our shields and Numerius, who was on the very corner of the hollow square, took a half step closer to me so that our three shields were tightly locked. Only my eyes were visible and a man on a horse had little chance of hitting those. I would trust to my helmet, shield and mail.

Legionary

I heard, from the rear, Optio Corbulo as he used his staff to push the rear ranks closer to the front, "The horses won't come close. Stand firm."

It was all very well him saying that. He was in the fourth rank. We were in the front rank. The horsemen did not charge us but, instead, rode through the gaps between squares and sent arrows and javelins at us. The missiles clattered into shields and clanked off helmets. Unlike our spears these were light javelins. Even those that stuck in our shields were not heavy enough to make our arms drop and when some of our slingers and archers sent missiles at the horsemen and had some success I felt a little more hopeful. I had more hope then when the ballistae cracked and men and horses fell. It was not like sending them into a packed legion where a bolt could transfix a few men. The bolts either struck a horse or a man. In one case a bolt went through a man's leg, his horse and, I suspect, his other leg.

One thing I had learned was that men with arrows and javelins have a limited supply of them. Once they had expended their weapons they had to move back and resupply. We had not lost many men and after removing the javelins and arrows that had stuck in we raised our shields once more.

We were then given a new command. Option Corbulo shouted, "Porcianus, take Ceres and lead her. The cohort will march in square."

I obeyed but I was aware that I was leaving a gap. Even as I untethered her I saw the men in the flank centuries turn and face west. The ones at the rear did an about face. When all were turned the order was given to march. It was a strange experience. The mule men along with the missile men were in the centre with First Spear, the standards and the cornicens. We marched in a hollow square. The ballistae were packed on to their mules and we were without the weapon that had accounted for thirty or forty men and horses. Ceres carried the water for our century and she was vital. We only travelled half a mile before we stopped to repel another attack. This time the mule men stayed in the centre and I was able to watch the attack. It sounded fierce but I could see that it was completely ineffective. Their horsemen were doing no harm and every attack saw their numbers lessened as slings and arrows took out one in five of the enemy. Passing between cohorts meant they were attacked on two sides for pila were used to thin their numbers too.

Their king, Hiarbas, decided to fight us with his infantry and we saw them as they advanced. The horsemen pulled back. The enemy had many more infantry than we did but we did not fear them for they whooped and cheered like wild men. They did not march in ranks and files as we did but came as a mob. The only force that looked in any sort of order were the three thousand Marians. The order was given to form standard lines. Centurion Bucco shouted to us, "Tether the mules and rejoin your centuries."

We tethered our animals once more and ran back to form our more traditional lines. This time our archers and slingers, their stocks replenished from their own mules, took their place before us. They would harass the enemy infantry and then take shelter behind our lines. We were in a slightly more open formation of four ranks and twenty files. The exception was the Fourth Cohort who would be facing the three thousand Marians. We were ready to fight. We had stood and endured attacks by their horsemen and sent a few spears back in anger. We would show these barbarians how a Roman army fought.

The men who charged us were led by their chiefs. Even as they raced recklessly towards us I saw the light glittering from the gold and silver they wore around their necks. Many of the men were half naked Nubians whose glistening bodies were well muscled. They had a variety of weapons, from long swords and axes to spears and pole weapons. They looked and sounded terrifying but the soldier in me knew that our discipline, training and weapons would see us victorious. We had endured the attacks of their horsemen and we were now on more familiar ground. The slingers and archers had time for just one volley and then they ran through our lines to shelter behind us.

When the enemy were just twenty paces from us the order was given, "Pila!" Our formation meant that every legionary could throw his weapon. There was space to pull back our right arms and hurl our pila into the air. Such was the mass of men attacking that every pilum would find flesh or a shield and the Numidians had no defence against the heavy, weighted spear. Such was the devastation that we had plenty of time to take our second pilum and present it.

Centurion Bucco said, "Close ranks."

We moved closer together. There were gaps between the centuries but they were filled by our slingers and archers. The Numidians hurled themselves at our solid lines of scuta and pila. Few of their men were mailed and every spear found flesh. The muscled Nubians fought on with bloody bodies but as spears from the second rank jabbed at faces with no mail to guard them, they fell and more came. My spear slew at least five before a blow from a club broke it. Hostius, standing behind me, rammed his spear at the man with the club and I had the chance to take my sword, one I had taken from the field at the Battle of the Colline Gate, and ensure that the clubman died.

When the fierce attack lessened, the horn sounded the advance. The front rank waited until the other three ranks had passed. We had no pila and we were the rear rank now. We moved over the bodies that littered the ground. We adopted a slightly more open formation as we moved over the terrain littered with human remains, the dead and the dying. The Numidians had sent their best and they had died. They now resumed the attacks of their horsemen but we were a solid line and I learned something that day. No matter how much a rider orders his mount forward it will not charge a man. At least the Numidian horses and camels would not. Spears rammed into horses and they died. Horsemeat would be on the menu that night. We moved inexorably forward.

Suddenly we heard, from the west, the sound of horns. Gaius turned to Optio Corbulo who had his staff pressed into our backs.

"Is that more enemies, Optio?"

He laughed, "No, Gaius, it is the sound of the end of the battle. The general has allies and we held the enemy until Bogud of Mauretania could attack their rear. We have won."

He was right and the enemy before us suddenly turned and fled south, into the desert. The horses and camels led the flight and many of those on foot clung to the camels' and horses' saddles. We had no opportunity to follow them. Nor did we have any inclination to do so for there was an enemy camp to ransack and a battlefield to clear. It was the Mauritanians who gave chase. Like the Numidians they were well mounted and would catch the weary enemy cavalry.

When General Pompey rode through we all cheered and gave him Alexander's title, "Pompey the Great!" It was a title he would enjoy until he died.

Ten days after the battle we marched back into Carthage. I had collected so much treasure in the enemy camp that I was forced to use Ceres to carry it. Luckily we had found oats and barley in the Numidian camp and she ate well. I looked after her. Numerius spent some of his money in the whorehouses but he was disappointed in the women that were there. He had expected more excitement and exoticism. He shook his head, "I only spent a few coins. I will save the rest for Rome. I know where the best lupanare is to be found!"

We had the victory but Pompey wanted a triumph and while the bulk of the army marched back to Carthage he and his officers went hunting with our new allies. By the time they reached Carthage they had captured and caged many animals, including elephants. They would make a great procession as they were led by the general through Rome. It would tell Rome that he had been to Africa and conquered.

Forty days after landing in Africa we boarded the ships to sail back to Rome. Sulla's ally, the deposed king of Numidia, Hiempsa, was placed on the throne and with a treaty made with Mauretania, Africa was safe once more.

Gaius took charge of Ceres and I, once more, led Hephaestus onto the transport.

The voyage back was a longer one. It took five days to reach Ostia and then a day more to unload the ship. I enjoyed the voyage as we ate better on the general's vessel than on the other transports and I also got to speak to him. I think he regarded me as something of a lucky charm. He made a point of speaking to me every day. It might have been that we were more similar in age than the officers with whom he travelled. We did not speak of war or weapons but he was interested in my life before I joined the legion. I discovered that the life of a young noble was not as wonderful as I had thought and he envied me the freedom I had enjoyed. I had not thought about it but the times I had hunted alone and walked in the woods were pleasures denied the young son of a successful general.

"You are lucky in so many ways, Lucius. There were no expectations of you but I am expected to be as great a general as my father."

I knew I was on treacherous ground here and I remembered that Pompey's father had died of dysentery and been so hated by his men that they had torn his body from the funeral byre. "Surely you have exceeded your father and his achievements, great though they were. It was you who was responsible for the defeat of the Marians. You took Sicily and you have conquered Africa."

He smiled, "And yet I have been given no triumph."

"Surely you will, General. Even Marcus Crassus has not achieved what you have."

"Perhaps."

I led Hephaestus from the transport and the general bade farewell to me. Another aureus found its way into my purse. We had profited from the war but Pompey the Great had taken an enormous treasure. He was even richer and could now afford more legions. We camped outside Rome. We were a victorious army but Sulla would not allow us into the city. Poor Numerius was beside himself. He had a purse full of gold and silver and he had nowhere to spend it. He was determined not to use the camp followers. When he spent his money it would be on a skilled artisan. Pompey sensed the anger and disappointment of his men. He paid, out of his own purse, for gladiatorial games. We had no amphitheatre but that did not matter. There were just two dozen gladiators but as I had never seen gladiators fight it could have been two and I would have been happy. The pairs were all identical. There would be a Thracian and he would fight one of the prisoners we had brought back. Not all the legionaries who had surrendered had been executed. The centurions and officers, not to mention the immunes, had been kept to be sold as slaves. The exhibition was for Pompey's legions. A small stand was erected close to the Tiber and food and drink were laid on. Looking back, I think that Pompey was still annoyed about his lack of a triumph and the games were a message for Sulla. They would only last one day and the cost to Pompey was a tiny fraction of the money he had made in Africa and Sicily. It was a clever move as it made the legions happy. Once the day was over it would be a different matter.

There was a great deal of anticipation about the combats. The Roman prisoners would be fighting in the mail that I wore and with the same helmet. They would be using the same sword and the same shield. The men fighting them, professionally trained at a ludus by a lanista, would be dressed as gladiators with Thracian helmets, a curved sword, a shield and a greave on one leg. There was both debate and bets placed about the outcome. The night before we sat around our fire drinking some wine which Numerius had acquired. We discussed the forthcoming fight.

"If they are centurions who are fighting, even Marian ones, they will be too good for the gladiators."

Numerius laughed, "Seer, these gladiators were all soldiers once. Some of them were the Samnites and Lucanians we defeated last year. You can bet that Sulla did not execute prisoners who could be sold to a lanista. The difference is that the gladiators have had a year of training how to fight alone. The centurions are used to fighting with a century." He took out a handful of denarii and counted them on the ground. "Here are five denarii on each fight and I am betting that the gladiators win all of them. Put your money where your mouth is Seer and match me."

Gnaeus Lamia coloured and reaching into his purse placed his own money before Numerius'. "There, Old Man."

"Any more takers?"

We all shook our heads. There were enough coins in all our purses but none of us had ever seen such games. Only a fool bet on something he did not know. Numerius said, "Mule Man, you are trustworthy. Hold the coins."

I was flattered that I was trusted and counted and then gathered the coins.

Gaius asked, "How do the fights work? Will they fight to the death?"

Numerius shook his head, "There will be an editor, I have heard that it will be First Spear, Varius Drusus. He will judge each fight. He can stop it when he thinks fit and he can order the victor to slay the defeated man but I doubt that will happen."

I asked, "Why not?"

Numerius rubbed his finger and thumb together, "Money. If they are centurions who are defeated they can be sold to the lanista. I doubt that we will see any executions. The centurions who win," he laughed, "and I have already said that there will be none, will become gladiators. The defeated ones, those who survive without crippling wounds, will also become gladiators." He shrugged, "Better than an execution."

Gnaeus Petronax, the one we called Nosey because of his crooked nose and the fact that he had a habit of sniffing, nodded, "Aye, and I hear that when they perform at funeral games, the night before the fight, after they have feasted, ladies often pay for them to come to their bedrooms." He gave a leer and grinned, "Fancy having a nobles' wife, a full belly and no chance of a dose of anything."

Numerius shook his head, "Nosey, the wife of a senator can be just as riddled as a whore in a lupanare."

I looked at Gaius who shrugged. We were both wondering how he knew that but neither of us would ask it.

We marched in a loose mob to the fields where the stands had been erected. Most of us would stand behind the palisade that had been erected around the elliptical circle. The officers would sit on benches. I was aware that we went as a mob but there was still order because we were Pompey's men. We walked in our tent groups for we were all close. The officers walked together but they were still with us. Enterprising Romans had set up stalls just before the place where the fight would take place. There was bread, pies, fruit, and wine. The fights would be spread out across the whole day. We found somewhere with a good view and yet close enough for one of us to be sent for food or drink. Old Man would not go. He was our Chosen Man but I was philosophical about it. I would need to make water sometime and when I did I would offer to fetch food and drink. I saw bets being placed between tents. Numerius cocked an ear and when he heard someone from the Second Cohort offering good odds he left us to place his own bets. He was away some time. There was a dais for General Pompey and his legates. We cheered them when they entered. It meant that the games would soon begin.

Gaius and I had both bought a beaker of wine and were drinking it. The wine was not the best but it had been cheap. We had bartered. "Well, Gaius, we are now proper legionaries, eh? We have come far."

Gaius nodded, "What I would like is to be able to travel home and show my family what their son has become." He looked sheepish, "And Flavia."

I smiled for he had voiced my thoughts too, "I would like that but more, I would like to see if the gods have rewarded my family for our sacrifice."

He looked wistfully at the sand on the ground before us, "But unless we campaign in Picenum that will not happen."

"And if we do campaign then it means that there will be war. I would rather we kept war from our homes."

"You are right and I am foolish. This is our lives and having survived when others did not I am grateful to the gods."

The order of the fights had been arranged, we later learned, by the lanista and First Spear. First Spear had visited the ludus and watched the gladiators when they had been training. He had arranged the fights in ascending order. It meant that First Spear thought the first fight would be the worst and the last one the best. The combatants all paraded before us. The Thracian helmets hid the faces of the gladiators but we could see the prisoners. All of them looked angry. I saw that none of them wore mail or armour. That gave an advantage to the gladiators whose right arm and one of their legs was protected. I thought that Numerius' bets had been a little premature. The gladiators had been trained but the centurions had something to prove and nothing to lose. I glanced over and saw the frown appear on his face. It would be good to see Old Man have some of his confidence knocked from him. When the men who would be fighting were taken from the arena to the sheltered area Numerius rose, "Just off to make water."

I watched him and smiled. He ran to some of the men who were still taking bets. He was anticipating losses and covering his bets. I was glad I had not wasted my money. I would enjoy the spectacle of two good warriors fighting. If nothing else I might learn some technique that might help me in the future. I had survived many battles and knew that I was better than the average legionary. The fact that five of my original tentmates had died was testament to that. However a man could always learn.

Numerius had returned before the first fight and he brought a small amphora of wine. "Here lads, never let it be said that Numerius Ennia Sura was tight."

We held out our beakers and he poured some in each of them.

The first two fighters looked to be equally matched. They were both of a similar size. The gladiator was confident and he waved his sword in the air as he entered, expecting a cheer. It was the wrong thing to do and some men booed. The two men faced each other and looked to the editor. First Spear looked pointedly at Pompey who stood and shouted, "Let the games begin!"

We all cheered. Some men had already drunk more than was good for them and would be lucky to see the afternoon.

First Spear stood back and said, "Fight."

I had never seen such a combat and I didn't know what to expect. Numerius had seen one before and said that whilst deaths could happen often they stopped when one man was disarmed or had an incapacitating wound. However, he had only seen combats between gladiators from the same school. It was clear from the first blows that this one would be different. The centurion wanted victory and he launched himself at the Samnite wearing the Thracian helmet. He punched with his shield and drove at the man. The gladiator was overconfident. He might have been still debating his best attack while the centurion just fought as he might have in the battle in the desert. He tried to defend himself and slashed with his sword. The centurion did not seem to care and took the blow from the viciously curved blade on his shield. Even so blood was drawn and there was a cheer. He was a centurion and an enemy who had been defeated. He was not popular. The cheers seemed to inspire him. He did a clever move, he back slashed at the leg which had no greave upon it. The gladiator must have been non plussed by his lack of success for he was slow to block it. This time the prisoner drew blood and I, along with a few others, cheered. There were shouts from some of the Third Cohort who clearly wanted the gladiator to win. I just smiled. I knew that the centurion would win. He wanted the victory more than the gladiator and he did not care if he died. That was clear from his reckless attack. The wound slowed down the gladiator. I think that but for the cheers for the centurion he might have thrown his sword to the ground and ended the contest but his support was not as widespread as he had hoped and he stepped back. He was now protecting his weakened leg and that gave his opponent an advantage for the centurion's wound was to his side and did not seem to worry him. The centurion feinted with his sword and as the Samnite raised his shield the prisoner punched with his own shield. He was a powerful man. I had seen the muscles on his broad back when they had passed us. The gladiator reeled and his weak leg was his undoing. He began to fall and the centurion did not hesitate. He lunged forward and stabbed under the ribs of the gladiator. He made a killing blow and the gladiator sprawled to the ground. He was dead. I stood and clapped as did others. The centurion did not milk the applause but merely stood. Some, especially in the Third Cohort, booed until Pompey stood and clapped. The centurion bowed and left the arena. He had survived and would now join the ludus of the dead Samnite.

Seer held his hand out to me for his winnings but I shook my head, "The bet was on all of the fights. I will pay out at the end."

I saw Old Man nod approvingly and Seer shrugged, "That is the shape of things to come, Mule Man. I can wait." He stroked his chin, "What shall I spend my winnings on."

He was premature. The next fight went the other way. Both fighters had watched the first combat and the centurion was the one who was overconfident. He was not killed outright but the slash across the stomach was a death wound. As he tried to stand the cry went up from the crowd, "Iugula!" We wanted him to be given the warrior's death. He raised himself a little as First Spear looked to Pompey who signalled with his thumb. First Spear nodded, and as the centurion exposed his neck, the sword was driven deep into body. He had a quick death. The other two bouts before the break for noon were not to the death. Both men fought hard and the loser in both cases, although wounded, was given the support of the crowd who shouted, "Mitte!" Pompey allowed them to live.

By the time we all went to make water Old Man and the Seer had both won in two bets. I told them I would not pay out until the end. Numerius had made side bets and was slightly in profit. I was enjoying the bouts and I had learned much. The feint was an action I had not tried. I knew it would come in handy.

The first bout after the noon break was a bloody one. Both men were well matched and fought hard. Although it was the centurion who lost and expired in the sand, he had hurt the Samnite and Numerius was not convinced that the man would live. "Even if he does he can never fight again."

Fullo asked, "What will happen to him?"

Numerius did not know for certain, "I don't know enough about ludus to tell you." He shrugged, "He might be killed to avoid an unnecessary expense or perhaps used as a slave by the lanista. He might not be able to fight in the arena but he looked handy."

The centurion lost the next fight but fought well enough to be spared. By the penultimate fight some men were so drunk that they had simply passed out and did not get to watch the last two bouts. The centurion who came out for the next to last fight had a determined look to him. He carried his helmet and he cast his gaze to Pompey. He seemed to be challenging him. I said nothing but thought it was foolish. No matter what the crowd thought the fate of the loser would be it was Pompey who would decide. The man donned his helmet and set about destroying the Lucanian he fought. He was slow and methodical. He never gave the gladiator a chance but the Lucanian fought well. In the end he was disarmed and lay on the ground. There was a mixture of support and opposition but Pompey spared the man.

The last one had a gladiator who was not one of the Samnite and Lucanian prisoners. He was a famous gladiator, so Numerius said, called *'The Butcher'*. He was enormous. The centurion was dwarfed by him. Numerius was confident now. He had the edge over Gnaeus Lamia and everyone thought that the famous gladiator would win. I saw some last bets being exchanged. Some had lost already and were trying to recoup their losses whilst others who had been successful were trying to make even more money. My purse remained unopened.

Legionary

This time the bout was cagey on both sides. The gladiator had not become as successful as he had by being over confident. He was called *'The Butcher'* because, according to Numerius, once he had the measure of a man he killed him piece by piece. The bout lasted longer than any other we had witnessed. As the gladiator begin to tire, I remembered something that Gnaeus Petronax had said. Famous gladiators were often wined and dined and then bedded by rich ladies. Was his night of pleasure coming to haunt him? The centurion would have been denied such a pleasure as he was a prisoner. Whatever the reason the centurion began to gain, surprisingly, the upper hand. He cut the gladiator four or five times. The prisoner was becoming more like the butcher. Numerius' face fell as it became clear that the wounds would weaken the gladiator and when he had his thigh slashed followed by a blow to the arm, which, although armoured, must have hurt then we knew the end was near. First Spear saw that the gladiator was unable to raise his sword and he stopped the fight and raised the centurion's arm. Once more there was a mixture of shouts. Cries for mercy and some for death. I happened to glance at the dais and saw the lanista wander over to Pompey and speak in his ear. I thought I knew what that was about and when Pompey allowed the gladiator to live I knew that the lanista must have offered money or a reduction in his fees to save the life of his most famous gladiator.

As Pompey left we all cheered. We had enjoyed a good day with no work, much wine and as Numerius and Gnaeus had honours even the atmosphere in the tent would not be tense. Numerius' side bets had meant he was in profit. As we walked away Gaius said, perceptively, "I wonder why Sulla was not there."

Numerius tapped his nose and said, quietly, "Pompey might have fought for Sulla but he is a rival. Men like Sulla can't afford to allow others to be seen to be more popular. Now that our general has won the war for Sulla he had best watch out."

That night, in our tent, the debate continued. No one actually knew what was going to happen. Would we have to fight the Sullan legions? Would Crassus favour Sulla or his rival, Pompey? Once more we relied on rumour and gossip. Over the next days we heard that Pompey had demanded a triumph but

Sulla was reluctant to allow one. Many of the veterans thought that was wrong and there was a great deal of debate about what we might do to ensure that a triumph was given. It might have been that Sulla heard the news of the discontent for he allowed Pompey a triumph as well as others for Lucius Licinius Murena and Gaius Valerius Flaccus. That did not sit well with our men for the other men had done nothing and it became worse when we learned that Pompey had been granted a triumph on the condition that he disband his army. There was a mutinous air in our camp.

Pompey was no coward and he and Legate Betto, along with the other legates, came into our camp. There were now four legions. We were the most senior for we had been the first legion that he had raised and Pompey stood before us to address us. He looked the complete general now. The young man I had seen at the harbour was a shadow of the man who stood before us.

"The war is over and peace is now in this land. You have all served me well. Now is the time for me to help Dictator Sulla to bring order back to Rome." He waved a hand and his slaves moved through us distributing coins. It was our pay and what seemed like a bonus. "I will need you again and when I summon you then I would have you come back to the ranks and fight for me again. It may not be for years but keep your bodies hardened and your minds sharp." He smiled, "Regard this as a holiday and a well-earned one at that. I will retain the officers and immunes at my expense. I would pay you all but that would be too expensive and I think my enemies would view it as a threat. Go and know that you have my thanks for all that you have done." He waved a hand and slaves appeared with amphorae of wine and baskets of food, "Celebrate this night and remember the ones who died."

He and the legates left us with our officers. The coins made our purses bulge and the discontent, whilst it had not disappeared, was masked.

I said, "Well, I shall go home and see my family."

Gaius nodded, "And I will come with you."

I turned to Numerius, "And you?"

"I will do as I said I would and enjoy myself but then," he jangled his purse of coins, "I might open my own tavern and whorehouse." He grasped our hands in turn, "But when Pompey the Great asks for his men again know that I will come back to the legion. After all someone has to look after you pair."

The tesserarius, Nanus Quietus, came over and he was leading Ceres, "The general favours you, Lucius Porcianus. He gives you another gift, the mule."

The gold was one thing but the gift of Ceres touched me more than I could put into words. We celebrated that night and, for the first time in my life, I became drunk. Gaius did too but Numerius looked after us. He turned our heads so that we did not drown in our own vomit and he ensured that no one touched our treasure. He was a true friend. The drunken experience chastened me and I never succumbed to drink again. It was noon before we were ready to leave and we bade farewell to Numerius who was keen to get into the city. We said goodbye to the officers and our comrades. With our mail, helmets and weapons packed on Ceres we wore just tunics and cloaks as we headed east to Picenum. As that was where the legion had been formed, there were almost a hundred of us making the journey. If nothing else it guaranteed that we would be safe from brigands and bandits. Ceres had the lightest load she had ever borne and seemed happy to be off on another journey with me.

It took a week to make the journey and as we headed further east so our numbers dwindled as men took the roads that would take them to their homes. When I parted from Gaius there was just Marcus Thurinius and I left, and when he headed for the port I took Ceres, now with a much lighter load, towards our farm. I felt lonely when Marcus went to his home on the coast. When I had joined the legion I had been used to being alone but now I missed the contuburnium and the order to my life. The seven days since we had left Rome had been in the company of soldiers but now I was in the civilian world once more.

As I walked up the narrow road to my home, the farm looked smaller somehow and it was definitely more run down. I saw just three pigs and the vegetable plot looked bare. My heart sank. It was my mother's face as she appeared at the door when she heard the squeal from the pigs as Ceres and I approached that made me smile. Her face lit up and crying, "It is Lucius! He is alive and he has returned."

She ran to me and with tears streaming down her face she embraced me. I saw that her hair was more grey than dark and she looked thin. The scream from my mother had been loud. When my father emerged, shakily, from the farmhouse, which looked even smaller than I remembered it, I saw that time had not been kind to him either. His hair was largely gone and he was coughing as he stepped into the light. His smile, however, was welcoming.

"You are grown so much. You left a boy and have come back a man. Are you home for good?"

I shook my head, "One day I shall return to the legion but you have me for some time and I do not come empty handed." I took the chest from Ceres' back and opened it. A shaft of sunlight from the west caught it as the gold and silver glinted. "This is for you. We can make the farm what it was and we can buy some slaves. The war is over and now we can enjoy the peace."

Chapter 11

My father was ill. He had almost fallen in the doorway when he had tried to greet me. I think that had I not returned when I did then he would have died. I carried him to the bedroom and laid him on the bed. My mother came in and touching my arm smiled, "He has not been well for some time but you, my son, are the best medicine he can have. Go and see to the animal you have brought and when I have tended to your father we can eat and you can tell me your tale." She squeezed my hand, "I never wanted the sacrifice and it has not worked."

I kissed her head and shook mine, "But it has. I have much to tell you."

We had space for Ceres and I tethered her and left her to graze. There might not be oats but there was grass. I ruffled her mane, "Your new home. I hope that it pleases you." I carried my clothes into the room I would use. My sisters were not there. That was no surprise. I just laid them on the chest that contained the clothes I knew would now be too small for me.

Mother was still with my father and I looked to find what food I could cook. I saw some vegetables chopped already. The fire that I would use to cook them needed to be fed and I did that before placing the pot on its top. The amphora with the oil was almost empty. That was a measure of how far the family had fallen. It had never been less than half full when I had lived at home. I put the vegetables in and went to draw water. The well was almost a luxury. It meant good water and had never dried up. I drew a pail of it and went back into the house. I stirred the vegetables and smiled as I did so. I took the small skin of wine I had brought and poured a beaker of it into the pot. It hissed and the smell became even better. Cooking had been the work of women when I had left. I had learned how to cook. My tent mates were critical eaters. I remembered the food I still had in my sack and went for it. I ladled some water into the pot. There was some sausage as well as a hunk of salted ham. I chopped them and put them in the pot. The ham would need more cooking to make it soft and to enrich the stew. I went outside and foraged

Legionary

for some wild garlic and herbs. I dropped them in the stew and stirred it. The aroma made me realise how hungry I was. I had not eaten at noon such was my haste to get home. Finally, I scooped more water into the pot and did so ladle by ladle until there was enough.

My mother's voice was filled with wonder, "My son can cook. What other miracles have the gods worked?"

I bowed, "I am not the boy who left. I am the legionary who has returned. Sit, Mother, you waited on me and I can see that the time apart has wearied you."

"Nonsense, I am as fit as I ever was."

The pain that flashed across her face told me the lie and I forcibly sat her down. "Father is ill and I am the head of the house until he walks upright and does not fall down when he sees his son. Besides, the stew is cooking and I shall sit." I poured us both a beaker of wine and sat. "I know not how long I shall be home but I am guessing a year or more. The general I served now seeks to become more powerful in Rome and one dictator at a time is more than enough."

Her face looked blank. We lived remotely and news from the other side of the country had clearly not reached here. As we drank the wine I told her my tale. It was not the tale of battles for the thought of her son being in mortal danger would give her sleepless nights when I left, but I told her of the return of Sulla, of Pompey and a little of Gaius and Numerius.

"They are your friends?" It was a question and I nodded. "Good, for I never liked your loneliness when you lived at home."

"I was content."

"But not happy." She took my hand in hers and stared into my eyes, "Now I see that you are happy." She took one hand away and waved it, "Not about this but, in yourself, you are content. Perhaps you are right and the sacrifice worked...for you."

The thought struck me that she was right. We had been advised to sacrifice me to the army or perhaps the priest had meant the slave market, I was still unsure. The farm had not prospered but I had. Squeezing her hand I stood and after stirring the stew went to my room. The chest I carried took two hands to lift and I placed it on the table. I smiled, "While I serve up the food, look within and tell me if the sacrifice worked."

I had my back to her as she opened the lid but I heard the intake of breath. "My son, where did you get this? I have never seen so many coins since…." I turned and saw her face. She looked to be overawed, "well, ever."

Sitting next to her I took the aurei I had been given and said, "The dictator Sulla gave me this one and these came from Pompey." I lifted the bag of denarii and dropped it on the table, "This is my pay and the rest…" I took a breath knowing that she was clever enough to see beyond the next words I used, "were taken after the battles that were won." I lifted the rings and jewels. "The Africans we fought wore many of these."

She studied my face and saw the white scar that ran there. She gently ran her finger down it, "And you have come close to death."

I laughed and stood to bring the bowls of food and bread over. I saw that the bread was not made with the best of grains. That would change. "I am still here for I am a good soldier." As I laid the food on the table I said, "A better soldier than a pig farmer. My future lies in the legion, Mother, but I promise that this farm will be bigger and better before I leave."

She took her spoon and tasted the stew. Her eyes widened, "This is good."

I laughed, "You sound surprised but believe me I learned how to cook with the most critical of eaters."

She still added garum but not much. I did not know if that was because she did not need it or we were running out. My coins would be spent in the market. When we had finished and I had mopped the last of the stew from my bowl, we wasted nothing, I said, "Now is the time for you to tell me all."

I knew the news would be bad for she emptied the beaker of wine. That was something else I would have to buy. Things had not gone well. The goats had died and while they had fed the pair of them for a while their diet had been diminished by the lack of milk and cheese. Had it not been for the vegetables then they would have starved to death. My father's health had deteriorated a few months earlier. They could not afford a doctor and their services were always suspect. The biggest fear was the lack of money to pay the taxes.

I tapped the chest, "There is more than enough here for that." While she had been talking I had been thinking and planning. I knew to the last denarii the value of my coins. The jewels I had were an unknown factor but I guessed they would be as valuable as gold. "Now here is what I plan. Until my father is well then I shall be the head of the house and make the decisions. I will buy slaves. We need them." I held up my hand to stop the arguments I knew she would raise. "You cannot do all on your own. I will buy more goats. We need the milk. I can see that the pigs you have will not bring us an income. Where is the boar?"

"He died too."

"Does Agrippa, on the other side of town, still have pigs?"

"You mean your father's friend?" I nodded. "I believe he does but I rarely go to town these days. We have no money to spend."

"We have now. I will go on the morrow and buy things that are urgent. When time allows and we have someone to watch over father while we are away you shall come with me and buy what is needed for the house. Your son is back, Mother, and you shall be repaid for what you did for me."

"Just being back you have done enough."

I was thrown into the running of the farm without a pause for breath. I had gold and I used it. The next day I bought two labouring slaves and a house slave. They came from the household of a man who had invested badly. He was also a Marian. I did not think they were expensive but my mother did. My father just nodded his thanks when I told him. He was still confined to his bed and clearly ill. Septimus and Decimus were young and had been born slaves. I gave them the corn store for their home as it was empty. Drusilla, the house servant, would sleep in the kitchen. She was young. Although barely twelve years old she was willing to work. I think her previous owner had tried to take advantage of her. I was lucky that he had fallen on hard times. He was a Marian and his family had been proscribed. The result was that he sold them cheaply and the three were happy to be working for me. When I bought them new clothes and sandals to wear they were even happier. Leaving

Septimus to help Drusilla to make good the repairs in the house that were needed, I went with Decimus to the market.

The goats had died and that meant no milk, no cheese and no butter not to mention a once-a-year meal of young kid. I bought a good breeding pair. I also bought pigs but this time I ensured I bought them from a man I knew. Agrippa Bantia Catalus had been a legionary with my father and I knew I would not be robbed. My visit lasted longer than I would have wished for he plied me with questions about the war. It had been fought far from Picenum and he wanted more than the results. I begged to leave and promised I would return when I had the leisure to give him more details. We spoke in the open, close to his pigs so that I could see them clearly. I had planned on buying more food and furniture too but we had neither the time nor the hands for that. As I walked home I wondered if I should have bought three slaves. I had more than enough money. The purchases I had made barely touched the gold and denarii I had in my chest. I still had the Numidian rings and necklets to sell. It was early days but as we headed back to the farm, I thought about buying more land from old Posthumus who lived across the valley. He had an olive grove. It was close to our land but it needed work. I thought I might also plant some vines. All that was for the future. I had plans and as I had told my mother until my father was well enough then I would be the one to make those decisions.

The first four months were the hardest. There did not seem to be enough hours in the day. The life of a legionary, when not on the march, was much easier. I toiled from sunrise to sunset. The house, as well as the animals and the land, needed work. It appeared more than a little run down. After I had repaired all that needed to be repaired I worked with my slaves to add a room. In the legion I had learned to build. Septimus and Decimus were interested in my stories of the war especially the African one. Africa seemed so exotic. I found myself seeking new words to describe all that I had seen, smelled and touched. Their questions and obvious interest made the days pass quickly but by the end of each one I was exhausted. My father became well again. He had not had to work since I had reached home and with a better diet and the care of my mother, who now had Drusilla to help her, he recovered. I forbade him to leave the house and I paid for a herb woman to examine him. He was given a draught and a lotion to put on his chest. His cough disappeared and with the better food I bought he improved and was able to come with me, as the new grass appeared, to walk the land and examine the olive grove and vineyard I had bought from the old man, Posthumus. I had bought them cheaply. The old man was dying and had no heirs.

"We do not need these, Lucius, we are pig farmers."

"And if the pigs become ill as they did once before? What then? We can eat olives, sell olives, make oil and make and sell wine. There are two slaves who are happy to work for they are treated better here than they were before." I realised my tone had sounded harsh and I softened it, "Father, when I return to the world of war and the life of a legionary, I want you and my mother to be safe and secure. These are good slaves I have bought and they are well treated. They will watch over you. Until the pigs died I did not see how we could suffer. Now I can and the olive grove and vineyard are there to give us all more chance of surviving disasters." I did not tell him of the lands that had been devastated by war. The Marians had destroyed crops and lands of the Sullans and we had done the same too. War was harsh and I was just happy that, thus far, the land of Picenum had been left alone.

I had deliberately made their lives as easy as I could for I had seen many slaves abused. There had been revolts of slaves who had been mistreated and I wanted ours to be happy. When I left they would be the crutches for my parents.

The goats were fecund and the nanny had young. There were three kids. The milk and cheese meant we ate better and so I bought another nanny. I also invested in a beehive. I wanted bees. The more things we could grow the better chance my family had of not only surviving but prospering. The honey was also liquid gold.

I visited with Agrippa six months after my return. I had felt guilty about not returning earlier but there was much work to do. I went because I thought to buy another sow off him. We were not ready yet to sell pigs to the butcher and were living off my gold. I was planning for the future. When Pompey recalled me to the legion I wanted my family to be safe. He had not given us a time scale but I did not think it would be within the year. I had learned a little of Roman politics in my time at the legionary camp and knew that he would need to build up allies in the deadly world of the Roman Senate. Sulla was getting old and once he died there would be a rush to seize power. I knew that my general would be as successful at that as he had been leading men. He was clever. I knew that I would not be robbed by Agrippa. I now understood about the bond between him and my father. It was the same bond I had with Gaius and Numerius. The pigs he had sold me had all been healthy and prospered.

This time I was invited into the home of my father's friend rather than his yard and there I met his wife and three daughters. His wife was named Cornelia and they had also named their eldest daughter the same. She was not a pleasant young woman. I took an instant dislike to her not least because of her habit of snorting. She sounded like one of her father's pigs and, if truth be told, her nose had a piglike quality to it. The second daughter, Aemilia, was much more attractive. Perhaps it was the contrast with her elder sister that made her so and the fact that she smiled at me and seemed attracted to me. The same was true of the younger sister, Claudia, but I was mesmerised by Aemilia. Agrippa opened a new amphora of wine and his wife brought out a well-made, air dried, sausage. The three girls sat there too and listened as I told my story. Of course, it was not the real story. That would be too gory and graphic for the women but I told them the parts I could and they were truthful. I had learned from Numerius how to tell a tale. Agrippa was especially interested in Sulla and Pompey. The fact that I had met them both raised me high in his estimation. He loved the story of Hephaestus. He had never seen an aureus and when I took the one given to me by Sulla from my purse he touched it as though it had some magical qualities. When I left he and his two younger daughters begged me to return saying that they had many more questions. The porcine Cornelia did not but I put aside my dislike of her for I wanted to see Aemilia again and I promised to return in a week.

I had visited Agrippa just as though it was a normal day but before the next time I went I visited the bath house and paid a slave to use a strigil and perfumed oil. I had my hair trimmed and was given a good shave so that when I returned to Agrippa's home I would make a good impression. I wore a good tunic that I had bought and new sandals.

Even the snorting Cornelia had widened eyes when I walked in. Both Claudia and Aemilia stared at me with unconfined joy in their eyes. That was the day I decided to make Aemilia my wife. She was pretty and I knew from my first talks with Agrippa that she was hard working. When I returned to the legion she could help my mother to run the house. Already I planned on extending the farm and I would use my gold to that end. In a year we would have a healthy income from the pigs, olives and wine. My investment would be repaid. Even as the thought entered my head I dismissed it. I did not want to be repaid. My gold was a gift. I would leave all my gold with my parents. Numerius was right, with a general like Pompey there would be more in the future. I was lucky that Pompey had let us leave the legion. It meant I could marry.

When the new pigs were born we ate one of the kids to celebrate. With the new nanny we would soon have a healthy herd. I made sure that the slaves enjoyed some of the meat. I also gave them half of the bones so that they could make soups and stews for themselves. The three of them had come from the same master and they got on well. Indeed, Septimus and Drusilla appeared attracted to one another. I also went to the temple and made an offering. This time I used some of the African jewels. The priest looked impressed and assured me that the gods would look favourably on such an offering.

The one blight on the year was the arrival of the tax man, the publican. I did not like Publius Rufio. I had never liked him before I became a legionary. Now I was a man and I was a different person. He had been an unpleasant boy and youth and, unfortunately, he had never changed. He had been my age, perhaps a couple of years older and his father was the senior tax collector. They both thought themselves above the rest of us and looked down their noses at us. That they were corrupt was clear for they lived above the means of such officials. When he came for the taxes, he did not know of my return. I was in the vineyard pruning dead wood when he came and Drusilla came racing down for me, "Master, Publius Rufio is here and he has two men with him." Her voice was urgent and told me I ought to rush.

Drusilla had fitted in well in the house and she cared for both my parents. There was something wrong.

By the time I reached the house I heard the publican's whining voice, "You have enough money to buy new pigs, goats and even a female slave. I hope that you have enough coins left to pay your taxes. If not then my men will have to confiscate your property to the value of the taxes you owe. Do so quickly for I like not standing in the sun. This is a hovel without even an atrium."

I was angry not least because it was my mother he was haranguing. My father was in the lower field with the pigs. Since he had returned to work he was determined that our pigs would prosper. He was the pig farmer. The law said that the publican should deal with the man of the house. I knew why he was speaking as he was, he was a bully.

My voice was that of a soldier. I had listened to the officers and even Numerius when they gave commands and that was the voice I used. "Publican, do you not know the rules of your office? You speak to the man of the house. In the absence of my father that is me."

He turned. I had grown since I had known him and I was now a head taller. The two men with him were paid muscle to protect him. They were large hulking brutes with clubs hanging from their belts. I watched his jaw drop as he saw me.

He regained his composure and like all officials who think they are better than others he tried to make himself taller. "Lucius Porcianus, I had heard that you were returned." He straightened himself and straightened his toga. His voice became even more self-important. "There are taxes that are owed. Last year they were little enough but I can see for myself more signs of prosperity. That means more taxes." His face showed what was going through his mind, "I hope you have enough coins to pay us or…"

I snapped, "Enough of this! Tell me how much you want, blood sucker."

His face hardened and he nodded to the two men, "I am a public official and not to be abused."

"Then act like a public official and do your duty. How much do we owe?"

"How many animals do you have?"

I told him and he made marks on the wax tablet.

"How much land do you own? When I visited Posthumus he said he had sold your father some land."

I told him.

"And how much income from the olives, the oil and the wine?"

I smiled, "As we have had them less than a year there is no income."

Septimus and Decimus passed through on their way to help my father, "You have slaves. That is more tax."

I sighed and waved my hand dismissively, "Just make an account and then I can pay and be rid of the stench you bring."

He did not like the remark nor the way I had answered him and he waved forward one of the men, "Teach him to mind his tongue, Brutus."

The man raised a fist thinking he would fell me in a single blow. He was strong but I had faced worse. I raised my left hand to block the blow and then punched him hard with my right hand twice, not in the stomach, which he had braced, but in the ribs. Throwing a pilum, using a sword and pulling Ceres had given me arms like young trees and I heard his ribs crack. The other knuckled his fists and I said, "Before you even think about helping your friend know that I did not hurt him as much as I could." He stepped back. I turned to the publican, "And your office protects your person and not the bodyguards you bring with you. The tax!"

I had clearly shaken him. Brutus was holding his ribs. I had hurt him. I was not afraid of what he might do. I was a legionary and the likes of the Brutus of this world were not a problem.

The publican held up the wax tablet for me to read and a confident smile appeared on his face, "Have you this amount?"

I went into the house and heard him say to his men, "We may have to drive animals back to the town. If we do then choose the best."

I took the coins from my chest. I counted out silver denarii for I wanted him to have the weight to carry. After he counted it out he smiled, "You are twenty-five denarii short. That is…"

Legionary

I dropped the Sullan aureus into his hand and folded his fingers about it, squeezing his fingers so that the edge of the coin bit into his hand. "This was given to me by Dictator Sulla for services against the Marians." I squeezed his hand tighter, "Let us call it paid in full. A receipt?" I saw the bodyguards' faces when I mentioned Sulla. They both looked to have been legionaries and knew that a man did not get an aureus unless he had earned it.

He nodded and went to the mule he had brought. He took out a lead tablet and with a stylus wrote on it the amount I had paid. He then took his stamp and made an impression on the lead. I took it and gave it to my father who had just arrived. Ignoring the publican I said to the two bodyguards, "And next time, let the publican come alone for if I see either of you again on my father's land I will give you such a beating that you will never work again. Do you understand me?"

They nodded.

"And you, Publican, remember you serve the people. Treat them with respect or else I might have to mention your behaviour to others." The fact I had used Sulla's name earlier was a veiled threat and I saw Publius pale and then nod. It mattered not that Sulla was in Rome and I would not be able to speak to him easily. The thought never entered the official's head. He was a little fish in a little pond. The last thing he needed was a bigger fish to be brought.

When he had gone my father said, "If you had not returned, Lucius, we would have lost the farm."

I nodded, "And when I am recalled to the legion then I will leave my treasure here. There is plenty left. Your days of making do are over. I have returned to make up for the time you suffered."

A year after my return I was married. Agrippa gave me a dowry. He had three daughters and there was little likelihood of his eldest ever marrying. I was more than acceptable as a husband. He made me his heir so that if he died I would take care of his family. He made me swear at the Temple of Jupiter and we both made an offering. I was more than happy to do so. I had proposed marriage a month before the ceremony so that I could extend the farmhouse. When we had been growing up we children had shared a room. I wanted more rooms. Thanks to Agrippa's dowry I could well afford it. My slaves and I did much of the work and I hired craftsmen for the things we could not do. I could not afford the fine frescoes I knew that some men had but I wanted the walls decorated. I hired a painter and he painted the walls in an artistic manner. This was not Rome and it was relatively cheap. Of course, we could not afford a marble floor but my slaves and I made one of broken pots in imitation of the mosaics I had seen in Rome. It was in the room that faced west where, in the evening, we could watch the sun set. I also had, in what passed for our atrium, an impluvium made. It collected rainwater and, especially in the summer, made the atrium appear cooler. We had always had an aedicula, a shrine for our household gods, but I had a small room built just to house the shrine. We had more gods now for we added those worshipped by Aemilia as well as Mars. That room was also decorated and this time the painter managed to add more embellishments. I think my mother thought it was coins that were wasted but I had plenty of gold and I believed my parents deserved it. Certainly my wife did.

My mother and Aemilia got on well and my wife liked Drusilla. When Septimus asked to marry our house slave I agreed. I knew that she would become pregnant and that would, perforce, mean less work but having a child would tie them to our farm and, in the fullness of time, we would have more slaves. This time the slaves would come without cost.

Our first grape and olive harvest was not a good one. That was the fault of Posthumous who had neglected both. Decimus knew the land and he and I had worked on the trees and the vines. We weeded and we pruned. We spread the sticky resin from pine trees on the lower branches to stop creatures from infecting them and we watched them every day. I knew that in future they would be better. We had pig, mule and goat dung to spread as well as a larger amount of human waste. We would prosper.

Aemilia was pregnant within three months of the marriage. I was happy but I knew, as there was a war in Hispania, that one day, and perhaps sooner rather than later, I would be recalled to the legion. I made sure that I did some training every day. I visited the market every couple of days and, in the Forum, heard

Legionary

news. One of the Marian rebels, Sertorius, had defeated the local Roman garrisons. He had fled Italy for he had been proscribed and he was now causing trouble in Hispania. The senate would have to deal with him.

The measure of time passing was the return of the publican. This was his third visit but he had learned his lesson. He came alone, as he had the last time, and was less arrogant. I paid the taxes and he left. My wife gave birth to Lucius a week after the taxes had been paid. It was as I visited Agrippa to tell him he was a grandfather that I saw the notice at the Forum. Imperator Gnaeus Pompeius was recruiting his legions. Old soldiers were recalled to Rome. I would soon be going back to the legion.

My wife, mother and even Drusilla wept copious tears at the news. I pointed out that I was still a soldier and that once I had served, I assumed in Hispania, I would return and with more gold. I hoped I was not tempting the gods with my ambitious claim.

"But I want you and not gold!"

"Aemilia, when I first met you I remember your eyes as I told you of my deeds in the war and in Africa. That was the man you wished to marry. I have not changed. I came home to help my family. I did not know I would be starting one of my own. I am pleased that I did and I will miss you but I am a better soldier than a pig farmer."

My father put his arm around my wife, "He is right, Aemilia, and we will watch over you and our grandson. Our other children never bring our grandchildren to see us but we can help raise young Lucius and when my son returns there will be more children and more gold. From what he has told me Pompey the Great is well named."

When my mother also put her arm around Aemilia then my wife nodded and smiled. "But come back, husband. I am too young to be a widow."

Chapter 12

Rome 78 BC

This time I was not a virgin. I carried my gear with me. I had left Ceres at home for she had been a gift from Pompey. It meant I had to carry my mail, helmet, shield and weapons and I learned how hard it was to carry the yoke with all the weight. I was just glad that I did not have two spears to carry too. I still had money. I had not given every denarii to my family. I had enough to pay for a place on a wagon that was going to Rome. Now that Sulla ruled Rome and there was peace in Italy then trade was good. I was disappointed that Gaius was not there. Had he decided to choose the path of peace?

I left the wagon at the Colline Gate as I spied the camp there. I was a veteran and knew the systems. I headed for the tent with the legion standards outside. I recognised First Spear. He did not smile. I am not sure he knew how to smile but his eyes were welcoming as were his words, "Good to see you back, Porcianus. The general will be happy. Go in there and you will be assigned. You can leave your armour and war gear out here. They will be safe."

"Yes, First Spear." Assigned? I had hoped that everything would be the same.

I did not recognise the clerks when I entered but they were efficient. "Name?"

"Lucius Ulpia Porcianus."

One of them scanned down a long list and finding my name slid it across. "Second Cohort, First Century."

Another clerk wrote it down and slid the parchment along, "Make your mark."

"I can write."

He nodded, "Then sign your name."

That done the last clerk waved for me to go to him and I swore the oath that was written on the lead tablet, "I swear to obey my officers and to execute their orders as far as it is in my power. I will follow Gnaeus Pompeius. I will not desert or do anything to break the law."

The clerk looked up at me, "Have you brought your weapons?"

"I have my sword and my dagger."

"No pila?" I shook my head. "Take two from that pile and I will deduct the cost from your pay."

I chose two good ones and when I returned to the table, he pushed over my pay for the first six months. When I had first joined the pay for my helmet, mail and the like had been stopped from my pay. I took the coins and slipped them into my purse. I was more than solvent once more.

When I emerged First Spear pointed, "The Second Cohort is over there." I nodded. I was desperate to ask if any of the others had returned to the legion but I was always intimidated by First Spear and, after nodding my thanks, picked up my mail and weapons and walked over. It was clear that I was amongst the first to arrive. The camp looked bereft of legionaries. I estimated less than a couple of cohorts were here. Perhaps that was why I had been promoted from the Ninth Cohort to the Second. It was a prodigious leap.

I recognised Centurion Bucco, Tesserarius Quietus and Signifer Gracchus. They were at the campfire with some legionaries I did not recognise. Their faces broke into smiles as I appeared. Signifer Gracchus said, "And now the lucky charm is here and First Legion will enjoy victories and I will garner more rewards for our standard."

I dropped my gear and smiled, "First Legion?"

Centurion Bucco nodded, "Of course, we were the first one raised and the general wished to honour us. That, at the moment, we are the only legion is immaterial."

"I was told to report to the centurion of the First Century Second Cohort. Where are they, Centurion?"

"Here you have found us."

"Congratulations on the promotion, Centurion. Where is Optio Corbulo?"

"He is now the Centurion of the First Century, Third Cohort."

The signifer said, "Aye, and there is another old friend there. Numerius has been promoted to Centurion of the Second Century, Third Cohort."

I was astounded. Numerius had made the leap from legionary to centurion and skipped the rank of Optio. "A mighty leap."

The centurion poured some wine into a beaker and handed it to me, "He was a good soldier and a natural leader. Of course, it helped that as he lived in Rome, he has a tavern now, he regularly saw the general. They trained together and became close. Numerius is an honoured confederate of the general."

I drained the wine. I had much to take in. "My tent, Centurion?"

"Take him, Signifer." As I picked up my mail and weapons he added, "You are now a veteran, Lucius. You will have virgins in your contuburnium. You are their leader. You served your apprenticeship well. Now you must mould young legionaries. You are a chosen man."

It was the first step to promotion. I knew from bitter experience that life could be short in the legion. Many centurions, optios and tesserarii had died in Italy, Sicily and Africa. It was why Numerius and Corbulo were now centurions. As we walked over to the line of tents I asked, "Who is the optio now?"

"Proculus Lamia."

"Numerius' friend."

"Just so."

"Why didn't the tesserarius get the promotion?"

"He was offered it by Centurion Bucco but he didn't want it. He is happy to serve the centurion as a tesserarius."

It made me think about my future. I was now the tent leader, a chosen man. Numerius had been the leader before me and was now a centurion. A centurion was paid much better than a legionary. I now had a wife and family. My visit back to my home had changed me. I could no longer just gather coins for myself. I had others to support.

The tent was empty but there were black feathers there. The tesserarius said, "The general wants those fixed to our helmets. When your tentmates arrive then show them how to fit them."

I had never fitted one, "Who will show me?"

He grinned, "You will figure it out. We all eat together at the moment. Avitus will sound the horn when it is time."

Legionary

After organising my gear I sat on the floor and worked out how to fit the black feathers. Sulla's legions had worn them, theirs had been white, but we had not. Was General Pompey making a statement? The black was a more threatening colour than white and he might be distancing himself from Sulla. They looked splendid but I knew that in the heat of battle it could become detached. It was something else to worry about. That done I sharpened my weapons. I had travelled with a dulled dagger and sword but now I needed them to be sharp.

When the horn sounded I took my eating tools and hurried to the fire. I recognised another twenty legionaries but none had been in our contuburnium. The bean stew had some meat floating but I could not tell what it was. Centurion Bucco saw me looking at it, "Porcianus, you are good with a sling, tomorrow see what you can bring down." I nodded.

The evening was a pleasant one as we caught up with one another. The officers had spent most of the time close to Rome. They had attended the wedding of Gnaeus Pompeius to Sulla's stepdaughter. She had died soon after the wedding in childbirth. The child was not Pompey's but the child of his wife's dead husband. There had been a second marriage, soon after. Gnaeus Pompeius married Metellus Pius' daughter, Mucia Tertia. Unlike me, men like Pompey married for politics. It allowed them to enjoy extra marital affairs to satisfy their needs and tied them to other families. I thought our way was better. The officers had all attended that wedding. I could see why they had been invited. Pompey was binding his officers to him. The First Legion was the first one that he had raised and the officers had all been selected from the other legions. He had paid them for almost the last three years and that must have been expensive. Pompey did nothing that wasn't calculated. I was flattered that I had been selected to be a leader.

Just before I retired I said, "Centurion Bucco, why has the general recalled the legion? Is war imminent?"

"We have a new consul, Marcus Aemilius Lepidus. He is supported by the general. Oh, by the way, you should know that the general's name has changed." He smiled, "You can blame his army. He is now Gnaeus Pompeius Magnus. He is Pompey the Great. Anyway there are rumours that the dictator is unwell.

Some say he is dying and when he does the general will want a state funeral."

I was confused, "And he well deserves one for he made Rome strong once more."

Proculus said, "Politics, Lucius. The consul was no friend of Sulla's and he will not want a state funeral. Our general was Sulla's man and he wants Rome to remember that. This legion is being readied so that in the event of a conflict there is muscle here to ensure that there will be a funeral." He shrugged, "And then there is the matter of Sertorius in Hispania. He will need to be dealt with. Hispania is a rich province and the rebels are denying Rome its prosperity."

The rest of the legion began to arrive the next day. I realised that having paid for my journey in a wagon I had stolen a march on the rest. After going into the woods to hunt some birds and take them to the communal pot I spent that first morning walking the camp to find familiar faces. Numerius was not in camp. I learned from his optio that, until the bulk of his century arrived, he would stay in Rome. Apparently he had Pompey's permission. He was favoured and I wondered how my friend had managed that. The new legionaries arrived and they were all virgins. I knew it from the way they carried both themselves and their equipment. They were struggling with it. I did not offer to help. The best way to learn was to do it yourself. I would teach them what they needed to know to become legionaries.

They presented themselves, first to Centurion Bucco who let them know that his word was law, and then the optio. The tesserarius would make himself known later. Quietus knew that they would be overwhelmed by the information and the orders they were to follow and obey. He was like the father of the century. Once they had found their place in the tent I called them outside.

"I am Lucius Porcianus and I am the leader of this tent."

One of them, Caeso asked, "Are you an officer too?"

I shook my head, "I am a legionary but unlike you, I am a veteran. I have fought in battles and defended the standard. The centurion has put me in charge of this contuburnium." I sensed that Caeso was questioning my right and so I put my face close to his, "Is that a problem?"

He shook his head, "No, I just wondered if I had to give you a title."

I smiled and stepped back, "No, Lucius will do." I was no longer Mule Man. I knew that someone would give me a nickname as there were so many others called Lucius but a man never chose his own name. Others did that for him. "First things first. Let me show you how to put on your mail." I demonstrated the best way to don it and they all copied me. I put on my sword belt and sword and they emulated me. Then I showed them how to heft the scutum and carry the pila.

When that was done Nonus asked, "What about the helmet," he hesitated, "Lucius?"

"Ah, normally you would have put it on already but you have a task to perform first. You need to fit the feathers." I took my helmet and showed them how to fix them. That done, and it was not a quick job, they put them on and I began the lessons in marching. I knew I didn't need to do it because the centurion and optio would do that in the fullness of time but I felt responsible and I didn't want any of them punished with a smack from a vine staff because of a mistake. I remembered Sertor. I took them through the two paces. By the end of two hours I could see the weariness on their faces.

As I let them drink from their water skins I said, "Of course when you march you will also have your kit pole and all the other equipment." I saw their eyes drawn to the poles they had been issued. There were groans. "You will get used to it."

Now that the new troops had arrived we cooked our own food. I had kept two birds from my hunt and I tossed them towards our pot. "Now, who fancies being cook today?" There was no answer and I sighed, "We all take turns but as this is your first day and I want a decent meal I will cook it but you all watch exactly how I do it."

I did not mind cooking but I wanted to let them know how we would be working. The next day First Spear began the training and I saw Numerius for the first time since my return. We did not have time to talk as First Spear was all business. My tentmates looked on me with gratitude as some of the others, notably a few who were in Numerius' century, incurred the wrath and vine staff of First Spear who did not spare the rod.

Legionary

After we had marched we practised with pila. I was proud of the distance I could achieve. I saw Centurion Bucco nod his approval when my pilum outdistanced everyone.

"I think I shall have to try my arm now, Legionary Porcianus." We all turned for it was Pompey on Hephaestus. He slipped from the horse's back and walked over to First Spear. "Legionary Porcianus has done well. Let me see if I can get close."

I smiled. I had learned that he had trained with Numerius. Numerius could not throw a pilum as far as I could but he made up for his deficiencies with skill. If he had taught the general how to throw then he would be good. The general ran and hurled the pilum using the mark we had all employed. It sailed through the air and landed a handspan ahead of mine. Everyone applauded. It was an act of showmanship. He was letting the new soldiers know that he was a fighting general and not some politician paraded at the head of warriors.

He came over to speak to First Spear, "I want this legion ready to march in a month."

First Spear nodded, "We are going to war, General?"

Pompey just smiled, "Just have them ready, First Spear. Legate Betto will be rejoining the legion when he returns from Hispania." He turned to me, "Come Legionary, greet Hephaestus. He saw you as we approached and he remembers his friend."

I went over and, sure enough, the horse seemed to nod and whinny to greet me. Animals, if treated well, could be very loyal. I stroked his mane and spoke to him, "No more sea voyages then, old friend?"

Enigmatically the general said, as he vaulted on to the horse's back, "Perhaps, we shall see."

That night I went to see Numerius. During the afternoon I had noticed my young tentmates viewing me differently. I was known to the general and he knew me. It changed their attitude. Numerius mentioned them when I went to his camp, "They have done you no favours with those babies. Are they old enough? I am not sure some of them have started to shave."

I laughed, "I think you said much the same about us." I looked around, "Have you see Gaius yet?"

He shook his head, "No, but I saw his name on the roster. He is in the Fourth Cohort. It looks like they are spreading out the men from our cohort."

"I hear your tavern is doing well." He nodded. "Then why return to the legion?"

"I am not yet ready to hang up the sword and mail. Besides I have spoken a few times with General Pompey and he is ambitious. I see more gold in our future. He is the best general I have served. He trained with me a little." He studied me, "And you, are you still a pig farmer?"

"First, I am married and have a son and now I own slaves."

He was genuinely pleased, "Well done. So why did you return?"

"Probably the same reason as you. I like the life and I want more rewards. And it is not just a pig farm. We have an olive grove and a vineyard. The vineyard needs work and time but by the time my son has brothers and siters we should have a decent wine."

Just then we heard a call and saw Gaius, his kit pole on his shoulder as he hurried over to us. He smiled, "I am glad you two are here but why aren't we all together?"

Numerius said, "We are making sure every cohort is as good as our last one."

"I thought you would have been here sooner, Gaius?"

His face darkened, "I buried my wife last week."

"Your wife?"

He nodded, "I married within six months of getting home. Flavia, you remember, Lucius, I told you about her." I nodded. "She and I had grown up together and was meant for me. She died giving birth to my dead son. There is nothing for me back home now. I will be married to the legion."

"But your family? Your mother, father...?"

"Seeing them would only make the remembrance worse. No, I shall join the ranks and gain honour. When I die, the son I never knew will greet, in Elysium, his father, the hero."

I was sad for Gaius but I also felt guilty. Aemilia had been blessed with an easy birth and I knew that she would be able to have more children just as easily. Poor Gaius had lost the love of his life. I was lucky and I knew it. If others knew that then my nickname would be Felix.

We had little time to talk for Gaius' centurion was annoyed at his tardy arrival and he wanted him to work with his contuburnium. As he left us I said to Numerius, "So all our lives have changed and the three men who returned from Africa are not the same men nor will we be together."

Numerius shrugged, "We are the same men but our lives have taken a different path. In Gaius' case I fear that it will make him more reckless while you will worry about your wife and son at home."

I said, quickly, "No, I will not." In my heart, however, I knew that there was a grain of truth in what he said. When I had fought to take the Marian standard I had not thought of living or dying. Now I might. I had, as Numerius said, a family at home. They didn't depend on me but as I had experienced with the publican, there would be times when the presence of Lucius Porcianus might be needed.

Sulla died at his estate close to Puteoli. I heard it was not a pretty death and his liver was consumed by worms. I had also heard that Puteoli was in a place close to something called the Phlegraean Fields. Sulphurous gases rose from nearby and I wondered why any would choose to live there. The consul did not want a state funeral for he had been an opponent of Sulla but Pompey had anticipated that there might be a problem and the legion was mustered. We did not enter the city but Legate Betto had us parade and march outside the Colline Gate. It was an ostentatious gesture and it worked. Lepidus agreed to a funeral so vast that no one in Rome had ever seen the like. We escorted the body to the Capitol. The senate, it seemed, had forgiven Sulla and his excesses now that he was dead. The other consul, Quintus Lutatius Catulus, supported Pompey and Lepidus lost. When, following the funeral, Lepidus tried to overturn some of the Sullan laws he failed and his time as consul ended in failure. I heard that at his funeral twelve bulls were slaughtered. The people of Rome ate well. There were also ten days of games but we were not allowed into the city and so we did not see them. I wondered if *'The Butcher'* and the other gladiators I had seen still survived. Perhaps they had earned their freedom and become lanistae themselves.

The general visited us often and we learned that he was raising more legions in Picenum. Most of our legion came from Picenum and we took it as a sign that he rated us highly. The general and the consul still butted heads but, at the end of the year when he was no longer consul and Lepidus became proconsul of Cisalpine and Transalpine Gaul, we thought he would be a distant memory. We were wrong.

Chapter 13

Mutina 77 BC

Lepidus tried to act as a petty king in Cisalpine and Transalpine Gaul. He was ordered back to Rome to answer to the senate. He refused saying he would only do so if he was granted another term as consul. The senate had tired of him and he was proscribed. Pompey was made military commander with orders to bring him back to Rome. Numerius would get his war. He had plans for his inn and they involved spending money. The best way to get money was through war. Pompey had never been defeated and we would be well paid and take from our enemies.

While we waited for the new legions to join us we trained under the eagle eye of the general. His time of peace had been a time when he could study the battles of the past and learn from them. He was something new. The old hands like Numerius recognised it. "The old generals, Scipio Africanus apart, were all politicians. Sometimes they were good but, as we found out with Hannibal, often they were awful. Pompey is a thinker and a planner." He rubbed his hands together, "I can almost taste the gold."

I remembered my own first months in the legion. Then we had been thrown into action and had to fight our way to meet Sulla. Much of my training had been on the march. I was determined to make the contuburnium the best in the century. Only three of us remained from that first tent and I wanted all seven of what I thought of as '*my men*' to survive. When the training ended for the day I continued the training with my contuburnium. The cook would be excused but the rest would practise all that I had learned. I taught them how to move from open to closed files seamlessly. I showed them how to throw their first pilum and then shift the other one quickly. We spent a long time learning how to draw the sword without taking our eyes from the front. That was not as easy as it sounded. I even taught them how to replace it without looking. That was even harder. When all that was done we would spar with wooden rudii. As I had learned a sword could save your life.

Legionary

It was only when the food was ready that we stopped and put away the weapons. They were all keen to know all the tales of my experiences, especially how I came to know Pompey. I gave them the facts without embellishment. I knew that Numerius was a better storyteller and he could keep men mesmerised with his words but I did not want one of the seven to become a glory hunter.

"We will be fighting Romans?"

I looked at Faustus. He was nothing like the first Faustus and I hoped he would enjoy a better fate, "Aye, but as they will have been raised in Cisalpine and Transalpine Gaul they will have Gallic auxiliaries with them. We should be able to defeat their legions but the auxiliaries can be a problem."

"How can you be so sure we will beat their legions, Chosen Man?"

"Simple, Arrius, we have Pompey the Great and he is the best general. If we had to face Marcus Crassus it might be a hard battle but we would win. Those two are the best generals." I smiled, "It helps that they are the richest too and can afford to buy good soldiers."

"How did they become so rich?"

I shrugged for while I had heard the rumours the reality might be different. I gave them what I had heard. "In the case of Crassus it was the acquisition and selling of slaves that brought him money. In Pompey's case it was his father Gnaeus Pompeius Strabo. He took towns in the Social War and threw the people from their land. He took everything. Our general does not do that but he knows how to profit from war." I nodded at their purses, "I know that after paying for uniform, equipment and food you have little from your pay but that will change once we fight the men that Lepidus brings."

While Quintus Lutatius Catulus raised more legions to protect Rome from Lepidus, we marched north. One thing I noticed, as we marched, was the coterie of young men who now flocked around Pompey. His martial success attracted the young nobles who sought to benefit from both his success and his skill. Often we would pass them as they took shade beneath trees to eat and enjoy wine while we marched. As Tesserarius Quietus commented, "It is like a school for soldiers." The tesserarius often join my tent as he did his nightly rounds to give the watchword. I think he liked me and enjoyed my company. I know I liked him for he was honest and funny.

It was a hard march for we travelled up the spine of Italy. We had scouts and from them we learned our destination. We were marching to Mutina in the north. Marcus Junius Brutus had taken the city and was squatting there with his legion. That meant a siege. When we camped at night I often visited either Gaius or Numerius. There were things I could say to them that I could not say to my young charges.

I confided my fears to Numerius, "A siege, Old Man, is that a bad thing?"

"It can be but it means we build one camp and stay there. The problem is always food but the general is no fool. He will keep us well supplied. No, Lucius, the problem as I see it is Lepidus. The senate is against him but now that Sulla is dead all Sulla's enemies are coming out of the woodwork and some of them are quite powerful. What mischief can he cause? Sertorius in Hispania has armies. What if they cross here, as Hannibal did, and join Lepidus?"

"Well why don't we stay close to Rome?"

"The consul can defend Rome. Our general is looking for victories. When we defeat Brutus then the revolt in the north is over and we can return in triumph. Lepidus will have more legions than Brutus. The First Legion apart, the rest of Pompey's legions are untested. This will show our general the measure of his men."

When we came to the end of the mountain chain we looked north and saw the city of Mutina. It rose between two rivers and had strong walls. The general rested us there, I think, to view the defences. I said to the optio, "Optio Lamia, that looks like a difficult place to assault."

"It does and that is why our general is being so careful to study it from here. At least we shall have water and the land looks to have crops and animals."

He was right but as we moved towards the city we saw a flood of refugees heading into the city and driving their animals with them. Signifer Gracchus said, "If we had some decent auxiliaries we might have taken those animals. It will be beans and grain again, unless, Chosen Man, you can bring down enough birds and kill enough rabbits to keep us supplied."

I nodded, "Perhaps I will see if my contuburnium have any skills in that area. If nothing else it will keep them occupied."

Our arrival was not contested and the cohorts were each assigned a section to build a camp. Our dolabra were put to good use for we had to cut enough wood to make a defence against an assault from the city whilst making sure we were defended from the surrounding land. Those who were camped by one of the two rivers had an easier task. We were to the south and Legate Betto ensured that we had a good ditch and a wooden palisade that would defend us. There were the usual offset entrances and sentries were set.

As we ate that night, we were not on duty, I studied the walls. They were a mixture of stone, wood and ditch. The ditches would have ankle breakers in them and be seeded with lillia, traps and stakes to catch unwary legionaries. The walls would have ballistae. We also had them but they would be less effective. The enemy could send their bolts at files of legionaries who were attacking and a scutum was no defence against such a bolt. I kept my fears to myself. I could see that the seven men I led were nervous already.

The next day was spent improving our defences on the city side of our camp. Centurion Bucco came to me in the afternoon, "Signifer Gracchus tells me that you think your men might be able to hunt?"

That was not exactly what I had said, "I said, Centurion, that I might be able to train them to do so."

He smiled, "And I have no doubt that you will succeed. Tomorrow is our turn to be sentries. You and your contuburnium can leave the camp and forage for food. Most of the farms have been abandoned but you never know. If you can find wood then gather it. Nights can be cold here in the north."

"Yes, Centurion."

That night, as we ate, I told them what we would need for our foraging expedition, "We will not need our scuta nor our pila but we will need our dolabra and slings. We will not waste our lead balls. We shall keep those for the enemy. Gather stones. We leave in the early morning. I have the watchword from the tesserarius. We will have better hunting around dawn."

"Will there be enemies, Chosen Man?"

I shrugged, "There could be, Publius, and if there is then we drop what we have gathered and fight as I have trained you."

"But we will not have our shields and spears, nor our mule."

I nodded, "We will have a gladius, dolabra and a sling. If we are attacked then heed my orders and we should survive."

"Should, Chosen Man?"

"There is nothing certain in this life, Faustus, except death and few men know when that will come. Know that if you do die, we shall share what is yours and if we can, give you a burial."

He shook his head, "That is a comfort."

"It is all that we can expect but know that I believe tomorrow night will see us back here and enjoying meat."

We had a frugal breakfast before the sun had risen and, giving the watchword, left the camp. I led and I had Appius at the rear. He seemed reliable but that day would tell me much about the men I would fight alongside when we stormed the city. We had our dolabra hanging from our dagger belts and had a sack over our shoulders. Without the kit pole, shield and spears we moved much faster than on the march. I took us, not on the road, but up across the uneven ground. It reminded me of the land near my home, in the east and I hoped we would find rabbits. The wind was coming towards us and when I spied the rabbits ahead of us I held up my hand and waved my arm. The skills we employed that day would stand us in good stead for no words were needed as my seven men took out their slings and without looking chose the roundest stone that they could find. I simply nodded and the stones were hurled. There were many rabbits and we managed six kills before the rest disappeared beneath the ground. We put the catch in our sacks and I took them into the woods.

The prey we saw were birds. It mattered not what type so long as they were big enough to eat. The smaller birds and songbirds were safe but magpies, crows, owls, hawks and pigeons were all acceptable. By noon we had sacks with enough birds and rabbits to augment the stews of the century for a week. We stopped in the clearing on the hilltop that afforded us a good view of the camp and the city. It was like the bald pate of an ancient man.

Legionary

There were trees below us but the rocks that were there had prevented large trees from taking root. After taking off our helmets and when we had made water, we ate. We had foraged berries and nuts as we had walked and they were eaten along with the hard bread and cheese we had brought.

The legions looked like ants from this perspective. I saw light reflecting from the weapons of the defenders in the city. We had seen, in the last couple of days, that the enemy had enough soldiers to man the walls. It would be a bloody assault. I finished eating and stood to view the contuburnium. It was my nose that alerted us to the danger. It was the smell of horses. I knew that Pompey had auxiliary cavalry and they would be scouting but it seemed prudent to be cautious.

Standing, I donned my helmet and after hissing to gain their attention put my finger to my lips. I put my sack on the ground and the others copied me. I drew my sword and took my dolabra from my belt. I listened and I could now clearly hear horses. Their hooves made a distinctive noise when it touched a stone. Then I heard voices. They were Gauls. That did not necessarily mean danger for they could be Pompey's men. I used my two arms to form the men into a line alongside me. I knew the direction from the noises and the smell. Friend or foe I wanted to face them.

The six Gauls who appeared looked surprised. They had cloaks about their tunics and on their heads wore the helmets favoured by such horsemen. They each had a javelin and long sword. Their shields hung over their left legs. I smiled and said the watch word. I saw their leader grin as he gave me the wrong answer. I also saw his hand going to his sword.

I shouted, as I ran at him, "They are enemies, kill them."

I moved really quickly and reached the leader before he had drawn his sword. I hacked at his right leg with the dolabra. I sliced through to the bone and thrust up with my sword to end his life. I whirled as the next Gaul lunged at my back with his spear. The dolabra swept it aside and I hacked at his thigh with my sword. It was sharp and there was no mail to stop it. It grated off bone and he fell to the ground. His horse charged off.

I heard the sound of a sling and then watched as the stone smacked into the head of a third Gaul. The advantage the horsemen had enjoyed was now gone as their numbers were depleted. Three men were down and there were eight of us. When Appius and Faustus attacked a fourth Gaul from two sides the last two decided that discretion was needed and they hurtled down the path; Publius' sling sent a stone to crack into the back of one of the Gauls. The stone did not kill him but his horse's missed footing made him tumble and when he cracked his head into the bole of a tree then he died.

I shouted, "Make sure the wounded are dead. Nonus, grab the horses."

I ran to the path they had taken. I saw the solitary survivor and three of the horses racing down the slope. If there were confederates there he would have stopped.

The seven of them did as I had ordered but their eyes were wide. None of them had expected to be fighting this day. I smiled, "You did well. Publius, you have skill, well done. Search the bodies and bring any coins and weapons to me." Faustus frowned, "So that I may share it equally amongst us all. We all shared the danger and we share in the profits."

"Sorry, Chosen Man, I…"

"No matter, Faustus. We will learn to trust each other as time goes on. The sword that is our contuburnium is being tempered already." Nonus had managed to secure three horses and along with Appius, led them to me. I nodded "These horses are profit. The quartermaster will buy them from us. Load the sacks and the weapons on the backs of the horses. The one thing we have not yet done is to collect wood. These trees look likely and we now have the backs of horses to carry them. Give me the reins of the animals and then start to hew."

I examined the horses and spoke to them. They were not like Hephaestus. They were smaller and little bigger than ponies. The javelins we would keep. Not as good as a pilum we would still be able to use them. The swords were the longer swords favoured by the Gauls. I reasoned that our own auxiliaries might be willing to buy them. When I deemed we had enough wood we loaded the horses. There was food on the horses too and we had made a good profit. I let three men lead the horses as I led us down the trail and back to the camp.

Centurion Bucco was pleased with the results of our foraging but concerned about the presence of the Gauls. He took me to Legate Betto and I gave him my report. He shook his head, "I knew we did not have enough auxiliaries. I will speak to the general but as we do not need the horsemen we have to assault the walls, they can earn their pay and keep these enemies at bay. Well done, Chosen Man, you are as resourceful as ever."

I had not expected that the day would be so rewarding but the greatest gift that came from the day was the bonding of the men I would lead. They had emerged successfully and without a scratch. They had obeyed every order and there had not been the slightest hesitation. I was happy that I had been sent to forage. I had also seen skills in Publius. He could make good decisions quickly and was an excellent slinger.

The rest of the century were more than grateful to us. We ate better for that first week as we toiled to make the defences stronger and to prepare for the attack. The general asked for the surrender of the town and, of course, they refused. Once those niceties were out of the way then we could begin to think about an attack. Marcus Junius Brutus, however, had other ideas. Centurion Bucco told us that the first assault by the First Cohort would be in two days' time. It meant they would have no duties for the next few days as, along with the other first cohorts, they prepared themselves for an assault. We had the nighttime duty and it was the first time my contuburnium had been on duty. I made it clear to them how we would watch.

"You look for shadows that move. You sniff the air. The ones in the city will smell differently from us."

"But, Chosen Man, we are going to attack them. They will not attack us, surely?"

"Perhaps not but there are sentries' throats to be slit. If the enemy can weaken our morale then we are less likely to attack."

I was more confident about my men than those who patrolled the sections next to us. We each had a one hundred pace section of the palisade to guard and that meant enough gaps for an enterprising assassin to use. It was the first time I had been responsible for a section of wall. When I had served before that had been Numerius' responsibility. I was nervous. I saw shadows that appeared to move and, more than once thought to shout out. Thank Mars I did not for they were just that, shadows.

It was Publius who touched my arm as I passed him, "Chosen Man, I might be imagining things but I think I can smell something."

"Something?"

He sounded embarrassed, "Perfume." He shook his head, "Mad I know, but…"

"No, let me sniff too." I went to the section of wall and sniffed the air. There was the smell of men but that could have been from our own lines. Publius was right. There was a whiff of perfume in the air. It was the smell from someone who had recently used the baths and a slave had used perfumed oil on their body. "Stand to."

I hurried down to Optio Lamia, "Optio Lamia, we have smelled perfume."

He nodded and said to the men near him, "Stand to. I will tell the centurion."

I went back to my men and said, "Get your spears and slings." I picked up one of the javelins we had taken from the Gauls. Lighter than a pilum it could be thrown further. The Parcae can be precocious and the moon which had been hidden by the clouds suddenly flared, albeit briefly, and showed the legionaries moving down the slope. They were carrying ladders to bridge the ditch. Even as I hurled the javelin and the moon slipped behind the cloud once more I shouted, "Alarm! Enemies come!" I had no time to tell the centurion.

My javelin struck a legionary and he screamed. All along our line I heard the sound of cornicens summoning the sleeping men to the walls. The legionaries who were approaching roared a challenge and ran towards us. I picked up and threw another javelin and then grabbed my scutum and a pilum. "Face the enemy!" My second javelin hit a ladder carrier and he was pitched forward to be impaled on the lillia in the bottom of our ditch. Covered in our dung they guaranteed death.

Publius' nose allied to my accurate javelin meant that we were not surprised but we had just one cohort to repel the attackers until sleeping men could be aroused. From the number of shadows that rose and flooded towards us I estimated that we faced four cohorts. This would be a test of our defences and our resolve. Faustus threw his pilum and I shouted, "Don't waste your pila. Stab with them over the palisade." We had made a small mound of earth, the spoil from the ditch and it meant we would have height advantage over an attacker.

I heard Publius' sling and the crack of the lead missile as it struck the legionary told me that Publius was using his head. The ladders crashed down across the ditch and one lodged on top of the palisade. It meant our height advantage would be negated. I rammed my pilum at the first legionary who negotiated the fat rungs of the ladder. He was holding his shield tightly to his body but I was below him and my pilum drove up between his legs. He threw himself, screaming from the ladder and into the ditch. I saw that the next men held their shields lower and so I dropped my pilum and grabbed my dolabra. I blocked the thrusted spear that was aimed at my neck and swept the axe head at the legionary's ankles. I chopped through and the man joined his companion in the ditch.

I heard Numerius behind me, "First Century, Third Cohort on me!"

Extra men were just what we needed. Thanks to our spears and Publius' lead balls we had halted the attack on our section of the wall. When the enemy cornicens sounded, just before dawn, then we knew the attack had failed.

Numerius was the senior officer and he smiled, "Well that was easy enough. It looks like we accounted for twenty men and lost none. Legate Betto will be pleased."

One of his men said, "And can we take their purses, Centurion?"

"These lads held the line and they get to have first choice but they won't have purses. They will have left them in their barracks. Still they will have mail, and weapons. The quartermaster might buy them."

When dawn broke we retrieved the enemy bodies and stripped them. We could use the mail, helmets and weapons. Even the caligae could be reused. Legate Betto told us to take the bodies to the river and hurl them there. They would be taken downstream towards the enemy. No one wanted the stink of burning flesh to permeate the camp.

When the tesserarius came along to give us the new watchword Publius asked, "Will the First Cohort still make their attack, Tesserarius?"

"No reason why they shouldn't. The attack last night won't be repeated. They have a finite number of men inside the city. Now that the general is the military commander he can summon more men. The attack will go ahead and we will support the attack."

"How?"

He nodded to the sling hanging from Faustus' belt, "With your sling."

Faustus looked at the walls, "They are a long way away."

"And that is why we won't waste spears but stones and lead balls are relatively cheap."

He was right. We had collected more than a hundred that had been sent towards us. We were all tired by the end of the day. It was not just that we had endured a sentry duty but we had fought as well. We collapsed into our tents and I hoped that the next century on guard duty would be as vigilant as we had been. The tesserarius was probably right, they would not make another sortie, but they might.

Each day saw us performing duties. We were not marching, building and taking down camps but we were working. Wood for the fires needed to be foraged. We were luckier than most cohorts. Thanks to our single scouting venture we had collected more than most but you could never have too much wood. Food had to be foraged. Often it was just greens from the river or, if we were lucky, creatures we took from the water. Our diet was dull enough as it was and anything that gave a different taste was welcomed. When we found the river crayfish, even though we had barely six of them, they were like a gift from the gods. They gave a different flavour to the stew and interest as we ate them. Those lucky enough to get a head sucked the flavour from them before chewing and digesting them.

The day of the attack I rose early. Dawn had yet to break. I was not one of those who would be attacking but I knew many of the ones who would and that thought had woken me. Some men alongside whom I had fought in Sicily and Africa would die. Being the first up I poured water into our cooking pot and fanned the embers of the fire beneath. It did not take much feeding to have heat under the pot and the water began to bubble. I poured in the grain to make the porridge. A healthy tablespoon of salt would give it some flavour. One luxury I had and kept to myself was the small pot of honey I had brought from home. I added some to my breakfast each day. I knew that it would run out soon and then I would search for the golden treasure when we ransacked homes. I hoped that when we took the city I would be able to find some within.

The bubbling pot and the crackling of the flames, not to mention the smoke woke the contuburnium. They dressed in their mail immediately. I had taught them that much. The weight of the mail did not seem so bad when you were used to it but the First Cohort would have not only their mail but they would be hefting shields and spears as well as climbing up a slope in the face of arrows, javelins, stones and ballistae bolts.

The attack was planned for early morning and even as we were breakfasting we could hear the sounds of men preparing just a little way along the front line. Ours would not be the only legion to be attacking. We had been told that General Pompey planned four simultaneous attacks at different places. We did not know those other legionaries. We were just concerned with the First Legion.

The cornicens told us that the attack was due to start and Optio Lamia shouted, "First Century, stand to."

I had finished my breakfast but Faustus had not and he laid his bowl down to take his shield, spear and sling and stand in line. We were next to the First Cohort and had a good view as they clambered through the gaps in the palisade. We had our own bridges to cross the ditch and once on the other side they formed up. They were in four ranks. Their centurions and signifers were in the front rank. Even as they were organised the enemy began to hurl javelins at them. Stones and arrows clattered against helmets and shields. To my right I heard the whizz of a sling and saw the lead ball sent by Publius at the walls. It was a good throw and the lead ball smacked into the head of the ballistae operator. The rest of our cohort cheered. I knew that the First Cohort would take heart from the cheer although they would not have any idea what caused it.

The First Cohort moved forward. I saw that behind them came the engineers from the legion. They carried ladders. They were as close to the rear rank as they could manage. They wore mail but they had no shields. That day was the first one I saw the deadly effect of a ballistae bolt at close range. It was not on the wall but before the wall in a sort of redoubt. It sent a bolt to plough through a file of four men and strike an engineer.

I heard Appius as he said, "They had no chance. How can a man face such a weapon?"

The death seemed to enrage the rest of the Fifth Century and they ran up the slope towards the ballista. They took the defenders by surprise and managed to reach the redoubt before the machine would be reloaded. The men inside the redoubt were butchered. The premature attack prompted a charge and the rest of the cohort hurried up the slope to place their ladders next to the walls. The engineers, their work done, scurried back down the slope to our lines. They left six of their number before the walls. The centurions led their men up the ladders. Their scuta gave them some protection but they were assaulted on all sides. The men waiting to ascend used their slings and men fell from the walls. The battle for the wall raged for an hour but it was clear that too many had fallen in the attack and the cornicens were sounded. I guessed that the other legions had the same difficulty as we for I heard their horns echoing. With their ladders and their wounded, the First Cohort descended the slope and we cheered them although, in truth, there was little to cheer. It was not a victory.

We went back to the dull work of a siege. It was depressing.

Chapter 14

Pompey did not risk more men on the attack. He had lost enough. We starved them out and he used his auxiliary cavalry to strip the land around us of food. It did not take long for starvation to take effect. The horns that sounded from the gates and the opening of them was the sign that they wished to talk. The meeting was held before the walls. We watched. The general and his officers returned to our camp and an hour later Marcus Junius Brutus and the senior officers left the city. The First Cohort were allowed in and followed the general. They had lost men and the city would be sacked by them.

Tesserarius Quietus shook his head, "The general must be getting soft letting General Brutus go. He will raise more men."

I asked, although I knew the answer, "And the garrison?"

He shrugged, "They will be given a choice, either join us or be executed or be enslaved." Less than forty chose death or slavery and the rest were more pragmatic. They joined our ranks. They were spread amongst every cohort. Men would watch them carefully until they had proved their loyalty. We followed the Prima Cohort into the city. There was still plenty of treasure to be taken. I did not take my contuburnium, as many did, to the better houses but, instead, the slightly more modest ones belonging to, not the nobles, but the shopkeepers. I found an amphora of honey and each of my charges made more from the houses than they had been paid for signing on. They were happy. I found even more coins for I knew where to look and I secreted them in my purse.

As we ate, once more in our camp, I asked Centurion Bucco where Marcus Brutus had gone. He waved a hand to the northwest, "Regium Lepidi." He shook his head, "A nest of rebels."

We prepared to leave for the enemy leader, Lepidus, was still in the south threatening Rome. Pompey the Great wanted to be there when his enemy was destroyed. As we were leaving some of the young nobles on his staff rode in from the northwest. The news they gave to Pompey was obviously welcome for he cheered. We headed south and west. It was on the march that we learned what had happened. Marcus Junius Brutus had gone not to a place where he could do no harm but a place where he could raise an army. The general had sent his friend, Geminius, to execute him.

When the tesserarius heard the report he laughed, "Execute my arse. The general had him murdered."

Execution sounded official and sanctioned. He was probably right and the death of Consul Carbo came to mind. Had that been an execution or a murder? I liked Pompey but he was a ruthless man.

We broke camp to head back to Rome. We were not privy to the missives and messages passing between the consul and the general but as we marched the three hundred odd miles to the centre of the world it was clear that Lepidus was far from defeated. Pompey gave us the hardest stretch first as we crossed the mountains and then we had an easier march down the coast. He had scouts out and when we neared Cosa, on the coast about eighty miles from Rome, we heard that Lepidus had been defeated by Consul Catalus outside Rome and was retreating towards the sea and his fleet. There was an increased urgency to our march thereafter. Pompey wanted his moment of glory and, just outside the port of Cosa, he had his opportunity. We caught Lepidus and his legions.

We were tired and so were the legions of Lepidus. There were two differences. They had been defeated and we had Pompey.

We camped and waited for the enemy to try to reach the port where they could take ship and leave Italy. The men I would lead were now slightly more experienced although they had never faced legionaries in open battle. The skirmish with the auxilia and the night attack were not the same.

As we lined up, as the right-hand cohort of our legion with my men in the front rank, I explained what would happen. "We will be in the front rank. Centurion Bucco and Signifer Gracchus will be amongst us and so there will be ten of us. We will be the first to throw our pila. When Cornicen Avitus signals then we will turn, presenting our shields to the enemy and pass through the lines to stand at the rear. When that happens then move quickly and watch your feet. Once at the back, if any are wounded, then you can be tended to by the leeches."

Marius Firminius was alarmed, "Wounded?"

I laughed, "They will not be using rudii but sharp spears and swords. Wounds happen." I paused, "Deaths happen. If you worry about such things then they will come to pass. Do your best to kill the enemy and to stay alive. Each battle we fight will see you and the legion become stronger."

Appius asked, "And when we win…if we win, then the war is over?"

"We will win. If you begin to doubt that then we are lost. When we win there will be recruitment and then the general will find another war for us." I remembered the time after we had taken Rome. We had not enjoyed, as many did, the joys of Rome but we had fought in Sicily and Africa. I could not see Pompey the Great being satisfied with the defeat of Lepidus. I had heard rumours that a Roman general, Quintus Sertorius, had gone to Hispania with some of the remnants of the Marian army. Perperna was said to be one of them. Pompey would want to defeat Quintus Sertorius and garner glory for himself. First, we had Lepidus to defeat.

Thanks to the forced march we reached the port before Lepidus did. Men could still board the ships but we would be able to destroy most of their army as they did so and they gave battle. We were equally matched in terms of numbers but as we had a few thousand who had fought for Marcus Brutus I was not sure if the numbers would help.

Centurion Bucco clearly felt the same. "When we fight these rebels, and make no mistake, boys, that is what they are, rebels, then we fight them and fight them hard. The last thing we want is to have to sail after the survivors as we did at Sicily and Africa." He glanced at the rest of the legion who were busy being marshalled. "We are the Second Cohort and in my view, the Prima Cohort apart, the best in the legion. We have two phalerae and I would like to earn more." There was a cheer from the century. These were the fighting words we want to hear. I noticed that he ascribed the phalerae that he had won, to the century.

Most of the new recruits had gone to the First Cohort as they had lost the most men at Mutina. It was telling that Pompey did not place them in the front rank as their status demanded. We were next to Prima Cohort and the Third Cohort. The First Cohort was in the third rank of our triplex acies. He assuaged their honour by saying that they had earned the glory at Mutina. We knew that was rhetoric.

The enemy were not fighting in legion formation but as a cohort; it gave more flexibility. We could tell that by the way they lined up and their shields. They had been badly handled by Consul Catalus in Rome and it showed in the way they were being lined up.

Centurion Bucco had given us the speech we needed but I remembered my first battle, "When they come, listen for your orders. Don't think about what they might do to you. Throw your pilum and then switch hands. Trust the men standing with you. They will not let you down."

I hoped that was true.

Pompey knew that we were tired but he gave us no respite. The horns sounded and were repeated by the signifers. We began to move forward. I was in the place of honour on the right-hand side of the line. I saw the Second Century just a spear's length from me to the side. Beyond them were the third. Behind us, in more open formation, were the fourth, fifth and sixth centuries. If the enemy tried to exploit the gap between the Second Century and me then the centurion of the sixth would move his men into the gap. As we moved forward I noticed that some of the enemy shields had been damaged. Ours were pristine. I also saw that some of their men had just one pilum. We each had two. They were small things but important, nonetheless. I saw their generals. They were mounted and behind their cohorts. Pompey was also mounted but he was with the Prima Cohort. He was a fighting general.

Neither side was racing. I glanced at our contuburnium. They had their pila ready to throw and were in step. They had heeded my advice well. Would the legate command us to halt or throw as we marched? I think that the command came from Pompey for I saw his arm move forward. The command for pila was given and we pulled back our arms. The enemy legionaries would know what was coming but they would await the order. Pompey and Legate Betto had gained an instant advantage. The throw, along our line, was not even but our eight pila went as one and I smiled as the other pila were transferred effortlessly and smoothly to our right hands.

The pila struck the enemy. The ragged nature of their striking worked to our advantage and some men were hit and shields drooped. When the replies came they were even more ragged for men had fallen and could not throw. Others were encumbered by bodies. I said, "Shields".

We lifted our shields and I felt a spear hit my scutum. I could feel the weight already. I had no opportunity to remove it and I gritted my teeth and held the scutum as close to my body as I could. I had to do so for no more than ten paces but they were the hardest ten paces I had ever marched. Luckily they only had one pilum each and if they had thrown a second I would have been in trouble. Ironically it was the coming together with Lepidus' legions that helped me. The pilum was at an angle and the end struck at the legionary I faced. The haft struck his head and he waved his sword to remove the spear. It fell from my shield and I thrust at him with my pilum. The enemy pilum, it might even have been his, had distracted him enough so that his shield was slow to rise. By such margins do a man's life depend. My spear drove into his cheek and I pushed through to penetrate the brain. He fell dead. The man in the file behind stepped forward. He had no spear either but the file behind all had spears. That would be a bridge we crossed later.

I was keenly aware that I was vulnerable to my right. The legionary on the left of the Second Century was protecting his men and he was a spear's length from me. I concentrated on pulling back my pilum and thrusting. I was pleased that my young charges were all doing as they had been trained. They had an advantage for they were fighting men with swords and we had the advantage of length. I saw Appius take a step back and shouted, "Keep your spears at their faces. Do not let them close." The voice I used was like the optio's and was more of a roar. He obeyed and the legionary who had seen the chance to step closer and gut the young legionary suddenly found a pilum in his shoulder. He wrenched himself free and then stepped back to rotate with the men behind.

"Push!" One advantage we had was that we were on the end of our rank. If we could push forward then the signifer and centurion would be better protected. When I saw the enemy centurion fall I knew that Bucco had won that duel. He and Signifer Gracchus could try to get at the enemy signifer. We were winning but the enemy knew that to get to the ships and escape Italy, they had to defeat us and they were fighting back hard.

The centurion of the Sixth Century, Centurion Davitus, must have seen something we could not for I heard his voice roar, "Sixth Century, close up. Advance."

I did not take my eyes from the man I was fighting but was aware of movement to my right. So far my opponent had managed to deflect my spear thrusts and I could see from his eyes that he was looking for an opportunity to gut me. As much as I wanted to get the fight over quickly I had to be patient.

"Sixth Century, pila!" Even as the Sixth Century's shields brushed mine I heard the sound of their pila being thrown. Half were thrown at the men we were fighting and the other half at those fighting the third. The effect was devastating. The enemy had their shields locked to help those in the front ranks. They could not raise them in time and men died. While the men were not in the front ranks they created a weakness in the homogenous nature of the century. Their centurion was dead. Their signifer was assailed and there were gaps to the left and centre of their line. They broke when their signifer fell and in that falling opened the door to the first, second and sixth centuries who found a gap. Their defeat by Consul Catalus now came back to haunt them. They were not fighting for their legion but their cohort and as the Prima Cohort destroyed the enemy elite cohort then men took to their heels. Even as I thrust my pilum into the back of the man who had foolishly turned to follow the flight of the others I saw Lepidus and his generals racing towards the waiting ships. They would escape. Their men would not but even the cavalry of Pompey the Great could not cut a way through the mass of defeated men in time to stop their leaders. Pompey would have his victory but the rebellion would continue.

When the fleeing men saw that they had been abandoned they began to surrender. I had never been one to kill such men but there were others who did and it sickened me to see it. The man who turned to me threw down his weapons and scutum, "Do not kill me."

I saw my young charges watching me. I nodded, "Appius, stay here and guard this man. When others surrender take their arms and bring them here." I rammed my pilum into the ground as a marker.

"Yes Chosen Man."

The legionary looked relieved. I warned him, "Any treachery will see you endure a worse death than you can imagine."

Other enemy legionaries saw what we were doing and surrendered. Centurion Bucco was also taking prisoners. Signifer Gracchus came over with the captured enemy standard. "I will stay here with Appius. Continue the pursuit, Porcianus."

I was relieved. Appius would be safe. We took over a hundred prisoners. Not all surrendered. One legionary faced me and my six men.

"Here is one who will not go quietly into the night. I will fight you all and die with honour."

I was not going to let one of my young comrades be hurt by a man with a death wish. I shook my head, "You will fight me and I will send you to Elysium."

The man grinned. He was a veteran and looked as gnarled as Numerius but if he was still a legionary then he had made mistakes and not been promoted. I was confident. I held my shield before me and kept my sword low. We circled each other. We were both looking for a weakness. I saw that the ground was uneven. Men had discarded helmets, shields and weapons. I would watch my feet. He took my cautious approach for fear and suddenly launched an attack. He used his scutum as a weapon and punched it at me. I did not risk stepping back but I did not want my hand to be struck by the boss on his shield. I pivoted on my left leg so that his shield hit nothing but air and I took my chance to ram my shield at him. I did not strike his hand but managed to hit his shoulder. He grunted and I saw caution creep into his eyes. He had seen my relative youth and taken that as his opportunity to win. It was time for me to take the offensive and I feinted with my shield. He stepped back and caught his foot on a helmet. He did not fall but had to take a longer step than he wanted to keep his balance. I simply stepped forward and slashed at his leg with my sword. His left arm had lifted his shield and the blade cut through to the bone. Blood pumped from it.

He nodded, knowing the wound was mortal, and said, "I have lived too long." He hurled himself at me like a man demented by drink. He was easy to sidestep and as he passed me I hacked at his back. I hurt him although I did not break flesh and, as he turned to face me I chopped across his throat to end his life quickly and, giving him a soldier's death, sent him to Elysium.

The other six all hurried to my side. They had been spectators almost as though they were watching gladiators. Faustus said, "Can you teach us to fight like that?"

I smiled as I sheathed my sword and searched the body for coins, "Were you not watching? That was the lesson. When you fight one to one you look for your chance. You use the ground and the weakness of your enemies and you fight cold. If you let the hot blood rush into your head, while it might aid your arm it will cost you your life."

We returned as darkness began to fall, having collected all that we needed from the field. We would share it with Appius. Signifer Gracchus and Appius had one hundred and ten prisoners. Legate Betto and Centurion Bucco came over. The legate said, "You are rebels and you have a choice. Join the legions of Pompey the Great or be sold into slavery."

Surprisingly eight men chose slavery. I think they thought they might have the chance to escape slavery while the legion was a sentence for life. They may have hoped to become gladiators who lived a life as a slave but a slightly better one than most. We marched, the next day, to Rome. Pompey was not given a triumph and we camped outside the Colline Gate. We were familiar with it. We were there for three weeks. I got to see Numerius and Gaius. Gaius was still protecting himself with sullen silences but Numerius was loving the life of a centurion. Like me he had profited from the battles at Mutina and Cosa. Pompey was successful and we had still to be defeated.

Pompey himself, along with Legate Betto came to address the legion. He rode Hephaestus. "We have won great victories. Marcus Aemilius Lepidus fled but you should know that he was defeated and killed in Sardinia by Valerius Triarius who was the pro praetor there. This rebellion is over." There was a huge roar from everyone and Pompey milked the applause then he held up his hand as Hephaestus stamped the ground with his forehoof. "However, while we have been dealing with enemies at home, General Quintus Sertorius has defeated our armies in Hispania Ulterior and Hispania Citerior. The senate has made me the military commander and commissioned me to defeat him and retake Hispania." There were more cheers but this time a little more muted. Hispania meant being away from Italy. "We leave in a month." He smiled and waved his arm, "We still train but the pleasures of Rome are here at your doorstep."

As we began to move away Centurion Bucco said, "Lucius, the general wishes to speak to you." He smiled, "You are a favoured son of the legion."

When I reached the general he and Legate Betto had dismounted. I saw that Numerius and Gaius were there too, along with two clerks and a pair of mules. Legate Betto said, "You three distinguished yourselves in the first war and the general has remembered you. You have been chosen by him for a task that is well suited to you." He stepped back.

"I want the three of you to return to Picenum. We were victorious at Mutina and Cosa but we lost men and if we are to go to Hispania then we need our ranks filling. Aulus and Servius are two trusted slaves who will accompany you back to Picenum. I wish you to recruit as many men as you can. You will be paid ten denarii each for every man you find who takes the sacramentum. You have three weeks for in one month's time we march for Hispania."

Numerius said, "General, my tavern?"

He smiled, "Will be watched over by my men. After all what better place for the men of the First Legion to use their pay than in the inn of Centurion Numerius?"

It was a bribe. Numerius would make a fortune and his inn would be safe. "Then what are we waiting for, let us go my friends."

I was being bribed too, for I would be, albeit briefly, with my family. The one who would not and the one who would suffer would be Gaius. He would be sent back to the place his wife died. He would come because of Numerius, me and the general's order but I could see that he was far from happy.

Chapter 15

We wanted a quick journey and so we used the horses I had captured at Mutina. They were the First Legion's and Legate Betto sanctioned their use. We hoped to make it back to my home in less than five days although the two slaves would not have a comfortable journey on the back of the two mules. We had authority from the senate thanks to the seal given to us by Pompey and that meant we stayed in the mansios along the way. They were comfortable and the food was adequate. It was pleasant to ride with my two brothers in arms. We were also amused by the two slaves who struggled on their mules. We spoke of life after Hispania. None of us thought that Sertorius would cause our general too many problems although, as Numerius pointed out, he was one of the few Marian generals we had not fought. Gaius was the quietest. I felt guilty because I had a family to which I could return, his wife and son were dead. He was philosophical about it all and seemed resigned to a life in the legion. "I hope that I can rise in the ranks. You have shown us both the way, Numerius. Both Lucius and I have tried to teach our charges the way you taught us."

He nodded, "Aye well, I have risen as high as I am going to and the pay is good. I think that the general may let me leave after Hispania."

I looked at him in surprise, "Really? You have not served long enough."

He tapped his nose. It was a habit of his, "When I lived in Rome I got to see a great deal of the general. I helped him with his training. Sometimes he drank in my inn. That was mainly as it was full of soldiers and our general likes the company of soldiers. We got on. He knows my age and he knows my mind. I have promised him that when I leave his legion I will continue to serve and recruit good men for him. I can spot good soldiers and I know how to make them into warriors. Look what I did with you."

The three of us rode in companionable silence as we each reflected on his words. I would still seek to leave once I had made my fortune. Gaius now had a future. His dead wife and son would never leave him but he could be like Numerius and make a place for himself in the First Legion.

What we could not know was that our occupation of such high-status places and the seal we used meant we attracted interest from the bandits, brigands and deserters who occupied the high passes. The civil war had created deserters. There were few soldiers guarding the roads and the Via Salara was not the Appian Way. We travelled at the pace of slaves on mules and did not move as quickly as we might. We were not travelling in mail. Our armour and helmets were on our horses. We wore just cloaks and woollen hats but we carried our swords and I had my sling. I learned much on that ride home. The last time I had used the road I had been in the company of legionaries. Now there were just five of us. There was a sort of brotherhood of bandits who had ways of passing messages that raced ahead of riders. Whatever the reason, word of our progress must have been known by those who lay in wait on the road for unwary travellers.

The bandits who stepped out from the rocks that flanked the road had chosen their ambush well. We were halfway between villages and it was lonely. The six of them stepped out on both sides to prevent our flight. Two had bows aimed at us while the others had swords, a spear and, in three cases, the vestiges of legionary clothes and caligae. The leader stepped down from the rock on which he had stood. He had a long sword which marked him as a former cavalryman. From the length and style of his hair he was probably an auxiliary. He addressed Numerius for it was Old Man who led us. The two slaves moved their mules closer together to have protection from attack by our three horses and bodies. They were not stupid but they were clearly terrified. The cavalryman smiled but I saw that it was a cruel smile. He had a long scar down his cheek and his arms bore evidence of old wounds. "Friends, you are well off. You have two slaves and mules not to mention three horses. I warrant that you have full purses too."

What he could not know was that we had a chest of denarii to pay recruits.

"We are not greedy men. We will take your horses and your purses. You can then continue on your way. We will let you live. Are we not kind?"

He turned and grinned at the others. Clearly they intended to kill us and take everything. The slaves would not fight and they outnumbered us two to one.

Numerius smiled back. His right hand rested easily on the hilt of his sword. I had already surreptitiously taken my sling from my belt and had a lead ball ready to use. He spoke reasonably and evenly, "We have a Senate Pass and serve Pompey the Great. You do not want to make an enemy of him."

"As you can see we no longer recognise the authority of Rome and Pompey the Great will never hear of this."

It confirmed that they were going to kill us but it was a slip. Numerius turned in his saddle and winked at Gaius and me, "What do you say? Shall we dismount and give them what they wish or…" In a flash he had drawn his sword and was galloping towards the leader. I fitted a stone and, whirling the sling, sent my stone to smack into the forehead of one of the archers. I had another ready but the second archer had sent an arrow at Gaius. My stone killed the second archer too but I saw that Gaius had an arrow in his leg. He bravely charged the other three. I could not let him do this alone and I drew my sword. Numerius was too wily a warrior to be defeated by a bandit. He rode his horse as though he was going to meet the man sword to sword and, at the last moment swerved to avoid the contact. He leaned over to smash the sword into the skull of the bandit leader who had underestimated the old soldier. One of those who remained tried to face Gaius but my old tentmate slashed his sword across the man's head, slicing deeply into bone. Numerius and I followed the last two across the rocky ground and our swords ended the bandits' lives. We smashed our swords into their skulls and they died instantly. It had been over so quickly and we had shown our skill yet one of us was wounded.

"Gaius is hurt."

"See to him." Numerius dismounted to examine the bodies.

The two slaves had dismounted and one was already taking honey and vinegar from the saddlebags. Gaius was bleeding heavily and I helped him to the ground. The arrow must have cut a vein for there was more blood than I expected. I tore some cloth from one of the dead bandits and pressed it to the wound.

"Give him wine." One of the slaves went to fetch the wine skin. I shook my head, "Sorry, Gaius, I was not quick enough."

He said, "It is me. I have enjoyed little luck in this life and that which I have is all bad."

The slave brought the wine and after he had poured a cup for Gaius I said to him, "Keep this cloth pressed against the wound while I remove the arrow." I gently lifted the knee. Gaius winced. I saw that the arrowhead was sticking out. That was a good thing. Holding the shaft tightly with my left hand I snapped off the head as quickly as I could. It still caused pain and this time Gaius could not control the involuntary shout.

Numerius, having searched the dead, came over, "How is it?"

I tossed him the arrowhead as I pulled the shaft out, "A lot of blood."

"Stitches then?" He examined the arrowhead and then slipped it into his satchel.

I nodded and said to the slave with the honey and vinegar, "Find the cleanest of the bandits' clothes and make bandages." I used my hand to press against the wound. Numerius had found the cat gut and bone needle. He threaded them but it would be me who sewed the wound. I had learned to do so on the farm. Animals were often cut and I was the one who stitched them. Numerius handed me the needle and gut and taking the bandage and cloths from the slave pressed the cloth into the wound.

I said, "Pour vinegar over the wound and then pack as much honey as you can into it." The slave looked at me questioningly. I sighed, hating having to explain, "It will slow down the bleeding." I made sure that the vinegar washed the wound clean. We did not need to have the wound become infected.

When all was done Numerius held Gaius' arms and I began to stitch. I was as gentle as I could be but the needle was not the smallest and when Gaius passed out from the pain it was a relief. I could work faster. When he was bandaged we bundled him onto the back of his horse and headed for the nearest town. According to the mile markers it was ten miles away. There was a village nearer but they would not have a doctor. We left the bandits to be consumed by the more natural scavengers. Their skulls and bones would mark where they met such an ignominious end.

I was worried for Gaius' breathing was uneven. Gaius remained unconscious until we were within sight of the town. We helped to make him more comfortable but the saddle rubbed against the inner part of his thigh and he was still having trouble with his breathing. We found a doctor and while the slaves used the Senate Pass to get us beds, Numerius and I helped Gaius to the doctor's. He was, like the best of them, a Greek. That gave me hope. There were many who fraudulently claimed to be doctors but were not. He gave Gaius a potion immediately and it must have contained something to ease the pain and to help his breathing for he lay back and smiled. The doctor examined him thoroughly. He put his eyes close to the wound and seemed to be smelling the wound as well as looking at it. He nodded, "You used honey and vinegar?"

"Yes, Doctor."

"The stitches are good but there is something…" he put his hand on Gaius brow and then close to the wound. He led Numerius and I from the room. "Tell me exactly what happened and what you did."

We did so and Numerius took the arrowhead from his tunic, "Here is the arrow."

The doctor took it as though it was a poisonous reptile. He looked at it closely and sniffed it. His face darkened, "It is as I feared, the arrow was poisoned. Your friend will die."

I said, "Can you not do something for him?"

"I can give you a potion to help him sleep. If you wish to hasten his end then the potion will do that too. The poison is in his body."

"Is there no antidote?"

"If I knew the poison that was used then perhaps but it seems to me that this might be lycoctonum, what we Greeks call wolf's bane. It is from the aconitum family and there is no antidote." We looked at each other and the doctor said, "Will you tell him?"

Numerius nodded, "We are soldiers and that is what soldiers do. They are honest and stay until the end. We will tell him." Numerius paid the doctor. He had not saved Gaius' life but he had been honest and done his best. He deserved to be paid.

Legionary

That night we ate and took food to him. After he had eaten Numerius and I looked at one another. Who would tell him? Gaius looked at us and said, "Speak. We have fought together and seen friends die. Speak. Come Lucius, this old goat is inscrutable but you and I joined up together."

There was no way of avoiding and as with anything the best way is often the simplest. I took his right hand in mine, "Gaius, the arrow was poisoned and you will die."

Surprisingly, he smiled, "Then I shall see Flavia and my son sooner that is all." He closed his eyes and I think he was picturing them. He opened them and said, "How long?"

"The doctor did not say."

"I will not delay you. We ride hard for I would be buried with my wife." He looked at me, "Lucius, you will do that?"

"I will do that."

Despite the pain he was in and the increasing shortness of breath, a sign the doctor had said of the poison, Gaius rode as hard as any of us and we made his home ahead of our planned time. He lived on the opposite side of the town to my father's farm. I am not sure that the slaves ever wanted to see the back of a mule again. It was almost as though his will had kept his body together. He had no sooner dismounted and his father, who had heard the clatter of hooves come to greet him than he fell into a swoon and I barely caught him. The joy on his father's face changed to one of bewilderment. As I carried him across the square to his father's house, Numerius told him what had happened.

"He is dying but he wished to be buried with Flavia."

"And he shall. Wife!" He looked at us and gave a sad smile, "You are his brothers in arms and I am grateful beyond words for the return of my son but, I beg of you, let his last hours be with us."

We both nodded, "Of course. I shall stay at my father's farm. Let us know…"

"I will."

Numerius said, "The slaves and I will stay at the mansio in the town. If nothing else Gaius' torment has shown me that you need all the time you can have with your family. We will use the square for recruitment. Come each morning and return home

Legionary

each night. Thanks to the attack we have less than ten days for it will take us longer to march the recruits back to Rome."

"You are sure?"

"I am sure and who knows I may be able to recruit some fresh whores for my inn." He grinned, "I shall let them all know that riches await them."

When we fought Numerius was just like Gaius and I but after that…

My family was delighted at my return but Aemilia was cross that I had not warned them. I shook my head, "We came as fast as any messenger. I can spend each night here on the farm but I must go to the town each morning. We have just the hours of darkness together." I did not tell her of Gaius. Those words would come but this was not the time.

She giggled, "Then we shall make the most of them." She handed me young Lucius as she and my mother went to join the slaves and prepare the food.

It was as I amused my son that I told my father of Gaius and the attack. He shook his head, "This is all the result of the civil war. I thought when Sulla became dictator that we would have order. We did here but, it seems, there are dark places twixt Rome and here."

I nodded and pulled a funny face for my son, "And we know that the creatures who inhabit those dark places are the worst of men."

To lighten the mood and to take my mind from the memory, he then told me of the improvements to the farm. All was good and the pigs I had bought from Aemilia's father had produced many young. The goats were fecund and the farm had enjoyed a good olive and grape harvest. There had been enough grapes this year to press five large amphorae of wine. It was a start.

The next day when I sprang onto my horse's back, wearing my mail and with my helmet in my hand, I felt light of heart for the evening in the farm had been wonderful. Lucius had even slept through our lovemaking. I think we were awake more than I had slept but it did not stop me feeling good.

That feeling evaporated when I reached Gaius' father's house. His father came from the house to speak to me when he heard the sound of the horse. My friend had died. He had woken once and, recognising his mother and father, they had told each other their feelings. Then he had slipped away.

"I want to thank you again. We bury him this afternoon. I know that you and Numerius have a job to do but…"

"We will be there." I led Gaius' horse and headed for the mansio. It lay on the road to the Forum and I was told that my friend had left early.

Numerius had set up the recruiting office in a small building close to the Forum. The Senate Pass had great power. He had bought an amphora of wine and every young man who passed was invited to drink. We told the tales of battle and by noon we had ten recruits. For the first morning that was a huge number. As we ate a lunch, in the open I said, "When we came to join we had a panel to impress. This seems more arbitrary."

"When we joined, Pompey was a young untried noble. Now he is a general and a great one too. He is the one who makes the rules. He wants as many men as he can get. When we are in Hispania we cannot raise more men. As we fight and lose men so our legion will shrink. He needs ballistae fodder."

"The funeral is this afternoon."

He nodded, "Then we will attend. We owe it to him as well as the others who fell and did not enjoy a Roman funeral."

In the afternoon, leaving the slaves at the Forum to take the names of any who wished to join, we went, in our mail and with helmets and swords, to the funeral. It was a small affair and just Gaius' and Flavia's family attended. However, the two of us attracted attention and as the priest spoke his words others were attracted to the columbarium. Gaius' body lay on the bier atop the firewood that would send his body to the heavens.

When the priest finished Gaius' father said, "Lucius Porcianus, I would be honoured if you would speak some words about my son."

I nodded and steeled myself, "Gaius and I joined the legion here in this part of Picenum. I am the last now for the others have preceded Gaius into Elysium. He was a good warrior. Like me he became a Chosen Man and had he not been so treacherously taken would, I am convinced, have become a centurion, perhaps even a legate. That hope was snatched away by a bandit's arrow but I will remember my friend each time we fight. I will remember when we took the standard. His name will not be forgotten." I do not know what prompted it but I drew my sword and, raising it to the heavens said, "Gaius Laelius Firminus, each time I go into battle you shall be with me." The words echoed in the cemetery and such was the silence that the sound of the sword being sheathed sounded loud.

"Thank you, Lucius. You are a good friend." There were tears in his eyes.

He took the burning brand from the slave and lit the firewood. We watched the flames lick around the body and then whoosh into life as Gaius was burned. The urn was ready at the side and I had seen the space next to the urn of Flavia and Gaius' son. His father had already arranged for a stonemason to carve the words on the stone that would mark it for all time.

As Numerius and I turned to return to the Forum Old Man said, out of the side of his mouth, "You have missed your calling, Lucius. You could have been an actor or a politician."

It was then I noticed some of the crowd who had gathered at the cemetery were following us. Our presence, helmets, mail and weapons, not to mention my speech had affected those listening. Twenty young men signed up that afternoon. The next day saw a steady stream of men, some older than the ones we had recruited the previous day, all coming to sign on. Numerius was delighted as we folded the table and the slaves placed the growing list of names in the chest along with the denarii. "If this continues we can be ready to go home in a week." I flashed him a look, and he shook his head, "Make the most of the time at home. Pompey wants us back. If we can get back early with plenty of recruits then we have time to train them."

He was right and I would make sure that I was with my wife and son as much as I could. I said, "Let us go to the columbarium. I would see Gaius' urn and…let us go."

He nodded and we returned to the place of the dead. Gaius' family were richer than mine and the niche was quite low down. I saw that Gaius' father had chosen an identical urn. It was good. I found myself almost welling up as I looked at it. This was foolish. I had buried others before him and yet…

Numerius' hand came around my shoulder, "Say goodbye and then put him from your mind. He is happy now and I know that he envied what you have with Aemilia and Lucius. Live your life for him. He is past pain. Make your life the one he would have chosen."

Numerius was wise. I also thought that he envied me too. He would never marry and sire children that he would raise, that was not his world, but he had genuinely liked Gaius and me. His words made me nod and I headed back to my home. I smiled at my parents but went directly to my bedchamber where Aemilia was preparing Lucius for bed. I felt guilty that my parents wished to speak to me more but I retired to our room as soon as I could. I made the most of my time with my family. Aemilia had been told of Gaius by my father and I just lay in her arms. She was silent and I was able to reflect that I had more than Gaius would ever have.

Numerius was right and seven days later we had four hundred and eighty men. That was all that we had coins for. I had to leave the farm well before dawn on that last morning as it would take some time to organise the men to march back to Rome. Aemilia kept trying to pull me back to bed but I shook my head, "With luck, when we return from Hispania, I might be able to leave the legion. Numerius says that after six years a legionary can apply to leave the legion if it is based in Italy."

"Six years is a lifetime."

"Poor Gaius would not have said so."

The thought made her realise how lucky we were and that we had enjoyed more time together than Flavia and Gaius.

With a cured piece of pork, homemade sausage, a jar of honey and a sack of cheese I left to lead our recruits home.

Numerius was almost as much a businessman as a soldier and he had procured a wagon for he had four young women who had agreed to work in his tavern. The slaves were delighted as it meant they did not have to ride the mules. Numerius rode at the head of our column and I brought up the rear. While the recruits chattered all the way west I enjoyed the solitude for my thoughts danced between the memory of Gaius' death and the time I had enjoyed with Aemilia. When we passed the place where the bandits had ambushed us we saw the remains of two bodies. Some creatures of the night had dragged away the rest to enjoy the bounty. The two bodies consisted of tattered and ripped clothes around bones. There was still some flesh on the bones and carrion scavengers would feed until all that remained were the bones that would gradually crumble and join the earth. No priest would say words over them and they would not be at peace. I touched the amulet of Mars I wore about my neck.

Pompey was not at the camp. He was in the Senate building being confirmed as military commander of Hispania with proconsular responsibilities. The latter was a rare honour for Pompey did not hold senate office and was still young but such was his standing that it was granted. Legate Betto was delighted with the recruits we had brought. The new men were sworn in and furnished with their mail, scuta, pila and helmets. Most of the equipment came from the legions we had defeated, Brutus' and those of Lepidus. The shields had been repainted and repaired as had any damaged mail and the new men were spread out amongst the cohorts that had lost the most men. Gaius was replaced by another and that saddened me. He had not had time to make his tentmates mourn him and his century had almost forgotten him already. He had been solitary when he had lost his family. Numerius and I were the only ones who would remember him and I was not sure how long Numerius would continue to do so.

By the time Pompey returned the legion was almost at full strength. Pompey made a point of thanking both Numerius and myself for our service. We were given an aureus each for our pains. He looked sad that Gaius had been lost. He knew the value of such men. His concern made me wish to serve him even more. It would have been easy for him to be like Gaius' new centurion and forget him immediately. Pompey was a soldier and valued soldiers. Before we left Numerius told me that his old friend, Proculus, who had been wounded in the battle of Mutina, had now left the legion and he would run the tavern for him. "He can keep the place orderly and Lucilla, the chief whore, can run the business. I will return from Hispania to the most successful tavern and whorehouse in Rome."

His friend had been replaced by Optio Decimus Cumanus who had been a Chosen Man in the First Cohort. He was a good soldier.

Legionary

I knew that Numerius had not forgotten Gaius. If anything the death of the young Chosen Man made his life even more precious and Numerius would enjoy a good life. When we had camped on the way back to Rome he had told me that Hispania would be his last campaign. "There is only a little more money to be made and, by the time we have won, I will have served six years. So long as we return to Italy I can apply to leave the legion. Right now I am at my peak but age is catching up with me, Lucius, and I want to enjoy my old age."

I, too, wished to leave and not only to enjoy old age but the rest of my life.

Chapter 16

Gallia Narbonensis 77 BC

This time we would not have to sail. The fleet that had taken us to and from Africa had been split up on our return. Instead, we marched. We took first the Via Aurelia and then the Via Aemilia Scauri to Genoa. While I had been recruiting, Centurion Bucco had worked hard to get our century to be the best in the legion. The young virgins I led were far from the untried boys I had been given. Not yet veterans, they now knew how to march and how to conduct themselves on the march and I no longer felt like their father. I was more of an older brother.

The army Pompey the Great led reflected his status. We had thirty thousand infantry and a thousand cavalrymen. We had the veterans of Sulla in our ranks as well as our own. I was one of the veterans. It was as experienced an army as it was possible to get and we were led by, in our opinion, the greatest general in Rome. Such a large army, however, does not move quickly and we had a long way to go.

The journey was lengthened when we reached Gallia Narbonensis. Although this had been one of the first provinces outside of Italy it was still heavily populated with Gauls. Most of them had adopted Roman ways but the rebellions of Carbo and Lepidus had created unrest and before we could leave the province we had to subdue the rebellion which had been festering for a while. We set up camp at Massalia and the cavalry were sent to find where the rebels were to be found. Massalia had been Greek and had often sided with the Carthaginians. By camping there Pompey was putting a stranglehold on the ones he considered were at the heart of the rebellion. In addition, being a port we could be supplied easier.

Centurion Bucco came to tell us what we might expect, "This time we are not fighting legionaries. There may be old soldiers amongst the rebels but they will not fight as legions." He smiled, "Imagine we are a dog who has fleas. We know where they are on our body but finding them and then removing them are two entirely different things. We need to be suspicious until it is proved that they are not rebels. We will not be fighting as a legion. It is cohort and century work. If I am to be honest with you this sort of thing is better taken on by auxiliaries. The enemy will take to the hills. They will try to cut our supply lines and Legate Betto does not want men wasted. We will be operating away from the rest of the legion. We will leave our mail behind and instead of two pila we will use one pilum and a pair of javelins. You will all need your slings. Perhaps we can see the skills once more of Legionary Publius and Chosen Man Lucius. It may well be that we end up fighting as contuburnia. That is no bad thing for the war in Hispania may well turn out to be a similar sort of war. Regard this as training. Each time we leave the camp a cohort will be left to guard it. We take with us enough supplies for a week in the field but we can take, especially from the rebels. Enjoy the food in camp while you can. Once we campaign we tighten our belts."

I was quite close to the tesserarius. He and Optio Corbulo had been good friends and he missed him. He and Numerius had also got on well. They both liked drinking. For some reason he found me to be good company and we would often talk around the campfire. I told him of Numerius' plan and that I hoped for the same. He nodded, "I was married once and, like Gaius, my wife and family died. The difference was that they were killed by Marian soldiers. The legion is all that I have. I like the life and when my twenty-five years are up I shall take the land offered in a colony." He gave a chuckle, "I am not sure I will enjoy it. Still, after twenty-five years I am not sure I will be in any condition to stay in the legion."

"There will be men we will be fighting like that, Tesserarius, men who were given land."

"And perhaps they were given land by Marius and that is why they are rebelling. Like him or loath him, Sulla won the civil war and there is no enemy to take on Marius' mantle. This Sertorius is little more than a warlord. He has the defeated Marian legions with him but his best troops will be the warriors of Hispania. Some have Carthaginian blood in them and their ancestors defeated the legions at Cannae and Trasimene."

Legionary

It was good to talk to the old soldier. I missed Numerius. The tesserarius did not have Numerius' wit but he had the same experiences and they gave me comfort.

Our cohort had a one-hundred-and-twenty-mile march to Cemenelum. It was loyal to Rome and it meant our camp there would be relatively safe and we would not be seen as oppressors. Our task was to go into the mountains and take the citadels that were there. Our work would be to end the threat and that meant killing the warriors and taking their weapons. If they had no arms then others could not fight with the weapons of the dead.

The town was close to a pleasant bay and there was plenty of fresh water. The Sixth Century was given the task of guarding the camp and that left the rest of us to split into five columns and seek out enemies. The Sixth Century would also forage for food. We, too, would collect as much food as we could while we sought and punished rebels.

Centurion Bucco took us up the path that led to the high ground where the people lived. It rose like a wall above the river valley and the tended fields. I could see why the people of Cemenelum had remained loyal. They had a good life. The centurion told us what he planned; he wanted to get, as he put it, *'the lie of the land'*. It also tested our strength to the limit as the path was very steep. Some of the older men, especially the tesserarius, were out of breath when we reached the top but we had a fine view and the centurion's decision was justified. He pointed to the northwest. We could see thin tendrils of smoke rising from some of the hilltop villages. He nodded, "Get your breath, boys and then we head for that first one."

As we marched I reflected that he had been clever. We had done the hard work while we were fresh. We had ascended the slope and while we might have to climb again it would not be a slog that would leave men incapable of combat. It took some hours to negotiate the paths. These were not Roman roads; these were the paths built by the indigenous people who had been conquered by Rome. I consoled myself that what we were doing had been done once before, twice if you thought about the time it was reclaimed from Hannibal's Carthaginians. If they could do it then so could we. Another advantage of the route taken by the centurion was that it was hard to ambush us. Gracchus, the

Legionary

signifer, led the way. The centurion had chosen to leave the standard at the camp. It effectively gave us another officer who was free to fight.

The first village was in a shallow valley sheltered between peaks. The sun's journey had determined the position of the houses and farms which lay alongside the narrow river. It was an orderly and peaceful looking village but our appearance came as a shock. We appeared through the trees almost silently.

The centurion nodded to Optio Cumanus who used his staff to wave us into two lines flanking the centurion, signifer and cornicen. He and the tesserarius waited behind us. We had our shields before us and held, not our pila but javelins. They were lighter to carry and we could throw them further. The men we saw were both unarmed and without a vestige of armour. Were they even rebels at all?

"Who is the headman here?"

A bearded man stepped forward. He wore his hair long in the Gallic style. "I am Brennus."

As with all non-Romans he used just one name. I vaguely recalled a story from the ancient times when a man called Brennus had sacked Rome. Was this an omen? "Proconsul Gnaeus Pompeius has sent us to ascertain your loyalty to Rome. Some villages and towns have refused to pay taxes and have rebelled."

Brennus scowled, "We pay too much in taxes." The centurion fixed him with his gaze and the headman nodded, "But we pay them and we are loyal."

While they had been talking I was counting the men and boys in the village. There were less than thirty. These were not a threat. The centurion thought so too for he nodded, "Good. Where is the next village?"

Brennus pointed to the southwest, "Vectis lies in that direction."

"And the people?"

He shrugged, "We get on with our own lives and do not worry about others. You will have to ask them."

"Thank you." He waved his spear and we moved in a column of twos from the village. I did not believe the headman and I don't think Centurion Bucco did either. Vectis would be belligerent.

We had lost a little elevation and as we began to climb once more I saw that this village looked to be not in a valley but higher in the hills. The farmer in me realised that the village would have the benefit of uninterrupted sun all day. The slopes were terraced and I guessed they would produce wine. The village must have been able to watch the path from Brennus' village. That became clear when, as we began to ascend the twisting path that climbed to the citadel, stones were hurled. The village was an old oppidum with ditches, ramparts and walls. We had warning for Signifer Gracchus shouted, "Shields."

Publius and I pulled up our shields and locked them above our heads. The stones clattered on them.

Centurion Bucco shouted, "Contuburnia one, two, three and four. Testudo on me. The rest stay here with the optio. Optio cover us."

"Centurion. Ready slings."

We were one of those conterburnia and Publius and I moved to flank the centurion and signifer. The cornicen was in the centre, his shield held above us. I was on the left and had the easy task of simply letting my scutum stay there. The centurion and signifer held their shields before them and Appius and Faustus hefted their shields above us. We were entombed in the protection of our shields.

"Nice and steady. Forward." This was where all our training paid off. Without another order being given we all moved as one and all used the same leg to do so.

I heard Optio Cumanus order, "Skirmish line, slings and javelins." Behind us the other half of the century would attack those sending missiles at us.

We peered over the top of the shields and I saw that this was an old-fashioned oppidum. There was a wooden palisade and a gate. The gate was closed and the walls were manned by men sending their stones, arrows and javelins at us. I almost laughed for the javelins were wasted. They were not pila and even if they hit and stuck, they were not heavy enough to cause a problem. They would have been better employed at close quarters. The stones and lead balls sounded terrifying as they cracked and clattered on the shields but they caused no wounds. As we neared the walls I saw the effect of the stones sent by Optio Cumanus and the rest of the century as they picked off the men on the wall who saw the testudo as the main threat.

The steep slope flattened close to the oppidum and I could see that the ground was relatively smooth, worn down by the constant passage of feet. Centurion Bucco said, "On my command we run. We will use our weight to smash open the gate." Mailed men with heavy shields and momentum were a powerful force. Were we enough to break the gates? We had trained to do this but never used the skill. "Run."

The ground was flat and without obstructions. We were doing something we had practised at the Colline Gate but, even so, I was worried that one of my young charges might trip. The gate loomed up and the shields at the front hit it so hard that the noise sounded like a thunderclap. There was a creak but I could see that the gate held.

"Back ten steps." The centurion was calmness itself. We walked back. "Steady and take a breath." It was nerve wracking as more stones were hurled at us. I felt one hit the shield above me and Decius' shield struck my helmet. It was not a lead ball from a sling. It was a large stone thrown from the walls. The cry and the thud that followed told us that the thrower had paid with his life. "Run!"

We had even more incentive this time for the stone that had hit us had been a warning. This time when we hit there was not only a thunderclap but a loud crack as the bar holding the gate broke. We almost overbalanced but Centurion Bucco saved the day by shouting, "Break and form a line."

It was as though the sun had broken through the clouds as the protective scuta were removed. We presented shields and I moved a javelin to my right hand.

"Aulus, the horn!" The cornicen sounded and I knew that Optio Cumanus would be leading the rest of the century to our aid.

A warrior wearing a helmet and with an oval shield raised his arm to hurl a spear at us. I saw that it was an old-style pilum. I was quicker for my javelin was lighter and he wore no armour on his body. As he pulled his arm back for a throw he exposed his body and my javelin hit him. The pilum dropped to the ground. It was as though it was the signal for the men of the village to attack. Even as I presented my pilum the mob of men who faced us ran at us. They clearly outnumbered us but we had helmets, mail and shields. We were the First Century, Second Cohort and we had never been defeated.

A brave young warrior wielding the two-handed axe hurled himself at Appius and me. My right arm darted out and the spear rammed into his throat. The speed of his charge and the strength of my arm conspired to drive the head through the neck to emerge at the back of his skull. I made a violent move to my right to throw the body from my spear head. Two things happened at once. The body fell before two warriors trying to get at the signifer and an enterprising warrior pulled back on a bow to send an arrow at me. My right side was exposed. My left hand moved almost as though it had a will of its own. That was our training. The arrow smacked into my scutum so hard that the head penetrated.

Optio Cumanus shouted, "Centurion, second rank in position."

"Century, forward."

We marched at the enemy. We were two solid lines and they were a mob. We simply drove through them spearing and stabbing until we reached the centre of the oppidum. The women and children had fled into the large longhouse there and the handful of warriors who remained defended it.

"Century, halt!"

We came to a stop and I was grateful for the shield felt so heavy I thought my arm would drop.

"Surrender!"

"Never, Roman, we are free from your yoke."

"Your warriors are dead and know this, if we have to fight you then all your women and children will be burned alive inside that longhouse. Vectis will cease to exist. Your bodies will remain unburied and when the weeds and tares have retaken this oppidum men will wonder at the foolishness of this opposition to Rome."

There were just twenty men left. The warrior who remained had a mail shirt and a Gallic helmet. He was clearly a leader.

"Our families will live?"

"You have my word."

He nodded, "Then we have no choice, we will surrender."

They dropped their weapons. "Optio Cumanus, collect the weapons and bind the men. Tesserarius gather the women from the longhouse."

"Yes, Centurion Bucco."

"Yes, Centurion Bucco."

"Signifer, take Porcianus' contuburnium and search the longhouse. When you have collected everything of value then burn it."

The leader who had surrendered shouted, "You said our families will live."

"And they will but Vectis will pay the price for rebellion."

The signifer turned to me, "Right, Lucius, stack your scuta and pila." We leaned the scuta against one another and while Appius held the pila and unused javelins we stacked them too. We entered the longhouse. The signifer had his sword out in case any had hidden inside from the tesserarius. It was empty and he sheathed it.

He said, "Publius and Faustus, look for food. The rest of you find where they hide their treasure. It will be under the floor somewhere."

We were lucky that this was a wooden building. We used our dolabra to hack up the floorboards and we soon found the chests containing the money that should have been paid in taxes. With the food collected the signifer said, "The rest of you outside. Chosen Man fetch a bucket of coals from the fire." There was a fire burning at one end of the longhouse and I spied a metal bucket with logs in it. I spread the logs around and then found a long wooden implement used to put bread into the ovens. I used it to shovel as much burning wood into the bucket as I could. When the wood began to smoulder I threw it onto the logs I had discarded. Smoke began to rise immediately. I saw a cloth and used it to grab the handle of the bucket. The heat was making it unbearable.

The signifer shouted, "Over here." He had gathered the ripped-up floorboards to make a pile. I barely made it before the heat was too much and I dropped it. He laughed as the burning coals spread over the piled-up wood, "Saved us having to spread it. Let's go. This longhouse will go up quickly."

I had not burned my hands but they were painful and I obeyed the last order with alacrity. Once outside I plunged my hands into a bucket of water. The relief made me smile. The smile left me when I looked at the prisoners. Each one had a bloody hand. When I looked I saw that the centurion had removed a finger from every warrior. He had kept this promise and the women and children were unharmed but the men had paid the price. Their hands would heal and they could work the land but they would never be the warriors that they were and their maimed hands would remind them of the folly of defying Rome. We spent the night at the oppidum. As we ate I asked, "Why did we not take the men as slaves? The general is not averse to selling such men."

Option Cumanus shook his head, "The centurion knows that we cannot afford to send men back to Rome with prisoners. Even Genoa would be too far. Our purpose is to recover Hispania. When we defeat them there we will take slaves and our general will become even richer."

The next day we headed down the mountain. The stink of the burnt oppidum was unpleasant. I also knew enough about farming to know that many would die that winter. The time and effort it would take to rebuild their homes would be time taken from the gathering of food. We had slaughtered and butchered their animals. Vectis would rue the day it challenged Rome.

We spent three weeks at our camp. The taking of Vectis was the only time we had to fight. For the rest we simply marched into villages and towns and accepted their surrender. Vectis had been a lesson for all. It was Geminus who was sent by the general to recall us. Winter was approaching and we had subdued the province. We were summoned to our winter camp at Narbo Martius. Thanks to our efforts we had plenty of food. Gallia Narbonensis would not and people would die of hunger but the rule of Rome was enforced. As the weather changed we built a camp that would keep us safe and secure until the new grass came. We would have a winter camp before we took on the mountains that were the Pyrenees. For us it would be an easy time. We would not have to take down a palisade each day and build a new one. We were close to the sea and could be supplied. All that we did was to train and hone the legion into the lethal weapon that would end the rebellion and retake Hispania. Numerius could go back to his whorehouse and, who knew, I might get a promotion. I knew that men might die in the battles we would fight. As I had learned it was the officers who were at the forefront and they were the ones more likely to die. There would be dead men's caligae to fill. I hoped it would not be our officers but war could be cruel and if the opportunity came then I would grasp it with both hands.

Chapter 17

The Battle of Lauron 76 BC

The winter camp was relatively pleasant. The sea was close enough for foraging parties to collect fish and there were hills covered with forests that allowed soldiers like Publius and me to hunt. We also trained. Centurion Bucco was never satisfied with staying the same. He wanted constant improvement. We had lost no men and so it was possible to hone the weapon that was the First Century Second Cohort into an even more powerful force.

It was in the winter camp that we learned of relative failures amongst the other legions. Perhaps the First Legion deserved the nickname they had been given, Felix Legion, for we were lucky. Other legions had lost men in ambushes and attacks when the rebellion had been quashed. The losses were not serious but as Felix had not lost a man it was something to consider. We were soldiers and we had to fight alongside other legions. What made us different?

When we sat and spoke about it the tesserarius, Nanus Quietus put it down to the training of men like Centurion Bucco. "The legate knows how to use men like the centurion. Optio Corbulo was the result of that training and Numerius too. He put you in charge of a tent of virgins and it paid off. He knows his men. We might be lucky but my belief is that the luck is earned. The gods favour us and that is enough for me."

Gnaeus Orestes, another veteran said, "The problem is when we face the rebels in Hispania. We have to stand in line with the other legions. What if they break? I have heard that the tribes in Hispania are fierce horsemen and that they excel in ambush."

Quietus smiled, "We stand our ground and do what we do best. We hold the enemy until they tire and then push forward and put them to the sword." He smiled, "They cannot be any fiercer than the wild Numidians and our general had the means to defeat them. You may be right and there may be surprises but I am confident that our general will deal with each problem as it comes. All that we need to do is follow orders and trust to each other." Men like the tesserarius were the backbone of the legion.

Legionary

They were solid and dependable. Standing at the rear of the century with the optio they were the ones who reacted to problems and it was their strength that enabled the centurion to forge ahead in battle.

The debate ran on each night. I think it was good to put fears into the open. We had been successful fighting rebels in Italy, Sicily and Africa. Why should Hispania be any different?

We left in Spring to climb the twisting roads that wound like hairpins through the Pyrenees. How Hannibal had brought elephants not only through these mountains but also the Alps was something we discussed as we slogged up them. It seemed impossible for the curves were so close that, many times, we had men above us and below us who were close enough for conversation. It was a relief to reach land that was relatively flat and where the air was not so icy. I was used to high places but not as high as those passes and the cold had seeped deep into my bones.

At our first camp, close to the Blue Sea, Pompey had a call for all the centurions. It gave us a day or so in camp and for that we were grateful. We could repair caligae and see to the mules which had suffered on the road. We foraged for shellfish and my men and I hunted for birds. Food and our stomachs were never far from our minds and we made sure that we did not waste a moment of the time in the camp.

Centurion Bucco was proud of his century and he liked to keep us informed. He was not a centurion like Numerius. Both were good leaders but each had their own methods. "Our old friend Metellus Pius is in the south of the land and we are to march to meet him so that Pompey can issue commands to the whole army." Even as we heard the information I was thinking back to the time when Metellus Pius and Pompey had been equals. Now our general led the older warrior. "The general has heard that Marcus Perperna has brought the last of the legions of Lepidus over to this land to join Sertorius." We knew that Lepidus had been killed but wondered what had had happened to the men who had managed to flee after Cosa. Now we knew. They were in Hispania and we would have to fight them, again. "The rebels are strongest in the west and the east of this land remains loyal to Rome. When we have joined up with Metellus Pius we will move west and destroy the armies of the rebels."

It seemed a simple enough plan and the next day we began the march to Lauron. It was over two hundred miles and the sun grew hotter each day as we moved south. It was not as hot as it had been in Africa but it was close. We were aided by the sea to our left and the breeze, when it came was a relief. We were used to marching in mail but the heat made it chafe and men had to seek medical help. We also had to forage each night to find supplies. While the camp was being built centuries would be sent out to gather whatever food we could. An army of thirty-one thousand took some feeding. Despite the heat and the hunger there was a confident mood as we headed south. Pompey was a popular general and he made the most of that popularity. Hephaestus, with the general on his back, would ride along our column and our leader made a point of speaking to veterans. My contuburnium were as proud as any when he spoke to me.

"My horse still remembers you, Lucius Porcianus." The white horse nodded his head and his forehoof pawed the ground. He remembered me.

I saluted, "He is a good horse, General, I am just sorry that I have no treat to give him."

"Like the rest of the army, Legionary, he must learn to tighten his girth until the last embers of this rebellion are doused." The last words were spoken loudly for they were intended for any who might be grumbling. He was telling them that we were all in the same boat. "Farewell and know that you shall reap a rich reward when this land returns to Rome." He made it sound as though it would be over quickly. The forty-day campaign in Africa had made our general confident.

We were in for a surprise when we reached Lauron. We expected to be able to use the city and enjoy fresh supplies but the enemy were there already and they had besieged the city. Their army looked to be the equal to ours but General Pompey was not discomfited by their siege lines. Africa had made him believe that he could defeat anyone. He camped as close to the enemy as he could without risking a sortie from them and he sent a challenge to General Sertorius to give battle. The enemy declined and Pompey waited for he knew that Metellus Pius was on his way north to join us.

We had to endure our marching camp. Of course, we had to forage and men were sent out each day to get what food they could from the surrounding areas. The enemy had many horsemen. It was an advantage they had over our army. They were more mobile and the foragers were often attacked. The losses were not serious, at least not in terms of men lost, but we were not fed as well as the general wished. To combat the losses General Pompey sent foraging parties further afield. Instead of hunting for food within sight of the enemy camp, where they could be seen, they ranged twenty miles or more. It meant they were away overnight but when they returned, normally in the morning, unharmed then Pompey decided that was the best way to proceed. We abandoned the local foraging and cohorts, largely from the veterans of Sulla, were sent out each day to find food for the rest of us.

The tesserarius snorted, "It would be better if he sent our legion for we have men who can use slings and bring back better food." He was talking about my contuburnium and I felt pride. He might have been right but I used the time in camp to continue my work with my young warriors. They were improving but I could see flaws and they needed work.

The first foragers who returned, as dawn broke, were laden. Centurion Bucco warned us that our turn at foraging would come soon enough. He gave us our instructions. "We will take scuta, swords and dolabra but not pila. We shall have enough to carry. We will also take the mule men." Ours was Appius. I did not think he did the job as well as I had done with Ceres for Diana was not as happy a looking mule. I had tried to teach him but he was not a natural. Diana knew that and she had proved obstinate on more than one occasion. When I had spent some time with her, in the winter camp, then she had behaved better. "Make sure your caligae are in good condition for the paths we shall take will be treacherous."

It gave us something to prepare for. I personally checked the caligae. I spent some time with Appius and Diana. I taught him to sing to her. He felt embarrassed but he did as I asked. Diana responded a little better to him. "The poorer root vegetables and hard fruits are a treat. Try to keep one with you." He gave me a quizzical look and I sighed, "Regard the treat as a beaker of wine brought to you by the optio on night duty." He beamed and nodded.

The night of the disaster we were the night guards. Our section of the camp faced the northwest. The duty would last until after breakfast for we had no camp to dismantle. We would then eat and get some sleep. It would not be enough but it would be rest.

I happened to be at the gate with Optio Cumanus when a mule man with neither spear nor shield rode in. We had heard the hooves of the mule. Both of us knew that it was a single animal but we stood to. The legionary had lost his helmet and that, alone, told us that there was a problem, "We have been attacked. First Spear Accius sent me for help. We are assaulted on every side."

It was confused and garbled. Attacked? Where? How many? He was a young recruit and not one of Sulla's veterans.

Cumanus nodded, "Porcianus, take command here. Have the men stand to and tell the centurion. I will tell the legate."

I shouted, "Stand to."

I was about to send a man to the officer when Centurion Bucco heard my order and raced down with the cornicen, "Why the order, Porcianus?"

"Optio Cumanus told me to, Centurion. He has gone to give the news to the legate. This man has come from the foraging party. They have been attacked."

"Sound the horn. Awake the camp." As the horn was sounded he said to the mule man, who had dismounted, "Tell me what happened."

The man had his breath back now and nodded as he spoke, "We were well loaded with supplies and had taken enough to feed a legion for three days. When we were heading back to camp we were suddenly attacked by lightly armed horsemen. First Spear tried to form battle lines but before we could do so, enemy legionaries charged at us from the woods. The charge broke our battle lines and routed us. We ran. It was then that the enemy cavalry started riding down our fleeing men." He shook his head, "It was a massacre." He pointed, "There are cavalry out there hunting down those that survived. How I managed to get through I do not know."

I smiled, "The gods wanted you to live."

General Pompey rode up. He had with him Legate Decimus Laelius. Pompey did not dismount, "What happened?"

Centurion Bucco answered, using fewer words than the mule man.

"Legate Laelius, take your legion and rescue our foragers."

"Yes General."

Pompey said to Centurion Bucco. "Have your cornicen sound the assembly. We may need to fight our battle today."

"Yes, General."

The horn sounded. I felt like a spare part. We would have to watch events unfold. We were the sentries and could not leave our position. We watched Laelius's legion as it marched out to rescue the foragers and, behind us, listened to the rest of the army as they prepared to respond to whatever happened. I ordered my men to take their pila and be ready to fight.

The sun began to rise although it was just a glow in the eastern sky over the city. As the sun rose we soon saw the fleeing troops racing for the safety of the camp and the enemy cavalry who were attacking them. There was a nearby wood and I saw some of our legionaries race there for shelter. It seemed like a good plan. They would have some protection from the horsemen. Legate Laelius had the men marching quickly towards the survivors and he had his men form their lines as fast and as efficiently as I have ever witnessed. I could not tear my eyes away from the unfolding battle but I heard Pompey forming up the legions behind us and wondered what our clever general would do. The enemy cavalry turned and fled. I lost sight of them beyond the wood. I began to breathe a sigh of relief. The legate might be able to salvage some of the foragers. It was then I saw the Sertorian cohorts forming up on the other side of Legate Laelius. The legate had to turn his men to face the new threat and it was then that I saw what he could not. Pompey could and he ordered the legions to march from the camp. The legate was about to be surrounded. The ones sent to rescue were now in more danger.

Legionary

The enemy cavalry had not fled the field but circled the wood and they now attacked the rear of Laelius' legion, caught in the middle of changing formation. That it was all planned became clear when the enemy legions also launched their attack. It was the Prima Cohort who took the greater casualties when the horsemen hit and as they died and their standard was taken so the rest of the legion broke. It was what the enemy cavalry had been waiting for and they tore into the legionaries.

The tesserarius was next to me and he said, out of the side of his mouth. "What will the general do, Chosen Man? Lead the legions to rescue Laelius and his men or stand and watch?"

In the end we did nothing for Pompey gave no order. We stood impotently to watch two legions destroyed. He had the remaining legions, minus ours who were still on sentry duty, in battle lines. We all watched the massacre as ten thousand of Pompey's men were lost. The survivors who made it were ruined as soldiers. They had seen their comrades die while the rest of us stood and watched. All that they would be good for, in the future, was sentry duty. I could not help but think back to poor Faustus Fullo. He had lost the rest of his contuburnium and it had torn the heart from him.

When Pompey brought his legions back to the camp we knew it was all over. Sertorius now had more men than we did. Pompey's hopes for a battle lay in ruins. We would have to await the arrival of Metellus Pius and pray that he arrived before we suffered another disaster. Two days later we saw Lauron burnt as it was taken by Sertorius. We could only imagine the slaughter that would follow and we waited our turn to be attacked by the general who had outwitted and outfought Pompey the Great. We had lost our first battle and I could feel the shock in the camp. When the enemy left the city and headed west we knew that Metellus Pius had arrived. Sertorius would not wish to be caught between two armies.

As we broke camp to enter the city I reflected that the only good to come from this was that the First Legion, in my view the best legion, was still intact and while we remained so there was hope but that hope was now slimmer.

In the end our cohort was spared the horror of entering a sacked city but we were given an equally horrifying task. We were sent to recover the bodies and as much equipment as we could from the dead who had been slaughtered. It was a grim duty. While the Prima Cohort formed a skirmish line facing west, the rest of us, in centuries, scoured the three-day old battlefield. It would have been bad enough immediately after the battle but the vermin and carrion crows had feasted on the dead. Our slings took some of the tardier ones as we scattered them. We had carts pulled by our mules to take back the weapons and armour. The bodies would be burnt and buried. We had priests with us and when we had enough bodies we buried their ashes in the graves hacked from the ground with our dolabra. Where we could identify them we wrote their names on pieces of wood but most of the dead were unknown to us. The exception was Legate Decius Laelius. We found his hacked body close to that of First Spear and the standard bearer. All had been hacked to pieces and their manhoods taken. Their three bodies, wrapped in their cloaks were taken back to the city. General Pompey would honour them.

In many ways the desecration of our dead hardened the resolve, certainly of our century. None of us had ever abused our dead enemies. We had treated them with respect. The Sertorian rebels had stepped over an invisible line. When next we fought then they would pay.

As we sat in our camp the tesserarius said to me, "Hubris, Lucius, that is the cause of this disaster."

Publius said, "Hubris? Tesserarius?"

"Aye, the general thought this was Africa all over again. We would have a short campaign and he would enter Rome with animals and trophies. He has made his first mistake and ten thousand of our men have paid the price." He lowered his voice, "I hope he has learned if not…"

"Surely Rome will send more men."

The tesserarius shook his head, "Politics. The men in Rome will wait. Marcus Crassus will be watching and his legions, as yet untouched, will only be sent when he is begged. Our general's star rose higher than his. There will be men looking to see if this is a comet that flares briefly and then disappears."

We spent a month at Lauron. We helped to rebuild its buildings and house its people but the heart had been torn from the town. When we left to move north and be closer to our supply lines in Gallia Narbonensis, I wondered how long Lauron would last. If Sertorius returned it could be easily destroyed again. We now had, in our army, six legions. Ours apart the rest were under strength. Metellus Pius had more and that gave us a slight advantage. As we trudged along the dusty road there were none of the songs we had sung on the way south. Defeat leaves a sour taste that precludes singing. Our legion had not lost but we felt tainted by the defeat and our march north, whilst understandable, felt like running away. We did not like it. We had also seen our mercurial general suffer his first defeat. That he had been outwitted was worrying.

One result of the mood was an eruption of arguments and fights in our camps. I was lucky, my young charges appeared to get on with one another and we had no such disagreements but others did. A legionary from the Eighth Cohort got into a fight with one of his tentmates; it was over the moving of a blanket. Such things, silly though they appeared, happened. The difference this time was that one of the legionaries died. The legion formed a hollow square as Legate Betto read out the charges. We all waited with bated breath. The death, whilst accidental, might result in the fustuarium. That was one of the most dreaded punishments and not just for the prisoner. The legionary would be stoned or beaten to death by cudgels, in front of the assembled troops, by his fellow soldiers, in this case the rest of the contuburnium. We breathed a sigh of relief when it was just whipping with the flagrum. The centurion who carried out the punishment did not spare the whip and the legionary had a back that was crisscrossed with bloody scars. I wondered if he had been ruined as a soldier. If we had to fight soon he would be incapable of wearing mail or fighting. However the punishment appeared to work and the minor disagreements became vocal rather than violent.

When we reached the colony of Faventia, it was autumn and any thoughts of further campaigning were ended. Metellus Pius and his legions joined us and that meant we were stronger but not yet in a position to face our enemy. Messages were sent to the senate for reinforcements and we prepared to spend the winter by the sea. I remembered what the tesserarius had said.

Legionary

While some were optimistic I was not. The army that had been sent was the one that would have to win. It was all down to the general once more.

Centurion Bucco kept us on our toes. When we were not on duty he had us marching and hunting in the lands to the west. Our supply situation was not the best and we would augment our food in whatever way we could. The marching to the places we would forage was to make us into a century with heart once more. We had witnessed disaster and there was little singing. Centurion Bucco did not like that and he made us sing. When we reached places to hunt then, while the hunters, men like Publius and me went to hunt, the rest were vigilant remembering the slaughter of the foragers at Lauron. The centurion made sure he spoke to every man during the day. The tesserarius and I got on and often Quietus would spend more time with me than the other contuburnia. He liked me.

"I think that the defeat has affected our general, Tesserarius."

He gave me a funny smile, "As I remember, Lucius, the only general who was never defeated was Alexander the Great but as that story is so far in the past it is hard to know if it is the truth or not. History is written by the winners and they do not like to admit their defeats. Perhaps Alexander the Great too made a mistake and lost a battle. The important thing about our general is that he is clever and will learn from this defeat. He was outwitted by Sertorius and that will hurt."

"You are saying that he will learn and we will not lose again?"

He laughed, "Every army can lose a battle. Hannibal defeated army after army until Scipio Africanus worked out a way to defeat him. We might lose again but I take heart from this, the Felix Legion did not lose. We were not defeated. Therein lies our strength. We just do our job." He smiled and lowered his voice, "It is good that you think about such matters but do not let your men hear the doubt. They take heart from your confidence."

I remembered Numerius when he had been our chosen man. He had never expressed any doubts. I resolved to mask my own fears. I could talk to Quietus and he would be the one to whom I would confide my fears. To my men I would be a stoic rock who blindly appeared to believe that we would win.

By the time we left the winter camp, our century was in better condition than most. We had hunted successfully and we had trained well. My men got on well with one another and I knew that other chosen men looked on with envy. We had come close to disaster but the enemy had not taken advantage of the defeat and I took hope from that. As Metellus Pius led his army to the west, we headed south to Valentia. Metellus had more legions and there were, in the cohort, some dissenting voices about the general's plan. He was splitting his army once more and the last time had seen disaster strike. Was he doomed to repeat his mistake?

Chapter 18

The Battle of Valentia 75 BC
The armies that awaited us were led by Marcus Perperna and Gaius Herennius. We had fought the legions of Perperna before. He had been defeated by Pompey at every turn and he held no fears for us. Yet Lauron haunted us. There was doubt even in the mind of the veterans. We hid it as best we could but it was there, in the eyes. The scouts we had sent out told us that they were waiting for us at the coastal city of Valentia and that they were equal in number. This was just south of Lauron and I did not like that. The ghosts of the dead legions would be close by. Before Lauron we would have had confidence in our general who had beaten Perperna before. Now that one defeat cast doubt on any outcome. I had learned that confidence in battle was everything and it was something we lacked. As we marched south it was clear that Pompey had also lost some of his confidence. Our flanks were closely guarded by the cavalry. They had managed to avoid any casualties in the disaster of Lauron and Pompey kept a screen of them to guard our flanks and to range ahead. He wanted to avoid an ambush. We met no opposition as we trudged our way south but it was a nervy march. Luckily Hispania was drier than Italy and we were able to march on the road.

When the Boeotian scouts found the enemy they were in the narrow gap between the River Turia and the city walls. The enemy clearly had confidence or else they would have squatted behind their walls and waited for Sertorius to come to their aid. Pompey had been defeated and Perperna thought to avenge his own defeat. We camped and Pompey gathered his centurions for their instructions. We would not be able to use our cavalry. They were placed behind us. The battle would be a simple one. We would have no room to manoeuvre and neither would the enemy. It would be the best legionaries who won. As we were the only legion anywhere near full strength we were given the place of honour and fought in the centre. The Prima Cohort was in the middle. We flanked them on one side and the Second Cohort stood on the other. While the rest of the army appeared to have lost much of their confidence, we had not lost a man in the last debacle and we were determined to show Pompey that his First Legion were still the best. We put our doubts deep inside us and adopted a confident air. The legate told us we would fight with our black feathers. We took them out, smoothed them and then fitted them. I knew that in the heat of a battle we could not guarantee their survival but there were always crows and jackdaws. Black could be replaced.

I could tell that Pompey was worried about the battle for he did that rare thing for him, he rode Hephaestus down the line of cohorts. He used fine words to inspire all of us. Hephaestus helped by prancing and tossing his head. The general spoke of how we were all veterans. He invoked the name of Sulla and, generally, flattered us all and promised the earth. I took solace from the fact that most of his words were aimed at the legions who had lost and not us. For us he used words like honoured and lucky.

After he had finished and rode to face us, he made Hephaestus rear and the whole army cheered when he raised his sword and shouted, "Victory!"

He rode Hephaestus behind the lines of infantry. His magnificent horse was too valuable to risk being hurt in a battle. He dismounted and stood behind the Prima Cohort with some legates and bodyguards. It was a simple gesture and we appreciated it for he had chosen to battle with us.

While I was in the front rank, on the right, my contuburnium were behind me. We made one file. Centurion Bucco had carefully chosen the eight men who would flank him and the signifer. He was not taking any chances. It meant that Publius would have to replace me when the order to rotate was given. As we waited for the horns I said, "Remember, Publius, pass to the right."

"Yes, Chosen Man, I will not let you down."

I knew he would not.

The horns sounded and Centurion Bucco waved us forward. The enemy did the same. I studied the shields of the men against whom we would fight and I looked at their standard. I did not recognise either. That gave me both hope and confidence. We had fought against the best already and the First Legion had always emerged victorious. The enemy would see our shields and the standards with the phalerae and know that they faced Pompey's best legion.

The enemy came forward. They were a wall of scuta. Our black feathers would stand out above our helmets but all we saw of the enemy were their helmets and their eyes peering over the tops of the shields. I had never thought of it before but as we approached men who had no feathers I realised that we looked bigger because of the plume. I now knew why Pompey had chosen for us to wear them. It was not just an affectation. He was telling the enemy who they faced. We were the one legion that had never lost a battle. We had never been broken and we had never fled. The black feathers were a sign.

The horns sounded again and both armies converged. Perhaps the commanders of the enemy cohorts were more nervous than their general, we shall never know, but whatever the reason they ordered the throwing of the pila too soon. They hit us but most of the spears struck the scuta of the front rank, including mine. The ones behind were unharmed. The one that hit mine hung limply. It had barely made it for it had been at the end of its flight and lacked power. Centurion Bucco had chosen, as had all the other centurions, the men in the front for their strength and skill. With a pilum hanging from my shield I could feel the strain already on my back and arm but I did not let the scuta drop. The enemy each had a second pilum. Would they throw it or save it to use as a thrusting weapon?

"Pila!" The command came as the cornicen sounded.

I pulled back and hurled my pilum. It sailed high in the air and flew over the front rank. I saw the enemy shields raised and I took the opportunity while my spear was in the air to reach over and pull the pilum from my scuta. The pilum was designed to break in the middle upon impact and it pulled away relatively easily. I dropped it and had my second pilum in my hand as we stepped closer. Some of the pila from our second rank had struck the enemy shields in their front rank and I could see not just eyes but helmets and, crucially, necks. Our spears had been sent from closer range and they had embedded themselves in the shields. They would not be pulled so easily. With our spears before us we advanced. I made sure that only my eyes were visible. When we clashed I thrust hard at the face before me. The enemy legionary did the same but he had a smaller target. We both raised our shields as the metal head of the pilum came close to my head and shield. The enemy legionary's shield was heavier due to the pilum hanging from it and it was slow to rise. My spear's head smashed between his nose and cheek and I drove it on to enter his head and he fell.

Publius, behind me had thrust his spear at the legionary next to the one I had slain. His spear caught the side of the legionary's helmet and the enemy soldier had to shift his position slightly, allowing Manus, Chosen Man, next to me to find the gap and to slay him. Two deaths had an effect for they made the enemy line ripple. Men behind tried to step into the gap but there were two bodies before them and Manus and I were able to ram our pila at the advancing men whose scuta were not properly in place. We caused wounds and a wounded man was always weaker. Even more important was the fact that their line was no longer intact.

The men to the left of Manus began to kill their enemies and Centurion Bucco roared, "First Century, advance!"

Our training came to our aid. We had bodies to negotiate but we all moved as one. We stepped forward using our right legs and as we gained the height we thrust at the enemy legionaries from above. We had more of their bodies as targets. I thrust down as I stepped off the dead body and my pilum entered the legionary's shoulder. The man had been, until a few moments earlier, in the third rank. His spear came up but struck my helmet and one of my feathers. The feather would be lost. As I landed on my left leg, the force of my arm and the weight of my body and armour drove my spear into his body. It was a good strike but it broke the pilum. I suppose I should have stepped back and allowed Publius to come to the fore as he had a spear and I had not but I quickly drew my sword and as I lifted my shield to deflect the enemy pilum up I drove the blade up. It was not exactly a blind strike, I was aiming roughly for his middle, but it was a hopeful one. The tip of the sword that had replaced my father's found a mail link and I pushed up. It tore some links and cut flesh. As the rest of my file were pushing against my back, as were those behind another Chosen Man, Manus, the enemy pila were of little use. The men facing us had no space to withdraw their spears and strike. They held them up above their shields and jabbed at our heads. They were easy to avoid. Manus was also using his sword. This was combat that needed little skill. It needed the memory of the practice we had endured in camp. We pulled back and thrust up and under the enemy scuta. Sometimes they managed to move their shields and block the blow and we pulled back. Behind us Publius and the others jabbed their spears at the enemy. If nothing else they were a distraction. We had the advantage that Manus and I could use our weapons above the enemy shield and it was one such blow that ended this particular combat. My new sword struck the enemy legionary's helmet below the rim. It was a hard blow and he must either have failed to tie the helmet properly or it had weakened thongs. Whatever the reason the helmet flew backwards and the legionary behind Manus took his chance and his spear skewered the rebel legionary.

    We had been fighting for some time and while all that I could see were the enemy before me, I had the feeling that we were winning. That became clear as the next man who came at me was unsupported and he was young. He was the first of the next cohort and seeing a gap had raced to help his comrades. He should have thrown his pilum. Had he done so then my shield would have dropped when it was impaled and he could have thrown his second one. He was young and, perhaps, had not been in battle before. Certainly his scutum looked pristine as though it had rarely been out of its cover. My scutum was faded by the sun and scored with marks. He raced forward and thrust with his pilum. I easily blocked the blow and saw that his thrust had exposed his middle. I rammed my sword to the hilt and watched the light leave his eyes. This might have been his first battle. It was certainly his last.

    The rest of the second enemy cohort was advancing more slowly than the reckless boy I had just slain. I sheathed my sword and picked up the two pila he had dropped as he had died. I hurled one high in the air at the advancing cohort and then held the second before me. We had destroyed the First Cohort. Men were already filtering back through the ranks of the Second Cohort. Centurion Bucco yelled, "Hold. Those without pila rotate!"

Legionary

I had a spear. Manus did not and he moved back to take his place in the rear rank of his file. The Second Cohort were like the young man I had killed. They had unmarked shields and the look of a freshly raised legion. These were not the veterans we had fought at Cosa or in Sicily. They came on bravely enough, encouraged by their centurion and signifer. It was the death of their centurion and signifer, slain by Centurion Bucco and Cornicen Avitus that broke their spirit. One moment they had been led by two veterans and the next they were leaderless and when Centurion Bucco shouted, "Charge!" it marked their end and a bloody one at that. We had seen the slaughter of our own legions at Lauron and while the men we faced were not the ones responsible they were part of the same army. We pounced like wolves on sheep whose guard dog has died.

I was tired but knowing that the walls of Valentia lay just a few hundred paces from me gave my weary limbs extra energy. My recently acquired pilum accounted for three men before it broke and I drew, once more, my sword. We were now in open order and I could use my feet. These were young men with the most basic of training that we fought and I danced around looking for an opening. When the young legionary thrust his spear where I had been, I hacked across his neck with my sword. It was not the thrust I had been trained to use but if I had learned anything it was to improvise. A veteran would not have given me the chance that the young legionary did.

The rest of the battle was a slaughter. We had lost ten thousand at Lauron. They lost that and more at Valentia, including one of their leaders, Gaius Herennius. Marcus Perperna did his normal disappearing act and fled with the handful of men who escaped the slaughter. Our century had light casualties. I saw just three cloak covered bodies at the end. I did not know the three well but we would make an offering at the next temple. We raced to be the first to enter Valentia. It was a port and those who could had taken ship and fled. The ones that remained surrendered. Pompey had them shackled and led from the city. They would be sold as slaves. There would be great profit for him and he would let some of the denarii filter down to us. The prisoners enslaved and the treasure taken, we were allowed to ransack Valentia.

Legionary

I had done this enough times before to know where to look and I led my contuburnium to seek gold beneath floorboards and under marked stones in the houses that we found. We took food and we took items of clothing that we could either sell or use. Had we been in Italy then I might have kept some of the clothes for my family.

Appius was disappointed at the first house for there did not seem to be much. "There is little here, Chosen Man."

I laughed, "I do not hope to find a Golden Fleece. We do not count what we take until we are back in the camp and we can share it. We just take what there is."

Faustus nodded, "We are alive, Appius, and we are victorious. Whatever we find is more than we had before the battle was taken."

"I suppose."

I was learning about my new men. Appius was half empty and Faustus half full.

I collected what might be loosely termed treasure. There were coins, rings, and jewellery. Some were simple and might not have had much value but I recognised some gold, a ruby and two emeralds. I had a home to improve and a family to support. My men took things that they either wanted or things which would make our lives easier. When the horn sounded for recall I was happy with what we had taken. We left the city. After we departed to follow Pompey it would be burned to the ground. It was too vital a place to be left so and we knew that time and effort would have to be put into its rebuilding, and that would take men who might be going to fight us away from the battlefield.

Our cohort had led the attack and it was the turn of the Seventh Legion, who had been largely bystanders, to be given responsibility of the guarding of the camp. We had our normal rations but it was augmented by food we had taken from Valentia. Anything that was able to be saved for another meal we put to one side but all that was perishable was consumed. One of the greatest treasures we found was a simple one. We had collected a dozen fresh loaves from the houses we had looted. We ate half of them and washed the food down with the wine we had taken. To a soldier bread and wine were real treasures. We also had some sausages and hams we had found. They were delights and dainties to be savoured. We would not gorge on them as some tents did. Both would last for weeks and could be carried on our mule to make our dull diet a little livelier. With fresh cheese, honey and figs to end the meal we felt like Pompey himself.

As we let the food digest I counted out the denarii and the jewellery we had taken. I made eight piles. The denarii were equally divided and we each gained sixty denarii. The rings and jewellery I would keep and dispose of the next time we found ourselves in a friendly town with a place where we could sell such things. My men trusted me to be fair. Even Appius seemed happy at the profit we had made. My coins would be kept for my family. I had no idea, yet, what my charges would spend their money on. We had not had much opportunity to have leisure time. I wondered now if we would be given the chance. Lauron had been partly avenged but I knew Pompey well enough to know that he would not be happy until he had defeated Sertorius.

We fired the city the next day and Pompey waited long enough to see it destroyed before we headed south. He was taking us back towards Lauron and the scene of his humiliation but it would also take us closer to the army of Sertorius.

Chapter 19

The Battle of Sucro 75 BC

We did not move far from Valentia. The general wanted to be close to Metellus Pius and we did not have to endure the long march to Faventia. The messenger who arrived from Metellus Pius had great news. His army had defeated Hirtuleius and Sertorius was bringing an army to face Pompey. General Pius was hastening with his army to catch Sertorius between the two of us. When Pompey was given the news I heard his cheer from the other end of the marching camp. I only found out later on the reason for the elation. That night, as we camped a few miles from the scene of the slaughter at Lauron, we speculated about the battle.

Tesserarius Quietus as usual was eating with us for he liked the company of my contuburnium. He was getting to the end of his twentieth year in the legions and perhaps he saw the young men as the sons he had never had. He liked me, too, as he had always got on well with Numerius. Whatever the reason he often came to eat with us and never came empty handed. He appeared to have a never-ending supply of wine. Perhaps when we had been in Valentia that had been the treasure he sought.

"At least we don't need to send out foraging parties like we did the last time. Valentia gave us more than enough food until we are resupplied from Rome." The ambush still haunted me. Every time we went foraging I wondered if our enemy was getting ready to ambush us.

Quietus nodded and downed half a beaker of wine, "And we have only had to march twenty miles. Sertorius has to march all the way from Italica in the south. If Metellus Pius can arrive before they do then we have the nut between our crackers!"

There was an optimistic mood about the camp. Ransacking a town had given each of us food and treasure that made the combat worthwhile.

Faustus, ever the optimist said, "Another victory like Valentia, eh?"

Nanus Quietus shook his head, "Sertorius is a better general than Perperna and we can't count on facing virgins again. It will be a hard slog." He smiled, "But you lads have done well." He nodded to me, "the slayer of cornicens and signifers has taught you well." I did not smile or respond for I did not wish to upset the gods.

There was silence and then Faustus, looking for hope said, "And our century has another battle honour for taking the standard."

"Aye," agreed the tesserarius, "as does the centurion. They are well deserved but the veterans who are coming with Sertorius will take that as a challenge. Whoever fights alongside the centurion when we battle next will need all their wits about them and more than a little help from the Parcae."

I nodded, "Don't forget that despite our victory we are still six under strength legions. Until the senate sends more men it will stay the same."

Nanus said, "Pompey has enemies in Rome. He also has friends who are not really friends."

"What do you mean?" Publius was a thoughtful soldier and he wanted as much knowledge as he could get.

"Crassus has lived in Pompey's shadow and he doesn't like it. Sulla favoured Pompey over Crassus and Pompey was given a triumph. Crassus, for all his money is desperate for one, too. There will be plotting in Rome to see Pompey fail. When he does then Marcus Crassus will bring his own fresh legions to Hispania. We will have done the hard work and thinned out the enemy ranks and he will garner the glory and the victory. That is what I think his plan is, anyway." It was speculation but since I had last spoken to the tesserarius I had learned that his instincts were right. Numerius, who had lived in Rome, agreed. We had met in the ransacking of Valentia. Numerius was my lodestone. He had never let me down and I trusted him completely.

"Then we shall have to stop him and defeat this Sertorius." I think because of our first meeting at the port, not to mention Hephaestus, I felt a close affiliation with Pompey. It seemed to me that our fates were bound in some way. Whatever the reason I was determined to do all that I could for Pompey.

Legionary

If we had enjoyed full strength legions there would have been thirty thousand or more of us to face the rebel general. As it was we had just four thousand men in our legion and the rest each had less than that. The auxiliaries and cavalry added another three thousand men. Normally we would not have worried about how many auxiliaries we had, we always felt that we did not need them but here, against an enemy with many auxiliaries, they might be the difference between victory or defeat.

Both generals were eager for battle. The two armies were arranged in roughly the same way. The auxiliaries were before us and the cavalry on the flanks. We were Pompey's favourite legion and he had us in the centre again. Pompey showed his confidence in us by positioning himself on the right and letting Lucius Afranius command the left. Legate Betto was a solid commander and Pompey trusted him to hold the centre. I did not recognise Sertorius but Centurion Bucco did and he identified the enemy general who positioned himself on the enemy right. "There is the rebel general. A nasty piece of work." I said nothing but I thought it strange. I had expected the two generals to face and fight each other.

We were in the same formation as when we had fought at Valentia. Why change something that was successful? We flanked the Prima Cohort and Second Cohort were on the other side. I was at the front of my file and found myself next to Manus once more. As we waited he said, "This time, Lucius Porcianus it shall be you and I who take the standard."

"Aye, but I think that our centurion is the one who will do so again. He seems favoured by the gods." Centurion Bucco was ambitious. When the centurion of the First Cohort fell then he would be promoted, perhaps all of us would be elevated.

"And that is good for us, is it not?" Manus had been a veteran when I had first joined. I wondered why he had not been promoted. He seemed a dependable sort. Then I remembered his words. Gaius and I had taken a standard. Manus wanted to emulate us and he saw promotion to optio as the result of taking a standard.

Whilst both generals appeared eager for war, the legates leading the legions and the centurions marshalling the centuries were all ensuring that their lines had cohesion first. This was a battle that had to be won for both sides. Another defeat would mean that we had lost Hispania. If the enemy lost then the war would swing the way of the senate. It gave me the chance to study the men opposite us. I had learned to do this since my first battle. I saw something interesting. The shields that faced us were not all the same. Someone had cobbled together a cohort. They looked to be veterans from different legions. Some were new shields and that suggested virgins. Some might say I was clutching at straws but I knew that in the heat of battle there would not be the familiarity as there would if they were the same cohort and legion. Neither side had a full complement of ballistae. We had both lost battles and, inevitably, the machines of war suffered. I was happy about that for the bolts seemed to me a lottery. If you were unlucky enough to face one then your life could be measured in moments.

 The horns sounded from the enemy ranks and ours followed a heartbeat later. Both sets of auxiliaries moved into the empty ground between us. They would duel with each other and, if they were successful, then rain missiles on the enemy legionaries. I saw Hispanians fall as did some of the Gauls who fought alongside us. In places men got through to send stones, arrows and javelins at the Fifth Cohort. Some of our missiles struck the enemy lines. When their supply was exhausted the survivors dragged back their wounded and returned to their ranks.

 Even before our men were safely behind the rear rank of our cohorts Pompey ordered the advance. He was keen to get to grips with the enemy. He was riding Hephaestus and his war horse looked eager for war too. He was leading from the front, surrounded by his young aides who were also mounted on fine horses. We began to march. This time we would have to face veterans and I steeled myself for a harder battle. The horns sounded and we advanced. Pompey rode the magnificent Hephaestus and he was just behind the leading cohorts on the right. He urged his men on. As much as I wanted to watch Pompey the Great I knew that I had my own battle to fight. The ground was littered with the bodies of the auxiliaries. They were dotted around and meant we had to be careful to negotiate them.

 Both armies were ordered to send their pila at the same moment. It could not have been by design and had to be the

Legionary

Parcae that decided. This time men and shields were hit on both sides. It was an inevitable result of the simultaneous order. The act of throwing a pilum necessitated the opening of the body. Even the best legionary would struggle to keep the scutum before them and make a good throw. Manus and I were lucky but the legionary next to Manus, Opiter, was not and the pilum hit his leg. Moving back through the file with a pilum hanging from your leg is not easy and it meant our advance slowed a little. The last thing that Centurion Bucco wanted was to strike the enemy line with gaps in his line. It meant that Pompey's wing struck first. The presence of Pompey must have had an effect for the men he was leading surged forward. Lucius Afranius was struck by Sertorius and his men and our line suddenly skewed with us as the fulcrum. One wing was ahead of the other. Perhaps the wound to Opiter had helped us. Had we kept moving at the same pace then we might have found our left in danger from Sertorius' men on our flank.

Then the battlefield narrowed from a mile wide to the width of a century and the eight men that we would face. We were evenly matched. Our pila and scuta clashed at the same moment. We had all trained the same way and fought in exactly the same manner. Luck would play its part as well as fitness. I was lucky in that we had eaten well. We had not marched as far as the enemy and as I looked into the eyes of the veteran opposite me, I was younger. A warrior looks for advantage and I spied one. I let him rain more blows on my shield and kept my spear low. Publius had long limbs and his pilum poked over my shoulder to attract my opponent's attention. The veteran's pilum was smacking a monotonous rhythm on my shield as he pulled back and struck. His head dodged to the side to avoid Publius's pilum and he forgot about my spear. Tiredness does that to a man and when I saw him raise his shield slightly as the legionary behind Manus thrust at the soldier's head I seized my opportunity. I rammed my pilum at his thigh. I found the gap and the pilum did what it was supposed to do, it drove into flesh and, as the shaft broke, the man clutched the spear and fell. As I drew my sword Manus also killed his enemy. It sometimes happened that way. When a man fell the soldier next to him became exposed and when Decius, next to Manus also slew his man then we were able to move forward and I saw the enemy standard pushed back. We had made progress. A battle is measured by such things.

We took their second rank by surprise for we had fought statically for some time. As I stepped into the gap I dodged the hastily thrust spear and rammed my sword up under the outstretched arm. He fell and I heard the enemy optio shout, "Reinforce the left!"

I saw that Pompey had pushed the enemy back and I heard the horns of Sertorius. We did not know what was happening exactly but it seemed that some reorganisation in the enemy ranks was taking place.

Legate Betto, who was mounted and had a better view of the battle, shouted, "First Legion, hold your position."

None of us wanted to obey the order. We had the advantage and the enemy were reeling but we were well trained and Pompey's finest. We braced. It gave the enemy cohort facing us the chance to reorganise and fill the gaps. I took comfort from the fact that the man I would next face had been three ranks back when the battle had begun and he knew that the man he faced had already slain two better men than him. He made his first mistake when he prematurely threw his spear before the order was given. He still had two and instead of hurling it at my shield he raised his arm to send it towards the rear ranks. The legionary behind Manus still had a pilum and his arm darted out as the enemy pilum was thrown. The spear head went into the throwing arm of the enemy soldier. It did not penetrate deeply but it was a wound. The man took his second pilum and I punched my scutum at his right side. He had to move his shield to block the blow and in doing so gave me the chance to stab at his exposed right side. It was not a mortal blow but a good strike and the mail was torn. There was blood on the blade.

I was almost distracted by the battle to my right. Pompey and the right wing had been forced back. We were still the fulcrum but now the line was skewed the other way and I could hear the cheers from Lucius Afranius and his men as they advanced towards the enemy camp.

The legionary I was fighting now had two wounds. Neither would kill him but they would weaken him. I, too, was tiring but so long as there was no blood seeping from my body then I had a chance. That chance came when he thrust his pilum at my head. I sliced the head from his spear as I chopped with my sword. Even as he dropped the now useless wood to the ground and reached for his own blade I punched at him with the boss of my shield. His hand must have been slippery with his own blood and he did not manage to draw the sword quickly. He needed a second attempt and I used my sword to strike horizontally over my scutum to stab him in the throat.

Any joy I might have had at a third dead enemy evaporated when I saw General Pompey pulled from his horse and surrounded by the enemy. He was less than one hundred paces from us and Legate Betto saw the danger. "Centurion Bucco, rescue the general!"

"First Century, cuneus on me!

I heard Centurion Drusus, behind us, shout, "Sixth Century, forward!"

They would take the place we vacated. Had we not enjoyed success against the enemy century then what we did would have been impossible but they were on the brink of breaking already and as we formed a wedge their will was broken. Centurion Bucco was the tip of the wedge and behind him were Signifer Gracchus and Cornicen Avitus. Behind those two came Agrippa, Manus and me. Publius and Manus' man were behind me.

"March!"

We all stepped off on our right foot and headed obliquely across the front of the Prima Cohort. They, too, were trying to rescue our beleaguered general but we were cutting through the enemy files and that gave us a chance. The men I encountered all had their right side to me. There were no shields to protect them. The Prima Cohort were pressing from the front and it was like a hot knife passing through butter. We were moving quickly but would we be quick enough? Already some of the bodyguards and finely dressed aides who had been protecting Pompey as he fought his way back to the Prima Cohort were dead and as the others tired they would soon follow. Pompey, of course, was fighting hard and I knew that he was a good warrior with the best armour but, even so, I knew that we would be lucky to reach him in time. Was this to be end of the general?

Legionary

It was Hephaestus that saved him. Some of the enemy, thinking that Pompey would be taken by others, led the war horse from the field. By such narrow margins are greater events decided. Centurion Bucco gave a roar and with a superhuman effort slew two men who stood in his path. Gracchus and Avitus slew their men and when I hacked into the side of the centurion who was raising his sword to strike Pompey in the back, then our century, or the remains of it, at least, were able to form a ring around the general.

"Steady lads and move back to our lines. Keep the general safe." Centurion Bucco's voice was steady. We moved back towards the safety of the Prima Cohort. The enemy were desperate to get the general who had nearly been taken prisoner. We were lucky that they were so reckless. We fought as one. Publius and Manus were at my side and our swords hacked and stabbed at the exposed flesh of wild men.

When First Spear roared, "Shields" we knew we were safe. We found ourselves, the fifty who had survived, standing alongside the elite of the legion. We had earned the right to be there. Hephaestus was gone but Pompey was safe. The battle was far from over. It was the sacking of the enemy camp by Lucius Afranius that ensured that we and our general would survive. Sertorius took a legion to prevent the legate from taking his camp and as they moved off, Pompey ordered a fighting retreat to our camp. The enemy threw all that they had at us but we were resolute and with scuta and swords stopped them from breaking our lines. Once we passed through the gates into the camp then the pursuit stopped and the enemy, who had been within a few paces of taking General Pompey, now hurried off to rejoin Sertorius.

When Lucius Afranius reached us we saw that his bold attack to take the enemy camp had cost us dearly. He brought back less than one depleted legion. We had lost ten thousand men. As we stood behind our wooden palisade we could see, from the enemy bodies, that Sertorius had lost about the same number but he held the field. We braced ourselves during a long night for an attack which would see our camp defences overcome and the campaign in Hispania ended. The sound of carrion scavengers feasting on the dead and the moans from some men who were wounded and

Legionary

would not see the dawn filled the air. It was the arrival of Metellus Pius and his army that was our salvation. As they approached from the south General Sertorius decided that he was in no position to fight two armies. Perperna had cost him half of his army and the rebels withdrew from the east of Hispania. We had not won the battle, in fact we had come very close to losing it, but we had won this part of Hispania back. Our scouts reported the enemy falling back to the Celtiberian heartland and the mountain fortress of Clunia.

We were left to bury our dead.

Tesserarius Quietus was dead. He had fallen in the last moments as we rescued the general. No one saw him die. We recovered his body following the arrival of Metellus Pius. There were other losses too. A whole contuburnium had fallen while others were depleted. We were lucky. Appius and Caeso had wounds. They were not serious enough to require them to be sent home but they would have to have light duties for a while. That was almost true of the whole First Legion. We had been the only legion who were close to full strength at Valentia but the two battles had cost us dearly. We would need time to recover.

There were men whose wounds meant that they had to be discharged and ships arrived to take them back to Italy. There were, however, no replacements for us. We would have to continue to make war with what we had. Pompey was keen to get to grips with the enemy and we left the east to march the sixteen days it would take us to reach Clunia.

That night we burned Nanus Quietus. Centurion Bucco was clearly upset. He gave me the sword of the tesserarius, "He liked you, Chosen Man, and this sword is a good one." He also handed me the tesserarius' purse, "and he named you his heir. His wine we will drink but the denarii are for you."

I was sad. The coins meant nothing and while the sword was a rich gift I would rather my friend was still alive.

Chapter 20

Two days into the march I was summoned to Pompey's tent. Legate Betto was there. The general had two slaves attending him and after they had poured wine they were dismissed and I was waved to a seat. I did not like sitting in the presence of the general. I felt uncomfortable and ran through all the things I had done to find where I had made a mistake.

"Legate Bucco said that you were with those who rescued me at the battle of Sucro. You and all your century will be rewarded and a phalera awarded to the centurion and the legionaries who fought so bravely."

I did not think that was the sole reason for the meeting. Unusually for the general, he looked to be uncomfortable.

"You know that Hephaestus was taken in the battle?"

I nodded, "I saw, General, and it was that which helped to evade capture."

He suddenly leaned forward as though to seize my words, "Exactly and I would have him back. Such a brave action deserves reward. I cannot bear the thought of him being a prisoner." He looked at Legate Betto. He wanted the legate to continue.

The legate had been wounded on the face in the battle and an angry red scar ran down his right cheek. The legate was a plain-speaking man and he said, "The general would like men to find and rescue his horse." He paused, "He wants you to take your contuburnium and return the animal."

I saw the frown that passed over Pompey's face when he referred to Hephaestus as an animal. He thought of his horse as a warrior.

I could not refuse and yet I did not want to risk my young warriors, "My men are young and two are recovering from wounds, General."

The legate simplified it all into numbers and said, "Six or eight men, it does not matter."

I remained silent for a moment or two as I pondered my response. When Pompey spoke his voice was almost pleading.

Legionary

He was not a man who was used to asking. He was one who gave commands and men obeyed. "You know Hephaestus, Lucius, and he knows you. The gods chose you for this task and you are the only man who can do this."

I looked for a reason not to do this. I thought it was impossible and would doom my wife to widowhood. "The men who took it could be anywhere."

"They will have the horse close to Sertorius for it is a trophy. He will be in Clunia." Pompey was eager as he pointed to the northwest, "We will take many days to reach it. We have some horses and you and your men can ride quicker than we can march. Find Hephaestus and bring him back." It was a command and I could not refuse.

It sounded easy but it was not and the idea daunted me. "For my part, General, I am more than happy to do this but I cannot order the men I lead. I will ask for volunteers and only take those that can ride. There is no point in taking men to an unnecessary death."

Pompey frowned but Legate Betto nodded, "Sensible." A practical man, he then went on to give advice. "I would suggest you pretend to be deserters. We have clothing from our own dead auxiliaries. They might help."

Pompey's eyes pleaded with me but his pride would not let him beg. "When you return you shall be the new tesserarius."

That was a minor consideration and I did not think I had any chance of succeeding. "If I return then it will be an honour that I do not think I deserve."

"Thank you."

The legate said, "I will walk you back to your camp." Once we were out of earshot of the tent he said, "You are wrong, you know. You do deserve it. I would not have you go on this hazardous journey thinking that. The rank of tesserarius is yours no matter what you do. The centurion and I, not to mention the other officers, are all agreed on that. The general would not like it if he knew I had told you but I am not a noble. I was raised from the ranks."

I nodded.

He smiled, "You will do it in any case."

"Of course, but it may be alone."

He stopped and faced me, "If you go alone then you will not return. I know that with every part of me. Take a few but a man cannot do this alone. You are a legionary and you know this. You have more chance with men around you, especially men that you can trust."

We continued and I was silent for I had much to think about. Centurion Bucco approached and said, simply, "Well, Legate?"

"He will do it."

He sighed, "Then he is a fool but he is a brave one."

The legate said, "I will send over the six horses, the clothes and weapons. If there are less of you then choose the best." He said no more and turned to walk away.

Centurion Bucco said, "I would rather have you stay here and replace Nanus Quietus. He saw you as his natural replacement, despite your youth."

"I will be honoured to take up the position, Centurion, when I return."

"It is an almost impossible task. It is not just getting through their lines, it is taking their prize from under their noses."

"If we had taken Sertorius' horse would we expect them to try to rescue it, Centurion?"

"Well, no but…" he smiled, "you may be right and you might have just enough luck to pull this off. I hope that those who go with you will also have that luck. Do you need me there when you tell them?"

"No, Centurion. They are my men and I will give them the truth."

The seven of them were watching me as I approached. They had seen me with the legate and the centurion. My men were not fools and they knew that something was going on. Appius and Caeso, having light duties, had been given the role of cooks. Appius said, as he stirred the pot, "Food is almost ready, Chosen Man."

I held my arms out and waved them to me, "Come closer I would speak quietly to you." I saw the concern on their faces. I did not want them frightened and so I came right out with it and told them what I had been asked to do. "General Pompey has asked me to take my contuburnium to bring back his horse. There are those who think that this mission is doomed to failure.

I will not command any to go with me; I want volunteers." They all spoke at once. I shook my head, "Appius and Caeso you are on light duties and I can guarantee that this will not be a light duty. Added to that I do not wish to aggravate your wounds." They looked disappointed. "When the horses come that will decide who I will take."

Faustus asked, "How, Chosen Man?"

"If I am not satisfied with how you ride you will not go. I need riders." Although I could see they all understood my reasons the looks on the faces showed me which of them had doubts. "Let us eat first."

The meal was eaten in silence. It suited me for I had much to plan. We had just finished when two Boeotian cavalrymen led the horses over. I recognised the decurion from our campaigns in Italy. He smiled in joint recognition, "I wondered which foot sloggers needed to disguise themselves as a horseman. I am not surprised." He stroked the horses, "This is our last act serving Rome. There are just four of us left and the general has allowed us to leave. We have land in Cisalpine Gaul."

"The rest?"

He gave me a sad smile, "This war has taken its toll. The clothes we bring are the clothes of those who fell at Sucro and these are their horses." He looked at me as something flickered across his mind. "The general could have let us go after Sucro but he asked us to stay for a few more days. What is it that you do?" I had not been told to keep it a secret but I think that the general wished the information confined to a handful only. The decurion saw my dilemma and said, "You can trust me for I want these animals to live and I may be able to help you."

I nodded and, taking his arm led him away. I told him.

"Now it makes sense. The horse is a magnificent beast but is it worth the lives of you and your comrades?"

"I gave my word."

"Then you are honour bound to do as you have promised." He nodded as he studied me, "Pretend you are deserters. Say that you are Boeotian. Use my name, Marcellus. Say I was a bad bastard and that you left because of that. It is believable. Two men did desert after Lauron. We slew them at Sucro. Their names were Cassius and Brutus. If you have to use the story then you have more chance if it has the ring of truth." I could not help smiling. He had given me the same advice as the legate but his idea had more credibility. He had given the story clothes. He glanced over at my men, "How many do you take?"

"No more than five and perhaps less if they cannot ride."

"I will stay until you know. The horses that you do not use will be ours." I cocked an eye, "You will not need them and what the general does not know will not hurt me."

I said, "Very well. Over here."

The saddles, thank goodness, were not Roman cavalry ones but simple leather ones that had a saddlecloth beneath them. They looked comfortable for the auxiliaries had been well used. The horses were little more than ponies but I knew from home that such animals could ride all day and not be fatigued whilst heavy cavalry horses, such as Hephaestus, could. I sprang on the back of the horse. Ceres had given me a good lesson in riding and taking the reins I slapped the horse's rump and trotted around the tent. I stayed on the horse and said, "Those who still wish to come on this quest, mount, if you are able, and then ride around the tent. Marcellus will decide if you come with me. He has a better eye than I do."

Nonus Rogatus struggled to mount the animal and as soon as he set off he fell. He lay there winded and then rose. He shook his head, "Sorry, Chosen Man, can I try again?"

I said, "No, it would not be right."

The others mounted and then all rode around the tent. Marius was the weakest of them but he managed it. The others grinned and then Marcellus said, "You may have to gallop. Ride your horses to the far end of the camp and then ride as hard and fast towards me as you can. I want to see if you are able to stop."

I nodded and turned my horse to lead them away. The rest of the cohort was now watching with interest. I saw money changing hands as bets were made.

Publius said, "I think I can gallop, Chosen Man, but how do I stop the beast?"

"Jerk back on the reins. I believe the best method is to pull so hard that you punch yourself in the stomach."

We reached the point two hundred paces from the decurion. The gap between the tents was only wide enough for two horses.

I said, "Good luck." I slapped the rump and the horse, whose name I did not yet know, took off like a startled deer. I was aware that if I failed then I would not be able to carry out the general's orders.

I grabbed the reins and, when I was twenty paces from the decurion pulled back so hard that the horse almost slid to a halt. The decurion smiled, "You will do."

The others followed with varying degrees of success. None rode as hard as me but three managed to stop.

Marcellus nodded, "Then you need four horses. That is handy as we have just four swords and four helmets. We use the same cloaks as you do."

Marius limped down towards us, holding his ribs. There would now be three of them on light duties. Marcellus stayed long enough to show us how to saddle and unsaddle the animals and how to fit the bridles and reins. He gave us the baldrics, scabbards and long cavalry swords and then, as he and the trooper mounted the two other ponies, he said, "These animals can eat almost anything that grows but they need water regularly. If you fail to water them then you will not succeed."

I nodded, "I was a mule man, remember? Thank you, Marcellus, and good luck to you and your men."

"It is you that needs the luck." He was about to leave and then he turned and smiled, "You had better know their names. Yours, Mule Man, is Mercury. As you discovered, he is fast. Yours," he pointed to Publius, "is Aries. Yours," he pointed to Faustus, "is Ariadne and yours," he pointed to Mettius, "is Leonidas. Look after them and they will look after you." They mounted their horses and led the spares back to their camp. They were going to a new home and their work was done. Would we get to see a colonia or would our bones be burnt in the Hispanian sun?

We spent the last hours of that evening getting to know the horses. Boeotians went bare chested but it felt uncomfortable and so we wore our tunics tucked into the feminalia that we now wore. We were lucky that the boots they left us with fitted. We tried on the unfamiliar helmets. They would alter the way we fought but, hopefully, it would not come down to fighting. If we had to fight then it was likely that we would lose. We had to be invisible and pretend to be deserters. It would be a hard role to play. I dismissed the thoughts. I was getting as bad as Appius. The dour legionary took charge of the ponies for he was the mule man. He led them to where they could graze and I sharpened my spatha.

The centurion came over, "We think it best if you leave before the camp awakes. There is already much debate about what you are going to do. We will wake you in the middle of the night and I will take you to the camp gate."

After he had gone I took a piece of wood and wrote a letter to my wife. I went to Appius and gave it to him before I retired. "If I do not return, this is for my wife and my treasure." I nodded to the small box containing what we had taken thus far in the campaign.

He nodded and then said, "How will I get them to her, Chosen Man?"

"You will find a way." I slept better knowing that there was a letter. The Parcae had taken an interest in me and they would find a way of delivering the message from the grave if it came to that. If nothing else I knew that Numerius would see it home. I did not make the mistake of seeking him and his advice, I knew what it would be.

We rose in the dark. Legionaries sleep deeply when they can and all we heard was the sound of snores from the legion. We saddled our horses and after taking bread, cheese and oats, we slung our water bags and followed Centurion Bucco to the gate. He was now the keeper of the watchword. When I returned that would be my task. It was only as we neared the sentries that I realised my promotion meant I would be leaving the contuburnium. I would sleep with the other officers. I would be Chosen Man no longer. Surprisingly that saddened me.

The watchword given, we stepped outside the camp. We walked a few paces and Centurion Bucco spoke to us, "You have all been granted an honour that I wish you had not. The four of you are amongst the best in the century and that means the best in the legion. As we are the finest legion in Pompey's army we need you. Come back. If the task proves likely to be impossible, Lucius, then return. The general will be disappointed but better that you live."

I nodded, "I am happy to obey your orders, Centurion. Know that I will only attempt to fetch back the horse if it is possible. Like you I think that our general has not foreseen all the problems that we might face. He is blinded by the need for the return of his horse."

He held out his hand and I clasped it. We mounted and walked our horses on the road north and west. When we were a mile from the camp I said, "Better we eat now while we are close to our camp. When daylight comes I would have all our attention on the road."

I knew that our scouts had already ridden this road the previous days and there were no enemies for twenty miles. However, I also knew that there would be enemy scouts there too. I wanted to avoid being seen until we neared the enemy camp and even then I wanted to be hidden as much as possible. The food helped and washed down with ale in our skins I felt better. The Boeotian cavalrymen tended to ride side by side. We wanted to appear as deserters and Publius rode next to me. We needed to play a part and we would do everything we could to aid that deception.

As the sun rose to our right we all automatically scanned the land around. Our noses were a good early warning system as were the horses. Marcellus had told me that they were clever animals. If they sensed other horses they would let me know. Daylight brought a land that had been ravaged by war. There were few people. Most had fled to those areas that were not consumed by war. Once Pompey was victorious then peace and prosperity would return to this disputed land. The pig farmer in me looked at the derelict farms, some of them already being consumed by weeds, and I felt sad. I became homesick. I yearned for my farm.

"How far will we travel today, Chosen Man?"

I had decided not to use the names Marcellus had given us to use. In the heat of the moment we might forget them. "We do not use titles. The Boeotian cavalrymen used just one name. Until we return to the legion I am Lucius and you are Publius." I raised my voice a little, "Do you hear?"

The two behind both said, "Aye, Lucius."

"As for how far will we travel…Marcellus said these animals can cover sixty miles and starting as early as we did then I think that is possible. Our backsides may be red raw and we might never wish to see the back of a horse again but sixty miles seems a good target."

He was silent for a while and then said, "So, will we catch up with them before they reach this fortress of theirs?"

"If we do not then we will have failed. Hephaestus will just be guarded with the rest of the horses until Clunia but after that he will be in the fortress and the stables and that would make rescue impossible. We have to catch their army while they are on the road. They have more men on foot and if they are making thirty miles a day then I will be surprised. Within the next two days we should begin to see their signs."

Mettius said, "There are signs already, Lucius, look."

I turned and saw him pointing to a mound of earth next to the road. The broken haft of a pilum was stuck into it. A wounded legionary had managed to make it all the way to here before he had died. Perhaps he had asked his comrades to give him a warrior's death. I had seen that in the arena. That had been one of the tales told by Numerius about his time with Pompey's father. Some soldiers knew that their wound would kill them and wanted rid of the pain. The sight of the grave was sobering for it showed us that we were on the right trail but was also a foretaste of what our ends might be. It also told me that the enemy was hurrying. He had been buried and not burnt. Speed was everything.

Chapter 21

That first day we rode more than sixty-two miles. All of us were in agony as we stiffly dismounted at the derelict dwelling that lay just forty paces from the road. There had been another place we could have used to rest just two miles down the road but it had been where the enemy had been camped. The stink of their latrines and the fact that there would be no grazing made us ride the extra two miles. Publius scouted out the buildings while Mettius sought water. Faustus and I waited with the weary animals.

"There is no one here."

"There is a well."

"Then fetch water." Marcellus' warning had been a good one. Every time we had passed water on our journey north we had stopped to let the animals drink. I think that was why they were in such relatively good condition. I spied a patch of ground which looked like it could be used for grazing. At some point in the past it had been used to raise wheat. The crop had self-seeded and while that made the wheat less useful for bread it would be nutritious enough for the animals. We led them to the field and we tethered them. They had enough rope to graze but not to wander off.

I pointed to the remains of a building that had a good view of the grazing animals, "We will eat there."

We each had a sack with supplies. While we were able, we would eat hot food. The enemy had passed north and should be more than thirty miles or more from us. Faustus started the fire and Mettius took the small pot that Marcellus had donated to us. It was smaller than the one we used but would be easier to carry. We filled it with water and poured in the grain and beans. Publius had gathered some wild greens and garlic while he had scouted and they were thrown into the pot. I still had some dried pig meat from home. It had been cured and was hard and tough. I cut off a finger's length and chopped it into the pot. It would flavour it. Finally, I sprinkled in some of our salt. We laid out our blankets around the fire. No one wanted to sit yet. Our backsides were still sore. We stood and watched the horses and the pot as it bubbled and gurgled.

As he stirred the pot, Faustus said, "I wonder what happened to the family who lived here."

I was the farmer and I looked around, "They had no animals here. I can see neither byre nor pen and that means they raised crops." I reached down and picked up a lump of soil. It crumbled in my fingers, "This is not good soil. You always need animals, even if it is just a goat or two. The dung can improve the earth. I am guessing that one year the rains did not come or perhaps they were raided. Farming is hard when things go wrong and this land does not seem as good as Italy."

"Then why did Marcellus take land in Cisalpine Gaul? Would not Italy or his homeland have been better?"

I smiled, "Mettius, do you not know yet how Rome works? They do not want warriors returning to their homes unless they were born in Italy and they are not going to give a foreigner land in Italy. Cisalpine Gaul needs warriors to protect it from enemies and rebels. Marcellus and his men will raise horses. I saw land, as we marched to Hispania, that would be perfect for horses. The Roman army always needs horses. Marcellus struck me as a man who knew what he was about." I had not known the man for long but sometimes you can know all there is to know about a man from one conversation. I felt that way about Marcellus.

Mettius nodded, "I have at least six years before I can go home and I am not sure I wish to return to Picenum. I did not like the family business. Tanning pays well but it is stinking work. The smell lingers on your clothes no matter how often they are washed and it taints the food." He stirred the pot and tasted it, "This might be simple food but it tastes better than food cooked close to a tannery!"

I was getting to know my men. We ate and used the last of the stale bread to wipe around the pot. It cleaned much more easily. We found some wild berries and ate them. They would help to loosen our bowels. We brought the horses closer to us and tethered them on shorter leashes.

"Do we need to take turns watching?"

"Not tonight but tomorrow, yes. The horses will alert us."

Legionary

I was woken by Mercury's neigh and I was on my feet with my spatha drawn in a flash. I sheathed it again when I saw the fox slinking away. The food in our sacks had tempted the creature. I did not want to go to sleep and so I rekindled the fire and put water on and oats. I gave a handful of oats to Mercury as a reward for his vigilance. I made water and found I needed to empty my bowels. I did so and used some large leaves to clean myself. I washed in a pail of water from the well and felt more refreshed than I ought to have done.

Publius woke when the porridge began to bubble. He stood and asked, "Couldn't sleep?"

"The berries."

"Ah!" He disappeared and when his horse whinnied as he passed, the other two woke.

Mercury had done us a favour by alerting us to the fox. We were ready to ride not long after the sun rose. The grazing had helped them and they seemed in good condition. As we gingerly climbed aboard the animals I was not so sure about us. I knew that within the next two days we would come across the rearguard of the enemy army. I wanted to avoid any confrontation. Accordingly we rode with our helmets tied to our saddles and our heads protected from the sun by the cowls of our cloaks. The Boeotian cavalry cloaks were better than ours.

That second day we met travellers. They were heading towards the coast. They had a sad mule which was pulling a cart. It looked to be a family. There was a young father who looked to be my age, a weary looking woman and three children who were barefoot but were happily skipping down the road. They were in direct contrast to the ones I took to be their parents. We were mounted and had they wished to avoid us it would have been impossible. I saw the fear on the faces of the adults as we approached. The children just stared in awe at our horses and weapons. I understood their fear. Deserters, if that was what we were, might be likely just to kill the children and father and then abuse the woman before taking all their belongings. If we were part of an army then the result might be the same. I had seen enough refugees to know that all they wished was to disappear.

I dismounted, grateful for the opportunity. I smiled, "Well, friend, where are you bound?" As with animals a smile always broke the ice.

I wondered if he would understand my words but Romans had been in this land long enough for it to become the standard. He pointed east, "The coast. We hear that Pompey has made it safe for people once more." He nodded behind him, "The warlord, Sertorius, just takes from the people. When my mother and father died it was time to leave." My smile and the fact that our weapons were still in our scabbards seemed to give him confidence, "And you?"

I just said, as I mounted my horse, "We are just enjoying the day. Is the warlord close?"

"He passed us three days since."

I nodded and pointed back down the road, "There is a deserted farm just ten miles away, on the road south. There are some ears of wheat and berries there. Your animals can graze."

"Thank you…friend…"

I waited until we were a mile up the road before I spoke, "We now know where Sertorius is."

Mettius said, "We have missed our chance for he is still days away."

I smiled, "Three days for the man and his family. Do you think they could travel sixty miles? They will be lucky to make twenty miles a day. They probably travelled forty odd miles in those three days. We will reach him tomorrow and that means we will need to leave the road after we camp. The time of leisure is over. Tomorrow begins the deadly business that brought us here." I saw their faces change. The last two days had been, sore backsides apart, quite pleasant. Once we neared the metal snake that was edging north and west then caution would be the watchword.

We met more travellers that day and the next but we did not speak to them. That was their choice as they cowered protectively when our horses approached. We had passed a large contingent, almost a convoy when I made my decision. There were too many people on the road. "We will leave the road and use the cover of the land to the north of it." I had spied some rocky and rough terrain. Wagons would not be able to use it and only those with hardy horses such as ours would risk it.

We began to zig-zag up through the rocks. I knew enough about riding to be able to give lessons to my young charges. "When you climb then lean forward and when you descend then lean back."

They were simple enough instructions and the three of them obeyed. They found the journey less alarming and hazardous for the hunter's trail we took looked to be barely used. Tell-tale horse dung was noticeably absent. As we climbed I saw, off in the distance, the rearguard of Sertorius' army. They were some five miles away. The light glistened from mail and weapons. We kept them in sight as we rose and fell in the rocky hills. When we dipped we lost them but when we rose or turned, they were visible. There were no people to avoid and no clear track to follow. That proved a problem on more than one occasion when I took a direction that ended in a dead end and we had to back track. Generally, however, I found a good path. One advantage we had was that there was wildlife and Publius brought down a couple of birds we could put in the pot. I also hit a rabbit. They could be skinned and kept for another meal.

When I saw the enemy stop as the sun dropped a little lower in the sky then I knew they would make a camp. Sertorius was too good a general to risk a night attack. He would want to be protected by a ditch and a palisade. We made another two miles before I decided it was time to make a camp. I found a dell where there was a rocky pool of rainwater that would suffice for the horses. The rocks meant we could light a fire. As with the previous night, however, we would each stand a watch.

As we ate I gave them my plan, "Tomorrow we get ahead of the column. We have to find Hephaestus first. I have no intention of putting my head in a noose only to find that which we seek is elsewhere."

"Lucius, they might have taken the horse ahead of the main column."

"I hope not, Mettius, for that would mean we had put our lives at risk to no good purpose but I believe that they will have it with them. Sertorius can use it to tell all that he came close to capturing Pompey the Great." They nodded. "Once we know that they have the horse then we can work out how to take it."

There was silence. Faustus used a bird's bone to pick a piece of meat from his teeth. He discarded the bone into the fire and said, "And how do you plan on getting the horse, Lucius?"

"That is a task for me, I am afraid. I was chosen because the horse knows and trusts me. Animals like Hephaestus are clever. If you were with me he might become a little nervous. You three will wait with the horses while I go to eliminate the sentries and take the horse."

Even as I said it I realised how ridiculously simple I was making it all sound.

Publius said, "And as soon as you kill the sentry then they will hunt us."

I nodded, "That is the reason I have brought us this way. Our army is behind us. They will be a couple of days away but if we can use this land to evade capture then we have more chance of reaching them." I paused, "Once we have Hephaestus."

I took the hardest watch, the middle one. To be honest I did not sleep much for we were now close enough to almost touch the enemy army and therefore we were at the crucial part of the mission. It had seemed impossible when we had begun but we could smell the smoke from their woodfires and the enticing aroma of food being cooked. We could hear, on the wind, the sound of their horses. We had not yet failed and we were within spitting distance of Hephaestus.

We were all nervous and had risen, emptied bowels and eaten a frugal breakfast by the time dawn broke and we heard the horns as the enemy camp came to life. This was a rebel army but it was still, largely, Roman and they followed the same systems as we did. The first legionaries would already be breaking camp to follow their scouts. By the time they reached the place they would use to make the next camp the last remains of the camp they had just used would be finally dismantled. We knew where the road ran and I took us to the east of it in the rocky gullies and hills that would deter and discourage any from travelling there. We passed the camp that was being dismantled and soon caught up with the advance guard. We hid in the trees. I left Mettius and Faustus with the horses and Publius and I headed down to a vantage point above the road. With the cowls of our dark cloaks over us and hidden by foliage we would be well disguised.

There was a gap before the next soldiers came up the road. It was a cohort of auxiliaries. They looked to be local men with the weapons and armour of the area. The rest followed. It was a testament to the ferocity of the Battle of Sucro that none of the cohorts looked to be at full strength. It was almost noon when the horse herd passed us. There were just twenty of them but, in the middle, I spied Hephaestus. His white colouring not to mention his height, easily marked him. They had the horse and that meant there was still a chance we could rescue him. I smiled for he was not cooperating and the two men leading him would be exhausted by the time they reached the camp. I frowned when I saw the angry red scar on his rump. He had been hurt. When they had passed us I tapped Publius on the shoulder and we made our way back up to the horses. Mettius had found some grazing and Faustus a water course. The horses had rested and would be able to complete the next part of the journey easily.

We followed the slow-moving column and kept pace with the horse herd. We only stopped when we heard the sound of the legionaries' dolabra as the advance guard cut down branches and saplings to use as their palisade. We had found where they would camp. There was no rush and the last thing we needed was to be spotted. We were closer to the horse now than I had thought possible when we had set off. We dismounted and I handed my reins to Publius. Signing for them to wait and with my cowl about my head, I moved closer to the legionaries. I watched from fifty paces away. I had the shelter of a tree and undergrowth that was thick and leafy. I could, however, hear them even when the bushes hid them.

A veteran centurion was in charge and when the mules were fully laden with wood he shouted, "That is enough, back to the camp."

I waited until the last man had left and then slipped through the trees. This was familiar territory for me. I had hunted in woods like this, many leagues across the sea to the east admittedly, but I had moved quietly and with purpose to hunt. I could do it almost instinctively. The boots I wore ensured that I would not hurt my feet as had sometimes happened at home. I stopped when I saw the land flatten and spied the legion at work digging the ditch and piling up the soil to make the ramparts and begin to embed the stakes. I found a tree which had new growth at the bottom and squatted as I awaited the horses.

I saw that they had chosen, for their camp, a piece of ground next to a narrow river. It flowed from the hills just to the north of me. Had we continued the way we were then we would have had to ford it. There was a small patch of grass there and then the fields of the farms. They had chosen their camp site because of the water and the small village that lay just a few hundred paces up the road. It must have been one sympathetic to the Sertorian cause. The first of the palisade stakes had been planted when the vanguard came. Hephaestus was still not cooperating and his antics had alarmed the rest of the horses. The horse herders were struggling to contain them.

I saw First Spear as he walked towards the horses. From his command I knew that he was acting as praefectus castrorum "You, horse herder, can't you control those animals?"

"It is this white one, First Spear. He is evil, the White Devil."

"Well, I am not having them in my camp and running amok. We have lost enough men as it is. Put them over there by the river. Your lads can make a pen for them. The people here support us and the horses will be safe. We only need a camp in case our enemies are closer than we imagine."

"First Spear, that means we will have to watch them."

"That is your job isn't it?" He sighed, "Just hobble them. That way they can't run, can they?"

"Yes, First Spear."

The horse herders led the horses to the water. Even Hephaestus cooperated, albeit briefly, and the animals put the heads down to drink. There were six horse herders and the leader, the one who had spoken to First Spear, was no fool. While Hephaestus drank and his mouth was occupied, they hobbled him. It took all six of them to do so but once hobbled he could only take small steps. He was led to a patch of grass and a stake driven into the ground. He was tethered to it.

The rest of the horses were similarly hobbled and they were tied to a long line. Only the White Devil was afforded special treatment and his stake was away from the others. He stood lonely but head erect. He was a fighter. The next part would be crucial. I watched as the men planted stakes and then ran a rope around it. It was an improvised pen. They were not building a defended camp. I did not blame them. For one thing they would need to leave access to the river and for another it was unnecessary work. Even as I watched I saw the mule men bringing their charges down to drink. That would continue right up to the moment the last legions arrived. The pen made, the horse herders made their own sleeping area and ignored the mule men. To my relief it was well away from both the river and Hephaestus. They intended to rely on the hobble to secure the animal. As I watched a steady stream of mule men bring their mules to drink a plan formulated in my mind. The auxiliary and legionary cavalry also brought their horses. All of them avoided Hephaestus. He might be hobbled but he still had teeth. The geldings ridden by the auxiliaries would be terrified of the stallion. The effect of so many horses arriving was to make the area close to the river a muddy morass. It would make people avoid it. The horse herders had a fire going and food was cooking by the time the last of the horses had arrived. It would soon be dark. The one thing I had not seen was where they would post their sentries but, if my plan was going to succeed, then I needed to get back to my men and tell them what I intended.

 I headed along the trees but took a path that was close to the river. After half a mile or so I found what looked like a hunter's trail that led to some stones across the river. I guessed that the villagers used the crossing to keep dry feet when they went hunting. I followed the path but kept an eye out for familiar ground that would tell me where my men were. I smelled the horses and human dung. It was fresh and one of my men must have emptied his bowels. We had foraged many berries as we had passed through the trees and shrubs. I saw movement and knew where the camp lay.

Chapter 22

I crept up on Faustus unseen and he jumped when I spoke, "It is a good job I am not an enemy, Faustus."

"Chosen Man! We thought you had been taken." I could hear the relief in his voice.

"Not yet. Come, I have much to tell you." The horses were eating from the smallest patch of grass I had ever seen. "Have they been watered yet?"

Publius said, "Just from our water skins."

I looked at the sky. Night was an hour away. "Then we have time to eat and then we will lead them close to the enemy camp. There is a river there and they can drink to their hearts' content. I think I know how we can take the horse and escape."

We walked back to the camp and the others looked up. I let Faustus sit and I drank from the wine skin. That done I said, "They have hobbled the horses and Hephaestus is alone. Publius and I will approach the camp. I need you and your sling, Publius." He nodded. "I will cross the river and take the hobbles from Hephaestus. You will cover me and immobilise any of their sentries who might raise the alarm. There are just six horse herders and I cannot see that they will have more than one guard. If we eliminate him silently then we have a chance. A better one, I think, than when we first left the general."

"And if they do raise the alarm?"

"Then Mettius, I may not be seeing my family again."

We ate another frugal meal but if truth be told I was too nervous to eat. By my estimate we were more than eighty miles from the nearest help. It would take more than one day to reach safety and there would be pursuit. Having taken the general's horse they would want to hold onto that prize. The enemy First Spear and the horse herders would not see it that way but Sertorius and Perperna would. My other fear was that when we took the horse the enemy might think the army was closer than we were. General Pompey was not expecting a battle, not yet anyway. Sertorius had outwitted the general once before and I did not want me to be responsible for a second.

Legionary

As darkness fell and the enticing smell of food being cooked in the camp drifted up to us, we led our horses towards the river. It was easier going once I found the path I had used. When we reached the stones across the river we let the horses drink. I had explained my plan in detail while we had eaten and there was little point in risking us being heard. We could hear the noise from the enemy camp. The river bubbled and burbled over the stones. In the forest there were the noises of the night and animals were dying but here, by the river, it was peaceful. The enemy would have scouts out from their camp and those within the camp, and by this river would feel safe, for this was their land and it was Pompey and Pius who were the intruders. Our army could only move at the same speed as theirs and they would feel secure. I nodded to Publius and with sling and stone in hand we walked across the stones to the other side of the river. It was dark but there was noise from the camp. We reached the bushes across from the horse herd. We squatted and waited. I saw that they had just one sentry. I could see the glow from the fire where the rest were in their blankets or drinking. It was hard to tell. I stared until I could make them out. I was relieved when I saw that there was one man still awake and the rest seemed to be asleep. The main camp was forty paces away and I saw the light from the fires reflecting from the legionaries' helmets as they patrolled their palisade. They would be less vigilant on the horse herd side as they would regard the horse herders as extra eyes and ears. The noise from the main camp told me it was too early yet to risk a rescue.

When the sentry was relieved, by the man who had been awake, I knew we had at least four hours before the next relief. We would never have a better time. I waited until the relieved man had settled himself down after his ablutions and rolled into his blanket. The new sentry walked the horse lines and checked the tethers and hobbles and then went to the river to make water. When he had hissed his water into the river he found a place to sit. There was a rock twenty paces from Hephaestus and he sat there. That way he could watch both the white horse and the rest of his charges. He jammed his spear, point first, into the ground. I saw that he had some nuts and was cracking them open and eating them.

Legionary

I touched Publius' arm and he nodded. We both rose and using the bushes and shadows for cover, made our way slowly and carefully to the river. The other side was a mess of hoofprints, caligae tracks and horse dung. No one would be able to identify our tracks. The sentry was working his way through the small sack of nuts. He occasionally looked up but it was perfunctory and such a quick glance that, unless we were actually moving when he looked, he would not see us. Publius could hit a bird in flight and the river was just ten paces wide. The sentry was a further five paces away. Publius judged his moment well. He stood, whirled and sent the stone so quickly that, even though I was expecting it, the movement took me by surprise. It smacked into the sentry's forehead and the man was dead before his body slipped from the stone to land softly on the sand. The only noise that could be heard was the sound of nuts rolling from the fallen sack to the ground.

I paddled across the shallow water. It came up to my knees and was icily cold. I bore it. Publius had another stone in case one of the others showed an interest in the noise of the nuts. I almost slipped on the muddy ground which had been churned up earlier but did not. If Hephaestus neighed then all was lost. I walked slowly towards him. It was almost as though he knew what was intended. His head nodded in recognition as I used my dagger to cut the hobbles. I didn't try to mount him but used his tether to walk him slowly back to the river. I did not cross to the other bank but walked up the river. Publius followed me. My calves were numb with the cold but I wanted to disguise where we left the water. The longer it took them to find our trail the greater the chance we had to escape. Mercury snorted as we approached and we used the stones to walk to the bank. Time was something we did not have and after giving Hephaestus a handful of oats I mounted Mercury. I intended to ride the general's horse but not for a while. I took his tether and held it. The rest mounted. I led and Publius brought up the rear. I had travelled this path twice before and I was the most familiar with it. We did not gallop for, in the night, that would be heard. Instead, we walked along the trail. We kept a steady pace. Once we could no longer smell the woodsmoke I knew that we were far enough from the camp to speak, if we had to. We kept silent

Legionary

and moved steadily on in the dark. Each pace took us further from danger.

I knew that the dead sentry would be discovered just before dawn. They would stand to and be ready to leave as the morning horn blew. They would spot immediately that Hephaestus was gone. Men would be roused and the riverbank searched for clues. I wanted to be hidden by the time daylight came. We would rest until noon and then risk moving in the late afternoon. It would still be daylight but night would be approaching and if we could reach the road by dark then we might risk using it. As we had followed the enemy army I had identified places that might afford us shelter. I had seen what looked like a cave up from the trail we had followed. It overlooked the road. I had no idea if a path went up to it but it was worth investigating. False dawn came and I had still to spot the cave. My imagination was playing tricks. I convinced myself that we had passed it already. Suddenly I saw it. It was a darker shadow that loomed into the side of the hill that was becoming a mountain. I dismounted and signalled for my men to do the same. We would be leaving the trail and I wanted the hoofprints to be less noticeable. Without a rider on their backs the tracks we left might be missed. I handed Mercury's reins to Mettius and led Hephaestus up the steep slope. I zig zagged to make it easier. The last part was the hardest part as there was a slight ledge but we made it. When the others joined me I waved for Publius to inspect the cave. If it was inhabited then we were in trouble.

He emerged with a smile on his face. "Empty and there is a pool of rainwater that has seeped through the rocks at the rear of it. The water tastes fine."

"Good." We led the horses in and I handed the reins to Mettius. I stroked Hephaestus. "This is Mettius, he is a friend." I turned to Mettius, "Stroke him and put your forehead next to his." He looked terrified, "Trust me."

"Yes, Lucius." He did so and said, "I will see you come to no harm, Hephaestus."

I handed him the halter. "I will go and disguise our trail. Rest while you can."

I went down the trail, aware that the sun was appearing behind the hills in the east. The valley would delay daylight for a while longer. After breaking a branch from a bush, I looked for hoofprints. When I saw one I rubbed it out with my improvised brush. Once I reached the part where we had left the path I walked back down to disguise the hoofprints, I could not totally eradicate them but anyone who was searching for us would have to spend some time deciphering the confusing clues. We needed that time. I went directly up the slope. It was not a path that horses with men could take. It was so steep that I often had to pull myself up by the trees. There was no way horses could come this way and I knew that the only ones who could catch us would be horsemen. As I passed one tree I saw some moss. It told me it was the north side. I took a handful.

I reached the cave and saw Faustus on watch. He grinned, "You did not catch me unawares this time, Lucius."

"Good. I will sleep. Wake me if you see or hear anything." I went to Hephaestus. I saw that the wound was still angry. I took the vinegar and honey from my bag. "This will sting at first but it will heal you." I poured a little of the vinegar on the wound and rubbed it with my hand. The horse's head came up in alarm but he made no sound, I risked a little more and my hand came away sticky. I had removed the surface blood and scabbing. I took some honey and smeared it on the wound. Finally, I put the moss on the top. "Good boy, now rest. Tomorrow will decide if we are to live or die."

I slept and dreamed of home. I saw a woman in the kitchen with my mother. I could not remember my wife's face. I knew it was her but her face was not there. I started.

"Lucius, there are men in the trees."

It was Publius who woke me.

"Where?"

"Down at the trail. Mettius and Faustus are watching them. They are not mounted and there are six of them."

I knew what he was thinking. We could mount the horses and escape but that was not the right decision. They would raise the alarm. I fastened my sword. "Silence and stones are needed."

We emerged into the light and it blinded me. It was early afternoon and if these men had been sent on foot then they had done well to reach us so quickly. They would be tired. Equally to have found us meant that they were good and it would not do to underestimate them. We moved from tree to tree. I saw Mettius and Faustus hiding behind two bigger ones. We had chosen a steep route and that gave us an advantage.

I saw, below me, the six men. They were local men. They wore no helmets and were barefoot. Each had a javelin. They were searching along the ground where I had disguised the hoofprints. Their attention was on the trail. I took my sling and fitted a stone. The other three looked at me. I pointed to which man I wanted each of them to hit. I wanted the four at the two ends hit. The last thing I needed was for one to escape and raise the alarm. The other three nodded. I waited until they had fitted their stones. We whirled our slings and, as I had expected, the noise made the six hunters look up. It gave an easier target. All four hit but only three were immediately mortal. Faustus' was a glancing blow caused when the man moved his head. The two unwounded men threw their spears and took to their heels. Publius sent a second stone to smash into the back of the head of one of them while the other escaped.

"Make sure they are all dead. I will go after the other. I will meet you at the cave."

I drew my spatha. I would have preferred my legion sword but that was back with the legion. One advantage I had was that I had walked the path in the dark. The man ran back along the path. I knew that there was a twist in the path where it turned back on itself and I risked running below the path in a straight line. It was dangerous as it was a steep slope and that was why the men who had made the path had put in a zigzag. The man was looking behind him. He saw no pursuit and made the classic error of assuming he was safe and slowing down. I reached the bottom of the zig zag before he did and as he saw me he tried to draw his short sword. One advantage of a spatha is its length and I swept the sharpened sword up and across his body. It hacked into his unprotected middle and his guts spilt like writhing snakes. He cried out and I could not avoid that. I made sure he was dead and then I ran back up the path. I saw that Publius and the others were mounted and waiting below the ledge we had negotiated the night before. I saw that they had killed the man Faustus had only stunned.

I sprang on to the back of Hephaestus.

"Faustus, take the reins of Mercury. We ride hard and fast. We will use Mercury as a spare and rotate the others. The man I killed cried out." I had used all my luck and now we would pay for the mistake.

I urged Hephaestus down the trail. Within a few hundred paces it flattened out as we left the steep slope. We could make better time. As I rode I tried to predict what might happen. If there were others in the woods then they would have heard. I consoled myself with the thought that they, too, would be on foot. They might not know the direction the hunters had taken. I might have been clutching for hope but it seemed a logical deduction. However, when they did not return the rest of the men hunting us would know where we were. How badly would Sertorius want the horse? Would he risk sending a large number of men to hunt us? I gambled that he would not. He would send auxiliaries and local men. His legionaries would be needed to fight Pompey.

It was late afternoon when we were close enough to the road to join it. I decided that it was worth the risk. We could switch one of the others to Mercury and ride hard. Hephaestus showed no signs of flagging.

As luck would have it there was a pool of water close to the road. "Water the horses. Mettius, switch to Mercury."

While the horses drank I took a swig from my own skin. I listened for the sound of hooves but I heard nothing. As soon as we galloped on the stone Roman Road we would be trumpeting our presence to any who were hunting us. I would ride until it was dark and only then seek shelter.

Had I been alone then Hephaestus would have easily outrun any pursuers but I was travelling at the speed of the others. My horse was making it look easy while the others laboured. When darkness came it was sudden. It was like the dousing of a candle. One moment the sun was there and then it dipped behind the mountains to the west. I stopped and looked around the gloom of twilight where the last light from the west afforded me a view. Up until now we had stayed to the north and east of the road. I saw a trail that led south and west. I took it. It was well worn and I worried it might lead to a village. When a spur came off to the left I took it and stopped when I saw the building.

Legionary

I waved Publius forward to investigate. He walked around the rear of it and then came back to the front. He cautiously opened the door. He was in there for some time. When he emerged he waved us forward.

"Is it empty?"

"Not quite, Lucius. There is a dead body within. It is an old man and I think he died in his sleep. The body does not yet stink so he died in the last day or so."

I looked around and, seeing the tools that lay there, and remembering the kiln outside, nodded, "A charcoal burner. Fetch his body from within. The stink might upset the horses. Mettius, we will take the horses inside when they are watered. See if you can find some grazing." I dismounted and stroked Hephaestus, "You did well, my friend and we are halfway home." I handed the reins to Faustus. "I will scout around to ensure that we are safe."

I took off my cloak for I was hot and sweaty from the ride. I drew my sword. I did not expect trouble but it was better to be prepared. The farm was a small one. There were signs that at one time there had been animals kept there but with no fresh dung it had not been for some time. The salad crops and beans showed me that the farmer had planted. I would pick some of the food for us. I walked to the end of the trail. The only prints I could see were the fresh ones we had made. There were no footprints. He had lived alone and he had died alone. We would bury him and say some words. I did not want the spirits of the dead to haunt us.

I picked some beans and some of the cabbage. I knew that my men would have lit a fire and have water on to boil. This was a house and, as the man had died recently and not been discovered, no one would wonder at smoke rising from it. With the horses hidden and if we kept indoors, we should be safe until morning and we needed the rest.

I gave the food to Mettius and then went outside with Faustus and Publius to bury the man. He looked old yet he had most of his teeth and he looked to have been a muscular man. Death could come from many places. Who knew what had taken him. As we piled the soil on the body I hoped it was not some pestilential disease. I said words I had heard the priest say when

Gaius had been burned. We could not burn the body and burial would have to do.

The house already stank of horse. We put the animals in the largest of the rooms used for sleeping and Hephaestus in the smaller room next to it. We had to move the old man's bed out. We used the wood to feed the fire for the cooking. There was food left in the old man's larder. Two game birds were hanging there and they fed the stew. It would be the best meal we had eaten thus far. As we mopped up the stew with three-day old stale bread that we found, I pointed to the door, "We take a watch but do so at the end of the path close to the road. There is an old tree there. It is gnarled and knobbly. With our cloaks about us we can be hidden. I will take the last watch. I nodded to Mettius, "You take the first watch, Faustus, the second and Publius the third. We should all be able to get some sleep with just a two-hour watch."

Faustus asked, "Have we evaded pursuit?"

I shook my head, "That is a dangerous road to travel Faustus. We might have but we carry on as though the enemy has sent an ala of cavalry after us."

Publius said, "You have done all that you could, Lucius. If we are hunted and caught then it will be the gods who wish us to be caught."

I rose and went to make water. When I returned I went into Hephaestus' quarters. It stank of horse piss. Better that than the risk that his white coat was seen. I used one of the old man's tallow candles to inspect the wound. It did not smell bad and while still red and angry it did not make him react when I lifted the moss. "Almost there. If your master has made the progress I think he might, then tomorrow you shall be reunited and I shall rejoin my legion."

Once again the animal nodded his head.

On my watch I neither saw nor heard anything. Only a fool would seek a handful of men at night. The chase would begin again in the morning. I woke the men before dawn. There was still some water from the stew in the pot and I had added oats and greens while I watched. We had a good breakfast and before the sun had even risen we mounted and rode. This time I

Legionary

mounted Mercury and led Hephaestus. We had the choice of changing later if we needed to.

We did not gallop. If there were hunters looking for us then the clattering of galloping hooves would trumpet our presence. We walked. I estimated that our army could be anywhere from forty to one hundred miles from us. I hoped for the former but was realistic enough to know it could be the latter. Pompey would have scouts out. They would be a mixture of auxiliary and Roman cavalry. They might range up to ten miles ahead of the main body. Once we saw a friendly face then we could begin to relax.

We continued our normal practice as advised by Marcellus and whenever there was water we stopped to refresh the horses. The gods favoured us for each time we halted there was grazing for the animals. It was little enough but seemed to keep them going. The horses we had been given looked to be doing well but Hephaestus was not. He looked thinner. The wound, the journey and the stress of capture was having an effect. Pompey would be angry.

At noon we rested beneath some trees and ate a meal from what we had taken from the old man. I was grateful to him and when I reached a temple I would make an offering for his safe passage to the other world. I did not know what gods he worshipped but Jupiter might think better of him with an offering. We did not leave in the noon day sun but waited an hour. The air was still hot but the sun did not seem to burn as fiercely.

We left when it was marginally cooler. I had rotated each of the three legionaries as the rider in the fore. It was to give them all the experience. When we returned to the legion all three would be better soldiers. They had performed better than any might have hoped and all acquitted themselves well. The road, thankfully, twisted and turned through a shallow valley. The road was Roman and largely straight but the rocks that jutted from the hillsides gave a few bends that were not normal. When the land was secure then a legion would be sent to straighten it. I say thankfully for the few turns and bends afforded shade from the sun. It was as Faustus turned a bend that disaster struck. He drew his sword and I knew there was danger. I pulled my spatha from its scabbard and urged Mercury on. As the three of us hurried to reach the isolated Faustus I heard hooves. There were horsemen and from Faustus' reaction they were not friendly. Even as we neared him I saw the two Celtiberian horsemen charge him. Faustus had courage and his spatha hacked into one but the other skewered him with a spear. We then saw the other four horsemen. There were five of them and just three of us. In his dying the ever-optimistic Faustus fought to save us. The horseman who had speared him thought that he was dead and rode at us. Faustus, falling from his horse lunged at the man and sank his spatha into his side.

   It meant that there were now four men and a wounded man against three of us. I let go of Hephaestus' tether. I could not fight and hold him. If he ran he might be picked up by a Pompeian patrol. Everyone knew Pompey's horse. The three of us charged the Celtiberian cavalrymen. They had javelins. We had a chance. That chance increased as they galloped at us and two of them threw their missiles towards us. One was badly thrown and Publius easily avoided the other. In the time it took the horsemen to draw their swords we were on them.

   First blood went to Mettius who avenged his friend, Faustus. He slew the wounded man with a mighty sweep of his spatha. I focussed on the two men who came at me. I was the closest to Hephaestus and when they raised their javelins then I knew they were looking for Hephaestus. The hunters had finally found us. One of the Celtiberians was closer than the other and I rode at him. He feinted with the spear and I moved. Even as I slashed with my spatha, the javelin entered my side. I was lucky that it was a light weapon with a small head. It did not penetrate deeply but it hurt. My spatha hit the man in the side and raked along his ribs. The second warrior had an easy target. My wound and the fact that I had slashed to my left afforded me no protection from my right. The Celtiberian pulled back his arm to end my life. Hephaestus' hooves crashed down on the man and the horse. The man died instantly and as his horse crumpled beneath him I knew that Pompey the Great's warhorse had killed them both.

   I looked at my two charges and they were both fighting for their lives. They were well out of the place where they were comfortable. They were more used to fighting on foot. Fighting from the back of a horse against skilled warriors doomed them. I urged on Mercury, aware that my wound was oozing blood. I owed it to them to do all that I could to save their lives. As I neared them I saw more horsemen appear. We had failed and the enemy would recapture Hephaestus. We would all have died for nothing. At least my end would be a glorious one and I would help them to slay these last two.

One of the Celtiberian horsemen heard the hooves and risked looking behind him. That was their undoing for in that distraction Publius slew him and I managed to reach the man whose sword was raised to strike the unprotected head of Mettius. I slid my sword through his body.

Even as I whipped Mercury's head around to face the new foes I saw that these were not the enemy. It was a turma of Roman Cavalry. Mettius and Publius saw them too. Mettius leapt from his horse and ran to Faustus' side. He felt his neck and rose, shaking his head, "He is dead."

I nodded, "He died well and we will honour him. Put his body on the back of his horse."

The cavalry reined in and the officer said, "I am Decurion Gaius Metellus. Is that the general's horse?"

"It is."

He grinned, "You have done well. We found the men you slew with another twenty close to our camp. They were scouts but we did not know why they were there. Now we do. They sought this war horse. We slew the others but these escaped. The gods smiled on you for you slew the last of them." He turned, "Gnaeus, secure the general's horse." As the man dismounted to take Hephaestus' reins the decurion said, "The general has pushed hard and the army is just twelve miles down this road."

We both turned as Hephaestus reared and tried to smash his hooves into the cavalryman's head. I sheathed my sword and slid from the back of Mercury. "It is better that I try,"

I walked over and passed the man who was shaking. He had come within an arm's length of having his head crushed. "Thank you, Hephaestus. I owe you a life. Now behave yourself. You shall be reunited with your master soon." He nodded and stood patiently while I took his tether and took him past the incredulous trooper.

As I mounted the decurion said, "You have ten miles or so to tell me this intriguing tale. You must be a horse master. What is your name?"

"Lucius Ulpia Porcianus, formerly a legionary in the First Century, Second Cohort, First Legion."

He laughed, "I think you have earned yourself a new cognomen, Equitatus."

Publius laughed, "Never was a truer word spoken, Decurion. Lucius Equitatus!"

From that moment it became my name. I did not choose it but the decurion and his men all used it almost as a mark of honour and when Publius told the rest of the century then I was marked for life. Just as Pompey had been given the honorary appellation, the Great, so I was Equitatus, Horseman.

His medical trooper tended to my wound. "It will need stitches but the doctors are close enough for that. I can stitch horses but I would be too clumsy to do a good job on a hero."

With a bandage around me I mounted Mercury and we rode back to rejoin Pompey's army.

Epilogue

Hispania, Winter 75 BC

The general himself came to congratulate me and my men. He greeted me with the title Tesserarius. I was formally promoted. However, when he saw the wound to Hephaestus, he became angry that his horse had been hurt. He swore vengeance on those that had done it. He was almost incandescent with rage. He asked me to tell him of the rescue. I did so and gave him details about the numbers that I had seen.

"Tesserarius, when you have had your wound healed I want you and your contuburnium to take Hephaestus back to my estate in Picenum." I saw his anger subside a little. "And you can take a letter to Marcus Crassus and the senate. From what you have told me I need more soldiers. Once you have delivered Hephaestus then you can return here. You can leave in the morning when my doctor has attended to my horse."

I was stunned. If I was to return to Picenum then I could see my family. It would, perforce, be a brief meeting but it was better than nothing. Even before I could tell both the centurion and my contuburnium of the orders we had a task to do. We buried Faustus. It was just my contuburnium who were there and we said goodbye to the youth with a permanent smile on his face.

It was only then that I had my wound seen to and Centurion Bucco and the other officers watched as my side was stitched. I told them of Pompey's orders.

Optio Cumanus laughed, "Well, Tesserarius Lucius Equitatus, perhaps we should name you lucky. You will travel back to Rome and be pampered on the voyage. You will get to visit your home and while we endure a winter camp you will enjoy your family."

The centurion nodded, "You deserve this and it is good that you take your contuburnium with you. They deserve it too. Your rank is assured but I will have another perform that office until you return. Manus is a good man too. This will be a long war and there are more promotions to be made. This century has shown what it can do and we will all be rewarded."

Legionary

    We left the next day. We had our mule but we left our spears and shields with the legion. I had not only the letters for the senate and Marcus Crassus but the Senatorial Pass from General Pompey. It assured me the right to food, shelter and passage, first to Rome and then to Picenum. I had come a long way since the day the pigs died.

The End

Glossary

adulescentulus carnifex - teenage butcher
atrium - a room in a Roman house which is open to the sky
aureus (pl. aurei) - a gold coin valued at 25 pure silver denarii
columbarium - niches for funeral urns
contuburnium (pl conterburnia) - the smallest Roman military unit: eight men
cuneus - wedge
duplex acies - a double line of cohorts
Faventia - Barcelona
feminalia - short trousers worn by cavalrymen
flagrum - short whip
immunis (pl immunes) - specialists in a legion: engineers, artillerymen, musicians, clerks etc.
impluvium - a pool in an atrium intended to gather water
Iugula - 'Kill him' - used in the arena
Mitte - 'Mercy' - used in the arena
Narbo Martius - Narbonne (France)
Optimates - Sulla and his supporters
Parca (pl. Parcae) - the female personification of destiny or the fates
pes - one Roman foot
pilum (pl. pila) - Roman spear
Populares - the Marians who opposed Sulla
Praefectus Castrorum - the third in command of a legion and the officer in a command of a camp
probatio - the time a legionary trained
rudius (pl rudii) - heavy wooden swords use for training
sacramentum - the oath of allegiance
scutum (pl scuta) - a curved Roman shield
simplex acies - a single line of cohorts
six pes - five feet ten inches
triplex acies - triple line of cohorts
Valentia - Valencia

Historical Background

The Marian reforms changed the Roman Army and the way that they fought. The old three types of legionary: hastati, principes and triarii were all merged into one based upon the principe. The contuburnium was the smallest unit. Ten of them made a century and six centuries made a cohort. There were ten cohorts in a legion but the first cohort was double the size of the others. Its name reflected its position and rank. It was the Prima Cohort.

When Pompey went to Africa his men did dig for treasure in Carthage and Pompey allowed it. The whole campaign lasted a bare forty days and animals were taken back to Rome for the triumph. Sulla, of course, was reluctant to allow his young lieutenant to have a triumph but he knew that Pompey's successful legions could make trouble. He demanded that Pompey disband his army. As the legions of Pompey were maintained at his expense and with no prospect of war it made sense for him to agree. Pompey the Great had just over two years of family life until Sulla died and Pompey had to assert his authority once more.

Funeral games normally involved gladiatorial combats. When bulls were sacrificed then the butchered meat was given away.

The Romans did not use stirrups. Their cavalry had a saddle with four horns which held them in place and allowed them to use javelins, shields and swords. Horses were normally vaulted to be mounted.

I have made up the rank of Chosen Man. The military historian in me cannot believe that the Romans did not have someone in charge of a tent. I hope I have not upset any purists but this was also a way to identify characters. The other ranks are all authentic ones.

It was Pompey's horse that inadvertently saved his life at the Battle of Sucro but the rescue of the horse is pure fiction.

Books used in the research

- The Complete Roman Legions - Pollard and Berry

Legionary

- The Roman Army from Caesar to Trajan - Simkins and Embleton
- Roman Battle Tactics 109 AD-AD 313 - Cowan and Hook
- Spartacus and the Slave War 73-71 BC - Fields and Noon
- Roman Legionary 109-58 BC - Cowan and O'Brogain

Griff Hosker December 2024

Other books by Griff Hosker

If you enjoyed reading this book, then why not read another one by the author?

Ancient History
Roman Rebellion
(The Roman Republic 100 BC-60 BC)
Legionary

The Sword of Cartimandua Series
(Germania and Britannia 50 A.D. – 128 A.D.)
Ulpius Felix- Roman Warrior (prequel)
The Sword of Cartimandua
The Horse Warriors
Invasion Caledonia
Roman Retreat
Revolt of the Red Witch
Druid's Gold
Trajan's Hunters
The Last Frontier
Hero of Rome
Roman Hawk
Roman Treachery
Roman Wall
Roman Courage

The Wolf Brethren series
(Britain in the late 6th Century)
Saxon Dawn
Saxon Revenge
Saxon England
Saxon Blood
Saxon Slayer
Saxon Slaughter
Saxon Bane

Legionary

Saxon Fall: Rise of the Warlord
Saxon Throne
Saxon Sword

Medieval History
The Dragon Heart Series
Viking Slave *
Viking Warrior *
Viking Jarl *
Viking Kingdom *
Viking Wolf *
Viking War*
Viking Sword
Viking Wrath
Viking Raid
Viking Legend
Viking Vengeance
Viking Dragon
Viking Treasure
Viking Enemy
Viking Witch
Viking Blood
Viking Weregeld
Viking Storm
Viking Warband
Viking Shadow
Viking Legacy
Viking Clan
Viking Bravery

The Norman Genesis Series
Hrolf the Viking *
Horseman *
The Battle for a Home *
Revenge of the Franks *
The Land of the Northmen
Ragnvald Hrolfsson
Brothers in Blood

261

Legionary

Lord of Rouen
Drekar in the Seine
Duke of Normandy
The Duke and the King

Danelaw
(England and Denmark in the 11th Century)
Dragon Sword *
Oathsword *
Bloodsword *
Danish Sword*
The Sword of Cnut*

Norseman
Norse Warrior

New World Series
Blood on the Blade *
Across the Seas *
The Savage Wilderness *
The Bear and the Wolf *
Erik The Navigator *
Erik's Clan *
The Last Viking*

The Vengeance Trail *

The Conquest Series
(Normandy and England 1050-1100)
Hastings*
Conquest*
Rebellion

The Aelfraed Series
(Britain and Byzantium 1050 A.D. - 1085 A.D.)
Housecarl *
Outlaw *
Varangian *

Legionary

The Reconquista Chronicles
Castilian Knight *
El Campeador *
The Lord of Valencia *

The Anarchy Series England
(1120-1180)
English Knight *
Knight of the Empress *
Northern Knight *
Baron of the North *
Earl *
King Henry's Champion *
The King is Dead *
Warlord of the North*
Enemy at the Gate*
The Fallen Crown*
Warlord's War*
Kingmaker
Henry II
Crusader
The Welsh Marches
Irish War
Poisonous Plots
The Princes' Revolt
Earl Marshal
The Perfect Knight

Border Knight
(1182-1300)
Sword for Hire *
Return of the Knight *
Baron's War *
Magna Carta *
Welsh Wars *
Henry III *
The Bloody Border *
Baron's Crusade*
Sentinel of the North*

Legionary

War in the West*
Debt of Honour
The Blood of the Warlord
The Fettered King
de Montfort's Crown
The Ripples of Rebellion

Sir John Hawkwood Series
(France and Italy 1339- 1387)
Crécy: The Age of the Archer *
Man At Arms *
The White Company *
Leader of Men *
Tuscan Warlord *
Condottiere*
Legacy

Lord Edward's Archer
Lord Edward's Archer *
King in Waiting *
An Archer's Crusade *
Targets of Treachery *
The Great Cause *
Wallace's War *
The Hunt*
The Prince and the Archer

Struggle for a Crown
(1360- 1485)
Blood on the Crown *
To Murder a King *
The Throne *
King Henry IV *
The Road to Agincourt *
St Crispin's Day *
The Battle for France *
The Last Knight *
Queen's Knight *
The Knight's Tale

Legionary

Tales from the Sword I
(Short stories from the Medieval period)

Tudor Warrior series
(England and Scotland in the late 15th and early 16th century)
Tudor Warrior *
Tudor Spy *
Flodden*

Conquistador
(England and America in the 16th Century)
Conquistador *
The English Adventurer *

English Mercenary
(The 30 Years War and the English Civil War)
Horse and Pistol*
Captain of Horse

Modern History
East India Saga
East Indiaman
The Tiger and the Thief

The Napoleonic Horseman Series
Chasseur à Cheval
Napoleon's Guard
British Light Dragoon
Soldier Spy
1808: The Road to Coruña
Talavera
The Lines of Torres Vedras
Bloody Badajoz
The Road to France
Waterloo

The Lucky Jack American Civil War series

Legionary

Rebel Raiders
Confederate Rangers
The Road to Gettysburg

Soldier of the Queen series
Soldier of the Queen*
Redcoat's Rifle*
Omdurman*
Desert War
An Officer and a Gentleman

The British Ace Series
1914
1915 Fokker Scourge
1916 Angels over the Somme
1917 Eagles Fall
1918 We will remember them
From Arctic Snow to Desert Sand
Wings over Persia

Combined Operations series (1940-1945)
Commando *
Raider *
Behind Enemy Lines
Dieppe
Toehold in Europe
Sword Beach
Breakout
The Battle for Antwerp
King Tiger
Beyond the Rhine
Korea
Korean Winter

Tales from the Sword II
(Short stories from the Modern period)

Books marked thus *, are also available in the audio format.

Legionary

For more information on all of the books then please visit the author's website at www.griffhosker.com where there is a link to contact him or visit his Facebook page: Griff Hosker at Sword Books or follow him on Twitter: @HoskerGriff or Sword (@swordbooksltd)
If you wish to be on the mailing list then contact the author through his website: Griff Hosker at Sword Books

Printed in Great Britain
by Amazon